Hannah Kingsley was a finalist in the 2021 Page Turner Young Writers Award. In addition to writing, she runs a special edition, sprayed-edges book business, where she has produced custom editions for Penguin Random House, Bonnier Books and many more.

Hannah lives in Wiltshire with her husband and Billy, their three-legged cat. *Soul Hate* is inspired by her frustration at the romanticisation of 'fate', when she believes that choosing who you love is far more romantic than destiny.

instagram.com/HannahKingsleyAuthor
tiktok.com/@HannahKingsleyAuthor

Also by Hannah Kingsley

Soul Hate

SOUL BOUND

HANNAH KINGSLEY

One More Chapter
a division of HarperCollins*Publishers* Ltd
1 London Bridge Street
London SE1 9GF
www.harpercollins.co.uk
HarperCollins*Publishers*
Macken House, 39/40 Mayor Street Upper,
Dublin 1, D01 C9W8, Ireland

This paperback edition 2026

1

First published in Great Britain in ebook format
by HarperCollins*Publishers* 2026

Copyright © Hannah Kingsley 2026
Hannah Kingsley asserts the moral right to be identified
as the author of this work

A catalogue record of this book is available from the British Library
ISBN: 978-0-00-870754-5

This novel is entirely a work of fiction. The names, characters and incidents portrayed in it are the work of the author's imagination. Any resemblance to actual persons, living or dead, events or localities is entirely coincidental.

Printed and bound in the UK using 100% Renewable Electricity
by CPI Group (UK) Ltd

All rights reserved. No part of this publication may be reproduced, stored in a retrieval system, or transmitted, in any form or by any means, electronic, mechanical, photocopying, recording or otherwise, without the prior permission of the publishers.

Without limiting the exclusive rights of any author, contributor or the publisher of this publication, any unauthorised use of this publication to train generative artificial intelligence (AI) technologies is expressly prohibited. HarperCollins also exercise their rights under Article 4(3) of the Digital Single Market Directive 2019/790 and expressly reserve this publication from the text and data mining exception.

To Alex
My Soulmate. My Chosen.

CHAPTER 1

Fate save me from this idiocy!

Though that would require Fate to have a sense of mercy, and I think he's proven he doesn't. At least not where I'm concerned.

I'm Renza Di Maineri. Fate does not care for me.

I pinch the bridge of my nose, summoning my dregs of willpower as the newly minted Electi Ulrico hogs the central white stage. Not even the gushing rainbow light pouring from the domed stained-glass ceiling could soften this prattle. I swear even the alabaster stone columns cringe as they listen, their tall trunks sluiced with shadows and dancing diamond flecks cast down from the artisanal heavens.

Ulrico speaks with no authority, not a shred of strength nor even a whiff of charisma. He has none of the gravitas of my former colleagues, who were murdered in the Grand Temple Explosion. It's more like pleading than persuasion, the words somehow falling clammy and clingy on the ear. His head flops up and down, nodding as though that'll make him more convincing. His beady brown eyes stare unflinchingly at the

Electi he's currently facing, before he wildly spins to unnerve the next.

Fate's Fury, how did this man win an election?

After the Holy States failed their brutal and violent attempt to take over Halice, the city fought back in the Great Rebellion. The people rose up against the Holy States' agents and militia, kicking them out of our home. And I was the only Electi left standing. To keep our democracy running we've held a few very speedy elections – five of them so far. Somehow Ulrico won his.

I mean, of course I know *how* he did it. I'm still in awe it worked. His sibling, Electi Yaleni, died in the Grand Temple Explosion – where the majority of Electi had been slaughtered along with most of their families and many others. Ulrico had leveraged the eyeballs out of the tragedy, lashing himself to the memory of Yaleni's good works for the rural districts, to scrabble together enough votes for a seat. Yaleni was an orator. Yaleni was raised for this office by a community that knew they would flourish and continue the hardworking legacy of their people.

Ulrico ... made me understand why choosing Yaleni hadn't been worth a debate.

But that was another time. A time before the Holy States conspired to murder my colleagues and weaken my city in an effort to destroy our independence. An independence we will never surrender.

Ulrico is now one of the six Electi that govern the free city of Halice. Six when it's supposed to be seven, because no one wanted to sit in the seat that used to belong to Bellandi the Traitor. After everything he did, from the calculated, heartless slaughter of the previous Electi, to positioning the Church Militia behind our walls and stealing from the city to pay a force to invade his own people – no one wanted the association. No one wanted to link themselves to such a great and foul traitor or his wretched legacy. The problem, however, is that leaves our sacred High Chamber off balance.

"Esteemed Members, I relinquish the floor," Ulrico finishes, eyes whirling to me, seeking approval. I force a tight smile, linking my fingers over my lap.

I've become used to that quick check my way to make sure the new Electi are doing it right. I try not to make it a big deal, but every time it rams the arrow deeper into my gut and makes my heart throb and my stomach churn: that I'm the longest serving Electi at only twenty-one years old, and the awful reason why. Thankfully, most of the newly elected have started to let it go.

I shift in my seat, the exquisite dark wood creaking softly as I move. Before I can stand, Electi Leone Strossi rises. My heart sinks as he strides forwards, vivid orange light sliding off his slick brown hair. His expensive brown shoes squeak as he walks, the sound like nails down a blackboard.

Leone Strossi, the replacement for Member Mortiselli. An absurdly wealthy young man with all the prejudice that comes from a long lineage of believing you're better than everyone else. He'd been my main opponent when I'd run for election almost three years ago, and he didn't take losing lightly. He rubs his stubbled chin, flashing a thoughtful smile around the room.

This man knows what he's doing. This isn't some new thought or unprepared speech as he tries to imply through body language. It's calculated.

I'm not going to like this.

I sit up straighter and narrow my eyes. I reach towards my side table, currently sprinkled with soft pink light from the stained window behind. I pull the papers on it closer, ready to take notes.

"Esteemed Members," he begins, voice crisp and warm, "it is no secret that we face a crisis in this city. Our biggest and oldest trade partner, the Holy States, will have nothing to do with us, and the other Independent States are afraid to provoke or anger the Holy States and the Holy Mother by increasing trade with us more than already exists – and even that is trailing away. As such, businesses are failing. Jobs are crumbling. Key resources are difficult to find. This crisis is of our own making—"

Trade. The bedrock of Halice. It had fallen catastrophically. Most of the trade that'd flowed through our city was en route between the Holy States or one of the other Independent States, nations like ours that had earned their freedom from the Holy States centuries ago. Our position along the Argenti Strait makes Halice the perfect stopping place.

"We did not invite violence here; it was forced upon us," comes Savino's voice. The quiet, stoic young man narrows his steely grey eyes. That unblinking gaze could unnerve mountains. Electi Savino is Captain Collier's son. Recommended for the seat by Idris, we'd both campaigned for him, and he'd won his election with ease, since both he and his late father are war heroes.

Savino firmly aligns himself with Idris on most matters, but I'd expected that when Idris made the recommendation. Still, throwing my influence behind Savino hadn't come without a favour of my own in return.

I can't help but let my eyes drift over to the empty seat strewn in a curtain of butter yellow. The absence of his tingling, blistering, caustic presence leaves a hollowness in my chest where a simultaneously comforting and pestilent knot of churning frustration should sit. I try not to think about it, about him. The infuriating man whose absence dominates my mind as much as his presence does. My Soulhate. I fail miserably.

He should've been back by now.

"Yes, of course. Thank you for the correction. Please forgive my careless words." Leone instantly agrees with Savino, playacting genuine sorrow. "What I meant to say is, that it is our responsibility to get our city's businesses and economy back on track."

"You have a suggestion?" chimes in Maggia with clipped words. Maggia had been my recommendation, and we were often on the same page with issues. The no-nonsense woman is in her mid-fifties, making her the oldest currently sitting Electi. She's sharp as a razor and beloved by the people of Halice. She used to be a teacher before changing path and managing several chamber-funded outreach programmes that help clothe, feed and bring medicine to the very poorest of our people.

Maggia is a walking saint, not that she'd be impressed with the comparison.

She sits in my father's old chair, elbow wedged on the arm rest, her chin resting on a closed fist. The blue light of the stained-glass window weaves like magic with the silver streaks in her brunette hair. She stares unflinchingly at Leone without enthusiasm, a man that symbolises everything she sees as wrong with this city.

"I suggest we lower some business taxes, to encourage business owners, to promote the idea of a strong, prosperous business scene here in Halice and get our economy growing again," Leone says.

"You want to give rich people more money, when the number of the poor and destitute grow in number almost daily?" Maggia can't keep the disgust out of her voice as she shakes her head. I shift in my seat, the wood creaking under my weight as I scribble down this suggestion. I keep track of all the ideas Leone has put forward.

"More money in the pockets of the people is more money they can spend at businesses. The money keeps flowing," says Leone.

"What exactly does this chamber do with taxes except spend them? On things the people in this city desperately need?

With key Halician businesses?" Maggia counters with a thin veil of calm that almost sounds like a teacher coaxing a student. Leone bristles at her words.

"Should not the people be allowed to decide where and how they spend their money?"

"They do – that's why they elect us."

I stand up. Time to interrupt before Maggia and Leone descend into their usual bickering that gets us utterly nowhere. Leone looks perturbed by my movement but nods in acknowledgement.

"Esteemed Members, I relinquish the floor," he says, striding back to his seat. He settles in the orange-clad chair, watching unhappily as I walk towards the central platform. Light ripples over my body as I take my place on the sacred, mosaic stage. I keep my stance relaxed, my shoulders wide and open, and a faint, welcoming smile on my face. I'm awash in every colour of creation as I speak, keeping my voice level and calm.

"Esteemed Members, I will not argue that Member Strossi makes a valid point," I begin, gesturing warmly to Leone. "We need to do more for the economy and businesses of Halice. I am a woman of business and banking; I have seen firsthand how people are struggling. Yet I do not believe this particular action to be the best way forward."

"So you won't even discuss it?" challenges Leone.

"Of course we must discuss every idea that might help our people." My answer holds a deliberate, barely audible undertone of weariness. "However, taxes are a matter of the budget, and the budget has already been agreed. If we were to open the floor to tax debates we would have to reopen the entire budget. The one we currently have has been very carefully reworked and already agreed by this chamber."

Being the one who spent countless nights reworking it, I will not let that bag of worms be opened again. It'd been a nightmare getting it to pass the first time, and that was when it was just Idris and Savino I'd needed to convince – Savino being the first member to get elected after Idris, making us a semi-functioning High Chamber again.

"Yes, when half the seats in here were empty," Leone counters unhappily. "This chamber is much changed since then. The voices of the people deserve to be heard."

"This High Chamber constantly changes. We set a budget once a year for good reason – because otherwise it would never be finished or closed. That is the law."

"Convenient for the woman whose bank holds the city accounts." Leone scowls.

I take a deep breath, fixing him with a level gaze.

"The Bill of Halice's Budget Reforms came into effect thirty-seven years after the founding of the city, with an amendment seven years later, for this exact reason. That's more than one hundred years before the Di Maineri Bank was created," I respond, quickly rounding the maths in my head. "While I hear your frustration, Member Strossi, the law is the law. It has not been adjusted or manipulated since—"

My words shudder and stop abruptly. I flinch. My breath is ripped from my lungs by hot, invisible fingers. Stinging goose-bumps erupt along my spine, snapping my back poker straight. My pulse turns molten, my heart hammers, my stomach convulses. Invisible boiling needles stab relentlessly into my fingertips, digging under my nails like scalding splinters.

Reflexively, I force myself to take a long, slow breath in, swallowing in vain to fight the bile blistering the back of my throat. I reach for mind-stilling – using breathing and logic to allow my head to fight the unruly, unreasonable emotions threatening to take over my body. I fight at the gnawing whispers beginning to echo in the darkest corners of my mind. I drop my head, unable to fight the relieved smirk pulling at the corner of my mouth. Behind me, a dark, pulsing star slowly grows closer and closer before stopping only a few tantalising, bruising paces away.

I lift my head, certain the Fated urges are now under control, but I don't see my colleagues. My only focus is the infuriating, tumultuous man hovering behind me like a dark hurricane. He's finally home.

My Soulhate.

I don't turn around.

"Are you going to take your seat, Member Patricelli?" I ask calmly, my words floating lightly around the hallowed hall.

He's back. He's here.

"I didn't want to interrupt you, Member Di Maineri." His deep rumbling voice, while abrasive, holds a note of amusement.

Steeling myself, I turn slowly. The blush-coloured silk of my dress slides soothingly over my tingling skin as I face the scorching dark fire of my Fated. Idris leans against the wooden barrier of the stage, arms folded, still in his travelling gear. His tousled blond hair gleams like the sun itself, his nose and brow tanned gold. His hazel eyes glint with light and the corner of his mouth lifts in a wry kind of smile.

My Fated has returned. My Soulhate. My predestined worst nemesis. The man Fate bound to me in an eternal, irrational bond of scorching loathing and violence.

The man who saved Halice with me. The one man I could trust when Bellandi and the Holy States were working to destroy us.

Our cursed bond has punished us both so fiercely, plaguing us with forces twisted and dangerous – brutal urges we constantly fight to keep in check. I'm grateful for mind-stilling, the breathing techniques that help my logical brain override the irrational, violent, Fate-driven part of my person. I reach for those techniques so often now, they're almost reflexive. But they do little to quash the borderline pain his presence creates.

And yet, there are times I am grateful for it – the agony of his closeness. Because when I'm struck by a myriad of familiarly heinous sensations, I know one unmistakeable, unchangeable fact.

Idris is with me.

Our eyes lock, and we stand in silence for a long, tenuous moment as rage and relief war through my bones. My pulse races, my throat itches. Venomous thorns bury themselves into my skin. I wrestle with the urge to close the distance to reach him, though whether in order to embrace him or beat him senseless ... it's a coin toss. Instead, I force myself to breathe slowly, in through my nose, out through my mouth.

Control my breathing, control my pulse, control myself.

I don't see a scratch on him. Thank Fate for his sparse mercies.

"Attempt unsuccessful, I'm afraid," I remark, before whipping back to face Leone. "As I was saying, the budget cannot be reopened. It's the law. But, Member Strossi, you make an excellent point. We should be considering all angles that might help our city and economy recover from the heinous crimes committed by the traitor Cardinal Bellandi before the Great Rebellion. Perhaps we can all think on possible solutions to the current problems, and bring our suggestions forwards soon?"

"What kind of suggestions?" Ulrico fires off instantly. The man always feels the need to ask some kind of question.

I shrug, hands open. "Whatever you think would serve the interests of our city. Perhaps in a dedicated collaborative session we can come up with some initiatives."

"When?" Leone demands unhappily.

"Shall we table it for a week? That'll allow us time to really think through possible options and consider the complexity of the situation."

"Two," barks back Ulrico, his voice unusually firm. "I want to consult with the farming and rural regions for their suggestions, too, as aid for them may need to be different than for the city."

It's always surprising when a startlingly reasonable and sane suggestion comes out of Ulrico's mouth. But I suppose he can't be without *all* sense.

"Of course, Member Ulrico. We must ensure all ideas for all peoples are taken into consideration. A fortnight it is. Now, Esteemed Members, it is getting late in the day. Shall we draw this session to a close?"

"Agreed," Maggia and Savino chorus in quick succession, with Ulrico fast to follow. Leone takes a deep breath and stands.

"Agreed," he answers, collecting his papers from his table.

I vacate the white marble stage, snagging my papers off my table. I try to organise them, but Idris's searing eyes carve a hole in the back of my head. Our invisible, molten tether is taut and tense, reeling me closer and closer with each beat of my heart.

Don't go over.
I shouldn't go over.
I want to go over.

The whispers purr so alluringly that my feet move of their own accord. I succumb, closing the distance. Idris and Savino are talking quietly, but Idris's golden eyes absorb my every step, my every breath as I step into hearing range. Both go quiet as I approach.

"Interrupting?" I ask from a few paces away, winning the tense fight to keep my voice steady. Proximity seems to be an exponential factor in the intensity of our bond. A few paces, an object between us, or simply not looking at each other all dulls the sharpness of the hot, fierce violence that bubbles between us. Idris and I had spent the months since the Great Rebellion navigating our bond almost daily, and the return of his fire broiling my skull was oddly completing.

My blood is rampant with angry, biting sparks and the urge to scratch away at the bare flesh of my throat. My breath is hot and clammy as it leaves my lips, but I force it to remain even and slow.

Control my breathing, control my pulse, control my mind.

"Not at all," Idris answers immediately, turning to face me properly. "Savino, old friend, we should discuss further. Meet at my home in an hour?"

"An hour. Perfect. See you then, Idris. Good evening, Renza." Savino nods warmly and departs. He's already mastered his new prosthetic foot, his gait betraying no hint of his lost limb.

"Do I want to know what that's about?" I ask, knowing full well Savino will be giving Idris a rundown of everything that happened in the High Chamber while he was away.

"Still don't trust me, Di Maineri?" Idris chuckles.

"Now why would you ruin a nice conversation with ugly questions, Patricelli?" I tease.

"Oh, nice evasive answer. You should go into politics." Idris smirks as the two of us walk towards the exit. Crossing the white and black tiled floor, we fall into silence for a moment.

I soak in the maddening mixture of relief and fury. When he's gone, my pulse is steady, my shoulders relaxed, my breathing easy. Yet a piece of me is missing. I toss and turn at night; during the day I can't settle, feeling constantly that something is misplaced or lost. There is a tugging, nagging sensation beneath my ribs, demanding I get to my feet and follow – but in what direction I cannot answer.

Yet with him close, my pulse is wilder than any storm. My muscles tense and jitter. I'm drowning in flames both uncomfortable and familiar. I have to force my breathing to remain calm and fight the ugly, deplorable whispers Fate puts in my head. But there's a sensation of being full. He brings a satisfaction akin to climbing a high mountain or completing a difficult day of work: tiring and exhausting, but also fulfilling.

The madness screams for me to run far away and yet seduces me to inch ever closer to him all at the same time. It's a war on every physical, emotional and mental level. Perhaps this is why they say denying Fate brings only misery. There's certainly a kind of masochistic insanity here.

"How are you?" Idris asks, quiet and serious.

I don't attempt to put words to the mixture of skin crawling and relief thrumming inside me like a stormy ocean.

"I'm not the one who's spent the last fortnight at sea. I thought you were only going to be gone ten days." I force my breathing to slow as I throw him a sideways glance. His face creases in a smirk as he leans closer.

"Worried about me?"

I roll my eyes.

"More like concerned you'd done something stupid, and I'd have to clean up the mess. It's a mercy no one wants to run for Bellandi's seat, even if it means we have to risk a split with every vote. I can't bear the thought of yet another Vote Day," I groan. Idris barks a laugh.

"It is a lot of effort," Idris agrees, "particularly when we can't agree on the candidate."

"Who says we have to agree? In the end you'll see I'm right," I retort, earning a snort from him. "Besides, I have a new suggestion—"

"Oh, let's not start this again right now." Idris half groans and half laughs. "I've only been on solid land for thirty minutes. Don't I get some adjustment time? Can't you ease me in gently?"

"Never. It's your fault for leaving. So what kept you?" I ask, dropping the mirth from my tone as we exit the chamber.

"Gathering details – what we could anyway." Idris's voice drops into that miles-deep whisper that tightens my throat and heats my breath. "We ran into ships from the Holy States. Alfieri's hunch was right."

"We're being blockaded," I hiss. What little trade remained in this city is being interrupted. This must be the Holy State's retaliatory plan. Isolate our economy and starve us until the city's resolve crumbles, then sweep aside the remains.

"Not officially of course, but considering how unfriendly our encounter was... There are definitely orders there. They wanted us to turn around. To abandon our cause. We only slipped through thanks to Barone family secrets."

The more I've learned about Alfieri's family business these last few months, the less I want to ask questions. The whole thing seems to be practically invisible – at least to the law. I've combed innumerable ledgers, studied a thousand documents, but the Barone family secrets are better buried than the foundations of this city.

If the Holy States are casting a net wide enough that even the Barone family's sketchy dealings are interrupted, we're in some serious trouble.

The wind rolls over my shoulders, sweeping a stray brunette curl across my face. I tuck it out of the way, turning my eyes from the painted steps of the High Chamber to the gentle blue sky, currently playing host to a number of rolling white clouds.

"Alfieri? Is he okay?" I ask, the breath hitching in my throat.

"Do you think I'd risk Emilia's wrath and bring him back with so much as a scratch?" Idris snorts gently. My shoulders drop, that hitch leaving my throat.

"Emilia? Wrath?" I snigger. Emilia would move heaven and earth for those she loved, absolutely true. But never with anything I could describe as wrath.

"It's the quiet ones you've got to watch. Listen, we need to talk but not here." Idris gestures around the open courtyard. People bustle about on both sides. Some watch us, covering their mouths to whisper with each other. I hate to imagine what stories they're concocting.

"Of course."

"Dinner at my place?" Idris suggests so casually, because it is.

Three months ago, before the Great Rebellion, I maybe set foot in the Patricelli family home four or five times in my life. Now I'm there at least twice a week, or he's at ours. Strictly for work of course. We couldn't afford any distractions; our city was in crisis.

The last time I had been distracted, I had been blinded. I had been taken for a fool by someone I thought I could rely on. My childhood companion turned lover turned malicious, manipulative murderer of my family and colleagues. A monster that stalked my nightmares.

Nouis's evil was dead, but the scars he left and the lessons he wrought don't need to be taught again. I won't be found so lacking a second time.

"Can't," I answer as I stomp the disappointment I shouldn't feel deep down in my gut. "I'm meeting the girls at Amica. You're welcome to join us."

"Thank you, but I have a few things I should sort now I'm back. Please send them all my best. Shall we meet up afterwards?" Idris suggests. I scratch the back of my head.

"I'll keep a nightcap for you." Idris chuckles, but I can see there is something serious he wants to discuss. I press my lips together. I shouldn't. I shouldn't tempt the bond; I shouldn't tempt Fate. I shouldn't test my own self-restraint.

Idris steps closer and my heart leaps to my throat as he lifts a hand up to my face. My skin shudders with hot waves as his fingertips brush the soft flesh of my cheek. He drags a stray lock of hair back behind my ear. My ear burns with his touch, my cheeks hot and flushed.

"I've been at sea for two whole weeks. Come, let me distract you from your problems for a bit."

"No distractions," I remind him and clear my throat. Idris smirks, mischief gleaming in his eyes.

"That's your rule. Not mine," Idris answers, trailing his hot fingers down the side of my neck before dropping his hand. "Still, come this evening. To talk."

"Okay," I agree. The small victory brings a smile to his face.

"Stay safe, Di Maineri," Idris whispers softly. "And when it's time for home, come find me."

Then he turns tail and disappears into the colourful Halician crowd.

CHAPTER 2

The Amica has changed drastically thanks to an absurdly good loan the landlady Paula secured from the Di Maineri Bank.

The entire building has been renovated and expanded into the building next door to create a beautiful kitchen, a large, open dining area and several private rooms for events. The inside is open and light thanks to the skylights during the day and lots of buttery candles on every table at night. Crocheted white tablecloths tumble off circular tables, surrounded by comfortable padded chairs and topped with crystal wine glasses.

The humming, warm space glows with amber candlelight. I take off my cloak as I sweep into the building. My lips widen as Paula hurries over.

"Signora, come in!" she says brightly, a stark contrast to the woman I first met when Idris and I secretly met here to fight against Bellandi's treachery. Paula is warm, funny and an absolutely brilliant cook, and the Amica has quickly become the spot for girls' nights.

"Paula," I greet, giving her a warm hug, "thank you for having us again."

"Thank you for coming, signora. The girls are at your table," she says taking my cloak and hanging it up.

She gestures through the crowded space to a large circular table. Giulia waves for me like I'd somehow miss my sister's signature golden hair glinting like spun sunshine.

"Thank you, signora," I answer before weaving towards the table. Michelle is seated on Giulia's right, hand lovingly wrapped around her girlfriend's. Serra sits with one elbow on the table as she holds her nearly empty wine glass and glares daggers at its dregs. Then comes Emilia, dark eyes bright as she flutters her fingers to beckon me over.

"Hi, how was your day?" Giulia beams, her pastel-pink silk dress swinging elegantly as she stands. The burns over her neck and left cheek have softened in the last few months, but the barbed silver snakes still remind me with every move of her head of the hell she's been through. Purple smudges lurk under her blue eyes; she's been working a lot of late nights recently. Hopefully girls' night will allow her some downtime. Moving with ethereal grace, she wraps me up in a warm embrace. I release her and smile.

"Idris is back," I answer.

"Yes, Emilia said the boys were back." Giulia chuckles as I sit in the spare seat next to her. Emilia beams, glass of red wine balanced between her fingers. The top half of her dark hair is wrapped elegantly back from her face, and a new set of jewelled silver earrings dangle from her ears.

"I'm surprised you're here and not celebrating Alfieri's homecoming," I tease, wiggling my eyebrows at her.

"He's got work this evening." She pouts. "I'll see him properly later, but look how pretty these earrings are."

"How did he get those? Weren't they on a ship for two weeks?" asked Michelle pouring me a glass of wine and sliding it over. As per usual, the slender brunette has her mass of dark curls bundled haphazardly on top of her head as she flashes me a welcoming smile.

"I think they ended up meeting some of Alfieri's *associates* on the trip," I say meaningfully, before sipping on my wine. Emilia sighs, biting her lips as though she figured as much but didn't like it.

"If you ask for the full story, does he tell you?" asks Michelle curiously, aware that the question is a little personal. Emilia nods, shifting uncomfortably as a brief, troubled look flashes across her features.

"Yes, of course, but I've decided most of the time I don't want to know. I really don't want to think about it, or the danger he's in. I can't talk him out of it. It's his family..." She trails off, tapping her wine as the thoughts spiral into her inner monologue.

"Oh, forget about that and tell us how the new sea defences are going," I say quickly to distract her. "Or the new alarm system you designed. It's ingenious." Emilia's small bell towers were being built all over Halice; tall posts, with ropes that could be reached from ground level, that house a glass-box pulley system that can raise and lower a candle inside a large stained-glass container. If you need help, you light the candle and use the pulley system to raise it all the way to the top. That way the watchtowers and City Guard can be alerted to issues sooner and come to handle problems. There were even different coloured glass containers to put over the candle, depending on the emergency and type of aid required. Accident, fire, crime and, of course, enemy soldiers – though those containers had thankfully not yet been used.

"Managing all these sites is a lot, but it's amazing," Emilia says brightly. "And I've just been asked to consult on strengthening the Old Bridge that goes over the River Vitta. I don't know how I'll have time for everything."

"All that money pouring into the Garden for defence is really paying off," muses Giulia. "Michelle's work documenting the Great Rebellion and inspiring Halician pride is just breathtaking!"

"Aww, thank you, love, but you'll always be the most breathtaking thing in the room." Michelle leans close and plants a sweet kiss on her girlfriend's cheek.

"How about you, Serra? Working on anything cool?" I ask, turning to my friend. She flashes a tight smile.

"Stuff," she answers brusquely, not inviting further questions. The silence stretches for a long moment.

"Let us know when it's done," I say brightly, hating the tenseness at the table. "We'll come and marvel."

Serra drains her glass in answer and nods shortly, refusing to meet anyone's eye as she reaches for the wine bottle.

I glance at Giulia who shrugs, worry lingering in her expression. Serra hasn't been the same since the Great Rebellion. Being arrested on suspicion of treason, and dumped in a dark cell, wondering if she was going to be executed for a crime she didn't commit, had left marks. She had seemed moderately okay, but this down spell seems to be lasting.

We'll have to make a concerted effort.

"So, Giulia, how's the bank?" asks Emilia, moving the conversation on. Giulia sighs, rubbing the burns on her jaw – a habit of hers now when she's troubled.

"Complicated," she admits. "We lost a lot of money and with everything ... it's tough to fix."

Michelle squeezes her hand.

Trying to plug the hole the traitor Bellandi left in our bank's finances isn't an easy task. He stole so much money to pay mercenaries to invade our city, to weaken it for a Holy States coup. And with trade dropping and work drying up, things aren't getting any easier.

"That's alright. No one expects it to happen overnight," I say encouragingly, knowing just how stressed she's been. Sometimes I find her in the small hours still poring over documents by candlelight.

"I'd take overnight in a heartbeat actually." Giulia snorts ruefully, but whatever she was going to say next falls from her tongue. Her brow pinches as her gaze locks on something behind me and I turn, spying a staff member from our home hurrying towards the table.

"Bruno, is everything alright?" I ask. He's panting hard, like he just stopped running. He nods to Giulia and me before starting.

"Signora, signora, apologies for interrupting your evening, but your aunts have arrived."

I bolt upright in my seat, blinking hard as my wine glass slams onto the table.

"Our aunts?" Giulia repeats, horrified.

"Which aunts?" I push, sharing her shock.

"All three, signoras."

Giulia and I exchange a wide-eyed look.

"Bruno, please hail us a carriage, quick as you can," Giulia instructs as I grab my wine, swallowing the last two mouthfuls as we get to our feet.

"Is everything alright?" asks Michelle. Giulia leans down, planting a tender kiss on her girlfriend's lips.

"Time to find out," Giulia answers ruefully.

"Need me to come with you?"

"No, dear, best we handle this first," Giulia answers, smiling away Michelle's concerns. "Di Maineri family politics can be tricky. I'll fill you in later." We bid goodbye to our friends and make for the carriage. Giulia and I don't need to exchange a word because we know the truth.

If our aunts are here that can only mean one thing.

We have good cause for worry.

CHAPTER 3

The night washes the creamy stone of our home with a layer of inky shadows. Torches glow orange as the flames fling themselves against their frosted glass prisons. They frame the warm wood of our front door and cast a rolling tide of vermillion and gold over the cobbled path from the street to the front step.

The carriage comes to a stop. Giulia and I don't hesitate. My boots thump quietly over the path, and I wipe my hand over the silk of my dress as I prepare for what awaits.

Giulia pauses, her hand on the twisted bronze front door handle. Her gaze snaps to mine, those blue eyes slowly turning to steel. She raises a delicate eyebrow questioningly. *Are you ready for this?* I let out the breath, straightening my shoulders. I give her a short nod.

Giulia pushes our front door open and we sweep into our warm home.

A sea of expensive leather trunks loiters on the pretty mosaic floor. Our staff dart about as they put them in various guest rooms. Amongst the chaos is a vaguely familiar face from the younger days of my childhood. Aunt Fiora.

Small and slight in stature, she has a dainty nose and arched brow. Her dark hair and warm complexion pair beautifully with large brown doe-eyes framed by fluffy dark lashes. Yet, for all her delicate appearance, she could be mistaken for a drill sergeant as she deftly imparts instructions to the staff, answering queries with effortless precision to move this pandemonium along.

She spins on the spot, her face melting into a smile of delight.

"Girls! Oh, look at you, so big now!" Fiora beams, hurrying over. She embraces me first.

"Renza, darling. Oh, so grown up," she says warmly, then pulls Giulia in a big hug. She pulls back, placing a hand on Giulia's jaw, inspecting the burns along her neck.

"Oh, my darling, look at you. You're such a beautiful young woman, don't you ever forget it," Fiora trills warmly. "I hear you have a girlfriend, too. I can't wait to meet her."

"Thanks, Aunt Fiora," says Giulia with a tight smile. "Are you alone?"

"No," chimes another voice, deep and tinted with humour. "We just know when best to leave her to her work."

Two women stand in the entrance to our living room. Aunt Rialta, the eldest of the three sisters, her dark eyes and thin lips pull into a smirk as she throws a sideways glance at Fiora. Her dark hair forms a braided crown on her head, studded with gold and silver pins that match long, draping earrings. Swathed in thickly embroidered satins with large, trumpeted sleeves and trailing skirts, she's embraced the lifestyle and fashions of her family in Galonga.

Fiora rolls her eyes.

"Well, someone needs to sort things. I put us in rooms to the north of the house. I hope that's okay?" Fiora says, looking to me for confirmation. After my father's death, I became Head of the Bank, and, as such, head of the family, given that most of the extended family tree consider them to be one and the same. I nod, trying not to fold my arms in hostility as I lean against the wall.

"Of course, this is a family home," I answer diplomatically. "If we'd known you were coming then we'd have prepared rooms."

"I thought Agosta sent word ahead?" Rialta frowns, turning to their youngest sister. The tall, lithe woman spins a glass of wine between long, dainty fingers. She laughs warmly, and shrugs her golden shoulders. Her brown hair gleams with dark red warmth, and her dark eyes match her sisters' and are framed with thick lashes that flutter like butterfly wings.

"Something must've happened to the messenger. Sorry, girls," Agosta answers with a small chuckle, "but it's good to have the family back together. Even if this home is hardly recognisable."

"Tomas made it his own, as is right. I love the changes; your mother did this?" asks Fiora, pointing to a beautiful mosaic wall of a peacock in a flower garden. My throat tightens as I nod.

"Yes."

"Such a talented woman," muses Fiora softly, shaking her head as she studies the piece.

"Don't lean against the wall like a common workman, Renza. Posture is self-respect," fusses Rialta.

Someone should have timed how many seconds we managed before the nitpicking started.

"Leave her alone, Rialta. She spent all day in the High Chamber. She's tired," Fiora retorts before I can speak.

"High Chamber, with that intriguing Soulhate the whole continent has heard about." Agosta slips closer like we're confidantes and it's the best gossip in the world. "I hear he's quite the charmer."

"Agosta!" scolds Fiora, horrified. "He's her Soulhate! It isn't like *that*."

Giulia's face flashes a smirk before she hastily covers it with a hand. Agosta notices, dark eyes glinting with mischief. Chuckling to herself, Agosta nudges me with her elbow before gliding away.

I want to slam my head into the wall, but that'll only start a barrage of scolding at my rudeness.

"So the Soulhate ... *thing* ... is real? You have a Soulhate and you're both ... what? Ignoring it?" Rialta frowns at me like it's absurd. "I thought it was made up."

"Of course it's real. I think it's brilliant." Agosta giggles, draining her glass of wine.

"Of course you do." Fiora scowls, shaking her head. "Perhaps your Soulhate can be spouse number four."

"Maybe they will," taunts Agosta, wiggling her eyebrows. "Maybe we'll be happier than even you and Arturo in your nauseating Soulmated bliss."

"Only problem is when this one dies, like your others, people will absolutely point fingers at you." Rialta snorts darkly. Agosta doesn't so much as flinch at her sister's harsh words.

"They did with the others, too, darling, but they were Fate-honest tragedies." Agosta inspects her nails like she's bored by the accusation. "At least with my Soulhate we'd burn hot and bright and brilliant, right, Renza?"

I. Have. No. Words.

Instead, Giulia and I walk in tandem towards the living room. I don't stop, heading straight for the drinks cabinet.

"That says it all!" calls Agosta as our aunts follow. Agosta drifts to my side as I pull out glasses and wine and sets her empty glass down for a refill.

"It's lovely to see you all but—" Giulia starts.

"Why are we here?" Rialta interrupts. "To give you our support of course. We've all just suffered a family tragedy."

"It's been three months," Giulia responds. Three months since the Great Rebellion. Three months since our father was brutally murdered in the Grand Temple explosion that claimed the lives of the previous Electi – and almost Giulia's, too.

"We had things to settle. I can't just leave Galonga with a snap of my fingers. As you know, I also run a very successful Di Maineri Bank," Rialta answers, folding her arms defensively, "second only to the Head Bank here in Halice."

"We know, Rialta. You've done wonderful work in Galonga with the bank branches out there," Giulia says, not holding back her eyerolls. "But you could've written."

"Loves that bank more than her daughter, I swear," Agosta whispers in my ear as I fill a wine glass. "I bet that's why she and her husband are estranged." I smother my smirk by raising my own glass to my lips and draining it.

They're estranged? I didn't know that.

"We all had issues to settle before setting off," Fiora explains, letting out a quiet sigh. "I know we missed the funeral, but I was hoping to visit Tomas's grave tomorrow to pay respects?"

"Of course," Giulia answers as I hand her the glass of wine. We tap our glasses together, sharing a look of steel before each taking a sip.

"So, girls, where can we help?" Rialta asks, rubbing her hands together expectantly.

"Help?" I repeat weakly. *Oh no, here we go.*

"Of course. We heard about everything. Money was stolen. The city was attacked and now needs aid. How can we help?" repeats Rialta. "That's why we're here."

"Help," I repeat, fighting the exasperated laugh threatening to spill over. "That's very kind, aunties, but given the hour, perhaps you should just settle in this evening. Besides, I have a work meeting I should leave for."

Giulia gives me a look of ultimate betrayal, and she's absolutely right. I'm a traitor leaving her with them, but I can't do this right now. Having all three aunties in one room is brewing the mother of all headaches.

"At this hour?" barks Fiora, concerned. "Where? What about? With whom?"

"I'm an adult, Aunt Fiora," I remind her, "and I'm going to discuss High Chamber business."

"Oh, you're so like your father! Always working," chuckles Agosta. "Chamber this and chamber that. Halice this, Halice that."

My stomach churns. Fate knows I wish Father were here. He would have been better for this city. He'd know exactly what to do. Perhaps he'd still be alive if I'd been sharper; been more aware of the manipulations and schemes of someone who tricked me – someone I should never have let as close as I did.

"Good. He was a good leader," I answer, draining my glass. "Giulia, a moment?"

Giulia and I step out into the corridor, closing the door behind us.

"Seriously, you're leaving me with this?" she hisses in outrage, gesturing to the door. I hold up my hands in surrender.

"Sorry. I said I'd meet Idris. I need to know what he saw out there. It sounded serious."

"Forget the war beyond the city, what about the war brewing in our living room?" Giulia scowls. "Those three under one roof? I can already tell you how that's going to end."

"Then let them fight it out. Maybe they'll kill each other? We can stand back and be entertained," I joke. Giulia throws me an unamused look. "We can't kick them out. It's a family home."

"This will end with bloodshed, mark my words," Giulia grumbles.

"Just don't let it start with you, that's all I ask. And if it does start, finish it." I wink as I head for the front door. "I owe you one."

"You owe me three," she corrects as I close the door behind me, returning to the serenity of the night.

CHAPTER 4

Halice slumbers as the night sky undulates between violet and sapphire. Stars cluster in bated silence, a captive audience to the scenes unfolding below. The full moon trails rivers of silver over the streets, pulling out the ridges and valley of our architecture like an expert painter. My beloved city has become a masterpiece of stone and starlight.

I turn down a familiar street, heading for the Patricelli family home. The grand building is made of the same pale stone as the rest of Halice, meticulously carved centuries ago by artisanal stonemasons. The filagree around the doors and windows is intricate, exquisite, but simultaneously understated. I could study it for hours.

I reach the large, dark wooden door and rap my knuckles against the polished surface.

My breath turns uncomfortably warm and itchy, my throat tightens, my fingers tingle hot and sharp. I turn in expectation as Idris opens the door.

"Did you walk?" Idris asks, his tone edged in disapproval. He stands back to welcome me in.

Gone are the tactical travelling leathers he'd worn in the High Chamber today. Instead, he's donned a pale, fitted tunic trimmed with red and blue brocade over dark trousers. His blond hair is carelessly tousled, hazel eyes studying my appearance. My throat goes tight because his gaze is like fire.

"Of course I did. It's barely a few streets."

Idris has always been protective. As a child he left Halice, travelling to strange cities and places, all to avoid our bond. And after all his adventures, after all he'd seen, experienced and learned, he'd returned with a solemn vow: he would never hurt me. He wasn't alone in his vow. I reciprocated the sentiment with an aggressive fervour – something beyond my wildest imaginings when we'd first met. But now? I couldn't deny it. A possessive need thrummed between us, and I couldn't tell if it was because of the bond or something entirely our own making.

But fierce as our principles are, intentions can rapidly burn to ash in the fire of a Fated bond. In my rational mind, I'd do anything it took to protect Idris. But the bond possesses no reason or logic, only pure rage, fire and destruction. But at least I didn't wage the war of two selves alone.

I step past him to enter. The air between us tightens and fizzes uncomfortably as I sweep past, refusing to look his way until I secure more distance.

"The Amica is hardly a few streets away. You girls must've had quite the session given the hour." Idris chuckles and closes the door. "I didn't think you were coming; I was just about to call it a night."

"I'm sorry. Want me to go?" I ask, my brow pinching as I cast my eyes down to avoid him. I breathe slowly, wrestling the bond into submission. I should want to leave, to relieve myself of the fury of the bond, the whispers rolling around my skull disturbingly vile and aggressive. I stretch out my twinging fingers and shift my shoulders to settle the discomfort.

"Never," Idris says seriously, his voice deep and warm.

My chest trickles with warmth as he closes the door. "Come through to the study."

The Patricelli home is beautiful. The creamy walls are examples of some of the oldest stonework in Halice. The masonry reaches to lofty, carved ceilings sprawling metres overhead. Warm wood panelling is affixed at the base of the walls, rising to chest height. The old wood is so well looked after that it's soft and gleaming like preserved silk. Large, patterned windows sit at regular intervals and the rooms are accented with exquisite furniture accumulated by generations of wealthy businessmen. The contents of this home are priceless and artisanal, and while the style varies, the exceptional taste is common amongst it all.

As we reach the study, I'm greeted by a crackling fireplace tossing fickle rivers of gold over the fitted wooden shelves that line the room. Idris sinks comfortably into the plush emerald couch, closing the leather-bound book he was reading moments before. I head for his drinks cabinet, snagging a bottle of wine and pulling out two glasses.

"More wine?" Idris queries gently.

"Girls' night was interrupted," I grumble, setting the bottle down. I push his glass towards him before grabbing mine and taking a hearty swig.

"By what?" Concern lingers in Idris's voice. I take a slow, deep breath.

"My aunts."

"Which ones?"

"All of them."

"All three of them?" Idris clarifies.

"Yes," I say on a sigh, tapping my fingers against my glass. "They descended upon Halice hours ago and are already turning my home upside down."

"They all arrived today? Together?" He frowns. I nod grimly.

"Which is weird given Rialta lives in Galonga, Fiora lives with her Soulmate in Nimal and Agosta – well, her last husband was a wealthy man from the Holy States, but where she's been since he died, I'm not sure. But it already stinks. They're up to something."

"Oof! Blood doesn't run so thick in the Di Maineri family?"

"Trust me, until proven otherwise it's best to consider my aunts what they most likely are. Threats." I shake my head at the sky. "If they're here, they're after something."

"What if they're here to mourn their brother and support their nieces?" Idris challenges quietly. I snort, rolling my eyes.

"You clearly haven't met enough of my kin."

Idris chuckles quietly, sending goosebumps flying over my skin. I understand why he'd suggest this – his family is nothing like mine. His parents loved him so much they changed the fabric of this city for him. They died in the same explosion that claimed my father's life. After so many years away, avoiding me, he had returned, only for them to be cruelly and brutally slaughtered.

I know how much family means to Idris. How their deaths torment him as much as my father's does me, but wishful thinking won't make my family any less a nest of snakes waiting to strike.

I take a deep breath, steeling myself, and lower my chin. I fix my eyes on my Soulhate, fire clustering into my vision and my pulse running molten.

"Alright, enough about them." I clear my tingling throat to no avail. "What did you see out there?"

Idris sits forwards, sets down his drink and links his hands over his knees.

"It's as we thought. The Argenti Strait is brimming with ships from the Holy States," Idris says. "They're discouraging trade." Idris gives a heavy sigh. "They're forcing ships to turn around and head back to their original ports."

They're trying to starve us. The Halician people see the Great Rebellion as a victory, winning our freedom from those who tried to steal it. But how quickly will that attitude change when they can't feed their children?

"We need to do something," Idris says. I nod, failing to dislodge the lump forming in my throat. "And that's not all."

"Not all?" I say, managing to keep my voice steady.

"I heard rumours... The Holy Mother is gathering her cardinals, and their armies of Church Militia, to the capital of Kavas."

I close my eyes, taking a shaky breath to steady myself. I should've expected it. I should've known this was coming. Starve us, weaken us, invade us. Conquer Halice undeniably for the world to see. Of course that was their plan.

"We can commission the Garden to create new, innovative defences. We can build more forts and strongholds along the coast and shore up our borders with infrastructure. But it's not enough, not with the time we have. Fundamentally, we do not have the fighting force to fend off an army, or the ships to stop this blockage." Idris says quietly, "We need more men."

He's right, though the bond shudders in revulsion at that acknowledgement.

Halice hasn't needed a real army in over a century. We're on good terms with all our neighbours – a crucial situation, given all the passing trade. Additionally, with the tail end of the Steel Curtain and the Argenti Strait flanking our land, a large force is not necessary as a deterrent – geography has already done that job for us.

Those days are behind us.

"You have a plan?" I ask. Idris nods.

"When you don't have something and you need it, you buy it," Idris answers.

I pause, blinking hard as I chew on his words. My chest tightens, the response springing to my lips.

"With what money?" I groan, rubbing my brows. "We have no trade. We have no money."

"If we have no city, we'll never be able to fix that," Idris points out. "Better debt than dead."

I set down my glass, resting my elbows on my knees. Oh, man, he's bringing on a headache. Why is everyone doing that tonight?

"You want to hire mercenaries?" I repeat, to be sure I understand.

"I know some really great candidates—"

"Idris, no!"

I press my lips together, throwing myself to my feet. I need to move. Need to release the pent-up angst of the bond. My pulse itches in my throat, embers roar in my palm. I pace in my usual spot behind one of Idris's sofas. The bond coils like a viper, tail flicking dangerously back and forth as I fight to keep my mind on track. The energy this bond generates has to go somewhere, and pacing works as an outlet.

My heart pounds at his suggestion. Fixing one problem by making another a thousand times worse can't be an answer!

"Renza, we need a military force we don't have!" Idris insists. "We're going to be invaded, and we will lose."

"Idris, we can't pay them!" I argue sharply. "How do you think mercenaries will treat this city when they don't get paid! Worse or better than the Church Militia?"

"We'll pay them—"

"With what?" I snap.

"We can work that out later," Idris says calmly. "But without an army we won't have a city."

"No. This is madness. We can't invite an experienced, foreign armed force into our city! Particularly not one without any loyalties to us! Particularly when *we can't pay them*!"

Idris sighs, sipping on his wine as he looks to one side. I pause my pacing, narrowing my gaze.

"What. Did. You. Do?" I ask tightly, the words snapping off my tongue.

"Well ... I hoped you'd see sense and it takes a while for people to travel," Idris reasons. "I've already sent the invitations."

Invitations? Plural?

I rub my temple. A brittle laugh escapes my teeth.

"And how many armies exactly have you invited to brawl over our city?" The anger boils on my breath. My skin itches, my pulse hammers against the veins in my throat, my mouth is dry and red-hot.

"Three, all of whom have the strongest honour code. The ones I trust the most," Idris answers steadily.

"You went behind the backs of the High Chamber, on your own, and invited *three foreign armies to our city!*" I shout the last part. I want to hurl something at his stupid, arrogant head.

"I'm going to bring the matter before the High Chamber tomorrow, and I was hoping to have you on side."

"No! No! No!" I shake my head frantically. Having a single army here is one thing but three? Three armies we know nothing about? Can't he see the disaster that's going to be? Three armed forces loyal only to gold in a city that *can't pay*! We don't have the soldiers or skills to keep them in line by force. If they decide to take what they feel they're owed, we're doomed.

"They're all good people, Renza," Idris insists, remaining seated on the couch. His blistering eyes trace my steps as I pace behind the sofa again, this time quicker. "I wouldn't invite untrustworthy monsters. I've fought with some of them."

I grit my teeth, raising my hands to my hair. I dig my nails into my scalp, the stinging a strange kind of relief.

"And exactly *who* have you invited to our city without the permission of the High Chamber?" I demand.

"We have the Salt Hounds; they normally fight up north. They make a lot of money from the various barons in Estrende and Agoa. Their leaders are two brothers named Panos and Solon."

"I've heard the name," I admit. How did Idris cross their path?

"Then there's the Galen Company. They have a leader named Briaggio, whom I've met a few times. Slightly older in years but his men are very loyal to him. Works mainly in Sovassa for their chancellor, handling inter-feudal disputes."

"And finally?" I push. Idris nods slowly before answering.

"Then I invited the Red Sands Bannerhood."

"The Red Sands Bannerhood?" I repeat. This must be the one he's really interested in. I can tell just by the way he said the name, that air of warmth and familiarity with it.

"Yes. From Coari."

I take a deep, steadying breath, placing both hands on the back of the sofa, my heart thrumming like a war drum. The Halicians have a long history with the people of Coari, and so does the Holy States.

Back when the entire continent was all under the Holy States' reign, previous Holy Sovereigns had attempted to invade Coari so many times we'd lost count. Their greed demanded they expand the empire to a new continent. Naturally the Coari people fought back, defending their home. Halice was the natural launch point for the invasions, given it was only on the other side of the Argenti Strait. Which meant the counter attacks launched by the Coari people had also been felt by the Halician people.

All of that quieted down after the Independent States secured their freedom, but the history is long and bloody and brimming with many scars that haven't been forgotten by either side. The Coari people are not friendly to us. They won't allow people from our continent to dock in their ports, even centuries later.

"From your time in Coari? I take it they're your friends." Fate's Fury, I hope that he hasn't invited strangers here! He can't be that nonsensical.

"Yes. They are. I trust them implicitly."

"How long did you fight with them?" I ask despite myself, stealing another small piece of Idris's life of adventure and mystery.

"Three years." Idris speaks quietly, his gold eyes watching me like a hawk. "They became a second family to me. Their leader is a close friend. It doesn't guarantee they'll fight for us, but they'll come, hear us out, and respect peace between all parties during talks."

The way he talks about them brims with warmth. Perhaps even hope. They were the family he'd been forced to find when he left Halice.

Because of me.

"Why'd you come back?" The question bursts from my tongue before I can swallow it. Idris shrugs, like the answer is obvious.

"Father called me home. We need the help, Renza." Idris stands. My eyes snap around, and I'm hit with a wave of nausea and bile. I focus on my breathing as he walks towards me, hands in his pockets. "I knew travel would take time so I sent the invitations before I left. These people are coming. We need to get on board with that."

"Because of you, Idris! These armed forces are coming here because of you!" I jab a finger at him, anger curling around my words. "You acted on behalf of the city without informing the High Chamber! That's inexcusable. It's grounds for a vote of no-confidence. You could lose your seat for this!"

"I don't trust anyone when it comes to Halice's safety. Only you." Idris closes the distance between us, each step making my gut bristle. I swallow the discomfort, stamping it down as I try and control my accelerating pulse. Idris leans against the sofa next to me and folds his arms.

"If I had gone to the High Chamber first, the Holy States' spies would've learned of our plans and moved to stop these potential allies from arriving. They would've shored up their blockade, making it impossible for anything to pass, and this opportunity would've been dead in the water. I had to make sure nothing could expose our plans."

"*Your* plan! Because you didn't tell me," I snap, digging my fingers into the velvet of the couch to keep from swiping at him.

"Because you—" Idris almost explodes in frustration, raking a hand through his hair as he stops himself. I narrow my eyes, teeth clamping together.

"Because I what?" I pushed.

"If they refused to come, I didn't want to add it to your plate," Idris mutters, looking away.

"Liar," I accuse. "Because. I. What?" He doesn't flinch, but his shoulders bunch as though preparing for a physical fight. He lets out a terse breath before speaking.

"You're not *doing* anything!"

The words certainly feel like a physical blow.

"It's like you're paralysed!" Idris growls out the words that have clearly been eating at him for a while. "You refuse to try anything unfamiliar, refuse to take any kind of risk! Everything is discussed endlessly for days and days. While they make moves, we dither!"

My cheeks burn. My throat tightens and my tongue runs hot.

"And that's my fault?" I hiss, the words tasting like smoke.

"Everyone in the High Chamber takes your lead! Fate's Fury, even I do half the time!" Idris groans. He reaches for me but I jolt backwards, not wanting to feel any more hurt.

"Renza," Idris says with a sigh, the word tinged with remorse, but I hold up a hand.

"No, let's hear it, Idris. Let's hear how I'm failing this city. How I'm blind and doing everything wrong!" I snap, my tongue running rampant as I take another step backwards. Idris's hands whip out to my shoulders. His fingers burn into my muscles as he pulls me to him.

"I didn't say any of that." He speaks in a low voice, almost seething. "Where did that come from?"

"You might as well ha—"

"No I didn't. Not at all!" Idris narrows those golden eyes, scanning me head to toe. I swallow, hating that he's right again. I had made that leap. I had said those words.

Words that had been churning in my head ever since the Great Rebellion.

Words Nouis had put there.

The childhood friend turned lover turned nightmare. The man who collaborated with Bellandi to slaughter my father, use my sister as a tool of manipulation, use me in ways I still don't understand. A monster I should've seen. Maybe then my father and Idris's parents and all my former colleagues would be alive. Maybe I could've stopped all this tragedy from happening. If I had just opened my eyes and seen that monster for who he really was.

"We're moving away from the point," I say with gritted teeth. "You acted without High Chamber approval."

Idris sighs.

"The invitations are sent. They are coming. So now we need to convince the High Chamber that this is a good plan. Will you help me?"

I shake my head, glaring at the low fireplace.

"No. I don't like this. I don't agree with it. Even worse, you acted on your own, risking our city, because you thought you knew best. We can't pay these dangerous people. We can't control them or ensure their loyalty. When they arrive, if I have anything to say about it, the gates will be closed and you can explain to your so-called friends how stupid and arrogant you are for inviting them!" I scowl, folding my arms.

Idris sighs and nods slowly.

"Okay, then I'll do it without your support."

I turn to lean back against the sofa next to him. I'm so close to him our arms almost touch. Sparks crack across the slip of air between us, tight and brittle, like one move and we'll shatter. The whispers of the bond hiss and purr in the vestiges of my mind, trying to draw me in with dark, satisfying violence.

Idris and I have disagreed on policy before, on how best to do things, on what we think is the right move. We have voted in ways that oppose each other. Often. But the High Chamber has always been respected, the vote has always been the decider. But this one ... to sidestep the chamber entirely ... this is a new low.

I shake my head. I'm so mad at him. I hate how mad I am at him. And that he felt he had to act without telling me. I hate the cracks forming in the trust I have in him ... and my own role in putting it there.

"I should go," I say sharply, loathing how thick my words feel leaving my lips.

"Stay," Idris counters softly.

It's not an unusual occurrence, me staying here. We often talk late into the evening, to the point of exhaustion. His spare room is quickly beginning to feel like a second bedroom. A second home.

"No." I shake my head. "No, I should—"

"It's late. Your room is always ready. You can shore up your battle plans in the morning."

"Idris—"

He moves. Suddenly he's in front of me, his arms resting either side of me, gripping the couch. I gasp, leaning back as a wall of fire races over my skin.

"Stay," he repeats. "I've been too long away from you. Please ... stay."

I only manage to nod once. A small smile graces his lips, his head dropping. For a moment I think he'll kiss me. No, we agreed we wouldn't. Yet I crave him. His smoke. His fire. His destruction.

He takes in a deep breath before he forces himself to straighten.

"Good," he says, his deep voice a touch strained, "You know where your room is by now. Let me know if you need anything." My heart hammers in my throat and clangs in my ears as he walks towards the hallway, firelight bouncing off his blond hair. Each step lessens the bond between us, diluting the dark, bristling flames. He pauses at the door, turns back and winks at me, that irritating, cocky, self-assured grin plastered to his face.

"Sleep well, my dearest nemesis. Tomorrow, we battle."

My stomach does flips and my mouth runs dry as he taunts the bond into a brief surge of new life. He doesn't let me answer before heading up the stairs like he's said nothing at all. I swallow, which does nothing to alleviate the dryness in my throat, and force myself to take a deep, calming breath.

That man is going to be the death of me, Fate knows it.

The High Chamber is majestic. Colours gush from the ceiling, wrapping their luminous, diamond-flecked tails around the creamy architecture. I stand in the middle of the grand hall, completely alone. The chairs are empty. The pews are silent. The bright warmth of the sun stained with vibrancy of the rainbow pours over my face.

I close my eyes and soak in that warmth.

But the warmth leaves. I open my eyes, gazing up at a ceiling again. Dark spindly fingers crack across the delicate art. Drop by drop, oily black rain falls from the splitting wounds, blooming like a poisonous mould as dark shadows crawl across the stone floor. Rivers of ebony ink weep from the roof, winding down the white stone columns, marring its perfection and flooding across the mosaic stage beneath my feet.

"Renza..." I spin, ensnared and hunted by that voice.

"Renza..." The hiss comes again. Something is moving behind me. I peer through the darkness. My heart throbs in my mouth, the scream barely held behind my teeth. Panting furiously, my eyes tear through the shadow, not daring to leave the sparsely illuminated central white stage, which is the only thing I can really see.

"Renza..." The voice is behind me now. I face it, the scream somehow stolen from me as a huge form grows from the slick oils on the floor. I scream and scream, but no noise escapes my lips. My feet are welded to the floor; I cannot run. The forming shape rattles ominously, hissing as it takes form. A huge snake, with three heads.

"Renza, Renza, Renza..." it snarls, gnashing its repugnant yellow teeth at me. It's going to eat me. It's going to consume me, blood and bones.

No. NO. NO!

"RENZA!"

Gasping, my eyes fly open as I bolt upright. Sweat coats my skin and my hair clings to my neck and back as my heart thunders in my ears. Hands burning like hot coals grip my shoulders as I look into two blistering hazel eyes.

Idris.

I wince and gasp again as revulsion rushes down my throat and sinks its claws into my stomach. I launch myself sideways, covering my eyes with my hands as I desperately fight the violent urges running through my mind – the desire to sink my nails into his skin, to feel the warmth of his blood dripping from my fists.

"Have you got this?" asks Idris quietly. "Do you want me to leave?" He's asking about the bond. Communicating is the key. I frantically shake my head as I grasp for control.

"I'm ... fine..." I manage as I fight to contain my lungs.

"It's okay," Idris says gently, rubbing my back. Only the thin silk of my borrowed nightshirt separates his searing touch from my skin. An inferno rushes to life up and down my spine, shuddering with rage. It's only then that I realise I'm still shaking. I swallow, my throat sore and swollen. I've been screaming.

That must've been what brought him in.

"Sorry," I groan, flinching as he eases onto the bed behind me. "I'm so sorry, I didn't—"

"It was a nightmare, Renza. They happen," Idris says calmly. "Do you want to talk about it?"

I shake my head, rubbing my eyes and brow as though I can throw the horrible experience away. But I can't. That three-headed snake thrashes about in my head like a poison.

"It was only a dream. It wasn't real," Idris says softly. I nod sharply, giving myself a little shake as I sit up properly. I fight to control my breath, summoning my will over my pulse and turn to look at him. I battle the wave of whispers that spring to my ears, the roaring black venom that wants me to go for his throat. I offer him a smile; it's weak at best.

He's shirtless and his chiselled chest is illuminated by a candle he brought with him. His deep-red scorpion-tail tattoo sits proudly below his left shoulder. I haven't seen him shirtless since the Great Rebellion. I forgot just how ... impressive he is.

I catch sight of a sword on the bedside table – he must've grabbed it thinking I was being attacked. If the ground could swallow me whole and save me the mortification, I'd be eternally grateful.

"I'm sorry I woke you," I croak, then attempt to clear my throat.

"Not a problem. Are you alright now?"

I nod, pushing my hair away from my face, unable to meet his eyes – and not for the usual reason. Idris nods, getting up to leave. As he reaches for his sword, my gasp slaps through the room like lightning, my gaze glued to the vicious raised scars streaking across his back.

"Renza—"

"Who did that to you?" I demand, voice quivering with fury. I bolt to my knees in the bed to see the savagery more clearly. My hand reaches out as if to touch, to soothe, but I pull myself back before I make contact. I can't bear to feel them, to force them to be real, to let this be something other than another nightmare.

These were made by a whip and though they're clearly years old, they tell a vivid enough story.

"Renza—"

"Tell me who did this to you!" I demand again, an inferno erupting in my stomach. Fury rushes in my ears, pounding as fast as a boxer punches. "Tell me now!"

I'm shaking with violence and with my desire to get my hands on the person who did this and return twice what they dared give Idris.

He sighs and puts one caustic hand to the side of my face and forces me to meet his gaze. Looking into his eyes is like staring into the unadulterated power of the sun, leaving me blind to all else.

"Who?" Fury makes my insistent word a thick whisper as tears of anger and horror quicken in my eyes.

"A dead man," answers Idris coldly. "It was a long time ago."

Dead. The disappointment wars with the relief. Because I can't give this beast my rage, but he didn't deserve to breathe a second longer than he did.

"Tell me." I'm practically begging. Idris sighs.

"I was leaving Chalgos, three and a bit years ago. I was on a trading ship bound for Halice. The plan was for me to come back here permanently, but we were stopped by a Coari ship just as we entered the Argenti Strait. They took the goods, the food and every life onboard as slaves. They already had other prisoners on board their ship whom they were going to sell at an illegal slave market in the south of their continent, so they just added us to the lot. Normally they wouldn't attack a ship on the strait, but it turns out they'd run out of supplies. We were dying of starvation and thirst, caged in like animals. I tried to get them to see reason, to at least allow us water to drink or we wouldn't make it..." Idris gestures to his back and shrugs. "They didn't like my thought process."

My eyes well with hot tears.

"How did you get out of there?"

"We were rescued, by the Red Sands Bannerhood. They'd come for the stolen Coari people, but rescued us, too," Idris answers, a warm smile flirting with his face. "Things unfolded and I learned they were heading to Malaya to study mind-stilling. I asked to go with them."

I let out a shaky breath, lifting my hands to Idris's neck.

All these terrible things he went through. Because he left. Because of me.

"Idris." The whisper is so sad, it cracks as it leaves my trembling lips.

"It's ancient history," Idris says, both hands reaching up to cup my jaw, setting off an invisible wave of burning sparks. "It's fine."

"No, it's not." I shake my head against his grip. "It'll never be fine." Fire writhes under my fingers, venomous snakes coil in my belly, my very teeth ache to fight back against the people who dared do this. Dared to touch him.

Idris leans closer, his forehead dropping to mine. His touch explodes like mini suns across my skin. It steals my breath, turning my blood into molten iron in my veins.

"Please, Renza, don't worry about it. It was long ago and I'm safe. I'm home."

"How can I not? You were almost—"

"Shhh," he whispers, his breath falling warm across my

nose. "Put it from your mind." A thousand stars fly across my flesh, dragging shivers deep from my bones.

"I can't think of anything else." My aching words shudder against my tongue. The fire, the black, dark loathing. How much of it is our bond and how much is the idea of those monsters I can't tell. I clamp my eyes closed as I reach up for him, digging my hands into his shoulders like I could pry the past and its horrors from him. Embers sizzle across my palms, sinking their tingling teeth into my flesh.

"I can fix that," Idris vows, his deep voice verging on a growl. Before I can answer, his lips close on mine.

His kiss is a poison that ignites every fibre in my body, scattering a thousand blistering needles through every dark crevice of my mind until I'm consumed. My fingers itch, my blood boils. A guttural noise rips free of my lips as I knot my hands in his hair. He can have my anger, the rage he provokes with his tortuous hands.

His fevered movements are hungry, his grip strong, rough and devouring. He throws us back against the bed, the sharp movement ripping the breath from my lungs. I don't recover before he pins me to the mattress, his muscled body pressing hard against mine to trap me beneath him.

My borrowed nightshirt rides up to my hips. His fiery hands run down the side of my body, slipping to my bare thighs. I fight my strangled moan as my pulse turns to thunder and stars. Only his linen pyjama trousers stand between my molten core and the thick, hard length of him. I can feel every hard ridge and bump through the thin material as he grinds it punishingly against me. His calloused fingers sweep over my sensitive, tingling abdomen, tracing blazing shapes into the soft skin and causing my hips to buck against him, pressing harder into his impressive manhood.

"Fate, Renza," Idris groans against my mouth. I gasp for breath, gripping him harder to me as I attempt to undo this man as much as he unravels me. To match his every relentless manoeuvre with a vengeful strategy of my own. To win this excruciating, exquisite battle of madness.

His fiery grip against my hips drags a hiss from my teeth, as I rip my mouth away, gasping for air as my vision swims red. He attacks my neck, devouring the sensitive flesh with blistering kisses. He drags his teeth against the side of my throat, that roughness my utter euphoric undoing. His hand slips under my arse, gripping hard as he continues to consume me body, mind and soul.

"Idris," I gasp as I yank his head back to mine. He catches my hands and pins my wrists to the bed. I hiss and buck, trying to free myself from his roasting grip, but soon his mouth is dragging strangled, cursed moans and inferno from my throat. This is a delicious, infuriating, insane torture.

Panting, he pulls his lips from mine, pressing them against my ear. The words are gloriously scalding as he whispers, "Say my name like that again, and I'll lose all control." He presses a long, slow kiss into my neck then lifts his trembling body away. He's fighting for slow, regular breaths, and I recognise the pattern. He's mind-stilling, but that doesn't wipe away the wicked smile twisting his lips.

I pant slowly, closing my eyes for a minute to fight the way my entire body roars for him. To dine on and dominate every part of him. To feed the fire raging inside.

Idris releases my wrists, the absence of his touch stinging like ice.

"Sweet dreams, Renza." He smirks, raking both hands through his hair as he retreats from me. I prop myself up on my elbows, watching him sweep through the door, leaving me alone in the room again.

What in Fate's Mercy just happened?

CHAPTER 5

"Don't you appreciate the absurdity of spending the night at the Patricelli house?" hisses Fiora in shock as we climb the steps of the High Chamber. "He's your Soulhate!"

I managed to wrangle the sarcastic reply back from my lips – but barely. I'd woken early and dashed home to change before I could see him. Only, rather than slipping in unnoticed, I'd been met with a family inquisition the moment I stepped through my own front door. The endless needling had eventually worn me down.

Now, amber sunshine rolls over the beautiful stone columns and gleaming artisanal roof of the High Chamber. A welcome breeze skips through the curving streets to twist around the lazy waves of my dark hair. Its cool, fleeting kiss against my bare neck is a pleasant distraction from my aunt's berating.

"It's not like that," I say tiredly, although last night certainly had crossed into territory we hadn't ventured into since the Great Rebellion. Every touch burned into my memory, repeating over and over again like a delicious, masochistic kind of plague.

Absence makes the heart grow fonder ... and the hate seemingly untameable.

Fiora hurries up the stairs after me, dark ringlets flailing in her outrage. We enter the High Chamber, a din of voices bubbling in the background from the spectator pews.

"Calm down, Fifi," chuckles Agosta, tossing her rich hair over her shoulder and winking at me. "Renza has a life. Let her live it."

"What about Fate?" Fiora snaps. "Fate has a plan! Fate has made a decree and flaunting your disregard—"

"I'm not having this conversation. I can't say the same thing any more times or in any other ways," I respond with finality, spinning on my heel and walking down the aisle towards the Electi chairs. Fiora darts forwards to block my path, putting her hand on the gate that separates spectators from Electi.

"You are the longest serving currently sitting Electi. You are a symbol, not just here, but across the continent. Halice needs you alive and well – we all do," Fiora says, holding up a hand to stop me. "Please don't take unnecessary risks, like spending time alone, tired and tipsy with your *Soulhate*! Don't tempt Fate to finish what he's started. Fate always comes out on top!"

I take a deep breath and level an uncompromising stare at my aunt. She doesn't flinch under my gaze, raising an eyebrow as though unimpressed.

Interesting.

"Why so little faith in me, Aunt Fiora?" I ask, narrowing my eyes. She shakes her head, her mouth twisting sadly.

"Fate cannot be ignored without consequences. Don't flirt with disaster more than you already are," she answers sadly.

"I have a city to represent. Please stand aside." She sighs and glides aside.

I cross the tiles to my chair. Goosebumps scatter up my arms and my teeth turn to daggers in my mouth. My breath is hot. Idris is here. He's close. The racing fire charring my bones brings last night back into blinding, caustic fury. His lips, his taste ... his hands on my body.

I close my eyes as I set my papers down, the mind-stilling and pulse-slowing techniques coming to me like a reflex. The motions feel natural after months of practice. Different days and situations deliver varying levels of success, but on the whole mind-stilling makes things substantially more bearable. Not comfortable by any stretch, and certainly nowhere close to pleasant, but I can bear the sensation of ants crawling over my skin, or the fire nipping at the tips of my fingers.

Once I'm sure I'll be fine, I cast my eyes to Idris. He sits in his father's old seat, the buttery yellow window highlighting the warmth of his golden eyes as he speaks with Savino. I swallow tightly as my gaze falls to the warm smile on his lips. The ghost of his mouth haunts my own, and my ear, and my neck.

Fate save me.

Why had Idris stopped so abruptly last night? Did I do something wrong? Doubt eats through me like acid, bubbling and hissing as the nagging questions erode my sanity. I bite my lip to keep myself from screaming at him.

I mean, he wasn't wrong to stop. Of course not. We said no distractions! And that ... that was more than a mere distraction. It'd been utterly consuming – at least for me. Even now, hours later, when it shouldn't matter anymore, I'm ensnared in the memory like an obsession.

"I don't like the look of Leone." Maggia drags me out of my wholly unhelpful private spiral.

I swivel my eyes over to Leone Strossi, who is nodding along absentmindedly to something Ulrico is wittering about. But his mind is clearly somewhere else. Somewhere smug. Complacent.

Maggia and I exchange knowing looks.

"Whatever it is, we'll put it down," I mutter quietly as I riffle through my notes, making sure the list of Leone's suggestions is within easy reach. "Also, Idris is going to bring forward a motion you're going to hate. Just know I'm right there with you."

"What kind of motion?" Maggia asks instantly.

"Idris took it upon himself to invite potential mercenary armies to visit, armies for us to hire to defend Halice. People he's worked with on his travels and people he trusts."

"He's already invited them?" Maggia hisses, throwing unhappy glances over my shoulder at the culprit. "Without a vote?"

"I gave him hell for it last night," I promise, "which is when I found out. Please don't think I knew; I assure you I didn't."

"That's not okay!" Maggia scowls. "Why didn't we vote on it?"

"For reasons of security – his argument not mine. I'm sure he'll explain his delusion soon enough," I grumble, shaking my head as I brush off the lilac silk of my tunic.

"It's outrageous." Maggia's lips purse unhappily.

"Agreed," I mutter. Maggia scowls as Savino clears his throat.

"I call this session of the Halician High Chamber to session," he says loudly from his seat. The din of the crowd instantly drops. Maggia and I exchange one final look before sitting in our seats. A chorus of "agree" goes around the room.

Idris stands immediately, colours rippling over him as he makes his way to the central stage. He is the spitting image of his father, only younger.

"Esteemed Members, I present to you today a problem but also a potential solution," Idris begins. "As you know, my recent absence was to investigate the rumours of a blockade by the Holy States preventing ships from arriving at our shores. I am sorry to confirm these rumours are true."

No one is surprised, the information having spread like

wildfire the minute their ship docked in port. Still, having it said in the Chamber does spur a round of quiet muttering. Idris ignores it, his deep voice stirring a low, boiling headache at the very tip of my spine.

"In my educational travels, I visited lots of places and I learned lots of things, but most importantly, I met a lot of skilled and talented people. People whom I came to know personally, people who may be able to provide our people with some much-needed relief."

"What kind of relief?" Leone fires back instantly with narrow eyes.

"The military kind, in exchange for currency of course."

"Our coffers are running on fumes, Electi Patricelli," Leone says, voice filled with derision, "and you want to buy military forces?"

"To defend ourselves while we build our own might. To defend ships travelling to Halice, and the much-needed resources that are on board," Idris says passionately, slowly circling the room as he speaks. "I've been very selective and chose only those with the highest honour, those I have worked with in the past and know, without a doubt, that we can trust."

"So would this be an army for Halice, or for you?" Maggia asks sharply. "Given you've apparently already invited them here."

More mutters go around the room. Idris nods slowly, a hand going to his chest.

"Yes, I invited my friends and acquaintances to the city. Given the harassment of the Holy States blocking paths of travel, I felt it was safer to move in a more clandestine way. Additionally, I was not the only person who knew about these invitations before they were sent. Electi Savino was aware and agreed to this proposal."

Of course he did. I shake my head, throwing Savino a dirty look. His grey eyes meet mine without hesitation and he flashes a smile that's only half-apology. He thinks what he's done is right.

"So the two of your conspired to get your own way? Without a vote?" Leone argues, his tone rising in volume. How in all of Fate's Mysteries, have I ended up agreeing with Leone Strossi? The world has gone mad.

"Not at all. There is nothing wrong or illegal in inviting my acquaintances to my home. Just because they are here doesn't mean we have to consider hiring them. That is what we need a vote for, to decide whether we want to receive them officially and consider them for the job."

"You sent out secret invitations to invite not one but three foreign armies into our city, during a time of military duress, and you don't think that requires a vote?" I ask in disbelief.

"I signed the letters from myself, not from the Electi," Idris counters smoothly, clearly prepared for my ire. "They are my acquaintances and friends. Do I need a vote to invite my associates to the city for non-business reasons?"

"When they come with fully fledged armies, yes!" Maggia snaps.

"Where in the law is that written?" asks Idris pointedly. I narrow my eyes.

"The last person to *invite* an army to this city without a vote didn't like the outcome," Leone said quietly, his words raising the hairs on my arm. "He was hanged for treason. You yourself carried out the order."

The hall goes silent as that fact sinks in. Idris's face begins to look drawn; his eyes narrow into slits as he stares the man down unflinchingly.

"Bellandi the traitor brought an army to slaughter, and the Militia to conquer. I'm not doing that. I would never do that," Idris vows, and no one could mistake the raw passion in his words. "My absolute desire is to defend this city and this chamber. Comparison to that stain of human existence is an insult."

"Leone states fact, and a history that is recent and painful to us all. You cannot blame him for his hesitations," said Savino quietly, tempering the passions crashing through the room. "But he also points out the piece many of you are forgetting. Halice knows how to handle those that outstay their welcome."

"My friends are coming. They will arrive soon. The question is, will we formally receive them?" Idris continues. "Or simply let them enjoy their holiday in our fair home?" He turns to look at me, those hazel eyes burning into my face like a roaring bonfire. I wrinkle my nose.

"This is surely grounds for a vote of no-confidence!" Leone snaps. I sigh, shaking my head.

"Unfortunately not," I grind out. "As he signed his own name, rather than on behalf of the High Chamber, he has technically invited people he knows to visit. It's not treasonous or illegal but it is on a knife's edge. However, should anything happen while they are here – anything at all – you are responsible for the outcome, Electi Patricelli. If there is a single act of violence, one broken law, even a whiff of intimidation or interruption to the processes of our city or our chamber, then you will be considered the responsible party. You will be held liable and prosecuted appropriately."

"I am aware and acknowledge that," Idris answers, the corner of his mouth pulling before he turns to face the other members. They all hold their tongues, wearing a mixture of expressions, outrage chief amongst them. I'm no different.

"We should consider them," Savino says evenly. "We need more military support. We can defend our city against criminals, but the Holy States are built for war, and they intend to break us, even if it means being underhand in their tactics. We are running out of resources; people are already feeling the strain of failing trade. We need our ships protected to get them moving again. Our people need to be safe."

"Halice has prospered for centuries on a bedrock of trade,"

Idris agrees, building off Savino's point. "We need this security to assure our trade partners that Halice is still a safe place to do business."

"Have you considered the appearance of arming up and readying for bloodshed? That image will raise already strained tensions," argues Leone, his tone quietly seething as he taps the wooden arm of his seat. "You are escalating the situation, not calming it down."

"Attempting to starve our people using their naval fleet makes it inescapably clear that the Holy States isn't seeking peace," Idris continues.

"I wonder if the wagons filled to the brim with gruesome art and a headless cardinal had anything to do with that!" spat Leone fixing his gaze on me. I meet his glare with a level, unflinching stare of my own. A beat passes before I ease to my feet, signalling I want the floor.

"Esteemed Members, I relinquish the floor," Idris says quietly, before retreating from the stage. I walk slowly towards the centre of the room, shoulders back and posture open. I take a deep breath before speaking.

"I do not like this proposal," I begin. "I don't like the idea of yet another foreign army in our city, even if this time they work for us. And if we pick one of these armies to stand at our side, what of the other two? They would have no reason to behave inside our city walls. And beyond that, as Member Leone previously stated, we cannot afford to pay them."

"We can work that out with time, when trade is flowing again. Debt is better than dead," Idris answers.

"Not if we're merely kicking the problem down the road, or exchanging one tyrant for another! We don't know these people."

"I do," Idris insists.

"Really? How well do you know them when promised money isn't on the table? When their payday is in question, can we trust them to be loyal then?" I take a deep breath and straighten my shoulders. "These armies are coming, friend or foe. We can't stop it now. If we welcome them but ultimately don't hire any of them, we can cross our fingers and hope they go away in relative peace."

"If they're coming anyway, we might as well consider it properly," Savino says. "What harm is there in hearing their pitches? They will have travelled all this way, would not hearing them out at least appease them? We wouldn't want to insult anybody kind enough to consider coming to our aid."

"We could hear them, if we were sure that their subsequent rejection wouldn't injure us or worse," I allow, slowly nodding my head. "But at the end of the day, this plan has a serious flaw. We have an inescapable, unarguable fact to consider: we can't afford it. We do not have the money nor the promise of trade to raise it. Esteemed Members, I relinquish the floor."

I walk back to my seat, sinking into the chair. I look to Maggia who nods at me.

"Anyone else wish to speak on this matter?" Savino asks, and gives Ulrico a pointed look. Ulrico shuffles in his seat, realising it's his turn to call the vote.

"Right, of course. Well, um, right. Time to vote," Ulrico babbles, squirming in his seat, "on this proposal. Do we formally host these visiting mercenaries? Vote yellow for yes with Member Patricelli's movement. Vote purple for no with Member Di Maineri's movement."

I select my purple stone from the chair.

We all wait, looking pointedly at Ulrico. He blinks before realising he needs to give the order.

"Cast!" he practically yelps as six stones fly across the room. They clatter in the central round stage.

Three purple. Three yellow.

Ulrico voted in line with Idris. And as it was his turn to lead the vote, his vote decides the split.

Idris has won. I have lost.

I sigh, leaning back in my seat. Leone glares at the stones, shuffling with pent-up frustration. Maggia's face is pulled tight as she folds her arms.

Idris's shoulders relax as he exchanges a warm glance with Savino and nods towards Ulrico.

"The votes are cast. A split," Ulrico announces. "The Patricelli movement wins."

Instantly, heated conversation explodes in the chamber. I rub my brow. Well, there's no use in crying about it. This is happening. Now I need to make sure Ulrico doesn't vote to actually give these guys a contract – or find some money to pay them.

Fate's Fury, what an absolute mess!

A huge noise blares from outside the High Chamber.

The entire hall falls silent and we turn towards the large, ornate doors. A small group marches forwards – four City Guards escorting two men. One carries a huge flagpole with two banners. At the top is a familiar black-and-white-striped flag bearing the likeness of a three-headed eagle – the flag of the Holy States. Below that, the second banner is white and painted with a green olive branch – the flag of diplomatic immunity. The other stranger is a messenger holding a scroll. The black-and-white-striped ribbon around the scroll screams the formal nature of this declaration.

My heart pounds. My throat closes as I track every footstep the messenger takes. Is this it? Is this a declaration of war? Is everything about to fall down around us?

The City Guard marches the messengers down the aisle towards the gate. They stop at the end; the guards hold out their arms and refuse to let the interlopers pass.

"I come with a message for the Halician High Chamber from the Esteemed Holy Mother herself," says the messenger, his voice trembling a little.

I take a deep breath. Everyone is frozen in their seats at this unexpected interruption. Slowly and uncertainly, Leone gets up. He looks at the rest of us with a wary expression as he crosses the floor towards the messenger.

Leone takes the scroll from the messenger's hands, cracking the wax seal then unravelling it to read:

"'I, Marchella Abbati, rightly appointed Holy Mother, Interpreter of Fate and Leader of the Great Holy Faith, and its subsequent land and holdings, do with a heavy heart hereby...'"—Leone trails off, horror flickering over his face. His fingers grip the page tighter—"'excommunicate the State known as Halice, including its cities, lands and people, from our Great Faith.'"

The uproar is instantaneous. The air is ripped from my lungs and alarm bells start clanging uncontrollably in my head.

"SILENCE!" roars Savino and the entire chamber quiets down again.

"Excommunicated?" Maggia breathes. My head snaps around. The horror on her face is a twin of my own.

Never had I thought the Holy Mother would stoop to this. To exile us from our faith. To take our connection to Fate, to our gods.

"Is that all it says, Electi?" Savino asks, face sombre and angry.

"No." Leone clears his throat. "It continues: 'After much deliberation, it is believed that many insults to Fate's Holy Plan and the gods themselves have been levied within this State. The people have turned their backs on the righteous and holy path. As such, the people shall be excluded from all religious ceremonies, institutions and preachings while they continue their path of impertinence. I therefore command the removal and return of all members of my clergy, until such a time we can be certain of the safety of our holy servants, and the true path of the Holy Faith is restored in these lands.'"

Leone's shoulders drop and he shakes his head, holding the

scroll out for someone else to take. Savino does, his eyes cutting over it.

"Well ... that's that then," says Idris unhappily.

The understatement of the century. This is another blow, another weapon against us to force us into submission.

I wish the Holy Mother's plan wasn't working so well.

CHAPTER 6

One week has passed since the vote. Yet it only took four days for mercenaries to arrive at our doors.

They were coordinated, turning up within days of each other. Idris planned it all so well, and every step of it behind my back.

Arsehole.

For two days I couldn't set foot outside my home without seeing a sell-sword or five exploring my beloved city, freshly sharpened blades shining at their hips or slung across their backs. The last mercenary army has turned up today – the Red Sands Bannerhood from Coari. Uneasiness hovers in the city air and we'll be lucky if tensions remain limited to dirty looks and muttered breaths.

"Well, they're here," says Fiora as we walk down the street. People flow around us in a myriad of colours. She's insisted on accompanying me everywhere – trying to stop me from seeing Idris alone. Some of her attempts are less than subtle, and all are getting on my nerves. But today, I'm glad of the company.

"Indeed they are," I answer. It's utterly ridiculous to be nervous walking around my own city. I know, rationally, I shouldn't be afraid. There is no reason for these soldiers to hurt me. In fact, it would be to their detriment.

Yet if they decided to, I wouldn't stand a chance. I don't have the skill, the strength, the threat. If they want to hurt me – hurt all of us – they can. That dynamic makes me incredibly uneasy.

I've seen Idris in High Chamber, but after sessions we barely share two words before we're interrupted. We still haven't really talked since that night at his house. Our unspoken business has turned tense and heavy. My stomach twists and gnarls; what in Fate's Mercy do I say after all this time? Do we pretend it never happened? Is that what he wants? Does he regret it?

Aunt Fiora is right – tempting Fate will lead to disaster. Yet the memory of his lips haunts me, the ghosts of his hands against the bare flesh of my body teasing my mind away from my tasks...

I'm in half a mind to march down to the docks and demand to speak with him. The bond purrs, urging me to do just that. To give him a piece of my unravelling mind. But I have far too much to do.

The pale midmorning sunshine soaks into the old buildings of our winding cobbled streets. The watery blue sky is splotchy with weak clouds as the air hangs limp and unmoving. The crowds bustle slowly about their business as we carve our path. Ahead is the end of a familiar queue. It's quiet, most people talking quietly, or embarrassed and refusing to meet anyone's eye.

"It's longer today." A chord of sadness hovers in Fiora's tone. I sigh.

"No trade, no jobs, no money, no food," I answer, a small lump forming in my throat. These are my people. I must help them.

"Then we'd better not waste time. For their sake." Fiora gives me a determined look that's almost a command. We enter the soup kitchen to find it thick with chatter and the smell of fresh bread and broth. Mismatched, rickety tables and chairs are clustered together, crammed with individuals tucking into their meals. I peer through the crowd for one person in particular.

Maggia is behind the counter, giving crisp orders to the volunteers, lists in hand. I step up, waiting patiently. She doesn't even raise her head to acknowledge me.

"They're here," she says irritably, marking something pointedly on her lists.

"They're here," I agree with a wry chuckle, folding my arms and leaning my hip on the sideboard. Fiora gives me an expectant look so I continue.

"Maggia, have you met my Aunt Fiora?"

"Nice to meet you." Maggia doesn't look up before barking orders at staff in the other room. Fiora stills as she studies my colleague.

"It's nice to meet you, too," Fiora answers graciously when we have Maggia's attention again. "Might I be of assistance? Standing around when work needs to be done has never been my forte." Maggia raises an eyebrow.

"We could use some help gathering dirty dishes."

"Consider it done. Let me know when you leave, dear," Fiora says warmly, squeezing my arm as she starts to gather dirty plates with the efficiency of a drill sergeant. Maggia folds her arms as she watches Fiora work.

"What's that about?" Maggia asks, suspicion flirting with her words. I don't blame her.

"Honestly, I could not tell you," I murmur, questions building in my mind. Maggia puts down her papers.

"Well, I'm glad you're here, to see this for yourself." Maggia gestures around.

"It's busy..." I trail off with a sigh. I press my lips together, imagining how much worse it might be over the coming weeks.

"Too busy. We're down to running one meal a day and checking off names and we're still turning people away, a lot of people..." Maggia growls, shaking her head. "We're trying to prioritise. Make sure children have meals, the sick and vulnerable, but more and more are coming all the time. We don't have until winter to sort this, Renza. People are starving now. By the time winter hits, we'll be out of food. Not just this kitchen but the city in general."

"I know." I sigh, rubbing my brow. "But without sorting this blockade what else is there?"

"We could attempt to trade with the Holy States."

Have I been slapped? Is this a joke? Maggia's suggestion certainly feels that way. I gape at her. Maggia sighs, and shrugs defeatedly.

"Look, I reacted poorly at first, too. I was certain they'd send poisoned grain or something." Maggia snorts.

"This isn't your idea?"

"Leone mentioned it in passing – not sure even he'd given it much thought," Maggia answers with a sigh. "But the more I think about it, the more I wonder if it might not be terrible after all. If we mend the relationship between us and the Holy States—"

"It's a reliance on people we cannot trust. It's giving them a foothold. It's—"

"Easy for you to say all of that. It's easy for you to stand on your principles when you aren't fighting to find supper tonight," Maggia interrupts. "You're not facing the very real possibility of watching your family go without a meal this very evening, not knowing if another will be coming soon."

My stomach churns at the precarious state of the bank. How things will get so much worse if Giulia can't work things out. If our branch collapses, it will be anarchy, and we're so close to the brink already.

I rub my eyes as I turn it over.

"Leone Strossi suggested it?" I ask carefully. Maggia nods.

"Yes. I know you two have a rivalry—"

"I don't like him; he wants to twist every bill in that chamber to enrich himself. He doesn't care about people beyond his gaggle of wealthy acolytes." I scowl, chewing on my lip.

"Agreed." Maggia chuckles. "But that doesn't mean he can't have a good idea once in a while."

"I'll hear him out. To feed our people."

"That's all I ask. Besides, there's something else you need to see."

I frown as she waves me into the back. I follow, squeezing through a slim door. She hands me a plain cloak and I throw it over my shoulders, pulling up the hood. For whatever reason, she doesn't want us to be recognised.

My heart picks up a few beats as she shows me through a back door. I trust Maggia, but I can already tell I'm not going to like this.

She walks me down the back streets. The filth is aged and clinging to every surface. Maggia and I dodge bins, buckets of foul water and piles of rubbish left to rot in the alleyways.

Maggia stops by a building a few minutes later. She pauses, her hand splayed on the simple black door and turns to look at me.

"Brace yourself. This is going to be nasty," she promises. I nod and she pushes it open.

The smell hits you in the back of the teeth and twists at your gut. The foul mingle of rotting and death clogs my nose and threatens to empty my stomach over the floor. I swallow down the disgusting bile swarming my throat and follow Maggia inside, pressing a hand to my nose in a futile attempt to stop the smell.

Rows and rows of bodies lie utterly still. Spread over the floor, some covered with clothes, some not. They're clustered, packed in tightly for any scrap of space. Decay has started for many, the putrid rot contorting their limbs and features.

I want to vomit. Three other people are here, too, weeping over one of the fallen. Their mournful sobs scratch at my insides. I look around and stare at Maggia, the horror of the situation punching me square in the face.

We've been excommunicated.

No weddings. No naming ceremonies. And perhaps most cruel of all, no funerals.

"The priests used to do all of this," I state. The realisation makes me want to hurl all over again. The absolute cruelty makes me want to scream. To lose someone and then deny their family a funeral, so their lost loved ones are left to rot in some warehouse.

"We've tried to bury as many as possible, but most want religious funerals. Death ... is often when we need spiritual comfort most. We have lost that. In times of hardship, people need faith. It stops atrocities. It stops hopelessness and despair," Maggia says, gesturing around her. "This is the tip of the iceberg."

Maggia is right.

This is dangerous.

Really, really dangerous.

The Holy States may have taken our faith, twisted and contorted it into a weapon to beat those who don't conform, but I refuse to let them take our hope.

I have to do something fast. If that means rekindling some kind of relationship with the Holy States then so be it. We can't let our people suffer. We can't let this get any worse and cruel than it already is.

But I hate it. I hate how much power they have – how much power we've continued to let them wield over the entire continent. Free? Independent? Was it ever true or merely an illusion we convinced ourselves was true while they smirked behind our backs?

I see clearly now. The strings of their influence shine bright and toxic. If I have to go back to the Holy States, I will not grovel. I will not surrender or plead. I'll have a few tricks up my sleeve. What are those tricks? I'm not sure yet. But that's never stopped me finding them before.

Idris will hate it. Hate it with a passionate fury. There is no way I'll convince him to make peace with the people that slaughtered his parents. The idea makes me want to rage, too. But the dead are at peace; it's the living who suffer. It's my job to fix that. Even if I have to do it without him.

I won't be what Idris accused me of. I won't be paralysed. I will act.

"Come on, let's get back. Before your aunt sends a search party," Maggia says. We leave the room, but the horror is fixed in my mind like a vile blister. I can't ignore it, I can't unsee it. It haunts me as we retrace our steps back to the soup kitchen. Stepping inside, I find Fiora giving out orders and holding Maggia's lists, not a dirty dish in sight.

"You're back!" She beams at us, relief palpable on her face. "You run a very tight ship here. I tried to follow your instructions while you were busy. I hope I got it right."

She hands the papers back and Maggia nods slowly, looking around, faint surprise hovering around her eyes. Maggia's impressed but refuses to show it.

"Thank you, Signora Di Maineri."

"No problem at all." Fiora turns to me. "Ready to leave?"

I nod, not feeling like talking. Stepping back into the sunshine, I slow my pace to an amble. I study, really study, the people around us. The absence of priests in their black and white robes hits like a sucker punch. The addition of these foreign mercenaries blinded me to the other massive change. Holy buildings are closed. Temples and monasteries are locked tight. Chipped wooden boards are nailed across the front doors, the windows boarded from the outside. Copies of the excommunication notice curl at the edges, lying limp against the wood into which they've been hammered. Where doors should be thrown open, welcoming people, offering solace, preaching and prayer ... there's nothing.

We have been abandoned.

"Where now?" asks Fiora brightly. I realise I've come to a standstill, staring at an abandoned church. I blink hard, shaking my head.

"The Garden." The words seem to spill out. I'm not sure why, but perhaps the most inspirational place I know will give me some idea of what to do next. "You don't have to come—" My aunt is already shaking her head. She flashes a small smile my way but her gaze flickers across to a group of strange soldiers walking by.

"I haven't been to the Garden in years. I'd love to see how it's changed."

I don't argue. It'd be pointless. We walk further into the city, navigating the familiar twists and turns.

"So how are Marino and Eliseo?" I ask, searching to take my mind off things. Aunt Fiora smiles at mention of her sons. Fiora found and married her second husband, her Soulmate, very shortly after the first died. The two had gone back to his home in Nimal and opened up a branch of the Di Maineri Bank there, which is now run by the sure and sensible hand of her eldest son, Marino.

"They're doing well, thank you," Fiora says warmly. "Eliseo will be turning nineteen soon."

"Oh, really?"

I've rarely met my cousins, but reports suggest Eliseo needs a steady, supporting hand. Wild and unpredictable, some might say he's naïve, but the impression I get is that he's easily filled with the romance of an idea but struggles with the practical realities of implementation. It's good he has a sensible, no-nonsense older brother to temper his passionate instincts. Together they will be good for the bank.

"Yes, and Marino is courting someone. But he won't tell us who!" Fiora says with a wry smile. "I think he should hold out for his Soulmate – the person Fate has determined to be worthy of him."

"We don't all find our Fated, Aunt Fiora," I answer. "It's rare that we find either our Soulhate or Soulmate."

"Yes, yes." Aunt Fiora waves this away. "One in ten, or so they say."

"I haven't seen any evidence it's not true," I chuckle. "And should he be alone forever if he doesn't find them?" We cross one of the stone bridges over the River Vitta. The clear water below swirls and dances as it races towards the port.

"Arturo and I are so happy together. I want that for all my family." Fiora's brow puckers. "I don't want Marino getting hurt when Fate shows him his part in the Great Plan."

The real, sickening worry in her expression has me unexpectedly linking an arm through hers.

"You're his mother. Of course you want him to be happy." I chortle. "I'm sure he will be – we'll make sure of it. Speaking of cousins, is Aunt Rialta really estranged from Cousin Allysa?"

"Oh, it's more than that, dear." Fiora sighs, patting my hand. "Your aunt threw her out and cut her off."

I almost miss a step in shock.

"What!" I gasp. Fiora nods with a grim expression.

"I've been sending her an allowance to live off, because Rialta completely ignores her. She's currently in Sovassa, sorting out some business for me there as a favour. But it's a crying shame. She's an exceptionally bright girl."

I've never met my cousin, though I'm aware of her existence. Reported to be a rare and great beauty with a wicked tongue, she's one year my junior. Still, it's a shock I've not heard any of this. Had my father known and just not informed me? I know he didn't keep close tabs on his half-sisters.

"What happened?" I ask, hastily covering how scandalised I am in my tone.

"That's the irksome thing. Neither will tell me." Fiora glares. "But the rage with which Rialta speaks of her only child – I can't imagine ever speaking about my own children in such a manner."

"Well, I'll be sure not to bring it up. Perhaps you can spend some of your time together to smooth things over for them both?" I suggest, not only because that might pry Fiora from my side but also because I can sense that it's something Fiora very much wants. Fiora nods slowly, mulling it over.

"I think time will be the key with that situation, whatever it is." Fiora sighs. "Hard to fix something when I don't know what's broken. Besides, the nastiness isn't one-sided. Lysa has some viciously choice words about her mother."

"That doesn't surprise me." I snort. "The Di Maineris seem to be born with claws and fangs."

"Aren't we just." Fiora laughs with dry amusement. "It would be nice if we sharpened them on others rather than ourselves."

"Oh, that would be very un-Di-Maineri-like," I say in mock horror as we turn a corner. The Garden stands before us in all her majesty. The gates are open wide, the smells and sounds of genius pouring over the large terraced homes that make up its colourful walls.

The two of us slip through the gate, and instantly a slither of stress is pried from my shoulders. My breathing becomes a fraction easier, my step lighter.

"It's so much more established." Fiora beams. "Father would be so happy to see it thriving."

Grandfather had campaigned for the Garden from the very beginning, financing the building of the High Chamber to convince the other Electi of its brilliance. It worked, securing the city funding these gifted artisans deserve. My father took up that mantel of being its champion, and now that responsibility has fallen to me. Rightly so. It's one of the most beautiful things about this city, along with our democratic High Chamber.

"I remember coming here with Tomas," Fiora chuckles. "When he first started courting your mother."

"Really?"

"Oh, how we teased him. He was head over heels the moment he set eyes on her. Constantly looking for excuses so he could speak with her, or even just see her. In the beginning, we all wondered if they were Soulmates. But your mother didn't want a bar of him. She wasn't at all impressed."

"Really?" I laugh. Fiora nods seriously.

"Oh, yes. She thought he was a cocky, rich boy used to having the world handed to him. Tomas had quite an arrogance as a young man and your mother was always uncannily perceptive. She was a reserved, thoughtful woman who loved her art, but Tomas had a way of bringing out the fire in her, drawing her out of herself, and when it got going, Fate's Fury, did it blaze!" Fiora chuckles, lost in the memory. "They knocked the corners off each other. He brought her out of her shell; she kept him grounded in reality."

A sad smile fills my face. My parents are both at peace now, reunited in the After. But I miss them both. I wish I'd been able to know Mother better, but the illness took her when Giulia and I were both so young.

"Is that Rugeiro?" asks Fiora, pulling me out of my stupor. I follow her gesture towards the familiar green workshop. Uncle Ruggie is bent over his forge.

"Yes, he makes the most stunning jewellery."

"He always did," she agrees. "He has a daughter, doesn't he? How's she doing?"

My mouth turns sour as I force myself to answer.

"Fausta died. She got injured fighting her Soulhate," I say quietly. "Technically she won, but her injuries were too severe, and she hated herself for her violence… It was like she stopped trying to live."

Fiora goes quiet, pressing her lips firmly together.

"I'm so sorry. I didn't know. Sometimes Fate's will is hard to understand," she says quietly, her voice smaller than normal. "But it's all part of the Great Plan, and Father Fate knows best."

"Agree to disagree," I grumble. Of course she would say that. She found her Soulmate, the love of her life, and has spent her existence in nauseatingly happy bliss. It's easy for her to think Fate is always right when she's only ever experienced his favour.

We continue down the winding, cobbled path. The leaves are shifting from green to amber, the early fallers already littering the ground. We pass a musician messing about with his violin and a few bars of melody. A writer is curled up under a tree, furiously scribbling in her notebook. A group have gathered, desperately trying to load a finished sculpture into a cart. I pause, realising it's not a sculpture but a large piece of complicated stonework for the new sea defences.

Amongst the helping hands are two familiar faces, currently brushing off their hands as the stone sits comfortably on the wagon.

"Need a hand or are we too late?" I ask, walking closer.

Emilia and Michelle turn around, both breaking into a smile.

"Oh, you timed that perfectly to get out of it!" Michelle laughs, flexing her shoulders. "That thing is heavy."

"Only three more to go now. Thanks, Omiros!" Emilia waves at the stone master as he starts to deliver his creation to the worksite.

"Aunt Fiora, meet my friends Emilia and Michelle," I say in greeting.

"Michelle? As in Giulia's Michelle?" asks Fiora brightly, giving both warm smiles.

"Yes, in fact I was on my way to the bank," Michelle says, holding up a basket spilling with food and a bouquet of zinnias – Giulia's favourite flower. "She's been so stressed lately she forgets to eat."

"That's so sweet of you," Fiora says with warm approval. "I'm sure she'll appreciate it. And you, my dear, what do you do?"

"I'm an architect," Emilia answers, a hint of blush staining her cheeks.

"Emilia designed New College school, and a lot of the new defensive structures in the city," I add, knowing Emilia won't blow her own trumpet. Fiora gasps in recognition.

"Oh, that new alarm system is you? My goodness, I love that! We might have to steal that in Nimal if you'll consult!"

"That sounds great, I've never been to Nimal." Emilia beams happily.

"It's pretty, but Halice is better," I tease as Fiora rolls her eyes.

"Are you off to the bank, too, dear?" Fiora asks. Emilia shakes her head, sunshine glinting off her dark hair.

"I was just about to pop in on Serra actually," Emilia says, her brow puckering slightly. "Invite her out for lunch. I haven't seen her lately."

"Neither have I." Michelle frowns. "I assumed she was in the throes of some new project. You know how she gets."

"Oh, that would be good," Emilia says, though worry isn't wiped completely clear from her expression. "Want to come with, Renza, if you've got time?"

"Oh, twist my arm." I chuckle as the four of us set off towards Serra's workshop.

"How are you doing?"

"Busy," I answer, the standard reply falling off my tongue without need for thought.

"With the mercenaries descending I'm not surprised," said

Emilia, pressing her lips together. "Alfie is all on board with Idris's plan. But I can't help feeling it's inviting trouble."

"Thank you! Where were you in the High Chamber vote?" I laugh as we reach Serra's workshop. The three-storey house is painted a rich burnt-orange. The entire downstairs has been converted into a workshop space with large wooden doors that swing out and lots of machinery and tools. But it's all locked up today, and I don't hear any banging or telltale signs of mischief inside.

We walk up to the front door and Emilia knocks gently.

"Serra? It's me," Emilia calls. We wait in silence for a long moment, the only answering sound is the rustling of the trees outside.

"Serra?" calls Emilia, knocking again. I exchange a worried look with Michelle. After a long pause, Emilia tries the handle. Unlocked. She pushes the door open, into Serra's workspace.

"Serra?" Emilia calls as we follow her. It's dark in here – not a candle lit, not a curtain thrown open. This isn't like Serra – it's the middle of the day. Where is she? A cold, churning burn takes residence in my chest.

"Serra?" I call, my concern etching deeper. Emilia pushes the door open to her study and her shoulders drop.

"Serra!"

Emilia sprints over to where Serra is slumped over her desk. Serra groans, blinking and squinting furiously as she drags her head from the mess of pages underneath.

"What? Why'd you wake me?" groans Serra, rubbing her eyes grumpily.

"We were worried. It's the middle of the day," Emilia says gently. The clinking of glass connects with my foot and I look down to see two empty bottles knocking together. I pick them up and see that drops of wine still cling to the inside. These were drunk recently.

"Don't be stupid." Serra scowls angrily. "I'm fine."

I look at the others, silently holding up the two bottles. Michelle points to two more. The concern on their faces deepens.

Serra has had her ups and downs in the last few months, but this is the worst we've ever seen her. She'd spent days locked in the darkness of the prison, wondering if that would be the day they executed her for a crime she didn't commit. Imprisoned because of her craft, for simply looking into the wrong thing at the wrong time. We'd rescued her of course, but being treated so badly for so long, left to live in abject terror, is bound to leave scars on the psyche.

"Hey, Serra." I aim to hit a cheerful tone as I put the bottles in the bin.

"Oh, you all came?" Serra hisses scathingly, flinching at the sound of the bottles clattering into the empty bin.

"Just popping around. What are you working on?"

"Nothing! I'm fine! Go away!" Serra snaps, bolting from her seat and gathering her papers as she pushes her unkempt dark hair out of her face.

"Okay, sorry," I apologise quietly.

"Renza and I are going out for coffee. Why don't you come?" suggests Emilia.

"Why in the hell would I want to do that?" snaps Serra.

"Because we're your friends?" Emilia's voice is small and verges on quivering.

"To hear you moan and gripe about your wonderful lives?" Serra huffs. "No, thank you."

"Serra, that's not—" I begin but she wheels around, glaring at me with a fury.

"Oh, shut up, Renza! Why are you even here? Shouldn't you be out fixing this blasted conflict with the Holy States? Isn't that your job!" Serra snarls. I step back, her words akin to a physical slap. I don't know how to answer that.

"I mean, that's why I have to spend my days designing

weapons isn't it? Because you can't do your damn job and keep us safe!" Serra hisses, picking up a handful of drawings from her desk and throwing them at me. "Well, here you go. Kill as many people as you like!"

"Serra, enough!" Emilia scolds firmly.

"Don't you start!" Serra snaps, jabbing a finger at Emilia. "It's a wonder you can even see me from your high and mighty horse—"

"Serra, stop it," I snap, walking to Emilia's side. "This isn't kind."

"This is *my* house!" Serra spits. "I didn't invite you here. Don't like what I have to say? Then get out!"

"Serra this isn't like you. We're worried about you!" Emilia says insistently. Serra scoffs and rolls her eyes.

"Don't bother! Go about your perfect little lives and leave me the hell alone!" she shouts, wincing as Fiora yanks the curtains open, raising a daring eyebrow at the young woman spouting vitriol. Serra throws her a scathing look.

"Just get out," Serra says witheringly before stomping up the stairs. The door to her room closes firmly, the sound a punch to us standing below.

We all stand still for a long moment.

"What did we do?" asks Emilia quietly, breaking the silence. I can't help but think the opposite; what didn't we do? What did we miss? How do we help?

"She probably just has a hangover and is still feeling the effects of last night," says Fiora, walking around with a waste basket rattling with bottles. "My advice is to let her sleep it off. I'm sure she'll come by and apologise soon enough."

Michelle crouches to the floor, collecting the discarded papers. I stoop to help, the three of us working in silence as we gather the half-completed designs and try to organise them on her desk. These aren't right. Really aren't right. I flick through, my heart dropping as vicious black ink slashes through designs, the quill digging so deep that the parchment is torn.

"Do you think it's designer's block?" asks Emilia, clearly seeing the same things.

"She's had blocks before," Michelle says quietly. "She gets frustrated, not vicious."

"How do we help?" I drop the papers neatly back on her desk before making to leave.

"How can we help if she won't let us?" Michelle asks. "When she's ready, she'll talk to us. She knows we're here for her."

"I hope you're right," I mutter, but a nagging feeling in my chest tells me that there's something going on here that she won't reveal unless we make her.

"Come on, why don't you all join Giulia and me for lunch?" Michelle says. "Get your minds off things? Sounds like we could all use it."

"Are you sure? We'd hate to intrude on your romantic lunch." Emilia smiles.

"Absolutely. I'm sure she'll be pleased to see us."

CHAPTER 7

We ascend the large stairs towards the Di Maineri Bank. The gleaming, blue-domed roof glints in the warm autumn sunshine, taking on a golden undertone. The painted blue columns are bright against the creamy stone as we stride through the glossy doors.

The bank is half-empty. The large, open hall is quiet as a library, the almost-silence held with the same reverence. It makes whatever construction is going on outside echo off the walls. People walk around with sombre faces, carrying ledgers and small stacks of coins.

Our bank is usually a bustle of activity. Not noisy but certainly there's more conversation than this. You couldn't hear someone thumping a ledger shut clear across the room like you can today – when a break in the construction allows for it. I'll have to ask Giulia what's being built out there.

My throat tightens as we pass accountants at their tables and head towards the stairs leading to my sister's office. Michelle leads the way, knocking brightly on the study door and pushing it open.

"Hi, sweetie," Michelle says as we walk into the room. Giulia looks up from the numbers, clearly dragged from intense thought. Mauve curtains hang under her blue eyes, her golden hair piled away from her face with little care, shoulders still hunched from her position over the books before her. She blinks at us, face falling.

"What's wrong?" she asks, voice tight.

"Nothing," answers Michelle brightly. We'd all agreed Giulia didn't need the added stress of Serra's outburst.

"Michelle brought you a romantic lunch, but we wanted to say hi," I say brightly, closing the door behind us. Giulia nods but turns back to the numbers on her desk, shoulders pinching together as she gestures to the papers.

"Sorry, but there's so much to do and—"

"Take a break to eat, dear," instructs Fiora gently. "You need nutrition."

"If you truly don't have time to stop, at least eat something while you work, hmm?" coaxes Michelle, setting down her basket and pulling out the food. She pulls the paper back from the sandwiches. "It's your favourite. My beef brisket with salad and a little caramelised onion."

"Oh, thank you, sweetheart," Giulia says quietly, leaning into Michelle's hug. Michelle places the sandwich down next to the work, and plants a kiss on the top of Giulia's head, rubbing her shoulders. Giulia's lips wobble as she leans into Michelle's embrace, burying her face in her shoulder. My pulse stampedes in my throat.

"Hey, hey. It's okay," whispers Michelle wrapping her arms around Giulia's shoulders. The door opens and in marches Aunt Rialta, another ledger in hand. She stops dead, seeing the group.

"Oh, you're here," Rialta says, her gaze cutting to Giulia. "Bad news?"

"No, no," Giulia says, breathing in sharply though her eyes have taken on a red tint. "What is it?"

"I found a few more accounts we haven't considered. I ... I've summarised for you," Rialta says, but studies Giulia for a minute before continuing. "But perhaps take a minute before giving it a look."

Giulia's face falls, her hands covering her face for a long moment as she takes long, deep breaths.

"Hey, hey, it's okay. We can do this," promises Michelle instantly.

"I'll take that," I say, stretching a hand to Rialta. She nods, handing it over. I scan down; my mouth goes dry as I drift over to the other documents on Giulia's desk. I riffle through them as Michelle quietly comforts Giulia. Emilia starts emptying out the basket of food on the sofa as Michelle manages to pry my sister from her desk chair and towards the plush seating.

"Why don't we give them a moment, Rialta?" suggests Fiora.

"We don't really have the time," Rialta says, matter-of-factly.

"You have the time for a small break," Fiora insists, refusing to be dissuaded. "Let's get a drink and give the girls a minute."

"Fine," Rialta says on a sigh. Our aunts leave, closing the door behind them.

"Giu, want to talk about it?" Emilia asks quietly. Giulia sniffs and shrugs, her posture one of utter defeat.

"The bank ... I don't know what we're going to do." Giulia hiccups. "I've already had to let half the staff go. We're running on fumes."

"What's the crux of the issue?" Emilia jumps into problem-solving mode at the drop of a hat.

"We have more money going out than we have coming in. Trade is dying, people want the gold they're owed, not to mention the huge hole in our accounts thanks to Bellandi's theft. I just..." Giulia shakes her head, worry robbing her of words.

Michelle wraps her up tightly, planting a kiss on the side of her head.

Everything inside me aches. My pulse pounds like a war drum, my skin itches for action. Anything to stop this, to stop the agony in my sister's voice. The stress lurking over her like a spectre.

"Your aunt is helping, right?" Michelle asks softly.

"Rialta is really good at this." Giulia swallows. "Like, really good. She's already getting on top of everything. The problem is it's only showing how bad things really are."

"Perhaps she'll have ideas, you know, once she sees the full picture. You said she runs a successful bank in the Wheel City," said Michelle. Giulia nods.

"How long do you think we have?" I ask quietly.

"Until ruin? Maybe a month? Month and a half?" Giulia manages to get out, hands trembling as she brings them up to her face.

I put down the numbers, my fingers shaking as they itch for action. My breathing is shallow and tight, my throat thick as I look at the destruction reflected in Giulia's tear-stained face.

"Hey now," says Emilia. "There's still time."

"Exactly. Much can change in a month," agrees Michelle, rubbing Giulia's back.

"All these mercenaries around the city are supposed to get things moving again, aren't they?" Emilia says. "Alfie says these guys really know what they're doing."

"Perhaps, but Renza's right. We can't afford to pay them!" Giulia hiccups.

"That's a High Chamber problem, not a you problem," I answer quietly. "Don't take on that burden."

"No, but the bank is my responsibility. It's our family legacy. I was entrusted with it ... and I'm going to be the one to lose it." Giulia's voice breaks as she turns towards Michelle, burying her sobs in her girlfriend's embrace. Michelle holds Giulia tight, whispering soothing words in her ear as Giulia dissolves into tears.

I can't bare this. Her pain, her anguish.

I want to run, to scream, to shout, to pound my knuckles into the ground until they're raw and bloody.

"Perhaps we should give those two a minute," says Emilia, gesturing for me to follow her outside. She's probably right.

"Are you okay?" she asks as the door closes.

"Why?"

"You look..." Emilia trails off as though she can't find the word. I wave her concern away.

"I'll be fine. I just ... need to find Idris."

Emilia balks at my words. "Are you sure?"

"Yes, I'm sure." I wave my farewell as I hurry down the corridor before she can call me out on my terrible lie.

CHAPTER 8

Salt trails through the air as I draw closer to the docks. The streets are wide and dirty, the cobbles ground almost entirely to dust after centuries of tread by generation after generation. The dock roads are some of the oldest in Halice. The knowledgeable dodge the occasional pothole; the less careful mutter about the wretched state of the roads as they catch themselves out. It's enough to make me grind my teeth, don't we have enough going on right now? Road quality isn't at the top of my list.

My pulse hammers in my ears, my breathing is short and shallow. My mind races yet is stuck fast on Giulia's tear-stained face, the visage welded to my mind's eye in vivid, heart-breaking detail. It bites at me over and over in time with each hurried footstep like an agonising blister. My strong, kind, beautiful sister is so stressed she's weeping. What do I do? How do I fix this?

There's a higher concentration of Coari mercenaries near the docks, which is unsurprising given their recent arrival. Weapons hang at their hips or are strapped to their backs. The blades curve in shape, rather than run straight like the swords on this continent. Oddly, I'm also struck by their boots – clearly good quality for travelling and fighting – in a strikingly familiar style. A style I hadn't seen until a Fated man returned to these shores.

I weave through the throng of people. Ahead, ship masts rock back and forth, accompanied by the giddy flapping of loose sails and the waves playfully slapping the underbellies of boats in their resting places. The breeze is briny and bracing as it plays with my dress, the loose blue silk frolicking behind me.

I head for Idris's offices, presuming I'll find him there. I don't know why. He can't do anything about the litany of problems piling onto my shoulders. He'll be busy planning the reception dinner for the mercenaries. This scheme is his idea, so I deem it only fair that he tackle the fall out.

Yet every instinct is screaming at me to find him, the bond purring as my chest thumps. A nervous sizzle has settled unwelcome under my skin. I need relief. To find that constant, familiar sensation that'll burn all else away. Something I can handle. I need our bond.

I need him.

The sun ripples off the water like liquid glass, glinting viciously in the corners of my eyes. The boats jostle upon their undulating bed, tugging at ropes that keep them safely tethered to the land. Workers hurry about, but there aren't as many as I'd expect. They're unloading a couple of boats that have just come in.

There should be more activity here. My throat clenches. People need work. No trade, no jobs; no jobs … disaster. My breathing accelerates, becoming shallow and fleeting. My throat constricts as I walk, my heart hammers loudly in my ears.

Goosebumps rise to attention on my arms. My breathing goes warm, my eyes itch.

He's close.

I stop by the water, closing my eyes and focusing on my

breathing. Warm itching stretches up my palms and familiar whispers swirl through my ears, quickly silenced by the steady sound of a gurgling tide mingled with my own breath and heartbeat. I force myself into the familiar sensation of Idris, allowing the unending fire to wipe away my frantic spiral.

I open my eyes slowly, searching for an infuriating blond head. Idris stands with Alfieri and a woman I don't recognise at the water's edge. Her attire tells me she's from Coari. Idris is grinning like it's the best day of his life, enraptured by the mercenary.

She's beautiful. Utterly and entirely stunning. Her dark brown skin glows with bronze undertones. Her eyes brim with warmth, vividly similar to dawn's first light glinting off fresh coffee. Her hair is black as onyx, forming large, bouncy curls that tumble over her shoulders. Piercings glitter all the way around the outsides of her ears, and a pretty, shimmering stud sits in her left nostril.

The woman laughs, her hand going to Idris's arm. Easy, familiar, intimate. They clearly know each other well. I swallow, trying to dislodge the fresh heat settling in my throat, an uneasy viper flaring to life in my stomach. I let out a short, sharp breath, my jaw clenching tightly as I ball my hands into fists. Who is she to touch him like that?

Alfieri looks well. His brow is sun-kissed, his usual cheerful expression hovering close to the surface. The top half of his long brown hair is pulled back from his face, and a short beard covers his square jaw – a permanent feature or just a necessity thanks to his journeys at sea? I'm not sure.

He's animated with Idris and this woman, gesturing about the boxes on the docks. They must be his. Meaning... Fate's Fury! I don't want to know what they are or why they're here.

The image of Giulia's tear-stained face explodes across my mind. My throat closes up. The stress eating her from the inside makes me want to scream. My mouth turns sour, the lump in my throat turns cold. A war of ideas clashes about my head, because one undeniable thought is slapping me straight in the face.

Alfieri has got these ships through the blockade.

Alfieri can move things.

But his business is illegal. I don't know much but I know enough. I don't ask, for a very good, very specific reason. I don't *want* to know for certain; I don't *want* to bring the law down on his head or on the heads of whoever else is implicated. He's my friend. He helped us in the Great Rebellion.

But the fact remains: the law is the law. It's there to protect the people of this city. It's the foundation of our great High Chamber.

Idris abruptly flinches, shoulders pinching and a wry smile flitting across his face. He slowly turns, searching for me in the crowd. His smile widens when he spots me but he folds his arms.

"Trying to sneak up on me, Di Maineri?" Idris chuckles. As they all turn to face me, the woman tenses and her hand drifts to the blade at her side. She watches me intently, opening her stance like Idris does when he suspects trouble. Her dark eyes study my every breath as though I am a wild animal that can't be trusted. Indignation rattles like a war bell in my chest.

How dare she? Who is she to come here and judge me! In my *city, with* my *Fated!*

I won't give this woman the satisfaction of my discomfort.

I meet Idris's hazel eyes, finding them gallingly bright and relaxed. He's in a good mood – probably because his friends have arrived, and the results of his win in the High Chamber are materialising. Fate's Fury, the man is more like his father than he realises.

I tear my eyes away, the hot burning tongue of our bond dancing uncomfortably across the back of my neck amidst a chorus of wicked whispers.

"Do I need to sneak up on you, Patricelli?" I ask, cocking my hip. I switch my focus to Alfieri who grins in friendly greeting. I wave back, forcing easy, smooth motions.

"I'd like to see you try," Idris answers, golden eyes glinting with mischief. "Let me introduce you. This is Tahira, leader of the Red Sands Bannerhood."

"Pleasure," I say, forcing warmth for the woman. She nods back, a small, bemused smile flirting with her lips as she studies me up and down.

"Likewise," she says, her voice rich and smooth like good wine.

My gaze switches back to Alfieri, partly to avoid the intense study of the Coari warrior, but also because I need to focus on what I'm about to do.

How can I do this? How can I ask? This isn't who I am. This isn't what I stand for. I am for law and order.

But if the bank collapses, it's more than just Giulia's stress at stake. The collapse of the Di Maineri Bank won't just be a disaster here but also abroad. Businesses will go under, people will starve, lives will be ruined and lost.

Surely that's far worse than a little undisclosed criminal activity? I won't be what Idris accused me of being – I won't be paralysed. I can do something to make this city safer. I have to do something.

"I'll finish up here and we can talk in my office, alright?" Idris says casually before I can say another word.

"Not everything is about you, Patricelli." I throw him a withering look, pretending he's not the very reason I came down here to begin with. "Alfieri, do you have a moment?"

Surprise breaks across both men's faces for a moment. Alfie cackles.

"Yeah, Idris, not everything is about you," Alfieri mocks as Idris throws him a scathing side-eye.

"Is everything okay?" Idris asks, concern bunching his brow.

"A moment in private, Alfieri, if that's alright?" I clarify brightly, fighting the urge to clear my throat. Idris again looks surprised, but this time worry thins his lips.

"Of course," Alfieri says.

"Renza..." Idris steps closer. "If you need help—"

"I don't have much time," I cut Idris off then turn back to the warrior, enjoying the exchange. "Pleasure, Tahira. We'll speak this evening."

The gnawing curiosity on Idris's face is unmistakeable, and the bond purrs at his fixation. I gesture for Alfieri to follow me back the way I came. Alfieri falls into comfortable step next to me. I throw a look behind me and realise Tahira has stepped to Idris's side and is whispering in his ear. The wicked grin that breaks across Idris's face make me want to leap for his throat.

I clamp my teeth down, snap my head back around and let out another sharp breath. This is ridiculous. This is beneath me; I barely spoke to the woman! Why am I reacting like a petulant child?

I need to focus, and not on whatever's happening behind me. Tahira isn't my business. Giulia is my priority. The bank and my people are my duty.

"So, this is unexpected." Alfieri chuckles, then his eyes go wide. "Wait, is it something for Emilia? I thought her birthday was in winter—"

"Don't worry, it's not Emilia. You haven't forgotten anything," I say reassuringly. "She loves those earrings by the way."

"Good. I saw them and thought of her so I had to bring them back. Anyway, what's going on?" Alfieri asks with a bright smile. He casually slips his hands into his pockets as we walk slowly along the port.

I hesitate, not sure how to begin. The sound of the docks swells around us, filling in the silence but only highlighting my nerves.

"I need to talk to you about something – not in my capacity as Electi," I babble out hurriedly, unable to meet his eye. I clear my throat, desperately fighting the urge to bite my lip or run away.

"Okay," Alfieri answers like he has all the time in the world. I hesitate, wishing words would magically appear.

"It's only me, Renza," Alfieri encourages. "What's going on?"

"I..." I sigh, swallow and then force out the first words I find on my tongue. "These are your boats, aren't they?"

"Maybe," Alfieri answers, an edge to his voice that kindly suggests I don't pry any further. I press my lips together tightly, casting my eyes to the floor. I shake my head.

Bad idea. I shouldn't do this. It's illegal, it's wrong, it's—

Alfieri's hand comes to my arm, pulling me to a gentle stop. I look up at him and he raises his eyebrows encouragingly.

"Renza, what is it?" he asks impossibly gently. "I promise, not a word will go anywhere. Not even to Idris."

"Can you get things into the city? I don't want to know how!" I spew quickly, forcing the words out as fast as I can, hating how they taste. Self-loathing rattles around my throat, but I can't take the words back now. I've said them.

This isn't me; this isn't what I stand for.

But the consequences of the bank failing would ravage so many. I can't let it fail. I have to do everything.

Even if I won't sleep at night.

Alfieri pauses, nodding slowly before replying. He slips his hands back into his pockets, keeping his shoulders open and relaxed.

"What do you need moving?" he asks quietly.

"The tithes from the other banks," I answer. "The bank is in real trouble, Alfieri. If it goes under, there'll be a catastrophe. I mean, starvation on a massive scale, riots and looting and ... chaos."

"The consequences would be horrendous," Alfieri agrees

quietly. "Emilia said Giulia has been stressed lately. I didn't realise things were that bad."

"We can't have people knowing it's bad. It'd cause widespread panic and—"

"No one will hear it from me, I promise," Alfieri soothes quickly. "So you need me to move tithes?"

"We can't take the land route. It takes far too long and with the raiders and bandits from Chalgos stationed en route, we'd lose more money than would make it here. But if you were to facilitate movement again..."

Alfieri doesn't speak for a moment. He pulls a face as he considers quietly, turning to look at his boats.

"If you don't want to, I get it," I babble, hating every word of this conversation. "Of course, we can't have any trace of this getting back to anyone. No one but the two of us can know. This would have to be entirely off the books—"

"Ten per cent," Alfieri quietly cuts me off. I stop, blinking hard.

"What?"

"Ten per cent of everything we move, we keep. That's our fee," Alfieri says. "No details, no discussions, nothing written down. Just ... taken from the top, shall we say."

I force myself to swallow past the lump in my throat. I take a deep breath.

"Five."

Fate have mercy.

"Eight."

"Seven."

"Deal," Alfieri finalises. My stomach churns. My blood runs cold. I've just struck a criminal deal.

What have I done?

I nod, unable to speak.

"Great." Alfieri smiles with ease, patting my shoulder. "By the way, I'm thinking of taking Emilia to the theatre tonight –

you girls didn't see *Lacrimae Rubri* while we were away, did you?"

I shake my head, fighting to clear my throat. I blink hard.

Emilia is going to hate me for this. She gets so upset about Alfieri's business. She worries about him so much, and I'm the one sending him and his men away this time.

Fate's Fury, am I a truly terrible friend?

"No, no, we didn't. Let me know if it's good." My voice cracks at the end. Alfieri's face pulls with concern. He opens his mouth but I speak before he can.

"I have to go. Look after yourself. Don't do anything ... reckless." I clear my throat, turning to run away.

"Renza? Renza?" Idris's voice is taut with worry, calling across the dock. I ignore him. I can't talk to him right now. I can't even look him in the eye. He'd pry this out of me. He undoes me completely, yanking my dark and dirty secrets to the surface. This one is too fresh, too sharp.

"Renza!"

I walk away, as fast as I can without running.

Did I just do that? Did I just break the law?

Oh my god, what have I done?

My heart is throbbing in my throat. I can't breathe. I can't think.

Oh Fate's Mercy, this isn't what I stand for. This isn't what I believe in!

I stagger through the streets of Halice in a daze, my stomach churning. I can go back. I can ask Alfieri to forget. I can ask him to pretend it never happened.

But the memory of Giulia engulfed in tears hits me like a sledgehammer and the guilt traces a noose around my throat. Pathetic tears cluster along my lash line like diamonds, each one sharp and salty. I refuse to let them fall. I can't be that pathetic. I can't be that ridiculous. I did this, I chose this. I can't cry about it. This is my choice, ghastly though it is.

My path is a blur. I don't think about direction, just the need to move, to walk and walk and keep walking. I feed that craving, desperate to quiet the circulating voices calling me a hypocrite and a criminal.

A crowd ahead brings me to an unceremonious stop and I realise I'm not far from the textile district. This can't be good.

But they're not yelling, not egging on a fight. No one is running away or charging through.

They're ... watching something. Swallowing tightly, my brow pulls together as I venture closer. The crowd stands shoulder to shoulder facing away from me. I slip between people. A voice floats above the silence. A woman's voice.

"Do not confuse the actions of a human for the actions of Father Fate. Do not confuse the words of a person on this earth for the words of the gods." Her words are so full and moving. I'm hooked.

I realise I'm not going to wriggle any closer to the front with how tightly people are packed. I spy a short wall, and hurry over. I pull myself up and stand on my tiptoes, pressing against a convenient column to keep my balance.

Over the turned heads of the crowd is a woman preaching.

A priestess.

She's a small, dainty person. She wears a simple black dress with a plain silver ring on her left hand. A white chiffon veil is pinned to her neat but modestly styled hair, which walks the line between brown and ginger like a tightrope. Her pale complexion enhances the roses in her cheeks. Her conviction pours out of her brown eyes. Such a small, delicate person houses such fierce passion and assurance.

"This is not the work of Father Fate," the priestess tells the crowd. "This is the work of the Holy Mother – a mortal woman. The gods have not abandoned us, a corrupt Church has. A Church that put their own power over the wellbeing of living, breathing people."

What is she still doing here? The Holy Mother told all Holy Servants to leave. They all obeyed.

Apart from her.

Why?

The priestess keeps talking.

"We're facing a time of hardship. We're all going to face challenges that will force us to examine everything we thought we knew." The priestess moves with extreme grace and speaks with real emotion and emphasis. "We thought we could trust the Holy Faith, but they abandoned us. We thought we could trust our allies, but they succumbed to their own greed. But while we examine what we know, we must not fall prey to those seeking to take advantage of your confusion, of your searching, of your questions. We are blessed because we know that the Church and the gods are not the same. No matter what the Holy Mother says. She can remove her servants. She can call us heathens. She can do everything in her earthbound power to drive a wedge between us and Fate, but she can never remove our connection to Father Fate and his Divine Daughters. Because they are in our hearts and they know us."

Wow. A priestess? Speaking against the Holy Faith? By Fate's Mercy I never, ever thought I'd see this.

My shoulders droop, my heart slowly crawls from my throat to my chest again as the thumping of my pulse weakens in my ears.

"A difficult road lies ahead. I don't know what will happen," the priestess continues. "Hardships are going to put decisions in front of us that feel impossible. They are going to put us in places where we feel there is no right answer. But we are Halicians. When we stand together, with our neighbours and for our neighbours, we are stronger. *We* are our community. *We* are our faith. If we do right by each other, then we do right by Fate."

Had a Holy Servant ever made this much sense?

Muttering catches my attention, and I see a few people

nudge each other and point my way. I don't want to interrupt this sermon, or draw attention when people need to hear this message. I surely did.

I hop down from my ledge and move away, a fresh lightness in my step and calmness filling my mind.

CHAPTER 9

The only thing I've changed in my father's study is his chair. I couldn't bring myself to get rid of that worn leather monstrosity; it reminds me too much of him. I moved it to the corner by the fireplace instead. I kept his beautiful desk, which is littered with the research and sketches Fiora has gathered on all of the mercenary companies we'll be entertaining this evening.

The speed at which my aunt gathered all this information is almost scary – and it's detailed, too. Information about the last conflicts they've been involved with, average price per soldier, numbers of casualties and specialised skill sets. It's especially impressive considering the Red Sands Bannerhood only arrived this morning, though admittedly the details on them are thinner.

A sketch of their leader graces my desk. It doesn't do justice to how stunning she is in person.

Tahira, the Princess of War. She'd saved Idris from slavers. Gone with him to Malaya to learn mind-stilling. Taught him at least part of his considerable skill with a sword – the skills that kept him alive. Kept both of us alive. I bite my lip, trying not to think about all the time she and Idris spent together. Close, fighting for their lives, on the brink of battle...

An uncomfortable itch rattles beneath my ribs and eats at my breath.

It's pathetic. It's ridiculous. I know nothing about it – about *them*. I'm in no position to have feelings about it at all. Logically I don't care – I don't! I am not this person; I've lived my life and have my own romantic history too – terrible though my taste apparently is and how blind it apparently made me. It's wrong of me to wish Idris's own history would stay far away, across the oceans.

Idris mentioned me before today. She knew who I was the second he said my name. She likely knew about our Fated bond before even I did, that galling fact twisting at my gut with nails of iron. What did she think of me? Me, the woman that drove her – that drove *Idris* – from his home and thrust him into danger? The memory of her hand on his arm makes me want to scream with exasperation – mostly at myself! At my untenable, unbelievably juvenile reaction.

"Renza? Ren—? Renza!" Aunt Rialta stands by the door to my office. She folds her arms, the trailing sleeves of her impeccable red dress reaching down to the floor. It is a popular style in the Wheel City, whereas here in Halice we prefer lighter fabrics, with smaller trumpeting sleeves made of free-flowing materials – so as not to irritate or overheat us more than necessary. Aunt Rialta's ruby satin is painted with intricate yellow flowers and depictions of brightly coloured birds, and her corset cinches her waist in so tightly I wonder if she can breathe.

"Do you have any idea what time it is? You should be getting ready!" Rialta says, exasperated, patting her tightly controlled dark hair.

"I can't be late to my own party, Aunt Rialta," I answer, but she's right. I ease out of my chair. Rialta sweeps forwards, picking up the papers from the table.

"Fiora's been busy," she muses. "I'd recognise my sister's handiwork anywhere. It used to be my life she snooped through and tried to arrange like this," snorts Rialta dryly. "Although, that implies she stopped."

Given the earlier conversation about Allysa, I elect to say nothing. Rialta throws a page of numbers down on the table.

"Regardless," Rialta says, sweeping me out of my father's study, closing the door behind us, "before your sister hears, let me state again that there is no way Halice can afford to pay these mercenaries. And more importantly, neither can the bank."

"Don't worry about that, and keep your voices down. Giulia's almost ready," Aunt Fiora chastises, descending the stairs. Her formal dress has a corseted waist with an A-line skirt and trailing sleeves. Halician fabrics, but still the standard formal dress.

I hate how much it reminds me of the Holy States. It's all inherited from them, lingering remnants from their time reigning over us almost two centuries ago, their styles imposed on us for all important events.

Fiora reaches the bottom step, her midnight-blue skirt fluttering around her feet. She eyes me with a bright smile as she turns to the mirror, holding up two earring options.

"Which do you think?" she asks.

"The left ones," calls Agosta from her position ensconced on the living room couch. "They suit your face shape."

"Thank you," Fiora calls back, meeting Agosta's eyes in the reflection of the mirror. "Not feeling better?"

"Nope," Agosta bemoans, sighing as she throws her head back onto the sofa with suitable flair. "I hoped spending all day wallowing would have me back on my feet for tonight."

Agosta discards a book, preferring to pass comment on us as we leave for the evening. She watches with a bemused expression and a nearly empty glass of wine between her fingers. She complained of a headache this morning at breakfast and took to her bed. Apparently, it hasn't cleared up.

"You *must* not be feeling well, passing up the chance of a party and gossip." Rialta snorts, walking over and taking the nearly empty glass from her sister, and draining its remains. Agosta pouts, pulling her blankets higher.

"I'm really not. My stomach is all over the place, too. So you must bring back all the messy secrets, okay? I want the dirt." Agosta grins.

"Me? Dirt?" Rialta asks disparagingly.

"I was talking to literally anyone but you. Renza? Fiora? Surely you loves will indulge me." Agosta sighs, leaning back on my sofa cushions and pulling the blanket up over her arms.

"Sure, Aggie, but no one has a nose for drama like you do." Agosta beams like it's a compliment and Fiora turns and flashes me a smile.

"Renza, dear, I'm happy to wait for you but I'm not sure what impression it'll give if we're late. Besides, we don't want Patricelli running the show without oversight."

"Oh, perish the thought," Giulia says, appearing like a golden goddess at the top of the stairs. She's wearing mottled, sweet blues and pinks, the colours swirling together like a flourishing spring sunrise. The trailing gossamer and silk shimmers like wisps of magic. Her golden hair is perfectly swept up onto her head, a few curls left loose to frame her face and a smattering of gorgeous butterfly pins to complete the look.

"Wow, Giulia! Michelle will be absolutely enchanted." I grin. Giulia laughs, the sound a soothing balm. She hasn't lost the dark circles under her eyes, though some clever make-up masks the worst of it. A fine pink powder glitters on her eyelids as she blinks.

"We decided to just enjoy tonight." Giulia turns and checks her appearance in the mirror. "Have some us-time, put work far from our minds."

"That sounds perfect. Exactly what you need." I beam, linking my arm with hers. "Music and food and dancing with pretty dresses. Very romantic."

"Yes, you should be relaxed this evening. If you look stressed people will think there is something to be stressed about," Rialta says. Giulia throws me a look. I mouth to ignore it, taking her hands and giving them a squeeze.

"Tell me you're not wearing that." Giulia wrinkles her nose.

"What's wrong with it?" I ask in mock horror before shaking my head. "No, I'm going up now."

"Want a hand? I can do your hair?" offers Giulia.

"That sounds lovely but don't keep Michelle waiting. Go have fun," I say, heading up the stairs. But Rialta's words come back to me.

"It used to be my life she snooped through and tried to arrange like this."

Is that what Fiora is doing? Trying to snoop and control me? Or is she genuinely trying to help? I suppose the two aren't mutually exclusive.

Why have my aunts come here? Rialta is clearly here for the bank, not out of concern for her two nieces. But Agosta? Fiora? What are their motives? My investigation will have to wait until tomorrow. Tonight I have to focus on the mercenaries and Halice.

CHAPTER 10

The High Chamber is brimming with amber candles. Dancing golden light soaks into every gilded corner and climbs every carved column. Rippling against the stained glass, each vivid pane is sprinkled with glimmering fire dust. The colours glow from within like magic.

The pews have been cleared, as have the Electi chairs, gates and all other furniture. Instead, surrounding the centre stage are smartly dressed musicians sporting strings, pipes and percussion of every name, playing joyful, elegant tunes. Large garlands of bursting autumnal flowers adorn the columns stretching for the ceiling. The black and white marble floors are freshly polished and gleaming as the opulent crowd mingle, dance and dine.

Idris has done a good job.

I don't spot him amongst the crowd, but I know he's here. My fingers tingle. My breath is warm.

I stride forwards, taking a crystal wineglass from a staff member with a smile of thanks. I catch my reflection in the mirrored silver tray.

Tonight needs a statement. Traditional formal wear is too

similar to the Holy States' favoured styles, so I've gone with something more Halician.

My dress is made from light, floating silks and gossamers in varying shades of rich green. The loose skirt drapes in uneven layers to my feet and is cinched at the waist by a swirling metalwork belt crafted by Uncle Ruggie. Embellished with golden beads and embroidery around the halter neckline, the dress flutters when I move. Golden bangles sit at my elbows and wrists, attached to a delicate, shimmering peace of translucent gossamer that floats and swirls as I move, the candlelight causing it to gleam as it dances and twirls.

My gladiator heels clip across the marble as I study the crowd. Dangling emerald earrings dance across my shoulders as I size up tonight's arena. My dark hair is pinned to my head with jewelled adornments fashioned after the sun and stars, with a few loose waves to frame my face.

Michelle and Giulia are already on the dancefloor, making me smile. They love to dance. They hold each other close, their embrace tender and sweet. The love in both their eyes as they twirl away warms my chest. When was the last time I saw Michelle this done-up? Her navy dress is simple and traditional, but it suits her.

It's good to see Giulia looking better. To see her smiling, the stress gone. Totally at ease and happy with her true love.

Fiora and Rialta chat with one group of mercenaries. I recognise one of the faces from Fiora's files. Panos Galannis from the Salt Hounds. He's wearing the traditional formalwear for men on the continent – a fitted jacket with flared sleeves from elbow to wrist over trousers and dance shoes. But where's his brother Solon?

"My-my, Signora Di Maineri, you look ravishing."

It's the man himself. Fate's Fury, there's no denying Solon is handsome. Tall, broad-shouldered and muscled, he has thick bronze hair with simultaneously sharp and twinkling blue eyes that promise mischief. He offers a rogue grin, the kind that has no doubt beguiled men and women across the continent. A few nasty but faded scars mar the backs of his hands, but somehow they only make him seem more daring.

"Signore Galannis, good evening." I smile back with warmth. "How have you been enjoying your stay in our city?"

"Oh, it's a beautiful place. It's not often our company has the opportunity to travel this far south," Solon answers, slipping closer to my side. I face him properly, smiling sweetly.

"I hear you've been working in Rhone recently."

"We have indeed. Have you been?" he asks, eyes glinting.

"Can't say I've had the pleasure," I respond.

"Ah, well then, you're missing out." Solon leans closer, his voice taking on a gravelly, whimsical quality. "It's cold and harsh, true, but the beauty is raw and wrenching like no other. Sunsets bleed over icy lakes... They'll stir your soul. The trees are so ancient they're thicker than a man is tall, stretching higher than any building could fathom. And if you're lucky, you'll see the wildlife. I once saw a mama bear with her two little cubs by a river, the children splashing about in the water as the mother secured supper. A sight for the ages."

"It sounds beautiful."

Solon grins. "It is. But it doesn't hold a candle to your beauty, signora."

A blush blooms across my cheeks and I tilt my face up to meet his gaze.

"Wow." A quiet laugh bubbles onto my tongue. Solon's eyes gleam as he steps closer, so close our arms are almost touching.

"Too strong?" he whispers conspiratorially. I shake my head, a wicked grin stretching across my lips.

"Not at all, just bold."

"Always be bold in the pursuit of what you want, signora. You would know a thing or two about that, I'm sure." He offers me a playful wink.

"And what is it you want, sir?"

"Well," Solon says, reaching for my hand. He slowly runs his coarse thumb over my palm before lifting the backs of my fingers to his lips. "Shall we start with a dance?"

I'm about to answer when my breath catches and my mouth goes dry.

Idris steps to my side. Idris in formalwear... *Fate have mercy!* His jacket is a rich, dusty amber, matching exactly the last rays of a summer sunset. The expensive satin is adorned in tasteful silver filagree and fitted to his muscular body, styled with two sets of jewelled buttons across his chest and long embroidered sleeves that modestly trumpet from the elbow to the wrist. The tails sit nicely over his smart, shapely dark trousers. His blond hair is carefully managed, glinting in the candlelight. This is a far cry from his casual tunic, trousers and marching boots.

I rip my eyes back to the mercenary in front of me, before my gawking becomes noticeable.

"Solon," Idris says in greeting, although his warmth holds an edge I can't place. He offers a tight smile and a flash of hardness in his eyes. Solon releases my fingers slowly, giving Idris a wild grin.

"Idris, you look well. Foreign sunshine must agree with you," Solon chuckles. "Speaking of, aren't your Coari friends supposed to be attending? I heard they were staying in your home with you."

Seriously? That's news to me.

I raise an eyebrow at the news, unimpressed, but Idris shrugs. His hand goes to my back, jolting me with red-hot pokers. He closes the space, barely a sliver of tense, brittle air between us.

"Some of my friends are," agreed Idris. "They accommodated me for many years; I wanted to return the favour."

"Ah yes. I've heard much about your famed ... ah ... *friendship* with the Princess of War." Solon grins wickedly. "That must be a fascinating story."

Friendship. Sure.

"Though I'm surprised to see you two so ... close." Solon gestures between us with narrow eyes. "Not tearing each other apart? I thought you'd be clinging to opposite sides of the room all evening. Perhaps switching in and out."

"Renza and I aren't strangers. We see each other every day," Idris says warmly. He steps forwards, between the mercenary and me, gripping Solon's shoulder in a way that I can't decipher. "Why would I ever avoid my Fated?"

Solon nods, questions lighting up in his eyes.

"Speaking of," Idris continues, "I did come over with a purpose. I must steal my Fated away. Please excuse us."

"I will speak with you again later, signora." Solon turns to take my hand, lifting it slowly to his lips and looking deep into my eyes as he kisses my knuckles. "I look forward to our dance."

Idris's tense smile wavers into a grimace, and something warm and devious spreads through my chest.

"I'd like that, signore," I answer, offering Solon a flirty smile before he leaves. I watch him go, aware of Idris's golden gaze devouring my expression. I don't acknowledge it, and instead turn back to watch the dancers twirling across the marble floor.

"So your friend, is he single?" I ask lightly. That cracks something in Idris, and he huffs irritably.

"In life, but his bed is rarely empty," Idris answers tersely. "It's how the brothers operate, attempting to seduce their patrons to secure contracts over the competition."

Is that why Idris came over here? Does he think I need managing now? I was blind where Nouis was concerned, true. But I won't be again. Never again. Indignation coils in my throat.

I shrug noncommittally. "It won't sway my opinion. But maybe I'll enjoy his efforts."

Idris clamps his jaw shut like he's biting back a barrage of barbed comments. The bond growls in my chest, egging me on. A small smile tugs at the corner of my mouth.

I spy Alfieri on the dancefloor, twirling Emilia under his arm. He gazes at her like she's the moon and stars walking, and in that gorgeous yellow dress she certainly looks the part.

"Why'd you interrupt?" I ask pointedly after a long moment of silence.

Idris leans closer.

"I wanted to check in. You looked … upset earlier."

He must mean at the docks when I took off without talking to him or Tahira. I roll my eyes.

"Do I look upset now?" I demand.

"No." Idris's voice is deep and guttural, sending shivers up my spine. "That's certainly not the word I'd use." The heat of his gaze brands the side of my face. The bond stretches and hisses, his attention both gratifying and gnawing.

"Good. I wouldn't want Solon's attention out of pity."

I pretend I'm unable to sense his biting frustrations. An eruption of laughter switches my attention to another group of mercenaries. Briaggio and the Galen Company appear to be indulging themselves, bubbling over with boisterous conversation.

"I take it you know them, too?" I say, gesturing discreetly their way.

"I do." Idris is practically grinding his teeth.

"You'd best get on with introductions, don't you think?" I say, my gaze flashing up to meet his. "I'd love to explore all options this evening." Something snaps in Idris's eyes, a fervid, sharp glint hiding amongst the gold. He chuckles once with wry humour and leans closer. The heat of his body radiates towards me, fizzing with tension so thick I can taste it.

"Admit it."

I raise a quizzical eyebrow. He drops his head inches from mine. His breath throws goosebumps racing over my skin.

"There are no options. Not Solon, not anyone else," he continues.

"Then why are they here?" I frown at him. "If they aren't options for Halice—"

"Not Halice. You. There are no options." My skin sparks with fire, the pain of his presence melting into my bones. His voice drops, becoming dark and quiet, only for me.

"Admit. It," he repeats, whisper-like, an addictive poison in my ear. I lower my drink. No options? Because my taste can't be trusted or because he considers himself to be my only real choice?

"If I wanted to, would you really stop me?" I ask without looking at him, hanging on his answer more than I'd like.

Idris runs a finger tortuously slowly from my elbow down to my wrist. My heart throbs against my ribs. Fire rages at his barest touch, sending waves of stars up and down my arm.

"Is this the game you want to play with me?" Idris murmurs softly, his deep voice vibrating through my head.

"Who said this is a game?"

"You're right, this is serious. How about we find a back room, and I'll take you very seriously indeed."

Okay, this was certainly about us and nothing more. My throat clenches, my stomach warms. It takes every ounce of my self-control not to react to his wicked words.

"No distractions," I remind him, clearing my throat. Idris sighs in mock disappointment, but he's not giving up.

"I thought we'd thrown that ridiculous rule away the other night."

"You left. Now it's back," I say shortly. Crap. This isn't how I wanted this conversation to go. Idris's intense scrutiny is a blister. I refuse to meet his eye. The air between us is so thick and tight I can barely breathe. I pinch my lips; I shouldn't have said anything. I shouldn't have let that stupid scrap of insecurity wriggle to the surface.

I take half a step away, hoping to put this interaction behind me. Idris steals the wine glass from my grip.

"Hey!" I protest as he sets it aside. He tightly snags my hands in his scalding fingers and spins me into the dancefloor. He pulls me flush against his chest, his splayed hands now blazing anchors at my back. His unyielding embrace fixes me against the inferno of his chiselled body. He lowers his head so his lips brush against my ear as he speaks, flooding my head with sharp, corrosive sparks. My blood is molten; my pulse is a warring hurricane in my veins.

"Are you mad at me, Renza?" Idris almost purrs, that hot whisper stealing a fevered breath from my lungs. "Did I leave you wanting more?"

"Don't ask questions you don't want the answers to." I scowl, instinctively straining back, but he refuses to allow the space. "My review might not be flattering."

"You already told me everything." His hand presses hard as it slides lower down my back. "I heard the noises, Renza. I was there."

I dig my nails into his hand, railing against his audacity. I glare at him.

"Then you weren't. End of story."

Idris smirks, the arrogant, irritating smile of a man enjoying this moment of power.

"You had a lot to drink. You'd been out with the girls, then you drank even more with me. I could still taste it on you. I was *trying* to be respectful." Idris is practically purring. "I can stop, though. I'll be utterly disgraceful for you."

I roll my eyes, but something in me softens. So that was why he stopped. I didn't do anything wrong. He was trying to be mindful.

Fate's Sake, why couldn't he have said it at the time?

"Don't lie, Renza. I watched your face when you saw me all dressed up. You like what you see." Idris chuckles, his lips brushing against my cheek, making every nerve in my face tingle with hot sparks. He's enjoying this far too much, and the bond bristles against him. My throat feels raw and hot. My tongue vies to lash out.

"Then you opened your mouth and ruined it all," I retort. "Besides, we're working. Get your head in the game."

"This is the only game I'm interested in."

"Idris—"

"Don't blame me. You started it. Coming here dressed like that... Fate's Fury, did you really expect me to keep my hands to myself?" Idris breathes against my ear, voice half a hungry growl. "A man only has so much restraint."

He shouldn't have handed me that amount of power. I smirk, a chuckle building in my throat.

"No distractions."

"Are you really going to torture me like this?" Idris asks again, his eviscerating hands starting to move over my back, eliciting sensations unsuitable for our public situation.

I stop us dead on the dancefloor, lifting myself up on my toes. My lips give the faintest brush against his ear as I whisper: "Suffer."

With that I turn and stride away, happy to quickly find Giulia and Michelle by a table with Emilia and Alfieri.

Idris's burning eyes follow my path. My lips curl confidently, satisfaction humming in my bones knowing that he's hooked on my every breath. Our obsession might be maddening, but at least I'm not descending the steps to insanity alone.

I fall into step beside Giulia, giving her a quick kiss on the cheek in greeting.

"Wow, Renza, you look amazing!" Giulia beams.

"Thank you. I thought I'd take a little risk," I chuckle.

"It's paid off," Michelle agrees vaguely, her eyes anywhere

but on me. I frown. She's searching through the crowd, but for what I can't work out. Her dark eyes run over faces again and again, almost compulsively.

"Thanks," I say, throwing a quizzical look at Giulia. She shrugs as if to say she doesn't know. Giulia takes her girlfriend's hand, giving it a gentle squeeze and rubbing Michelle's knuckles with her thumb.

"Has anyone seen Serra this evening?" I ask.

"No," Emilia sighs. "We tried to call on her before coming, but she wasn't home."

"She doesn't sound like she's doing great at the moment," Alfieri says soberly.

"How do we help her?" I ask, hopeful he has suggestions. "If she doesn't want help?"

"She does, she just doesn't know what she needs. And what she needs depends on the problem. Just ... keep showing her that you're there for her and eventually she'll open up."

"Fate's Fury, I hope so," Emilia says, a dent forming in her flawless brow.

"This is a happy evening," Alfieri reminds us. "Laughter, music, refreshment. Speaking of which, would you like a drink, my dear?" Emilia nods with a beaming smile.

"Anyone else?" Alfieri asks us. After polite refusal around the group, he walks away with a bounce in his step to find refreshments.

"Emilia, you have a good one," I say, remembering his kindness this afternoon.

"He's been showing her off to everyone," Giulia grins. "Alfie is enamoured."

"Yeah, he kind of is, isn't he?" Emilia blushes deeply, undiluted happiness flooding onto her face.

"Awww! You have it just as bad, huh?" I give her a quick hug.

"He met my mother yesterday. He was so sweet with her,

and she really likes him." Emilia's voice is quiet like she's terrified it'll all break and slip away.

"That's a really good sign," I encourage.

"I hope so. I just worry, because ... anyway, what do you think?" Emilia says, looking to Michelle. Michelle doesn't seem to notice. Her eyes are still cutting through the room, searching through the crowd for something.

"Michelle?" I ask. Michelle snaps around and flashes a smile.

"Sorry, what?"

"Are you okay, darling?" Giulia asks, concerned. "We can go home if you're feeling rough?" Michelle shakes her head, gaze turning back to the crowd obsessively. Her brown eyes jump from face to face. Her hands clench in and out. Her breathing is short. She's searching for something like it's haunting her. Something unsettling. Something she can't put her finger on.

Oh no. No, no! Horror swirls through my stomach. This is far too familiar.

"Run!" I say, firmly grabbing her wrist and hauling us towards the door.

"Why? What's wrong?" Michelle babbles as Giulia and Emilia run to keep up.

"You feel antsy, right? Like something hasn't been right for hours but you can't determine what. Like a thousand ghostly eyes are watching and waiting with bated breath? Like there's someone in the crowd staring at you but you can't quite catch them." I stride as quickly as I can. "I remember it all too well."

A Soulhate? In a room filled with mercenaries? This could go wrong very quickly. Emilia swears under her breath and Giulia grips Michelle's hand, her face rippling with determination.

"Don't worry, darling," promises Giulia, "I won't let anyone hurt you. I have you. I love you."

"Fate's Fury, are you sure?" Michelle whispers with wide eyes, fear blooming across her face.

"Better safe," I answer certainly. "Run, now!"

A new group enters the High Chamber and Michelle freezes like she's been turned to stone, eyes fixed on one person in particular.

She's stunning. Tall, athletic and covered in vibrant tattoos. They decorate her honey-gold skin like a walking canvas, their colours vivid, bright and expertly woven. Her silky raven hair is fashioned into many tight braids then gathered into a high ponytail, the tips reaching down to her waist. Her septum is pierced with an ornate silver ring. Loose trousers bunch tightly around her ankles and navel with large heavily embroidered cuffs. Her top is all jewels and beads, fixed in intricate patterns that wrap beautifully around her arms and shoulders. At her hip sits an ornately jewelled dagger.

I tense, ready to throw myself between this stranger and one of my best friends.

Instead of blind fury, her shoulders slacken and her rich brown eyes go wide and round as they lock onto Michelle. An utterly absorbed smile blooms across her face. I look between the two women. Michelle's shoulders drop and a sweet, peaceful breath is pulled from her lungs. But there's no anger. No blood-curdling rage.

This stranger walks calmly towards Michelle as though in a trance.

A different kind of sorrow sweeps through my veins, turning my pulse cold and bittersweet. I was close. So close and yet so, so wrong.

Giulia.

My sister's face almost stops my heart. Her agony rips me apart. The pain so raw and devastated etched across her features makes me want to scream. A flood of tears starts to break free of her blue eyes.

"Hi," the stranger says, still smiling at Michelle like the

whole world begins and ends with her. Like that, the spell breaks.

Michelle swallows, jolting back and blinking rapidly. She gasps, shaking her head. Horror washes over her as she wheels to Giulia. Giulia clutches her mouth with both hands as though to physically hold back her sobs. Every limb is trembling as my sister races for the door. Michelle desperately takes after her.

"Wait, wait!" The stranger tries to follow. My hand moves of its own accord, leaping out and roughly grabbing hold of her wrist. I yank her back with all my strength, glaring at the interloper.

"Don't you dare!" I hiss with all the threat I can muster, before hurrying after my sister. Emilia and I run through the door of the High Chamber and into the cold embrace of the night. The steps are lit by a thousand slender torches. A few paces away, Giulia is in a broken, hysterical state. Every breath is shredded with grief as Michelle tries to take her in her arms.

"No, Giulia, please listen to me," begs Michelle, as though she herself were falling apart. "Please."

"She's your Soulmate!" Giulia's voice is ragged and raw, her spirit breaking in every note.

"I'm so sorry."

"Your Soulmate!" Giulia collapses to the steps, folding over her knees, crumpled by the heartache. Michelle kneels in front of her, trying to take her face in her hands as Giulia pushes her away.

"She means nothing. Nothing. I love you. You are my everything, Giulia," pleads Michelle as Emilia and I descend towards them. Michelle desperately looks at us for help. She latches onto me like a lifeline.

"Please, please tell her. Please explain that nothing has changed," Michelle sobs. Emilia looks to me, waiting for me to work out what to say. I take a deep breath, slipping to sit down next to Giulia on the steps. The coldness of the stone leaks through the fabric of my skirts as I wrap my sister in my arms, pulling her close.

"It's going to be okay," I whisper softly, holding her tightly as she sobs uncontrollably into my shoulder. "Remember what you told me when I met Idris. You have a choice. This is something you and Michelle get to choose together."

"Giulia is my choice." Michelle is in tears as she grips hold of Giulia's hand and presses it close to her heart. "Please, sweetheart, please believe me."

Giulia grips me tighter as her entire body shakes under the weight of her heartache.

"This doesn't have to be the end of anything," I murmur softly, a lump swelling in my throat. "Remember how much Michelle loves you. Remember how much you love her. Don't let Fate steal something so beautiful from you both. You're strong. You're Halician. You're Di Maineri. You can fight this."

Giulia nods into my shoulder, breathing uneven and ragged.

"Oh, my darlings." Fiora hikes up her skirts as she sprints down the steps, brow creased with worry as she throws herself to her knees before Giulia.

"I heard what happened," Fiora whispers gently. She presses a hand to the side of Giulia's face. Giulia can't form words in her heartache, and the worry on Fiora's face morphs into determination.

"Let's get you home, dear," Fiora instructs, manoeuvring Giulia into her embrace. "I'll make you some of my sweet tea – it's just the thing to calm your nerves. It's okay, it's normal to be in shock. Come with me. Home will make everything feel easier."

Giulia nods numbly.

"Please, Giulia, please look at me. Please believe me!" Michelle begs as Emilia holds her. "I love you. I love *you*!"

"I think what's best is some space for the evening. Alright?"

Fiora says firmly but not without some kindness as she pulls Giulia to her feet.

"I'll find us a carriage," I say to Giulia. "Fiora has you, okay?"

"Renza, it's lovely you want to come, but it's not smart for you to leave," Fiora counsels, keeping a motherly arm around Giulia and gently rubbing her back. "You have three sets of interviews to get through. You need to be here in your capacity as Electi."

"But Giulia—"

Fiora holds up a hand.

"Giulia is going to come home with me. We're going to drink sweet tea, bundle ourselves under blankets and settle our nerves. We'll be there when you're done. Nothing will change in a few hours, I promise."

"Giulia needs me."

"So does Halice."

"My sister comes first."

"That's very sweet," Fiora answers warmly, "but there is nothing you can fix for Giulia right now. You can do more good here."

I look at Giulia, who nods.

"She's right," Giulia hiccups raggedly, "go do your job."

"You are my priority." I take her hands and squeeze. "I'm happy to come home. Idris and Maggia and Savino – they can handle this."

"No. Stay." Giulia lets out a shuddering breath. "I'll see you later."

Giulia and Fiora descend the steps in search of a carriage. Michelle breaks down, clutching Emilia like a lifeline. Her sobs crack against the cold silence of the night. Emilia holds up a hand to me as she rubs Michelle's back.

"I've got this," she mouths, then gestures a thumb back towards the High Chamber. The large arched doors hang open, jarring laughter, music and warmth rolling through the decorative opening. It is a violent clash with the splitting grief outside. I take several deep breaths, shaking. I should go home. I should be with my sister as she deals with this world-crushing pain.

But Fiora's words stick in my mind. The city needs me to do my job as Electi. I need to talk to these visiting mercenaries. This is for my city; to break the blockade and hopefully end that awful deal I made with Alfieri. Once this is done, these mercenaries will leave.

So I force my feet forwards and I head back inside.

~

As I re-enter the party, half the faces turn to look and whisper. I pretend I can't hear them or feel their eyes. My head held high, I keep walking, trying not to let my sombre mood leak onto my expression.

Idris and Alfieri are lurking close to the door. Idris walks over, offering me a full glass of my favourite red wine. I take it, nodding in thanks as I drain half right then and there.

"I think your night is over, Alfieri, sorry. Emilia is looking after Michelle," I say tiredly. Alfieri nods, expression taut.

"Understandable," he says quietly, without hint of irritation for which I commend him. "Am I needed, or would I be interfering?"

Emilia really does have one of the good ones.

"I don't think Michelle wants an audience," I say. Alfieri nods.

"Are you okay?" Idris asks intently. I let out a rueful laugh.

"Do not ask me that question," I answer shortly.

"If it makes things any better, Royah is a really great person—"

"Idris!" I snap. "My problem isn't with her personally. My sister is heartbroken. Her loving relationship is one of the few things holding her together through a mountain of stress I'm terrified will destroy her. It's one of the most important and treasured things in her life and it's been upended! Not to mention, one of my closest friends is also completely distraught. While nothing is your friend's fault, and I'm sure she's lovely, right now everything is too fresh. Everyone, including me, needs a few hours to process. Understood?"

I sigh and pinch the bridge of my nose, instantly regretting my outburst. Idris doesn't deserve my anger. But it reminds me far too vividly of our disastrous meeting on the steps of the Grand Temple, the violence and terror that followed, the way our families pried us apart. Everything is painfully fresh.

I drop my hand and take a deep, calming breath and try to focus on mind-stilling. I look around the room and frown, realising one of the mercenary groups is missing.

"Where are the Salt Hounds?" I ask.

"They left." Idris narrows his eyes unhappily. "Apparently Panos is under the impression we can't pay for their services."

"How has that rumour got around?" Alfieri frowns.

"I'd look at those who don't like this plan." Idris glowers at Leone who stands in the corner with his rich buddies.

"Don't go starting anything without proof," I counsel quietly. "We spoke about it openly in the High Chamber. It could be anyone."

"I think Briaggio is waving us over," Alfie says quietly.

"Alright." I force a smile to my lips.

"No, I've got this," Idris strategises. "You take a minute's breather, then come and get me."

"Smart, we'll need the out. Briaggio witters." Alfieri throws me a wink before disappearing. Both clearly know the man. I wonder what shenanigans happened during those months they spent in Chalgos in their errant youth.

I head for the food table. I don't even see the array of delicious dishes because my mind is racing home to my sister.

At least with the Salt Hounds gone, that's one less group I need to charm and feel out. All the quicker to get back to Giulia.

One of the Coari party breaks away in my direction. Of course it's Tahira.

Tahira looks even more beautiful than she did at the docks. She wears embroidered turquoise trousers, exposing her toned naval with a heavily beaded top displaying glittering shades from mint through sapphire to amethyst. The outfit highlights her incredible curves. Her hair is pulled back in a slick ponytail; the dark curls tumble down her back like a jubilant waterfall of onyx. She's traded in her nose stud for a beautiful sapphire hoop, and her ears sparkle with the multiple piercings.

"Hello again." She offers a guarded but warm smile. I smile back.

"Hello to you, too." That's when I noticed the dagger at her hip. It's unlike any dagger I've seen before. Wide yet short and curved and absolutely covered with jewels and precious metals. It's so ostentatious it must be something meant for display. Curiously I turn my eyes back to the Coari group, but only see two others sporting a similar blade at their hips. Interesting. I also note that Michelle's Soulmate – Royah, Idris called her – is nowhere to be seen.

"Is everything alright?" Tahira asks tentatively. "I fear we made quite an entrance."

"It's no one's fault; these things happen." I refuse to let any lingering bitterness leak through. "It's just ... extremely painful for people I love a great deal."

"Idris explained briefly." Tahira's face creases with sorrow. "If it makes any difference, Royah feels incredibly guilty."

"Fate is no one's fault. I would know." I shake my head wryly. "I would love to have a few choice words with him one day, when I reach the After."

Tahira laughs, a slightly bitter look fleeting across her face.

"You and me both."

"Excellent. We'll do it together then."

"You're on."

"If I'm going to give a god a telling-off, I'd rather do it with the Princess of War by my side," I say measuredly, wondering how she'll react.

"Great Spirits, has that name travelled all the way here?" Tahira snorts and rolls her eyes.

"Blame Idris. He can't help but name-drop."

Laughter explodes from Tahira, the sound free and inelegant but absolutely infectious. A smile cracks across my own face as we step closer, as though we are confidantes.

"I am so glad it's not just me that sees it!" Tahira snickers, then covers her mouth like she shouldn't be saying it. I grin with her.

"It's so funny!" I say conspiratorially.

"I'm not sure he's aware he does it," Tahira whispers, casting her eyes over to where Idris stands with Alfieri.

"Oh, rest assured, I've called him out on it. Several times. I've decided if I mock him enough, he might stop."

"I like that strategy. I'm on board." Tahira nods.

"Perfect, I'll drink to that." I laugh as we tap our glasses together. Tahira grins, shoulders dropping as she shakes her head.

"Before I forget, thank you," I say, clearing my throat. "I owe you a debt of gratitude."

Tahira looks surprised, brow arching in a silent question.

"For keeping Idris safe while away from home," I explain quietly, watching Idris talk with Briaggio and Alfieri. My blood grows hot, my pulse picking up the crash against my ribs. Tahira lifts her head as though pleasantly surprised.

"Rest assured, we have exchanged life debts a few times over the years. We stopped keeping track long ago," she tells me.

"Still, my thanks are sincere," I say insistently.

"You're welcome."

"Now, I would love to meet the rest of your party, but I promised Idris a timely social rescue. So if you'll excuse me, we'll circle back in a minute or two. It'll give you a chance to come up with the best stories to embarrass Idris. I expect all the dirt, no holding back."

"I have plenty to choose from, so I'll look forward to it," she says warmly by way of goodbye.

I can't help but issue a small internal groan.

Fate's Fury, I like her. She's smart, funny, confident. Not that I expected Idris to be friends with an arsehole, but it would help me feel a lot less stupid for my reaction to her.

Damn Idris and his good taste in people.

I head towards Idris with a polite smile fixed to my face. Every step prickles, the muscles in my limbs twitching uncomfortably. Each breath turns warmer and warmer until hot coals glow in my throat. I control my breathing, swallowing against the bile bubbling up my gut.

I step beside Idris and start to open my mouth when I catch the reflection in the window behind him. An archer in the rafters, a curved blade at his hip and arrow poised to fly, pointed at—

"IDRIS!" I scream, throwing myself at my Fated as the archer releases his arrow. Vicious pain slices through my arm, dragging a painful scream from my lips as the two of us tumble to the floor.

Screaming and shouting swallow my ears. Idris rolls me off him, away from the danger, shielding me with his body. In a flash, his golden eyes capture the threat.

Thwack.

An arrow finds a body amidst a roar of agony as I start to pick myself up. Idris wraps a strong hand around my arm and hauls me behind a large column. Another arrow whistles past our position on the floor, bouncing off the polished marble.

My entire body roars with flames as Idris presses me against the decorated column, his scalding inferno at my front and cold, unyielding stone at my back.

Gasping for breath, I turn my head to the side.

"You got this?" Idris's breath heaves.

"Just," I gasp back. Blood drains from my face at the body on the floor, a crimson puddle collecting on the black and white tiles. Briaggio's eyes stare unblinking at the wall, an arrow protruding like an enemy's flag from his back.

Dead.

Oh, Fate's Fury, no.

"Idris!" Tahira shouts, racing against the crowd madly scrambling for the exits. She dives for cover behind a column next to Alfieri, the two just about fitting behind the ornate stone.

"Get to the rafters!" shouts Idris, pointing at a door near where they're both taking cover.

"Got it!" shouts Tahira, hand going for the jewelled dagger on her belt before both she and Alfieri throw themselves at the door, narrowly missing the volley of arrows that thud into the ancient wood in their wake.

"Idris—"

BANG. BANG. BANG.

Suddenly we're swamped in itchy, awful white smoke. Hacking coughs threaten to swallow me whole. I can't breathe; the air is blistering as the world starts to spin.

Idris throws me over his shoulder, holding his breath as the plumes of white smoke smother the room. I can barely see my hand in front of my face, but Idris runs. I can't see his feet in this thick smog, but I'm jolted up and down amidst a storm of fire as we pelt forwards. The world is churning; I can't breathe but suddenly we explode out of this burning white cloud and down the steps of the High Chamber.

The air is clear again. Cold and night-tinged, soothing

against my blistering lungs. I gasp and struggle to breathe and fight to keep my vision steady.

Idris sets me on the floor, panting furiously. His eyes are red, his skin irritated as he crouches next to me. He cups my face with his hands, but his eyes drop to the wound on my arm. His face contorts with unadulterated fury.

The world won't stay righted; I desperately try to focus on Idris but everything keeps moving.

"Get her to Taio," Idris shouts at someone I can't see. "Straight there now!"

Idris stands, turning back to the nightmare inside as a large man from Coari takes his place in front of me.

"No! No, Idris!" I slur my protest. Idris doesn't hear me. He charges headlong back into the poisonous white smog of the High Chamber. I stare in horror at the wide-open doors as my vision spirals.

"Idris! Idris!" I try to scream, but instead the world turns red and foggy before fading to black.

CHAPTER 11

Ow.

Ow.

Fate's Fury, this hurts. Why does breathing hurt? Fate have mercy.

Blearily I open my eyes. The world takes a second to reach me. I'm lying on the couch in Idris's study, a wriggling blanket of firelight frolicking over the homey room. A stranger leans over me, prodding at the large, ugly wound in my arm.

I gasp, bolting upright as I study the older Coari gentleman. He has greying hair, a dark complexion and finely creased features suggesting an age of late fifties or early sixties. His dark eyes brim with wisdom and secrets as he holds up his hands calmly to steady my panic.

"You're okay. You're safe," he comforts, his words faintly accented. "I'm a doctor."

"Doctor?" I repeat coarsely, blinking hard and begging my brain to start working again instead of cowering like a sluggish lump. My fingers dig into the plush green velvet of Idris's couch as I try to throw off this lingering smog of confusion.

"Yes," the doctor says warmly. "How are you feeling? Any nausea?"

I shake my head, leaning back against the cushions of the couch – that movement makes the world shake more violently than it should. The doctor nods, content, pausing a moment before going back to the bleeding wound in my arm.

"You should be in bed, young sir," he says without looking up. My head snaps to the door, mouth slipping open and stomach rolling when I see a child.

He can't be more than eight or nine years old. He looks so much like Tahira it's startling. Rich, dark skin and brown eyes framed by thick lashes. His dark, curly hair is cut close to his head and he wears loose linen pyjamas, holding a stuffed animal in his hands as he looks at me inquisitively.

"Hello?" I offer, uncertain why he's studying me with such intensity.

"You're Idris's Soulhate," he says in that blunt fashion only children can get away with.

"Yes, I am. Are you one of his friends?"

"Yes. I'm Karrius," he says and cracks a cheeky, adorable grin, showing a gap between his front teeth.

"Go back to bed, young prince," says the doctor, giving him a firm look. "I mean it. Now. Don't make me tell Tahira you didn't behave."

I stiffen, replaying the moment again in my mind to be certain I didn't mishear the doctor.

Prince? Prince?!

Idris Patricelli... What. Have. You. Done?

Karrius gives a huge sigh before stomping off down the hall again. I blink, turning back to the doctor who's currently finishing his work on my arm.

"I'm Taio," the doctor says. "It's nice to meet you, Renza Di Maineri."

Okay ... clearly Idris has mentioned me to more than a few people. What did he say? What do these people think of me?

"Likewise," I manage. "Um, where's Idris?"

As if waiting for his cue, I hear the telltale signs of the front door swinging open. Goosebumps spring along my skin, my palms itch furiously, my eyes feel too big for my head. He's not alone; there are other voices.

"Taio?" Idris calls out.

"Here!" the doctor calls. Idris and Tahira hurry to the door, along with the large man I saw just before I passed out.

"You're awake! That's impressive. I thought you'd be out for longer!" Tahira smiles, folding her arms as she leans against the door frame. What is she *doing* here? Her people just attempted to kill us! I saw the assassins – they were rather identifiable.

"What's going on?" I manage to grind out in shock. Idris doesn't say anything, walking further into the room, eyes glued to the aching wound on my arm. I look down at the mess of blood and pain. That barbed arrow has ripped the once flawless flesh apart, and was clearly coated in something that irritates and bubbles over the skin like acid. Taio has applied an ointment that's soothed the brutalised skin and is currently adeptly stitching my arm back together.

"You passed out, breathing in too much Witvuur smoke," Tahira answers warmly, walking to sit on the back of the sofa. She shrugs nonchalantly. "Happens to all of us. Take it from me, the first time feels the roughest. But given you're already conscious, you're handling it like a champ."

"Witvuur smoke?" I repeat, swallowing as my patience cracks at the seams. My mouth is dry; my head is pounding. My skin itches furiously, stinging in odd places like I'm being bitten by tiny invisible bugs. How much is caused by the drug and how much by my stupid, arrogant Soulhate standing barely two feet away? The doctor finishes wrapping up my arm.

"It's a powder, made from various plants and rocks found in

Coari," Idris answers, voice quiet and hesitant. His eyes are fixed on me like I'm a rabid wolf about to leap for his throat. He's not wrong.

"It burns with thick, itchy white smoke," Tahira continues. "It's great at filling a room and blocking lines of sight and causing panic, but inhaling too much will knock you out, which can also be useful."

I swallow tightly, my blood practically fizzing with anger. I glare at Idris, my jaw locked so tightly I might break my teeth.

"That's why I thought it best Taio look after you," Idris says. "He knows a lot more about Witvuur smoke than a Halician doctor. Plus, he's a good friend; I trust him." Idris gives the doctor a friendly slap on the back.

"I'm Bash by the way," says the tall man who brought me back here. "Nice to meet you."

If looks could kill, Idris would be cinders by now. I take several small breaths, fighting the urge to get up and punch his stupid face. His stupid, selfish, arrogant face.

"Tahira, Taio, Bash ... give us a minute." I manage to grind the words out with the last ounce of politeness I can scrape together. Idris flinches.

Good.

"Have you ... got this?" Idris asks quietly. *How dare he? How dare he!*

"Now," I growl, my anger leaking out.

"Are you sure? You seem pretty..." Tahira trails off. I fix her with a fierce glare so threatening that she, the Warrior Princess of Coari, actually winces and steps back with her hands high.

I turn back to Idris who is still as a statue. The only sounds are Taio quietly gathering up his things and the fireplace, which also seems to have shrunk lest it too becomes a target of my ire.

I seethe; the image of that archer distorted by stained glass is burned into my brain. That attire made it clear those fighters were from Coari. That image is violently smothered by one of

Briaggio on the floor, a bloody arrow protruding from his back. We were almost killed. Idris was almost shot! Then he dragged me outside and dumped me in the cold with a stranger as I passed out, before charging back into unknown danger like a moron.

Idris brought these people here. Idris brought this violence not just against my colleagues, not just in the most sacred place in all Halice. But against us. This is his fault.

The door latches with a quiet click and my fury fights for the first words off my tongue. I'm losing my control. *How can I even start to convey everything I need to? My justifiable rage?*

I glare at Idris, the seconds stretching like eternities. The blistering heat of his gaze feels like scalding daggers across my skull. My skin writhes with needles, my breath turned short puffs of fire coiling in my throat.

Idris folds his arms, hands clenched into fists.

"Tonight was—"

"No!" I snarl, holding up a hand. I snap to my feet. Idris takes in a deep breath, steeling himself.

"First"—I reach a point of such absolute fury that a wave of insane calmness sweeps through my chest and my words fall from my lips sharp and clean as a razor—"do not lie to me. Is there or is there not an actual *child prince* upstairs right now?"

Idris's eyes narrow for a split second, realising he's been caught, before it flees his expression. He takes a deep breath before giving a curt nod.

"Yes. Karrius is Tahira's half-brother. Where she goes, so does he."

The exasperated half-scream that leaves my body holds so much force it could rip out a lung. My fingers spasm of their own free will, pain radiating from their tips all the way up to my elbows as I raise them to my hair, trying to wrap my head around this.

"We have an actual foreign child *prince* in our city – making us responsible for his safety – *AND YOU DIDN'T TELL ME?*"

The words roar from my mouth with such violence they burn the back of my throat and shake my entire body. Idris bristles before answering with maddening calmness.

"Karrius goes where Tahira goes. It's ... complicated."

"Complicated?" I bite back at him, narrowing my eyes to slits. "Complicated? If anything happens to that child while he's here then we're responsible! You thought it a good idea to bring him here? In the middle of this brewing war?"

Idris growls his frustration, ripping his eyes away to glare at his wall of books instead. I grit my teeth together, heaving furious breaths as I wait. For an apology, an explanation, a denial – anything. But he says nothing.

"Fate's Fury, Idris! Has that smoke robbed you of your tongue? Fogged over your senses?" I shout at him, wishing I could hurl this entire couch at his head. "Do you have nothing to say?"

"What do you want me to say?" Idris snaps. I could explode; I'm boiling over with anger.

"EVERYTHING!" I scream at him so loud it could rattle the walls. I march closer, letting the rage flow so freely I'm shaking from the excursion. "You promised me this wouldn't happen! You promised me *exactly this* wouldn't happen! The trained killers that *you* freely invited into our home, persuaded me would be safe around my loved ones, decided to go on a slaughter spree. Why, Idris? Why the hell did they do that?"

"I don't know!" Idris snarls, and it's clear that fact is eating him alive. Good. He deserves that. He deserves that guilt.

"That all you have?" I shout back. "Why aren't they under lock and key or packing their Fate forgotten bags and leaving this very night!"

"Tahira wasn't part of this. This wasn't on her order; these men were rogue traitors acting against her explicit instructions. She will investigate—"

"No! Enough! Your words mean nothing. Less than *nothing*! I want them gone. I want them all gone," I demand, panting hard.

"No," Idris bites back with the fury of ice. "They can't now. The Salt Hounds and the Galen Company will want answers, and Tahira has to provide them."

"For Fate's Sake, Idris, you just started a mercenary war in our city!" I scream, my throat raw.

"No, it won't come to that. I promise."

"Just like you promised *this exact situation* that I *warned you* about, wouldn't happen? Your arrogance is astounding!" I snarl. My exasperation twists all the air in my lungs as I close the gap between us, glaring up at him.

"We'll work it out," Idris insists. I bark a shocked laugh.

"We? We'll work it out? Oh, so now you want to be a team? Now you want my help, after running around on your own and making everything a thousand times worse than it already was?" I might expire at the sheer audacity of this man.

"Renza—"

"Shut up!" I cut him off. I want to see every crack and tremble in his face for the next part. He meets my eyes with that blistering golden gaze of his.

"That doesn't even touch the fact that after I saved you from that archer, you dragged me out of the High Chamber, injured and drugged to the eyeballs only to *abandon me*. You dumped me in the middle of the night, vulnerable and panicked. Alone."

"You weren't alone—"

"Then you ran right back into that poisonous white smoke" —I'm practically nose to nose with him now—"charging recklessly into a fight and abandoning me!"

"You were safe. You were with Bashran—"

"You left me with a stranger, from the same strange army

that *just tried to kill us*!" The words are shrill and sharp as I throw my hands hard against his shoulders in shock, horror and trembling rage. My arm screams with pain but I eat it, I savour it, the release filling a twisted, satisfying need. "You don't know these people! You can't trust these people – they literally tried to kill you seconds ago!"

Idris doesn't surrender an inch from my assault. His strong hands leap forwards, grabbing my elbows, his fingers digging into the flesh of my arms. His touch burns, setting wildfires raging across my chest. He pulls me closer, our faces almost touching. His eyes are hotter and more blistering that staring into the sun.

"I know Bash. Personally. I was certain you were safe. I would *never* gamble with your safety. Ever."

"Like you were certain nothing would happen?" I spit back venomously. "You abandoned me to go play soldier with your friends again! You're an Electi! You endangered yourself needlessly and recklessly and you left me in the hands of an enemy we cannot trust."

"What was I supposed to do? Take you with me? You were unconscious," Idris shouts, trembling with anger. His words are loud and abrasive on my ears.

"You did what you have done so much recently. Acted on your own!" I snap back at him. "Tossed me aside. Disregarded me entirely. Went behind my back or ignored me. You invited these people here, you're harbouring a foreign royal child, you left me and ran back into the fight. All things you did without involving me! So what? Did our partnership end when Bellandi was hanged? Forgive me for thinking we were moving forwards united. Illusion successfully shattered!"

"It was a fight, Renza, a real fight! Did you want me to stop and chat it through before saving you? The killers weren't going to wait! Every blade and every man makes a difference. I had to help. For our people, for our city. I had to act, I had to stop it! The stakes were too high, I couldn't hesitate. Not when it comes to you. The last time you distracted me I lost the fight. I couldn't let that happen again," Idris snaps back, but his face changes when he realises what's come out of his mouth.

Now it's my turn to be verbally slapped. That awful night with Nouis by the dock replays in my mind. Idris hitting his head, collapsing to the floor as Nouis stood over him with a blade. The blood on my fingers, the dagger pressed into my hand.

My heart is fizzing and threatening to explode from my ribs. My pulse is racing, the whispers of violence now a great roaring chorus.

I take in a long, shaky breath, pushing my hands up against his chest to shove Idris away as roughly as I can. He staggers back, shaking his head like he's trying to take his words back. I'm panting furiously, hating the cold, cracking sensation in my ribs.

"No distractions. Got it." My answer is cold, divorced from the thick emotion in my throat by my calm, quiet tone.

"No. Renza, that's not what I—" Idris holds out a hand and steps towards me. I take three steps back, jolting as I wrestle for self-control. Idris freezes like I hit him.

"You want to work alone? Wish granted, you're now distraction-free!"

I turn sharply on my heels and march towards the door. I pause with my hand on the handle, turning back to glare at him.

"And for the record, when you were the one unconscious, I didn't leave your side for a moment, no matter how much pain it caused me."

Idris flinches and I tear open the door of his study, swinging it so hard it slams against the wall.

In the hallway outside, clearly able to hear everything, stand Tahira, Royah, Bash and Taio. Of course they're hovering, ready to protect Idris if I lost my composure. Because *I'm* the violent one here. I shake my head, a wry laugh falling from my lips.

I do not have the energy for this. I march to the door.

"Renza! Renza, stop!" Idris hurries after me. His hand catches on my arm and pulls my wound. I yelp at the surge of pain, and Idris drops me like I'm venomous. I look down to see blood already seeping through the bandages Taio provided.

"At least stay the night," Idris continues, ignoring his friends. "You're injured, you were drugged—"

"Your house is full," I remind him with a scowl.

"Your room isn't," Idris answers. The audacity of this man. I glare at him, my lip curling.

"I'm going home. My family might be a bunch of wolves, but at least I expect them to lie and betray me."

Idris's chest caves inwards slightly.

"Take my carriage. You are not walking tonight." Idris speaks softly, but the steel in his eyes can't be missed. This is his surrender, and given everything I'd be a fool not to take it.

I yank open the front door and slam it shut behind me, wanting to scream out into the darkness.

Stupid. Arrogant. Arsehole!

His words play over in my head, stuck like a snake eating itself over and over. I dig my nails into my palms, the sting bringing tears to my eyes as my breath comes short and sharp. I gasp in the cool night air, hoping it'll soothe my frayed nerves.

The door opens behind me. It's not Idris. Quiet footsteps approach me on the small path where I wait for Idris to organise his carriage.

Tahira steps up next to me. We're both still dressed in our finery, but looking decidedly more rumpled than during our last conversation. I don't speak, arms still folded as I glare forwards.

What can she want? To defend her friend? To finish the job her people failed at this evening?

"You have no reason to trust me or my people," Tahira

begins, her words tentative but earnest, "but please know, I had *nothing* to do with what happened this evening. I would never do something so honourless, and certainly not in the home of one of my dearest friends. The people that did this betrayed me and dishonoured themselves. They are traitors to the Red Sands Bannerhood."

Tahira pauses, as though waiting for my acknowledgement. I say nothing. The cold night air sinks into my skin, a chill setting at my fingertips. The inky night sky dances with silver stars, the fickle breezes jostle sleeping flowers tucked into their slumber by a navy blanket.

Tahira continues, her words uncertain.

"I've already started the investigation into what happened. The culprits have been caught or killed, and those that knew anything about their plan will be questioned extensively. Every answer I get will be relayed to you. You have my word."

The sound of carriage wheels rattling draws closer until it stops right before us. The carriage boy quickly hops down and pulls open the door for me.

Not having the energy for this conversation, I walk towards the carriage without another word.

"Renza, please." Tahira hurries two steps forwards. I pause, hand on the carriage handle, already hoisting up my long skirts to get in. I look at her. Backlit by the candles burning around Idris's front door, her hair gleams with rivers of orange and gold. I raise an eyebrow.

Tahira takes a deep breath.

"I'm sorry," she says, her dark eyes meeting mine. I pause for a long moment, wondering how to respond. Because I am exhausted. I nod once, slow and sharp.

"We'll speak tomorrow in the High Chamber. Your presence is required. No excuses. My advice is to have something of substance to share – real, tangible proof you were not part of it. If your sorrow is genuine, then prove it. Do what it takes to ensure no further violence comes to this city because of your people. Do whatever it takes to leave as quickly and peacefully as possible."

Tahira nods, swallowing tightly.

"Understood."

I turn around and get into the carriage, shutting the door behind me.

As the carriage pulls away, I lean back into the plush seats, closing my eyes for the journey. I need to not think, just for ten minutes. But I can't. Instead, Idris's words repeat over and over in my mind until I think I'm going crazy.

He could've left me in the smoke and run off and killed those men, but he didn't. He got me out of there. I'm alive because of him. Even if he did abandon me afterwards.

Did I say thank you? In my anger, I'm pretty sure I forgot.

I press my hands to my face, hating how my chest clenches and my throat is so thick and tight that every breath feels sticky. My eyes sting as water wells. My mouth trembles as I fight my body's reaction. But I can't fight anymore. Tears break free of my eyes and start rolling down my face.

Furiously I wipe them away, only to be mocked by their replacements. I gasp for control in the darkness of the carriage. The night is quiet. No one else is on the roads. There is no one to hear my quiet, private sniffles. I draw a deep breath, and focus on mind-stilling. I breathe slowly, relaxing the muscles of my body one by one – as much as the uneven carriage ride will allow.

It works – sort of – and I take one last shuddering breath before opening my eyes. I lean towards the window and gaze up at the constellations, doubt lancing through my stomach like a riptide. How do we handle tonight? How do we move forwards? How do I make Halice safe?

The carriage turns a familiar corner. I take three steady breaths and check my eyes for remaining tears. The carriage stops and I exit. Slowly I open my front door, closing it quietly so as not to wake anyone.

"RENZA!"

Giulia sprints towards me. Her face is red and blotchy and she wears a pink silk robe fastened tightly around her waist. She throws her arms around me and crushes me in an embrace.

"Where were you?" Giulia demands, hands going to my shoulders as she scans me up and down. "We were so worried."

"I passed out," I explain, clearing my sore throat. "The smoke ... I inhaled quite a lot of it. I saw a doctor."

"Your eyes are red – are you okay?" She narrows her eyes suspiciously.

"Blame the smoke for that, too, and my throat is on fire," I groan. "Apparently it'll pass."

"Come in, have some water," Aunt Fiora says from the doorway. She's standing with her sisters, all three of them watching me. I look to Rialta.

"Are you hurt?" I ask. She was the only other family member still there when the attack occurred. Rialta shakes her head and folds her arms.

"I was a bit woozy after a lungful of that awful smog," she admits, "but that's quite cleared up now."

"You should've stayed!" accuses Fiora, simmering with rage. "Instead of running home you should've found Renza and brought her back, too! Not left her with Fate knows who!"

"Idris took me to a Coari doctor who knows about Witvuur smoke," I answer. That doesn't make Fiora feel better.

"After everything they did this evening?" Agosta says in shock. "You trusted them like that?" She doesn't hold her usual composure. Braided hair pulled over one shoulder, her robe tied loosely over her silk nightie, she looks pale and sleep-deprived.

"I was unconscious. I didn't make the decision. And trust them? Fate's Fury, I'm not that stupid," I say dismissively.

"What did their doctor say? Are you...?" Agosta gestures to the bandage on my arm. I nod.

"I'll heal."

Agosta smiles tightly, folding her arms as her shoulders drop.

"We'll get our doctor to confirm," Fiora answers sharply. "Can't trust your Fated for anything like that."

"No need. I'm feeling well."

"Tomorrow then." Fiora doesn't like it but she clearly knows it's not a battle worth having right now. "So what's the plan?"

"Yes, what are we going to do?" Rialta says. "How do we handle this? What's the strategy?"

I sigh, leaning down to unclasp my shoes. I kick them off and straighten, hand going to the back of my neck. "I'm going to bed. I'm tired, and I will be better prepared to attack this situation tomorrow with a little more sleep and a lot less rage."

I take the answering silence as everyone accepting my plan. My aunts nod, bidding their goodnights as they filter up the stairs. Fiora pauses in front of me, one hand going to my cheek as she studies me for a long moment.

"I'm so glad you're okay, sweetie," she says gently.

"Thanks, Aunt Fiora," I answer before she walks up towards her room.

Giulia follows me to my own room, not saying anything as I start pulling off my jewellery. She stands behind me, quietly helping take down my hair, which is an absolute mess. It's clear her mind is a million miles away, her heart, too. My throat clenches.

She wasn't there this evening, thank Fate for his small mercies, but I can't forget why.

She was crying long before the archer released that arrow.

"Giu," I say softly as the last pin is pulled free. Giulia meets my gaze. Her blue eyes are red. She blinks rapidly.

"Yeah?" Her voice is quiet and thick.

"I'm so sorry," I whisper. Giulia's lips tremble and she rips her gaze away as her hands fly to her mouth. She tries to swallow a sob but her shoulders collapse inward.

"No, I didn't mean to—" I wrap her in a hug, wishing I could put this back together for her. But I can't. No one can.

"What do I do?" Giulia sobs quietly in my ear. "Her Soulmate, Renza. It's her Soulmate."

"I wish I knew," I whisper. She sniffs hard, pulling free of my embrace. I sit her down on my bed and find a handkerchief.

"Want to have a sleepover? Like when we were little?" I ask softly. "I don't really want to be alone tonight."

"Yeah," she says with a watery smile. "Yeah, okay."

I change into my nightdress and the two of us climb into my bed. I blow out the candles and we lie there, both awake and staring at my ceiling, now lit only by the moonlight filtering through my curtains.

"Tonight was awful," Giulia whispers in the darkness.

"Without a doubt."

"One of the worst nights ever."

"Agreed," I say, putting my arm under my pillow, hoping the cool silk will help me sink into something resembling sleep.

"What are you going to do about the mercenaries and Idris?"

"I don't know. Maybe I shouldn't do anything." I sigh, eyes stinging. "Maybe I should step down and let Halice find someone who knows what they're doing."

Giulia stills.

"Why would you say that?" she asks, shock rippling in her words.

"I just"—I blink back tears—"I feel so lost. Like every action I take has an awful consequence I can't see coming."

Giulia sighs.

"Is this about Nouis?"

Nouis. That vile ghost stalking me even now.

"You know his betrayal wasn't your fault, Renza. He was practically family – we'd known him since he was a child," Giulia reasoned softly. "You had every reason to believe he was genuine. We all did."

"I should've seen it," I breathe.

"Why? No one else did."

"Idris did."

"I don't think he did, at least not like you think he did," Giulia counters. "He didn't like Nouis, and was set against him before any of us had any proof of his schemes."

"But he knew. Maybe it was history or instinct," I whisper, a tear leaking from my eyes. "I didn't have that instinct."

Giulia goes quiet, allowing me to continue. I stare up at the dark ceiling of my bedroom as I dare to speak the thoughts that have plagued me since the Great Rebellion.

"Everyone has always said I'm a natural politician. From childhood, all I heard was that I was talented and destined for the High Chamber." I swallow, hating how my words tremble. "But I didn't see Nouis for what he was. What won't I see next? What if they're all wrong and I let everyone down again?"

"Renza," sighs Giulia. "Instinct, talent – they don't make you infallible. Mistakes happen; I'm certain Father made loads when he was younger. I didn't see Dorado's betrayal at the bank when he colluded with Bellandi to steal all our money. Do you think I am a terrible banker and should stand aside?"

"No!" I gasp, horrified. "You're fantastic at your job."

"And you are great at yours," Giulia insists. "One mistake doesn't define you, unless you allow it to. Halice needs Renza Di Maineri to be fighting fit. Don't let Nouis steal another thing from us."

I stay silent for a long time, smiling as a sliver of resolve warms my chest. *If Giulia has faith in me, who am I to argue?* I reach for my sister's hand and give it a squeeze.

"What would I do without you?" I ask, reaching up to wipe the water from my eyes.

"Or me without you?" Giulia chuckles wryly before groaning. "You should've seen those three earlier."

"Bad?"

"They were awful. First Fiora and Agosta arguing about..." Giulia's thick voice trails off, unable to even say Michelle's name. "And then when Rialta turned up and told us what happened, they wouldn't stop fighting. Bickering and picking at each other and shouting. It was horrible."

"I'm so sorry, Giulia. I should've been here to dilute it."

"Don't worry about it. I just..." Giulia turns over to face me. I look at her. Her hair is a mess but there is an effortless elegance in the way it tumbles around her face which is cast in moonlight.

"Yeah?"

"Promise me, no matter what ... it's you and me," Giulia says. "No matter who comes, who goes, it's always going to be you and me. We will *never* be like that."

I take her hand in mine, linking our fingers and squeezing tightly.

"You and me. Always. I promise," I answer, a smile filling my face. It's a small promise in the scheme of things, but one of immense personal value.

Win or lose, come or go, we will be each other's constants. The person we can count on no matter what.

CHAPTER 12

The High Chamber's usual serene majesty is in shambles. The building is crammed to the brim and everyone is yelling. Voices clash against the gilded columns and domed ceiling, the very air teetering with the promise of violence.

I stare down the pandemonium from the doorway, papers balanced in my good arm. Fiora and Agosta are by my side, struck as speechless as I. Swallowing, I study the throng of angry soldiers. Sunlight fills the teeming space that bore witness to a massacre barely hours before. The decorations and frivolity have evaporated. Groups of angry mercenaries are held apart by some of the bravest City Guards I've ever met. They hold out their arms, forming a thin line between the arguing parties, stopping potential fights as swiftly as possible.

"If this gets too ... rowdy, you should leave," I tell my aunts, clearing my voice in a futile attempt to ease the thickness.

"What, me?" Agosta chuckles, straightening her shoulders and flashing a cheeky wink. "I love a good fight."

"We're here to support you." Fiora gives her sister a long sideways glance.

I start forwards through the crowd.

"Excuse me, excuse me!" I try to squeeze past the two lines of the City Guard.

"MOVE!" roars Fiora, shoving her way ahead. My smallest aunt becomes a human battering ram as she carves our path. I follow closely, vile itching spreading across my palms. The heat settles uncomfortably in the back of my mouth and drips corrosively down my throat.

Idris is on the other side of this mob.

I don't know what to say to him – if I can even look at him.

We argue. A lot. Sometimes it gets heated. It doesn't surprise me; we're Soulhates. We're designed to aggravate each other, destined to destroy each other – but there was something particularly painful about last night. All morning my mind circled our fight over and over – truly one of our worst. I've heard every blistering word a thousand times. It hurt no less with repetition.

We push to the gate. Turning back to my aunts, I consider the angry mass behind them. I'm tempted to ask if they can come with me, for their safety. After all, they are family. But it's against protocol to have anyone but the Electi this side of the barrier.

Fiora smiles and gestures me to go ahead. I nod, slipping inside.

"Are you alright?"

Maggia hurries over the minute I close the Electi gate. Ulrico and even Leone aren't far behind. Maggia takes my face gently in her hands, scanning me up and down.

"I'm fine. And you?" I ask.

"I have a cough from that dreadful smoke." Maggia sighs, dropping her inspection and folding her arms. "Nothing more. Apparently it'll fade in time."

"We happened to be standing relatively close to the door,"

says Ulrico gesturing to Leone and himself. "We were able to get out without much bother."

"We got lucky," Leone agrees quietly, shaking his head. "Are you alright?"

Alright? Fate's Fury, no! I woke up in absolute agony. Vivid purple and black bruising swarms my upper arm, and the wound itself is angry and red. I can't move my arm without sharp pain shooting up into my chest, but I'll heal. The doctor Fiora summoned before breakfast assured us of that.

I've chosen my outfit with care: a light shawl over a halter-neck dress, the pretty yellow silk adorned with beaded blue and purple flowers. The shawl covers my ugly wound, keeping my pain private but with easy access for care. I've pinned my hair up, like I wore it last night, to remind people I was there and injured — even if my pain isn't on display. The yellow colour is bright, to draw the eye, but it also clashes with the blue and purple of my wound, highlighting its brutal colours if needed — which match the hues of the embroidered flowers, to keep my injury in mind.

Politics has many weapons and appearances are everything. I have bled for this city; I might as well use it to my advantage.

"It hurts," I admit. Understatement. My arm aches with the fire of a thousand suns. "I'm right-handed, too, so it's inconvenient."

"But nothing permanent?" Leone asks. I shake my head, and both his and Maggia's shoulders drop.

"Let's just ... get these people out of Halice. As fast as possible," I offer with a tight smile.

"Agreed, I'm the speaker today. I take it you have a motion ready?" Leone asks. I nod. How am I, yet again, in agreement with Leone Strossi?

"It's not much. I had a lot on my mind, but give it a quick read before we start." I hand it to Maggia. "It should contain everything we need."

"Hmm…" Maggia reads it quickly. "Short but sweet—"

A brawl breaks out in the spectator seats. Everyone turns as the City Guard wrestle the offending parties apart.

No. Not here. There's been too much violence in this sacred place already.

Suddenly a deep horn blares out. I wince, dropping my papers and throwing my hands over my ears. Every voice falls away; every head turns to the source of that terrible sound.

It's Royah, blowing into a large black trumpet. Idris has already invited the Coari delegation past the gates? *Fate's Fury, what was he thinking? That's against the rules!*

Irritation licks the back of my teeth as I set my jaw. He ignores the laws of this city like they're nothing! Arrogant, stupid, careless man. This is a chamber of law and order; he can't run around as the lone, rogue soldier making unilateral decisions. Not here.

Royah sets down the black trumpet and gestures to Idris. He nods his thanks before addressing the room.

"Okay, everyone. Let's start." Idris's voice carries over the crowd. "Please, can each party send their delegates up so we can begin discussions?"

"Discussion?" shouts a voice. "This was a freaking massacre! We want justice!"

A roar of agreement erupts.

"I understand your anger!" I shout over the crowd, walking forwards and holding up my good hand. "I am also angry. I want justice, and I know you want that, too. Please, give us a chance to follow our processes. Send your delegates forwards, and let's get the satisfaction we all deserve!"

Amidst grumbling and complaints, the soldiers start shuffling and their leaders progress towards the front. I rub my brow as a headache brews. Maggia gives me an encouraging nod and a pat on the back as all the Electi move to their seats.

Once seated, Leone speaks.

"I call this emergency session of the High Chamber to order."

"Agreed," I add my voice to the chimes around the chamber. Leone stands up.

"Due to the nature of the issues today, I invite the delegations from the Galen Company, the Salt Hounds and the Red Sands Bannerhood to pass the gate so we may engage in meaningful discussion. All in favour?"

"Agreed."

The City Guard open the gate, allowing the small groups past the barrier. The Salt Hounds come first and Solon catches my eye and flashes me a wink before falling in step with his brother. The Galen Company are simmering with rage, faces dark and gloomy as they stalk across the floor.

Tahira steps forwards with Royah and Bashran. Now that last night's drug isn't rattling around my head, I can see him clearly. Mid-twenties. Built like a mountain, and tall enough to contend with one. He has deep brown hair that swings around his jawline and a short, neatly trimmed beard. His eyes are dark and warm, twinkling like a dancing night sky.

"Excellent," Idris says, walking forwards and gesturing towards the Galen Company. "Oviedo, I take it you're acting as interim leader?"

A man I recognise from last night gives the shortest, sharpest nod in history. His thick black beard melts into his long hair. A buckled scar cracks across his nose to amplify his sneer. He glares at Tahira as though he wishes he could rip her apart with his mind. She meets the violence in his gaze with a calm self-assertion that's terrifying in its own right.

"Oviedo will speak on behalf of the Galen Company," Idris says, gesturing between the groups. "Panos and Solon speak for the Salt Hound. Tahira speaks for the Red Sands Bannerhood."

"Screw your introductions!" hisses Oviedo. "Why aren't

these murderers in chains? Why isn't this their execution?" A roar of assent rolls amongst the watching soldiers.

Tahira steps closer, holding her hands up before folding them over her heart.

"I swear my words to be wholly true." Tahira's steady voice holds so much heart intertwined with her own hurt beneath the surface. "I had no prior knowledge of the cursed events of last night. I swear, on the honour of my blade, that this act of violence was done by disloyal traitors. I will find everyone responsible, and punish all associated. Swift and final, there will be no mercy. You have my word."

"Your word is worthless!" snarls Oviedo. "Your forces are your responsibility! Leadership, honour and a code of conduct are what separate mercenaries from bullies and heathens. Your people broke that code! Your people murdered my uncle and three of my closest friends!"

"We found this," Tahira continues calmly, like Oviedo never spoke, and Royah holds up a purse. She throws the heavy bag onto the floor. It clatters and jingles as a pile of gold coins spills across the black and white tiles. One coin rolls close to my chair, glinting softly. It's not a Hali-pound, but I know that currency.

Gold Aureus from the Holy States.

"All three men who committed this betrayal had their belongings seized and searched last night," explains Tahira. "We found this amongst their possessions. We came straight from Annen, a large city in Coari, to here. The only place they could've got this gold is here, in Halice. Someone in the city must've approached them and paid them off. That would've been noticed, and my men will talk. Because if they do not, I will assume them to be guilty, too, and ensure that they face punishment."

"You're going to blame this on Holy States spies?" asks Panos, raising an eyebrow in scepticism.

"My men are responsible for their own actions. But this does illuminate possible motives," Tahira answers. She's not wrong. That does make sense.

"My friends, please think from the point of view of the Holy States," Idris says walking forwards. "They don't want you forming a working relationship with us. Not one of you will deny that this city currently stands alone, and that with any one of you we'd be stronger. They want to conquer Halice. Of course they'd disrupt our attempts to secure allies. For the Holy States, this plan works in their favour regardless of outcome. Their best-case scenario is that we start a four-way power struggle that destroys this city, so they can claim the remains. In their worst-case scenario, they strain a valuable relationship and you leave, and we still stand alone."

"Allies you can't pay," Panos said sharply. "Or is that rumour false, too?"

"Payment will be discussed before contracts are signed," Idris answers simply. "But we're not talking about that. We need to focus on the task at hand."

"I don't care about the Holy States, or Halice. Those people murdered my uncle!" shouts Oviedo, his face growing red with anger as he jabs an angry finger at Tahira. "If you won't deliver the justice my uncle is owed, I will take it."

"Try it, and your company will be a footnote in history," Tahira promises with venom.

"Enough!" My voice rings through them as I stand. Their heads snap to look at me as I walk slowly, deliberately towards the group. I take my time, holding their attention, deliberately meeting each and every one of their eyes. "If you want to kill each other, go right ahead."

"Renza—" Idris starts.

"I'm speaking." I hold up a finger to shut him down, and don't bother to look at him. I keep my focus on the angry mercenary leaders. "I mean it, go ahead and kill each other. I don't care. But you will not do it in my city."

"You don't get to—" Oviedo starts.

"QUIET!" I scold. I throw off my shawl, exposing my arm. The entire chamber falls deadly silent; people stare at the agonising wound on my arm as I gesture to it.

"Look at me!" Rage simmers in my voice like molten steel. "Look at the justice I am owed. I want the men that did this found, and I want them punished."

I pause to look at each and every one of them, ignoring Idris's presence entirely. I speak with calm authority, aiming for a fair but firm tone.

"You are in my city," I say. "You're standing under a Halician roof. You were all invited as guests, in good faith and peace. That peace has already been broken once. Don't be guilty of breaking it again."

"We weren't the monsters that broke conduct," snarls Oviedo. "Hand over these barbarians, and we will consider the matter handled."

"Barbarians?" hisses Tahira, anger bristling on her tongue. "My people will not stand for this insult—"

"Wrong," I answer, moving to block Oviedo from her view. "Because you owe me, maybe more than you owe them, because *I'm still alive and still in pain.*"

Tahira sighs, looking away as a war breaks across her face. *No, that won't do.*

"Look at me. Look at my arm," I instruct, walking the line between request and command like a tightrope. "Look at the damage you are responsible for. We invited you, hosted you, threw a party in your honour. Every step made in good faith and a promise of peace that *your* people broke. Your responsibility. Now you owe me a debt. You will repay that debt by refusing to bring further violence into *my* city or to my people, no matter the circumstances. I don't care what insults or behaviour you receive. You will not start fights. Be better. Do I make myself clear?"

Tahira takes a deep breath, her eyes narrowing before a small smile curls at the corner of her mouth.

"We won't be the first to raise a blade. That is my oath."

I turn back to Oviedo. He glares at Tahira. I walk towards him, forcing him to look at me and not her. I smile softly.

"We are united in our desire for justice. But let's make sure we get the right people. We do not need to continue a cycle of hurting the innocent," I say to Oviedo. "You are a man of honour, and you know there is no benefit in this. So, I propose the Coari contingent will have until noon on the second day to find their traitors. After that time, regardless of the outcome, you will all prepare to leave this city with no further violence."

I face Tahira again to explain my plan further. Suddenly, a mercenary standing next to Oviedo lunges for me. I gasp in pain as he grabs hold of my bad arm, yanking me back to look up at his mountainous form. His hand digs into my wrist, burning across the already tender skin there.

"Briaggio is dead and you want to let them go?" the mercenary snarls, shaking with rage. Idris leaps forwards and my free hand snaps up, crashing into Idris's solid chest and pushing him away. Idris is furious, his body heaving against my palm. Lightning roars up my limbs as I ignore him. I keep my focus on the mercenary giant.

I level a cold, sharp gaze that has him loosening his grip before I turn to Oviedo. I fix him with an unmistakeable stare; he is on his last warning.

"Restrain your man," I say quietly, the words falling like poisoned honey. "Don't make me stoop to threats. Don't make me remind you that Halice doesn't take kindly to foreign forces bringing violence to our streets. Don't make me remind you that Halicians are inventive, creative, and have perfected the art of holding a grudge and spreading compelling stories. Don't make me remind you that I'm the Head of the Di Maineri Bank, and what a shame it would be if you, or anyone working with your company, were blocked from all forms of payment, account holdings or dealings in the future with *any* Di Maineri Bank in any country or city on the continent. Don't. Make. Me."

Oviedo's eyes go wide, particularly at that last one. The Di Maineri Bank is the major bank of nearly every city in the Independent States. If they refuse to touch him, he'd never work again.

Oviedo grabs his associate gruffly, snarling in his ear about dishonour and disgrace. The man drops my arm like it scalds him. Oviedo pushes him away, putting his body between us before slowly facing me, and taking a deep breath to steady himself before speaking.

"You have my sincere apologies, signora."

"Emotions run high," I say graciously, fixing him with my winning smile. "I understand mistakes happen *once*."

"Thank you, signora. There will be no further initiation of violence from anyone in the Galen Company while we are here."

"Good." I turn to the Salt Hounds. "Solon, Panos, will your honour be satisfied with finding the traitors, those guilty, then receiving due punishment?"

"Yes," answers Solon, his eyes twinkling as he folds his arms. Panos looks a little miffed but nods, agreeing with his brother. I turn to Oviedo.

"And you? Same question."

"I want to see the evidence and the punishment with my own eyes," Oviedo answers.

"Entirely understandable. Which is why we'll allow the Red Sands Bannerhood until noon on the second day to conduct their investigation on Halician ground. They must present the rest of the traitors, with proof of their crimes, by then. After that, regardless of the outcome, everyone will leave this city in peace."

"And if she magically cannot find any more traitors?" snarls Oviedo.

"I'll find them," Tahira promises, venom in her words.

"If you still require satisfaction, what happens outside our territory is not our business, Oviedo," I answer. Tahira folds her arms. "All I ask is that you not hurt innocent Halician people in pursuit of this matter. We are willing to allow Tahira time to prioritise this hunt for traitors on our soil, but if this cannot bring the required outcomes, I ask you take the matter elsewhere."

Oviedo meets my level gaze, his anger fading slightly before he nods.

"We agree to this."

"Then it is agreed by all," I announce. "And we can call this open emergency session to a close. Electi Leone?"

"Indeed." Leone smiles at me. "All for closing part one of today's emergency session?"

A round of quick agreements runs around the room.

"The open part of this session is now over. Due to the sensitive nature of the matters next up for discussion, we will be closing this session to anyone not an Electi."

Idris hurries over as talk bubbles amongst the crowd, the wave of his fire crashes over me.

"Are you alright—"

I ignore him, heading for my seat as the soldiers file slowly out of the room.

I pull my shawl back into place, glad the thought I'd put into this outfit paid off. Revealing my injuries had the impact I needed it to. Satisfaction blooms across my chest, the knot of uncertainty Nouis had buried deep in my bones starting to uncurl.

My father would be proud.

Heat flares up my throat, and the dark star at the side of my vision moves closer. I refuse to look at Idris as he steps up to my seat.

"Renza," Idris begins quietly. "Your arm... Taio can—"

"No," I answer curtly, using my left hand to pull out a fresh piece of paper.

"Renza," Idris pleads softly. "I am so sorry. I didn't mean—"

"Yes, you did," I snap back, locking my eyes with his and letting the rage flare in them. "Now sit down."

Idris takes a shallow breath and retreats to his seat. I shake my head, wincing as I write down the details of the open session.

Finally, the City Guard leave us alone, standing at all entrances and exits to the chamber. It's just the six of us.

The air is thick and quiet as Leone clears his voice.

"I open part two of this emergency session."

"Agreed," we chorus.

Idris clears his throat and gets to his feet.

"I think we've heard enough from you at this time, Signore Patricelli," says Leone.

"He's an Electi and has the right to speak," Savino counters quietly.

"Seriously? He still has your support after all this?" Leone asks, incredulous.

"This is not on him. We all voted. We should've realised that it was a prime opportunity for an attack, and that there would be Holy States agents trying to undermine our efforts."

"As Captain of the City Guard, please can you confirm, are we already conducting our own investigation into the events of last night?" I ask Savino. "And the information supplied by Tahira will be used to aid tracking down Holy States spies?"

"Of course. Tahira asked the City Guard to accompany her people as she conducts the investigation – to ensure that proof she collects can be verified by an impartial set of eyes. I have agreed."

"That's fair. She wouldn't want to be accused of planting evidence," says Maggia.

"What we need to do is discuss your conduct, Signore Patricelli," says Leone.

"My conduct?" Idris demands, narrowing his eyes.

"You invited these people to this city without the knowledge of this council, forcing us into a corner where we felt we had no option but to entertain your plan. Now we have three armies of angry sell-swords spoiling for a fight, and if it weren't for the talented efforts of Electi Di Manieri, today's session would likely have ended with mercenary warfare."

Talented? Did Leone Strossi actually call me that?

"That's melodramatic," Idris answers. "It's neither fair nor apt to place the blame on me. I didn't attack anyone. We voted to hear their pitches. Just because you don't like the outcome of a vote, doesn't mean that it wasn't legal or that you weren't part of it."

He's got a point.

"Besides, my suspicions were proven correct. We now know definitively that Halician spies operate in this city."

"That was a pretty safe bet," Maggia responds unimpressed. "Bellandi didn't work alone. He had loyalist support here."

"But now we have proof."

"And we can use it how?" asks Leone incredulously.

Idris shakes his head. I force myself to look at him, to watch the debate behind those blistering hazel eyes before he speaks. His head dips, and he closes his eyes.

"None of you have seen war before," Idris says quietly. He takes a deep breath, opening his eyes before looking straight at Leone, then moving his attention around the room. "I have. We've seen the Great Rebellion, and that was violent enough but believe me when I say that was nothing compared to a real battle. A real invasion. None of you have seen what happens when a city gets sacked. None of you have smelled the odours of rotting flesh, heard the screams of a thousand dying soldiers, seen mangled limbs and blood smeared across every broken surface. The horror of real warfare is coming to Halice. Quickly. We've spent weeks doing *nothing* but sitting on our hands, debating this or that. While they're making moves, we are sluggish and slow to react. I'm telling you outright; we're not going to win this war. Not without taking a few risks, and unfortunately sometimes those risks won't pay off. That's why they're risks. But it's the only shot we have."

"That might be true," Maggia says quietly. "But they are risks this *chamber* is set up to vote on."

"But it's moving too slowly! We talk and debate and allow time for spies to pass messages back to the Holy Mother and her cardinals in Kavas." Idris's voice is gruff, his words tight. His back is poker straight as he speaks.

A brief, poignant pause echoes around the room. Idris is right. It's only been a week since knowledge of these mercenaries was brought to this chamber, and the Holy States already had time to dispatch orders to sabotage the whole thing.

"It almost sounds like you're petitioning for a Maestrus," Leone says quietly. My mouth runs dry, my eyes widening.

"Absolutely not!" Idris answers, visibly shaken by the idea. I don't blame him. A white-cold shot cracked across my chest as well. A Maestrus? Back before we earned our independence here in Halice, we had a Maestrus. A single ruler with absolute power over the city, appointed by the Holy States to run things.

The premise still exists in law. In a time of emergency, this chamber can vote in a Maestrus – someone in charge absolutely until the danger has passed. Supposedly it'll allow for decisions to be made quickly and for orders to be carried out using a quick and clear chain of command. If an army were at our gates and Halice about to face a battle, it would make sense … but it would also render this chamber entirely obsolete. This High Chamber, our democracy – one of the most precious and important things in our entire city – would be gone.

"Then what do you want?" Leone asks, tapping the arm of

his chair. "You're talking about how you have seen things we haven't. How you understand things we don't. To what end?"

"I want to start making some real moves. We're not going to win this if we don't start acting. This will come with risks and challenges. We can't turn against each other and start pointing fingers when those risks are realised," Idris answers, his words tight and hard. "I don't see anyone else securing potential solutions, or coming to this chamber with actionable suggestions to handle the very real, very violent army that is marching for Halice. Last night was horrific. But worse is coming, and I am doing everything I can think of to prevent it. If this didn't work, fine. But what alternatives are there? Please, someone tell me how you plan to defend this city. I will gladly jump on a realistic plan and do my part to make it work. Any of you. Tell me."

The chamber is quiet for a long time.

"Anyone?" Idris half demands, half pleads, the words echoing around the empty hall. He turns slowly, making eye contact with us all. He's not wrong, and Idris has always been a man of action. He was that way in the Great Rebellion, too. I take a deep breath.

"We all voted to hold last night's party," I say quietly. "Idris is not to blame for what happened. Idris has done nothing against the law, and we can all agree that his intentions are good. But we cannot ignore the precipice edge from which we just took a step back. What if the Galen Company had decided to take the honour they feel they're owed? What if they'd decided to do it last night, or still today anyway? Or tomorrow when they aren't satisfied with Tahira's proof?"

Idris's eyes pummel the back of my skull. I turn to meet his gaze.

"You're right, winning this war will involve risks and sacrifices. That's a problem for tomorrow. These people are the problem we face today. We can make threats and placate wounded egos only for so long. We need to get these mercenary groups out of Halice, without opportunities for violence."

"And leave us without a real army? Leave us vulnerable?" Idris asks, half furious, half incredulous.

"We couldn't afford them to begin with! You heard Panos just now. He was offended that you asked his army to travel all the way here to pitch for a job when we knew we couldn't pay. Honestly, I don't blame him," I answer. "It's not a smart business practice on his part, not to mention the danger it's put him in. We're lucky they aren't asking for compensation or damages!"

"If the answers to our problems were easy, convenient or comfortable, we'd already be doing them," Idris answers shortly. "A bad solution is better than no solution."

"That depends on the solution, and who pays the price," I retort.

"Electi Di Maineri is right," says Leone quietly. "Over the next few days, let's focus on ensuring peace between these separate groups. After that, when our city is ours again ... then we can talk about de-escalating the current conflict with the Holy States. Perhaps negotiate peace talks or a new treaty."

"What?" Idris almost expires at the concept. He wheels around to me, expecting me to join his outrage. I sigh and shake my head.

"Some of us have been talking," I say quietly. He physically recoils from me, shocked, angry. He looks almost ... betrayed.

"If we can resolve this without bloodshed, surely that's the best path," Leone reasons. "Not to mention it can open up trade routes again, get money flowing."

"Our people are in desperate need of food," Maggia says. "We won't survive winter if we don't find a solution."

"They tried to take our city by force! They slaughtered all of your predecessors!" Idris seethes. "They murdered my father and you want peace?"

"They murdered my father, too," I say quietly. "Everyone that died ... I knew them well. I worked with them every day for years. I cared for them. Including your father. Jacopo and I weren't always on the same page, but he was a man who would do *anything* to protect this city. Including swallowing his pride and making peace with his enemies. For the people."

Idris looks like I've shoved sand down his throat.

"Electi Strossi has a strategy that could end this conflict without bloodshed. We would be fools not to explore it."

"Who knows if they'll even talk to us?" Savino ventures. "They want to conquer, not placate."

"Perhaps," Leone explains soberly. "But at least we'll have tried."

"Even if all we buy is time, it's something we could really use right now," I add.

"I'm calling this motion to a vote. Am I authorised to reach out and attempt peace negotiations with the Holy States? Vote blue for yes, vote yellow for no," Leone says.

"Wait, you must share all letters to and from the Holy States with every member of this High Chamber. Every single letter must be observed before it is sealed and sent with a trusted courier, and the same for any received. We must see the wax seal being broken with our own eyes," Idris insists.

"Don't you trust me, Electi Patricelli?" demands Leone.

"We have spies in our midst. We can't afford to lose sight of the chain of custody," Idris answers diplomatically.

"That's a fair request," agrees Maggia quietly.

"Alright then. Let's cast," Leone says. The stones fly across the room.

Five blue, one yellow. Even Savino has voted with us.

"I'll start immediately. I call this session to a close," Leone says.

Six rounds of "agreed" chorus around the room in quick succession. Idris makes a hasty exit before anyone can say any more. As the fire of our bond fades from my blood, my shoulders drop. I didn't enjoy that at all.

I get to my feet, cradling my papers in my good arm.

"Signora Di Maineri, wait a moment," calls Leone Strossi. He strides over, a small smile on his lips. He reaches my side, hands slipping into his pockets.

"I just wanted to thank you."

"For what?" I ask warily.

"Your support. I did wonder … I realise what I said might have been going too far for you. I know you and Idris have a … complicated, paradoxical … understanding at times."

"I care about Idris," I answer carefully. "He is a friend, colleague and was a rare, dedicated ally during the Great Rebellion. But my personal feelings cannot interfere with the running of this city, and Idris has been acting too much the free agent. Choices have power, but they also have consequences. This is what his choices have brought. What you said … held truth."

Somewhere the sun burns cold.

Leone chuckles.

"I know our first election seasons pitted us as opponents when we were both much younger, but after today I can't help but wonder if we could agree on more. Perhaps there are more ideas we can collaborate on, for the good of the city."

I doubt it. The instant thought springs to my mind and I chastise myself. Leone is being civil. He's inviting cooperation and my eyes on his politics.

"That would be good," I agree. "I look forward to collaborating in the future."

"As do I. Well, I must see if I can get these peace talks arranged. Good day, signora," Leone says, before walking away with a purpose in his step. Leone is my ally. Idris is pitted against me.

The world really is turning upside down.

CHAPTER 13

The fireplace crackles. Sunset invades my living room through the tall arched windows, bold gashes of amber and vermillion coating the plush sofas and tall bookcases.

I'm sitting with warm tea in my hand, reading over Maggia's report from the foodbanks. It paints a dire picture. I sip on the sweet, hot tea. The warm liquid runs down my aching throat, weakly soothing the anxiety racing through me. I savour the silence in my house – too rare these days. My aunts appear occupied, by some rare mercy of Fate.

Rialta and Giulia are still working, having requested use of the study. Seeing the hanging curtains under Giulia's eyes, the paleness of her face ... of course I gave it to her. I would give anything right now. The money will start arriving soon. Alfieri won't let us down. I know it.

"Ah, Renza. There you are," says Fiora, drifting into the living room.

"Hello," I answer, not looking up from my numbers.

"I have something for you," she says, coming to sit at my side. She holds a small pot in her hands. I raise an eyebrow.

"It'll help with the bruising," she explains. "It'll take some of that sharpness out of the pain and clear it up more quickly."

"Oh, thank you," I say, surprised. "What is it?"

"A mixture of things to form a paste," she says, taking off the cover. It smells like they somehow made mint spicy. I wrinkle my nose as she takes some of the paste on her fingers.

"You warm it up a little, and then just rub a fine layer over the bruising. Don't get it anywhere close to the open wound," she instructs, rubbing it over my arm. My skin feels a little tingly as it's applied, simultaneously hot and cold. But within a few minutes the pain does dull.

"Wow, what is that?" I ask, impressed.

"It's a new tincture from Nimal called Soldier Paste. A doctor in the army invented it. I never go anywhere without it now. It's great for clearing sinuses," Fiora chuckles. "Hopefully you'll feel a bit better."

"Thank you." I let my shawl drop back down to cover my arm again. Fiora smiles softly, putting a hand on my shoulder. She looks on the verge of saying something before she shakes her head.

"Of course, dear," she says quietly, standing up. "I'm here for you."

As if on cue, the study door opens and out walk Giulia and Rialta. Giulia makes straight for the wine.

"Hey," I say, pushing my papers aside and sitting upright. Giulia throws me a vulnerable look and pours herself a generous portion.

"Good evening, Renza," Rialta answers, rubbing her brow.

"Any news?" Fiora asks. Rialta shakes her head.

"No. We are ... out of options." Giulia releases a shaky breath. She takes a deep swig of her wine.

"Perhaps it's time we discuss ... limiting the damage," Rialta suggests tentatively.

"What do you mean?"

"The Di Maineri Bank is continent-wide," Rialta says. "Halice ... Halice's branch may very well go under, despite our best efforts. But ... that doesn't mean the rest have to."

"You want to cut off the Head of the Bank?" Fiora asks sharply.

"I want to save the rest of our family, our legacy. It's something to consider. Just because things are bad here doesn't mean they have to sink our entire extended family!" Rialta answers hotly. "We can rebuild here once the turmoil is over. There will still be Di Maineris in Halice, as I take it Renza and Giulia aren't going anywhere."

"But it wouldn't be the Head Bank."

"No. That could be elsewhere," Rialta answers. "It's just an option. It's unpalatable, I agree. But we might not have many other choices."

Giulia doesn't answer. Instead, she stares at the bracelet shining on her wrist, lost somewhere in the recesses of her mind. Michelle got her that bracelet for her birthday three years ago – she never takes it off. My heart cracks open as I slide off the couch, walking over to her as Fiora and Rialta start bickering.

"Hey," I whisper. "Are you okay?"

Giulia blinks hard, tears lining her eyes.

"I'm losing," she whispers. "I can't make this work. I can't think straight. I can't focus."

"Okay, okay." I wrap my arms around her and hold her close. "Just hold on a little longer. A little longer is all I ask; things will get better."

"How do you know?"

"Because I did something."

Giulia pulls back, frowning.

"What?" But the question didn't come from her. It came from Rialta. I turn to see both aunts staring at me.

"It doesn't matter," I say firmly. "Just hold on, okay. A few more weeks and things will look a lot better."

Giulia sniffles and rubs her jaw. A frantic knock comes to the front door before she can respond. Fiora answers it.

"Please, I need to see her."

Giulia flinches, closing her eyes as Michelle's voice splits through the air.

"Dear, this isn't a good time—"

"Is she here? Please, I *need* to talk to her." Michelle's distress is thick in her tone, in her desperation. Giulia's shoulders tremble and she shakes her head, lips wobbling as fresh water wells in her eyes.

"I can't. I can't," Giulia whispers, practically begging. "I can't."

"Okay. You don't have to do anything right now," I promise, holding her close as tears slip down her cheeks. Her shoulders buckle inwards as she silently sobs into her hands.

"Please," pleads Michelle. "I need to see her. Please."

"Maybe another time, dear," says Fiora firmly.

"No, no please—" Michelle's pleas are cut off as Fiora shuts the door on her. Giulia sobs even harder, pressing both hands to her mouth like she can physically hold back the sobs.

"Oh, sweetheart," Fiora sighs softly and walks over to Giulia. "I'm so sorry. This is so difficult."

"I love her," Giulia sobs, face red and slick with tears. "She's my everything."

"I know, sweetheart. But Fate knows best. It's for your own good. Hers, too. It doesn't stop the hurt, but in time you'll heal and find someone else. Maybe your own Soulmate, hmm?"

"What are you talking about?" I ask, shocked at Fiora's answer. "Giulia and Michelle have choices. They don't have to break up. They can work it out if they want."

"Renza..." Fiora's tone verges on scolding. "Fate has made his will clear. It's for the best."

"Best for who?"

"Everyone, but especially the girls. You might see fit to tempt Fate and his vengeful wrath, and on your own head be it. But don't drag anyone else into your futile tussle with the Great Plan." Fiora changes her attention to Giulia. "Come on, dear, let's go get you cleaned up. I'll ring for a hot bath, some tea and then you should try to get some sleep, hmm?"

Fiora takes Giulia's hand and pulls her towards the stairs, rubbing her back gently.

"Don't be surprised, Renza," Rialta advises, studying me. "Fiora believes strongly in the will of Fate being right. She has to."

"She has to?" I ask perplexed.

"Because of what happened with her first husband," Rialta answers with a short laugh. I frown.

"He died."

Rialta pauses, narrowing her eyes at me, before realisation downs on her face.

"Tomas never told you the full story?"

I shake my head. Rialta actually looks sad for a moment. She gestures me over to the sofa. She hesitates before speaking, folding her hands delicately over her lap.

"So, you know Fiora was married before?"

"Yes, to Uncle Carlo. He died."

"In a duel with his Soulhate. Your Uncle Arturo."

My mouth falls open, eyes popping wide. Uncle Arturo, Fiora's second husband? Her Soulmate and the love of her life?

"What?"

"Yeah, that's where they met. At the duel. Fiora went to support her husband in his duel to the death and found her Soulmate, Arturo. Arturo was the victor, obviously. Fiora was almost destroyed with the guilt and self-hatred. Were she not already pregnant with Marino, I don't know what she would've held on to."

"Wait, Cousin Marino is Uncle Carlo's baby? Not Arturo's?" I gape. Oh my gosh, how did I have no idea about any of this? Why had Father kept this secret?

"Exactly, but I think Fiora, even now, tries to forget," Rialta says evenly. "She loved Carlo intensely. But given all the... She clings to Fate and the Great Plan. It helps to make sense of her loss and upheaval. She's happy now, really happy with Arturo. She deserves that."

But the guilt, being happy with the person who murdered your first husband... No wonder...

"Poor Aunt Fiora," I whisper, looking towards the stairs.

"Yeah, so cut her a break when it comes to Fate things," Rialta suggests quietly. "She means well."

"Thank you for telling me."

"Of course—"

"RENZA!"

Agosta is screaming as she sprints through the door, panting furiously.

"Aunt Agosta, what—"

"Executions!" Agosta gasps, bending over her knees for strength. "At the High Chamber. The Coari are carrying out executions."

"What?" I shout, horror flooding my bones.

"Take my carriage – go!" Agosta shouts as I sprint through the door and back into the carriage that Agosta has just vacated, and set off to face this horror.

⁓

I'm tossed about like a leaf in a gale. The horse gallops, losing the race with my heart, which throbs in my throat and threatens to explode out of my mouth. My fingers dig into whatever purchase I can find. The city races past the window amidst the desperate clatter of wooden wheels and horse hooves.

The square around the High Chamber is crammed with mercenaries. Bathed in a bloody sunset, they face the building. Tahira stands at the top of the steps with a sword held high. Six of her men are bound and on their knees with wounds on their faces. Oviedo, Solon and Panos are at the front of the crowd, watching this all unfold with solemn expressions.

No. No.

"STOP! STOP!" I barrel through the crowd. I push and shove my way forwards. This isn't Halice. This isn't what we do! There are processes, a court of law! This is madness! This is illegal! Practically murder!

Just as I break through the front, boiling hot arms come out of nowhere. They wrap hard and unforgivingly around me, hauling me off my feet and away from the proceedings. I'm crushed against a devastating marble chest, a noxious hand clamped tight around my lips. That vile touch pours vinegar down my spine and bites at my eyes. I'm drowning in acid and fire as I thrash against my assailant.

"Renza, stop. Stop!" hisses Idris urgently in my ear, dropping his hand from my mouth as he secures his grip against my struggle.

"For your acts of treason, for the dishonour of your actions, for the disloyalty to your brothers and sisters in arms, I sentence you to death." Tahira continues like I haven't spoken, walking up behind the first man. Tahira raises her blade high.

"NO! This isn't how we do things!" I shout at Idris, fighting against his grip.

Idris wrestles me off my feet, dragging me around the side of the building. "You can't interfere!"

I fight against his every step, but it's like battling a statue.

"No! This isn't right! We have processes, we have law! You can't let them, Idris! Stop—"

Idris throws me up against the cold stone of the High Chamber building, his caustic body on top of me again – this time at my front and pressing me into the prison of his grip. His blistering hand returns to my mouth, silencing me as he drops his head to mine.

"Don't." Idris speaks low and insistent. "Renza, we have to let this happen."

I shout but his fingers muffle the extremely rude and vile words I hurl at him.

"Interrupting Tahira's justice would be challenging her strength and leadership! You have to let her punish her own people," Idris hisses at me, eyes burning with a touch of fear. "You don't understand."

A wet thwack comes from the other side of the building, followed by the thump of a body hitting the steps. Then another. I sag against the scorching jail of Idris's arms, fighting the vicious nails dancing a symphony across my limbs.

I'm too late.

Fresh rage pours through my bones. Shaking and betrayed, I fight him. Idris refuses to let go as I throw all the strength in my body against his. I manage to get an arm free and shove and beat his shoulder to get away. Gasping for breath, my head spins. Idris removes his hand from my mouth, instead pinning my wrists firmly to the cold stone wall behind me. My lips tingle against the cold air as my eyes water with anger. Is this what we have become? Is this what Halice has been reduced to? Executions without fair trials?

"You let them do this," I accuse, a sob teetering on my tongue. "You sullied our High Chamber with even more blood. We don't do this; we don't perform executions without trial in Halice."

Idris sighs, dropping his head.

"Do you have any idea what you almost did? Tahira's power over her people cannot be questioned, not publicly, not ever. If I had let you interrupt, she would have had to assert her power and leadership. She'd have to fight you. To the death."

My blood runs cold. I shake my head, my throat running thick.

"So no one can ever question her?" I demand.

"Of course they can, but not like that," Idris answers, fighting for controlled breath.

"What other choice was there? I had to do something! If you understand so much, then you shouldn't have let this happen—"

"I have to let Tahira handle her own people," Idris huffs, frustrated. "They aren't Halicians. This is what they understand and respect. The Coari have their own practices and culture. If Tahira hadn't done this, it would've made her look weak. That would've got her killed. This is how it is with mercenaries. Let them handle their own affairs."

I shake my head, loathing bubbling up inside me like a viper wanting to bite off his head.

"You really stand for this? You really think that was okay?" I demand, my voice catching. "Using our High Chamber as a stage for murder without trial!"

"It's the way things are done," Idris snaps, grinding his teeth. "I don't have to like it to accept it."

I shake my head, bile sour and thick in my mouth.

"You really are one of them, aren't you," I spit. Idris narrows his eyes at me, fire raging beneath his expression.

"That ridiculous rhetoric? Really, Renza, I thought you were above that," Idris snarls, his hands tightening on my wrists painfully. "I am Halician. I was born here."

"You certainly don't act like it," I scoff. "Because Halicians don't accept things we don't like about the world and move on. We change the world for the better."

I shove with all my strength and Idris staggers back barely a pace. That's all the space I need and I yank myself free and march away, unable to look back at the bodies now being cleared from the steps. Unable to look at the man I thought I could trust with something so important. Unable to face the High Chamber itself, a building of democracy and progress, knowing what just unfolded here. A betrayal of its values. An undermining of its tenants. On my watch.

Unable. That's how I feel.

And I hate it.

CHAPTER 14

Halice brims with activity the following morning. People hurry along the familiar stone streets as golden sunshine pours down. The autumnal warmth soaks into my skull, dripping comfortably down my neck.

I've just seen Savino, to discuss the City Guard. Like most of the things in Halice, it isn't going well. Thank goodness for the crisp sunshine and lazy breeze, here to sweep all the awful things away. Even if just for a walk.

I have a million things to do, but I walk slowly. Leisurely. Stealing a few minutes to recharge before facing the thousand problems demanding my attention. Everything feels brittle; everything is on a precipice.

I round a corner and am met with a crowd. For a second my heart drops, but everyone is standing still. A familiar voice rises above the others, a gentle voice.

The lone priestess.

"Love is pure and selfless, light and good. With Agoi, the day of love, drawing closer we should all turn to love. Not just our Soulmates, but love in all its shapes and forms. Love is what binds us, as families, as friends, as a community."

I find a space to listen. The priestess is sitting on the edge of a water fountain, helping to distribute the freely available drinking water to those struggling to reach it. Sunlight bounces off her pale face, filling her creamy cheeks with roses.

"In the cycle of love and hate, Agoi reminds us that love is as strong as any force in this world. Father Fate sent us his Divine Daughters in equal strength," the priestess continues. "On the sacred day of Agoi, the bonds of love will be at their strongest. You are more likely to find your Soulmate, or if you know them already, that bond will be at its strongest. We will all be filled with love for our fellow man. Remember that feeling, celebrate that feeling. Because it is what makes us great."

Her words soothe a rough wound I hadn't realised was hiding in my chest. I smile, but two people whispering catch my eye. My mouth drops in surprise at the sight of Tahira and Royah listening to the priestess. The two women smile tentatively, lifting their hands in greeting. I nod in return. They start making their way over and my heart sinks. I really don't want to talk to either of them. Not after everything.

"Morning," Tahira says. I smile tightly, nodding back.

"She's quite the speaker," Royah says quietly. "Idris said you'd been excommunicated. I thought your holy people had left."

"She stayed," I answer.

"Why?"

"I don't know. But I'm glad," I murmur, and realise we're drawing daggers from the crowd. I wave my apologies and slip towards the back. Tahira and Royah follow.

"Sorry, we didn't mean to interrupt if you wanted to listen," Tahira apologises.

"It's fine," I answer evenly, though I wish they hadn't interrupted. "I have things I should do anyway."

"I never understood the draw of your faith. Idris's brief explanation and the little pieces I've come across make it feel unforgiving and rigid. Almost punitive," Tahira ponders, but then gestures back towards the priestess. "But listening to her wasn't what I expected."

"Yes, well, I suppose your interactions with men from the Holy States and our faith haven't been stellar," I allow, folding my arms. "Malaya sounds like it was a disaster." Royah laughs, pushing her long braids back from her face.

"Idris told you about that?" Royah chuckles. "Idris ate himself alive after that. But hey, there are arseholes of every faith, nationality and creed in the world."

"That's true. Nouis king amongst them," I grumble.

"How do you know him?" asks Royah curiously.

"I killed him," I answer, deciding to forgo the history of my relationship with my toxic, manipulative, dead ex-lover.

"You?" Tahira asks, delighted.

"What?" I say, offended. "Idris never told you how I saved his life?"

"Wow, good for you. I just didn't peg you for it." Tahira shrugs. "Idris chewed me out yesterday after the execution. I've never seen him so angry. And given your protest—"

"Let me stop you right there." I hold up a hand firmly. "If we start down this path, it will end in an argument. All I'll say is that violence is a last resort when words fail. My words rarely fail."

Tahira nods slowly. Royah grins.

"I take it you're preparing your departure?" I say, clearing my throat.

"Yes. Although I want to apologise for, well, everything since we've been here," Tahira says. "Things haven't turned out as anyone hoped."

"I appreciate it, and you're not solely to blame," I answer. "Things are what they are."

"How's the arm?" Royah asks. I look down at the pretty pink shawl covering the worst of it.

"Recovering. My aunt has a fantastic salve that's working wonders," I say, lifting the shawl to show them. "It's called Soldier's Paste, a new concoction from Nimal."

Royah and Tahira's eyebrows shoot up studying the wound that is already shrinking in size and vicious colour. They lean closer to inspect it.

"That's remarkable." Royah whistles. "Might need to snag some of that."

"I'll send you some," I promise. "Are you shopping for anything in particular? Or just enjoying Halice?"

"I broke my Dolk," Tahira sighs, pulling out her beautiful, bejewelled dagger. The one she wore the night of the massacre. She turns it over, showing where some of the sapphires have fallen out.

"Dolk?" I ask.

"It's a dagger gifted by family and friends to those who pass Nakari," Tahira explains. I blink, the question still clear on my face.

"Nakari is a series of trials you must pass in order to become an elite warrior," whispers Royah conspiratorially. I nod, new understanding dawning.

"So your Dolk is a badge of honour," I venture carefully. Royah nods.

"Your Dolk *is* your honour. It's given to you by those that love you, so you can defend them. Ceremonial, really, these days – you're not supposed to actually use them in a fight. But it was the best I had to hand." Tahira shrugs. "This one was my father's."

"Well, I know a jeweller who can fix this no problem. My Uncle Ruggie."

"Seriously?" Tahira's face brightens. "You're sure he can work this intricately?"

"Easily. I'll take you—"

"Signora! Signora Di Maineri." A gangly teenager pushes

towards me. I know him. He's Meo, a dishwasher from the Amica. Panting, he comes to rest his hands on his knees.

"Yes?" I ask, hand going to his back to help him catch his breath.

"Paula needs you. It's urgent."

Paula? Oh no.

"I'll go now," I say.

"Sounds like trouble. Mind if we come?" Tahira asks. I hesitate, but what kind of trouble could Paula be in that she asked for me? It wouldn't hurt to have armed backup.

"Quickly," I agree. We speed walk to the Amica. My heart pounds in my ears as I weave through the people. Our steps are hurried and determined; I barely acknowledge the people who call out in greeting as we sprint past.

We get to the Amica quickly enough. Meo knocks firmly on the door. Telltale clicks of the locks rattle and the door is pulled open by Paula. She looks relieved to see me.

"Thank you for coming, signora," she says. "She's through here."

"She?" I frown, walking into the room. I follow her gesture and stop dead.

Serra is slumped over a table, propping herself up with a sluggish elbow as she nurses a shallow glass of wine. Five empty wine bottles lie discarded on the floor beside her.

"She broke in?" I ask in disbelief. Paula shakes her head.

"No ... she was here last night, drinking," Paula explains. "I thought she'd left, but apparently she just fell asleep under the table. She's clearly..."

Paula trails off but I sigh, reaching to the purse fixed to the beaded belt at my waist and handing it to Paula.

"For her tab and your kindness," I say with a sigh. I approach Serra, who finishes pouring the last of her wine into a shallow glass. Spotting me, she rolls her eyes, lurching alarmingly from side to side.

"Of course, they told you," Serra slurs, lifting up her glass. I firmly take the glass from her fingertips. Serra pauses, swaying in her seat when she realises her drink is gone. She scowls, jabbing a finger at me, that then drifts around the room.

"You can't tell me what to do," she argues.

"This place is closed, and you should be at home," I say firmly. Serra narrows her eyes at me, anger filling her face.

"Working. I know. I should be working. Working on weapons. Working on war. For a city that threw me in a dark cell." Serra spits in disgust, slumping forwards on the table and gripping her head with one hand as the other picks at a large chip in the wood.

I take a deep breath, pulling out a seat next to her.

"No! No!" Serra argues belligerently. "I don't want you here."

"Serra." I ignore her. "Honey, what's going on?"

"You won't get it," Serra hiccups. "None of you get it."

"Come on, love, try me," I say gently. "I want to help. You know how much I want to help."

Serra sighs, tears forming in her dark eyes.

"You're all just moving on. Moving forwards. You're Electi again, Giulia and Michelle have each other, and Emilia has everything she's ever wanted. Acting like it never happened, like I was never locked up in the dark, alone, knowing I would be killed..."

Royah goes still at the mention of Michelle. Serra wasn't there the other night. Clearly, she doesn't know.

"You're only part right," I mutter. "Serra, sweetie. Look at me. Tell me, what's wrong?"

"I just told you, and you don't get it!" Serra bemoans. "Everybody just moves on. Forgets. But it was so dark, stuck in a cell without light. Left to think again and again about how I was going to die, framed for a crime I didn't do. I didn't do it. I didn't do it."

"Serra, I know. I know you didn't. We got you out, remember?" I say softly, trying to soothe her.

"I was there because of my work! I was going to die because of my work!" Serra's eyes brim with tears as she furiously wipes them away. "I don't want to die. I don't want to die."

I close my eyes, finally getting it.

"Okay, let's get you home," I say gently.

"No! No, I won't. Not back there," Serra babbles amidst hiccups.

"Only to sleep, Serra. Not to work, just sleep," I promise, easing an arm under her and pulling her to her feet. She staggers, almost pulling me down with her.

"Okay, easy does it," I say to steady her.

"Want a hand?" offers Tahira. I nod gratefully. Serra will be mortified when she's sober.

"Best not mention this again," I say to them as Tahira gets Serra's other side. "Pretend it didn't happen."

"Of course, signora."

We manoeuvre Serra into a carriage, Tahira and Royah looking out the window as we rattle along on our journey. The closer we get to the Garden, the more beautiful the world becomes. Art pours from every crevice, vivid murals and intricate cobblestones in gorgeous patterns. Sounds and smells leak from over the painted walls and homes, mingling like a cacophony of genius on the breeze.

We stop outside the Garden gates, and stagger down the path with a now unconscious Serra. I couldn't have asked for a more vivid display of brilliance. The workshops are all open and busy. Statues, art, music, genius of every kind is on display everywhere you look. The leaves of the blossom tree in the courtyard are turning a deep ruby. The wandering path winds around the busy artisans.

At Serra's workshop, I find her key, letting us in. We get her up the rickety stairs, putting her swiftly to bed. Tahira and Royah go back downstairs as I roll her over, take off her shoes and place a bucket by her head.

I sit by her, sighing at her slack, slumbering face. How did I not see this pain sooner? How have I not done anything about it? Am I a bad friend? So self-absorbed with my own issues I'm blind to those I love?

I lean down and press a kiss to her brow.

I'll speak with her properly when she's awake, and sober. Right now, she needs sleep.

I head back down the stairs and find the girls looking through Serra's designs.

"Wow, these are cool!" Tahira grins. "Do they work?"

"Yes. Serra's brilliant, and not normally a drunk," I'm compelled to explain. "She's been through some tough stuff recently." I look through some of her half-finished work, most of which have large crosses through the designs. I move to her bin, pulling out crumpled papers containing more designs like her firework catapult or traps, torn and discarded. My heart sinks.

"Sounds it," Tahira says, putting a hand on my shoulder. "War is tough on everyone."

"She was one of Bellandi's first targets," I explain quietly. "She was arrested after the temple blew up. We broke her out, but..."

"Solitary confinement?" asks Tahira with a puckered brow. I nod.

"She was arrested on suspicion of treason," I answer. Royah sighs.

"That'll mess with anyone. You know, mind-stilling might

help her," Royah suggests as she wraps a braid thoughtfully around her fingers. "Idris says it helps with his nightmares."

"It helps with grief," I agree. "I'll lend her my books."

"Doesn't work for everyone. I never really clicked with it," Tahira adds, and narrows her eyes at me curiously. "So the mind-stilling, it helps you and Idris to coexist?"

"Some," I answer honestly. "Idris swears by it, and the exercises do help. But it's not like the urges vanish. Every interaction is a battlefield. His presence causes me physical pain. Communicating about how we're handling the bond is essential. Respecting it, respecting ourselves..." I trail off, thinking about how much respect we've shown each other lately. I bite my lip, shame flooding my cheeks.

"So what would you suggest, if someone else were to try fighting a Soulhate bond?" asks Tahira.

"That's tough. A Fated bond is so personal, so unique to the two people it's between." I think carefully as I set about cleaning up Serra's room. "With the Great Rebellion, Idris and I were forced into proximity under duress and given a purpose greater than ourselves. It forced us to the point of make-or-break. To save Halice, we had to be around each other and fight *for* each other. Logically we never wanted to hurt each other – I've never wanted to hurt anyone – but the bond is something feral and entirely consuming. Mind-stilling, in general, is good. It doesn't erase the bond, or the strength of it. It's more like ... making sure my calm, rational side is in control of my actions rather than my instinct for violence. It takes that edge off the pain. But it's still a fight."

Tahira nods slowly, considering that. I almost ask her about the interest, but something tells me it would be too personal. My eyes drop to the dagger on her belt.

"Come on," I say. "Uncle Ruggie should be able to help with your Dolk."

We close the door behind us, and I slip the key back under

the door. Locked up safe and sound. We walk to Uncle Ruggie's workshop, barely a few hundred paces away. He's outside by his forge, a few moulds in boxes on the floor. He looks up as we approach, a grin stretching his time-lined face.

"Renza!" he says, setting down his tools and yanking off the thick gloves on his hands.

"Uncle Ruggie!" I laugh, hugging him tight.

"Oh, good to see you! I heard about the party. Are you alright?" he asks. I nod, and he releases me.

"These are my friends, Royah and Tahira. Tahira has some work for you, if you can?" I say. Tahira hands over her Dolk, pointing to the damaged area. Uncle Ruggie holds it close to his eyes, nodding slowly.

"Hmmm, I see. Yes, I can fix this," Uncle Ruggie says. Tahira's eyebrows jump up in shock.

"Are you sure? It's intricate work."

"Of course." Uncle Ruggie waves off the worry with a warm smile. "Come inside. Do you have the stones or will you need replacements?"

"Replacements," Tahira sighs. "I couldn't find them when we looked."

"Come and choose the stones then, I have a wide range you can pick from." Ruggie invites us inside. I smile and mouth my thanks at Uncle Ruggie as we enter his home. There are boxes and boxes of jewels everywhere, his pieces littering every surface. I walk over to the stove, fill the kettle and place it over a gentle flame. I think all of us could use a cup of tea.

Royah bends over some of the pieces, picking them up with care as she inspects them. A small, awed smile spills over her face. I chuckle to myself, walking to her side.

"He's talented, right?" I whisper to her. Royah nods, inspecting the most beautiful bracelet formed of intertwined silver and gold rivers studded with diamond clouds and topaz stars.

"Stunning. The detail in the metal work..." Royah sets the box down. "He's an artisan."

"Only the best here in the Garden," I say proudly. "The best and brightest of every ilk. Geniuses each and every one."

"Anyone here do tattoos?" Royah asks excitedly. "I love learning from other artists."

"I don't think so. Tattoos aren't popular here in the south of the continent, but if you travel to Rhone or Agoa they are much more prevalent," I answer honestly. "Are you an artist?"

"Yeah." Royah beams, showing off her arms. "I've collected these from artists I've met and admired. See this one"—she points to the vivid depiction of butterflies on hothouse flowers that graces her shoulder—"I got it from a master in a city called Alverga. He taught me so much about movement in my pieces."

"Wow."

"This one I got while we were in Malaya. They don't do tattoos over there the way we do in Coari. They only have black and white ink, and their technique takes hours," she says, pointing to a gorgeous depiction of a dagger wrapped in thorny vines with tiny, delicate flowers that graces the back of her forearm. "So I drew this and did it over time on myself. Non-dominant hand, too."

"You tattooed yourself?" I gape. Royah chuckles.

"You're not supposed to. But I had to try their technique, and no one volunteered to be my test subject." Royah grins. "Most of the crew have been at the mercy of me and my needles at some point."

"Did you do Idris?" I ask.

"Yeah. He just wanted a straight scorpion tail, nothing else. I wanted to add some flourish but he said no." Royah rolls her eyes like he was boring. "Why? You want me to get out my needles for you?"

"I'll pass right now, thanks. But they're beautiful," I muse, knowing someone who would love these. An artist who lived only a few doors down. Fate really was playing his games. "Let me show you one of my favourite pieces Uncle Ruggie's done."

I head to one of Uncle Ruggie's cupboards. I sink down, tugging open the draw and riffling through the boxes. I bring out a large flat box and tug off the lid. Nestled in the black velvet bed is the most gorgeous necklace. A bursting bouquet of flowers – tulips, daffodils, crocuses and snowdrops – runs like an explosion of springtime in the most intricate, delicate network of silver.

"It reminds me of flowers in the snow," I admit. I've only seen snow once, when we went to stay up near the mountains on holiday as a child. But I've never forgotten it.

"By the great rivers!" breathes Royah, her mouth falling open.

"They're glass of course, not real jewels. He made this as costume jewellery. An experiment a few years ago. But I still think it's phenomenal." I smile. Royah takes the box, holding it up to the light as she watches the sparkle dance.

"If your uncle ever decides to go to Coari, he'd clean up! People would go mad for these," Royah says. I raise an eyebrow.

"Really?"

"Oh, yeah." Royah nods. "People wear their wealth in Coari."

I blink, an idea taking root in my mind.

"What's the food like in Coari?" I ask, hoping to strike a tone of only mild curiosity.

"Well, Coari is mostly desert, but we have a few great rivers that have large tides," Royah explains. "The wetlands are rich with all kinds of foods. Wheats, fruits, veg, spices. Why?"

"I love exploring my palate." I wave off the question, but a plan is beginning to form.

"You and Idris share that in common then." Royah chuckles, her mind's eye skating somewhere else. "He was always cooking or eating. Everywhere we went, he had to try everything. It's a miracle he isn't the size of a ship!"

"Okay, sorted." Tahira smiles, coming to join us. "These are incredible."

"Thank you." Uncle Ruggie beams.

"Can I buy these?" asks Royah, picking up a box. Inside are a set of earrings, the dangling jewels reminding me of frothy ocean waves rolling over each other.

"Of course," Ruggie says brightly. "Those are studded with sapphire and aquamarine, set in mother-of-pearl."

It doesn't take long for us to finish up business. We walk out of Uncle Ruggie's house in a bright mood. I pause outside Fausta's mural. I clear a stray fallen leaf from a nearby tree and whisper a quiet prayer before heading up the path again.

"Thanks for the directions," Tahira says brightly.

"No problem. Getting lost in Halice can be wonderful, but sometimes the direct approach is best."

"Oh, I believe it..." Royah trails off, her eyes catching over my shoulder. I spin to see Michelle. She's frozen on the path, like a rabbit aware she's been spotted by the wolf. Fate's Fury, she looks pale.

"Wait," Royah breathes, pushing past us. Michelle stumbles back, frantically shaking her head.

"No! No, I don't..." Michelle throws up her hands, shaking her head frantically. "I can't."

"Please. I just want to talk," Royah breathes. Michelle turns tail and runs for home. Royah takes off after her.

Tahira swears as the two of us break into a sprint down the path. Royah is fast, her dark braids flying in the wind. Michelle gets to her home and slams the door shut behind her with such fury that every inch of the wood shudders.

"No, please! Please just talk to me," Royah begs through the door. "Please let me explain."

"Go away! Go away!" shouts Michelle over and over again, her voice torn apart with sobs. "I love Giulia!"

"I know. I know that," Royah says morosely, her face contorted. "I just want to talk. To apologise or explain or ... just talk." Her head drops and her eyes close.

I bite my lip. Michelle is my friend; I love her to pieces and she's hurting so badly right now. But Giulia is my sister, and she's hurting, too. How do I help them both? How do I show them both I care?

Tahira sighs, looking at me.

"How is your sister?" she asks tentatively. That is a loaded question. I can't find the words as a lump forms in my throat. I answer with the only words I can think of.

"Giulia and Michelle are what true love should be."

I swallow, realising how combative my answer is. But Tahira doesn't seem to mind.

"Good," Tahira answers as she considers her friend. "Then they'll get through this. Royah would never want to get between anyone."

I sigh, hating how aggressive my words were even more. Royah steps away from the door, her shoulders slumped. She doesn't look at us; her bright mood has evaporated.

"Let's go," she says, wrapping her arms around herself.

"I'm going to stay," I answer. "But ... perhaps we can do dinner? Tomorrow evening, say? If your preparations aren't finished by then?"

"No, we need two more days," Tahira says suspiciously. "Dinner tomorrow sounds good. Where?"

"My place? I'll send the information. Idris can come, too – and feel free to bring your brother. There'll be plenty of security," I promise. "Until then."

I bid them goodbye, and watch them retreat. Maybe this is the answer I've been looking for. A new way of looking at the problem.

First, I need to talk to Idris. If he gives me the answers I need, this might just work.

And save us all.

But first things first, Michelle and Giulia.

I turn back to the front door and try the handle. Locked.

"Michelle, it's just me. They've gone. I promise," I call through the door. No answer.

I sigh and start walking around to the window by the kitchen. I reach down and grab a stick from the ground then use it to nudge the lock open and wiggle the window up. The things I do for my friends!

I clamber into the house.

"It's just me!" I call as I right myself in the kitchen and close the window. "I am not leaving till we talk."

Michelle appears at the top of her stairs, looking a terrible state. Her hair quivers with the intensity of her breaths, and she swallows tensely. I force myself to smile.

"Tea?" I offer.

"How's Giulia?" Michelle begs, tentatively descending the stairs. She holds herself tightly as though it's the only thing keeping her together.

"Not good." I decide to answer honestly. "She's heartbroken and under a lot of stress."

"She won't talk to me!" Michelle sobs, fresh tears rolling down her face as her shoulders tremble. "I have tried and tried! She won't speak to me."

"She's not got a lot of space mentally right now, and the pain is so fresh." I walk closer and try to hug her. Michelle steps back, shaking her head.

"I didn't do anything, I swear it!" Michelle's pleads. "That woman is leaving and never coming back. Please tell Giulia."

"I know." I try to soothe her. "I know. You two need to talk. Properly."

"I'm trying!"

"I know!" I talk over her. I take her shoulder and lead her to her kitchen table where we both sit down. "Giulia is *so* buried in stress right now, I think she's terrified she's losing you on top of everything else."

"She's not!" Michelle hiccups. "I love her. Nothing has changed for me."

Is that true? Has nothing changed for her? When I met Idris, everything changed, but then I wasn't mortal enemies with anyone else. Does the introduction of a Soulmate diminish the love you have for another?

"Tell me," I say quietly. Michelle lets out a shaky breath and rubs her forehead.

"You wouldn't get it."

"Wouldn't I?" I challenge. "You know anyone else defying a Fated bond?"

Michelle swallows, hesitating.

"You are my friend, Michelle. I want the best for both you and Giulia," I remind her. "Tell me what's going on with you. I want to help. Maybe start small. You still love Giulia?"

"Yes!"

"And what do you feel for Royah?"

"I feel … I feel…" Michelle grips her head in anguish.

"It's okay. You can say it," I coax gently.

"Drawn to her," Michelle says, wincing like she said something awful. "But not like Giulia. It's not … it's not the way I adore Giulia. It's more like I met a part of myself I didn't know I was missing."

"You want to talk to Royah?"

"Obviously, but it's not worth losing Giulia! I love Giulia so much I'd rip out my heart and hand it to her if she needed it."

Michelle drops her head, her shoulders slumping as she breathes deeply. She turns her head a fraction, fixing me with a questioning gaze.

"What if ... our understanding of Fated bonds is wrong?" she asks softly.

"Wrong?"

"Wrong," she breathes. "What if Soulhates aren't always destined to destroy? What if Soulmates aren't always destined for romantic bliss?"

"All I know about Fated bonds is that they are unique to the people they occur between," I say quietly. "What that means for you, Giulia and Royah is for the three of you to decide."

"I can't if Giulia won't talk to me."

Michelle looks at her hands, her sigh large and heavy as water leaks from her eyes. I rub her back gently.

"I'm hoping things at the bank will start looking up soon," I admit quietly. "Then she'll have space to talk and work through her emotions. Don't give up. You two are special. Don't lose that."

"How do I fight for us when she won't fight with me?" Michelle's voice crackles.

"She wants to but she's terrified," I counter. "So you have to be the one to show her how."

Michelle swallows, eyes drifting away to a half-finished portrait. I follow her gaze. The image could tear out my throat and stomp on my organs. It depicts a woman raging, the colours bold and brash as they're delivered to the canvas. Devastation cast in oils.

"Write her a letter," I say. "I'll give it to her."

"Really?" Michelle hiccups. "She hasn't responded to my others."

"I'll make her read this one. I can't promise more," I say quietly. Michelle walks to her table and picks up a few pages.

"I wrote this earlier..." she whispers, folding the pages and handing them to me. "Is it too late? Have I lost her?"

The naked pain in her eyes makes me hesitate. I don't want

to promise on Giulia's behalf. I can't – that would be wrong. But I can't believe it's over. I simply can't.

"Either way," I say as kindly as I can, "we'll find out."

CHAPTER 15

The walk to Idris's house is a long one, but I barely notice it. After leaving Michelle, I force my mind away from their heartbreak, onto a possibility that'll make things better. I'm wrapped up in my small idea blooming through my mind, testing it and probing it from every angle I can find. The more I work it, the larger is grows and the more promise it holds. This could be it. This could be what we're looking for.

I knock sharply on Patricelli's polished front door. My pulse runs a mile a minute, impatient to get the answers I want. I take a deep breath, waiting for him to arrive. When he doesn't, I knock again. Harder, insistently, refusing to go quiet.

Finally goosebumps flood up my arms, my lungs run hot, and my teeth feel like oversized blades in my mouth.

He's home.

Idris opens the door sharply, no doubt a witty remark poised on his lips about my impatience. I don't want to hear it, so push past him into his home.

"Do you have books on Coari here?" I ask as I head for his study.

"Um, no," Idris answers, confused as he closes his door. "What?"

"Then fill me in. Coari, what does it have?" I press, continuing down the hallway.

"Have?" Idris hurries the few paces to my side. "Take a few steps back and take me on the journey with you, please."

"Answers first. Coari, what resources does it have?"

Idris flounders for a minute before speaking.

"Um, precious metals. And jewels. Sapphires, rubies, diamonds—"

"So they're rich?" I press. Idris nods slowly, irritation rife on his face. He raises his eyebrows in question, clearly expecting me to explain myself.

"And Tahira, is she really a princess?" I continue. "Or is it just a moniker?"

"It's complicated." Idris steps towards me, head ducking expectantly as he folds his arms. "Want to elaborate on where these questions are coming from?"

I levy a look, wondering where to begin. The last time I stood in this house comes flooding back. His anger, my rage. Our barbed words. My throat tightens as I step back, claiming space between us before the flames in the dark corners of my mind can really sink in their blistering teeth. I head to his study, not looking back as he follows. Idris closes the door with more force than is necessary, and I put his velvet green couch between us.

"Renza?" I wrestle back the vitriolic indignation at his almost commanding tone. I will not be controlled or commanded. But he does need to know my idea if he's to support it.

"We need to replace the Holy States as a trade partner, preferably with someone who has a navy that will allow us to regain control of the Argenti Strait," I explain. "I just spent the morning with Royah and Tahira."

"You did?"

"Yes, and they were really interested in Uncle Ruggie's work, and Serra's, and this salve my aunt got from Nimal. We have things they want. There have got to be other things people in Coari want, or need. Things the Independent States can get them, things we can trade with them."

"Lumber. Sturdy lumber is in short supply there, and they need it." Idris's hazel eyes shine brightly as he catches on. "And dyes for fabrics. Ours are so much better. They would love them over there."

"Lumber we can start quickly; Rhone and Nimal are land trade routes!" I say excitedly, already planning to corner Fiora. She can arrange things with the Nimal banking branch.

"So back to my question, is Tahira really a princess?" I push. "Can she authorise a trade agreement?"

Idris rakes a hand through his hair, the muscles of his arms jumping beneath the fitted green tunic, the pins at his elbow glistening like a cluster of stars. I force my eyes away, my throat bobbing as I try to ease the clenching in my stomach. Idris pauses, tilting his head as he searches for the right words.

"Tahira's mother, Akilah, is Queen of Coari. But that's the case because Akilah married the King of Coari, Makram, when Tahira was three years old."

"So Tahira's stepfather is the King of Coari," I follow. Idris nods. He slowly walks in my direction, rubbing the back of his neck, his mind's eye a thousand miles away. He takes a deep breath and hesitates, trying to work out how much is okay to tell me and how much is really for Tahira to divulge.

"Tahira's blood father fell in battle with the Red Sands Bannerhood when Tahira was only nine months old. He was the commander and, on his death, Akilah ran it until her marriage to the King. Then she was forced to relinquish it. When Tahira passed the Nakari, she challenged the former commander for her birthright as her father's heir and won back her father's mercenary company."

"Oh, wow." I gape. "Did you see that happen?"

"I didn't." Idris sighs ruefully. "That was six months before I met her."

"So the Princess of War thing, that's where it comes from?"

"Yeah. Makram loves Tahira like a daughter. In the eyes of the King, she is a princess. But technically she's not even of noble blood."

"Does she have enough sway for a trade agreement?"

"We might not need one. If Tahira wants to trade using the Bannerhood, it would make them all rich. There's no law preventing them from trading. But if we want an official trade agreement between nations we would need to get her stepfather involved..." Idris trails off, the idea spinning around his head.

Idris smiles, rounding the sofa towards me. The air grows thick and fizzy. My heart picks up its pace. He folds his arm, leaning against the sofa back, a wicked smile spilling over his lips.

"So rather than buying them as mercenaries, which we can't afford, we create a mutually beneficial, ongoing trade agreement that gives us all the resources and trade we need, but is also in their interest to actively defend." Idris chuckles, shaking his head in wonder. The infectious energy of a good idea thrums in both our veins, building and building.

"While respecting the sanctity of this city because we are the only people who can get them what they need to sell," I add.

"This is brilliant! Renza you're a genius!"

"I know," I jest, running my hands over my head as I analyse all the ways we could convince Tahira to jump on board. The Red Sands Bannerhood is not a trading company. Tahira might be reluctant to enter that space.

"Now we get it to work," I murmur. "The sooner the better.

People are hungry and desperate. No weddings, no funerals, no work with trade drying up," I sigh.

"We'll get food, if Tahira agrees," Idris reassures, flashing a tight smile and scratching the back of his head.

"It doesn't fix the faith aspect," I answer. Idris wrinkles his nose.

"The people don't need a viper like the Holy Faith in our city," Idris murmurs in disgust. "They saw what those power-hungry, self-righteous zealots are like."

"Did they? Or did they believe the story we told them?" I point out quietly. I dig my fingers into the velvet couch as I speak. "People need something to believe in when times are tough, and those times are here."

"They can believe in us. In Halice."

"Patriotism? That's a message you want to push?" I bite my lip. It could work, I suppose. But Idris has never been as religious as I am – or, well, as *I was* before events quite literally blew up in my face. Even with the bitterness and ugliness we went through, I can't deny that there is a small niggling hole where my faith used to sit, filled with questions and cavities as it was. Would patriotism really be enough to fill that?

"I'll talk to Savino," Idris says, snapping me out of my musings. "Given the rising tensions in Halice, I think it best we arrange for some guards to be with you at all times."

"No!" I almost vomit the word. "I don't need personal guards!"

"Renza!" Idris argues, a tether tightening between us, humming with dark whispers. "You were shot—"

"Yes and I'm fine," I retort.

"Your arm argues otherwise," Idris snaps. The air around him fizzes aggressively. My nails are scalding in my fingertips.

"That wasn't done by Halicians," I remind him curtly. "If I take on guards, people will think I'm scared. People will think there's a threat."

"There is a threat," Idris says as though I'm slow on the uptake.

"I'm not having guards," I answer flatly; our lips are barely inches apart.

"Your safety isn't a negotiation."

"You're right. *My* safety isn't. *Mine*. I decide." Idris narrows his eyes, his frame physically shaking with restraint.

Suddenly he grabs my shoulders and pushes me against the bookcase. The shelves dig into my hips and back, the books shuddering as my head tilts back to see Idris. His gold eyes glare with a fury that could melt iron and freeze lava. His nose almost brushes mine, lips pulled back in a grimace. His voice is a low, dangerous growl as he talks like he's on a razor's edge.

"You're selfish," he accuses. Outrage and shock leap from my bones. The bond roars in my blood, my heart throbbing in my temples.

"Me?" I laugh, the sound hollow.

"Your safety isn't just about you; it affects tens of thousands of people. Most of all, it affects me. Do you even care what the idea of you in danger does to me?" Idris's fingers weave through my hair as he tugs my head closer to his. His touch burns, seeding embers through my scalp. I'm trapped by him, my entire body running like a river of molten metal. Breathing is hard and hot, like my lungs are shrinking and bleeding and fighting for air. A strangled gasp leaves my throat and Idris flinches.

"That sound," Idris's voice is a quiet, almost reverent, agonised groan, "the look on your face that night when you saw Nouis..."

His face ripples with horror. Idris closes his eyes, screwing up his face as he tries to wipe away what he sees in his mind.

"Idris—"

"You were terrified," Idris whispers, his words betraying his pain as his thumb runs over my lips, planting red-hot sparks across the tender tissue. "I was supposed to protect you and I failed."

I blink hard, shaking my head. His fingers tighten in my hair, the tugging setting off a cacophony of flames and daggers racing down my head and neck. But he needs to know. Needs to understand.

"No, Idris. You didn't fail. We protect each other. It's mutual. That night was simply my turn," I murmur softly, pressing my hands against his chest. I tear my eyes from his, unable to mask my shame. Because if I had listened to him, it wouldn't have happened. Idris knew Nouis was a snake from the beginning.

The relentless, infernal heat of Idris's body soaks into my hands with painful fangs.

"We defend each other."

Idris's hand moves to my jaw, his fingers tight as he forces my face up to look at him. "You should never have had to. Not like that."

"It's history," I counter, the words a whisper.

"Not when it still stands between us. Not when the last time you were in this study, I said something careless. Something that didn't express what I meant and it hurt you!" Idris whispers passionately. "Don't you understand? You are my priority. How can I be anywhere else, think about anything else, when I can't stop picturing you in danger? When I don't know if you're safe?"

Idris's hands are trembling. I swallow tightly, though it does nothing to relieve the raw scratching of my desiccated throat.

"That night was my fault," I whisper thickly. "I was the burden. I was the one who made the mistakes. Carelessly tugging on the bond by accident – it was stupid and brainless." I hate the torn breathiness to my words and hot tears filling my vision. I shake my head as I continue. "I was an idiot. A stupid, pointless distraction."

Idris's brow creases like my admission causes him physical pain.

His muscled body presses harder against mine, leaving no room to breathe. My limbs shake from the wild flames charring deep in my bones. The blistering, blissful tingling dances in a maddening, addictive symphony, corrupting my blood.

He lowers his face, his mouth hovering over mine, his breath cracking across my sensitive lips, casting them into an aching blaze. His voice is a whispered groan, as though I'm prying his confession syllable by syllable from his tongue.

"You're not my distraction Renza; you are my devotion."

His lips pounce on mine. A bonfire rages through my stomach; my spine crackles with fireworks. Every corner of my head burns so bright I'm blinded and consumed. His lips battle over mine, tugging and demanding. They devour every push and pull, unyielding in their attack.

I throw my arms around his shoulders, refusing to lose the battle. My hands dig into his hair as I kiss him, launching counter manoeuvres of my own. The feral blaze surges up my body, the pain and pleasure mingling in poisonous euphoria. I'm ravaged by his touch. I bite down on his lip and the mixed growl and groan melts through my stomach. His hands sweep over the curves of my hips like a scorching wave, sending lightning jolting through my every fibre.

My head rolls up, eyes closed as his lips drop to the tender flesh of my neck. His hot breaths and torturous lips pry a strangled moan from my mouth. One hand slips around my front, under the hem of my tunic, and travels upwards. The agonisingly slow path of his bare, calloused palm up my stomach is delirious and devastating, moving higher and higher until the tips of his fingers brush the undersides of my breasts. I buck, arching my back as his lips return to punish mine, his tongue dancing wickedly in the fray. His fingers circle my nipple, the frustration building like hot, boiling bubbles inside me, desperate for his attention.

My core is absolutely molten. All thoughts have burned to ash. There is only Idris and this fire that promises to destroy me entirely.

"Idris?" The quiet, childlike voice leaks through the door. I'm drenched in ice and bile crawls up my stomach, the agony too much to bear. I lurch away from Idris, panting wildly as I fight with every instinct inside me the desperate urge to wrap my hands around his neck, to feel his hot, sticky blood under my nails, to slash and beat and bruise until this dark desire is stated.

I force my breathing to slow, battling with the monster inside that pleads to turn around and batter my Soulhate over the head while he's distracted.

Idris pants behind me, bent over to grip the sofa as he regains his control.

"Idris?" comes the voice again. Karrius. Idris groans quietly before speaking.

"Yeah Kaz?" he calls. The young boy pushes open the door, smiling brightly as he walks into the study.

"You said you'd help me with my footwork. Hi, Renza!" Karrius waves brightly, holding a wooden sword in one hand.

"I'll be right there, buddy, just give me a minute with Renza, alright?" Idris answers warmly.

"Are you two friends again?" Karrius asks, blunt curiosity in his eyes. "You were yelling the other day."

The honesty of children is so refreshing after the secrets and manoeuvrings of politics.

"Don't worry." I walk over to Karrius, glad to put more distance between Idris, myself and the devastation that just passed between us. "We yell at each other a lot. But we're always friends, even when we fight."

Idris chuckles, shaking his head.

"Yes. Friends," he repeats dryly.

"Like me and Father?" Karrius asks, voice full of hope. "He loves me even though he can't be with me?"

The pieces of the puzzle tilt and slip into place. Of course. Now everything makes sense. Why a Prince of Coari is travelling with a bunch of mercenaries instead of growing up in a Coari palace. Why Tahira was heading to Malaya to learn mind-stilling even before meeting Idris. Why she is so interested in how Idris and I are handling things.

Karrius is so young. When had the Soulhate bond between father and son snapped into place?

"Exactly, buddy," says Idris quietly, realising I've worked it out. We exchange a long look, his hazel eyes blistering like staring into the sun.

"But you two can be together," Karrius says quietly. I take a deep breath, before taking the young Prince's hands.

"Listen to me, little man, I'm going to tell you my most important secret," I say gently. Karrius grins brightly, showing off that toothy smile that melts my heart.

"The future is full of possibilities. It's full of questions, full of mysteries we get to discover. But the most magical part is that we can change it. Our actions today can reshape tomorrow. If we act today with fear, then tomorrow there will be more things to be afraid of. But if we act today with hope, then tomorrow we are one step closer to making that hope become real. So if there is something you want, act with hope. Then, maybe, Fate will make it real."

Karrius beams brightly.

"Come on, buddy, let's go fix that footwork of yours," Idris says quietly after a moment. Karrius nods and bounces out of the room. Idris walks towards the door, pausing with his hand on the doorframe.

"Act with hope, huh?" he says, looking back at me before a soft smile fills his face. "I'll remember that."

CHAPTER 16

If I'm to present this new trade deal with Coari to the High Chamber, I need numbers. Numbers mean I need Giulia.

Sure, I'm pretty good at maths. But Giulia has a brain for it like no other, and with something so vital I'd trust no one else.

Not to mention that this trade will hopefully flow through the Di Maineri Bank. It'll certainly move a lot quicker if we can leverage the other family branches. It should also settle the problems the bank is having and remove a lot of things from Giulia's plate.

I swear Giulia had silvery tears of relief in her eyes as I pitched the plan. Her voice held a long-absent brightness as we worked all afternoon in her office. The two of us crowded around her desk, calculating delivery times and potential price points and a thousand things Giulia knew to consider that hadn't yet crossed my mind.

Shoulder to shoulder with my sister, working towards a solution at long last, was so therapeutic. The sky slipped from yellow to lilac as the loud banging of construction outside stopped and the stars sprouted from their burrows in the sky.

Giulia finally sets down her quill, handing me her latest page of calculations.

"There. I think that does it," she breathes. I nod slowly. This is brilliant. These proposals could get our finances back to where they were before this stupid tension with the Holy States.

"This could work," Giulia says, throwing both hands over her eyes like she's fighting back tears again. She leans back in her chair, taking several long breaths. The relief flooding off her makes me want to laugh for joy; just watching that stress leaving her body makes the world seem so much lighter.

"I'll make it work," I promise her, squeezing her shoulder. "The Di Maineri sisters are unstoppable when we work together."

"I can hold on until the new cash flow is here." Giulia chuckles, shaking her head ruefully. "I really thought I'd have to close this branch of the bank. I mean, Rialta was making so much sense that I started looking into separating it from the rest of the business. I mean, this changes everything."

My eyes catch on how pale her skin is, the thick violet bags under her eyes and the red skin on her knuckles. The ink coating her fingers looks almost permanent at this point.

"Giu," I start gently, my chair creaking as I lean forwards. "Can I ask you something?"

Giulia nods, pushing a stray lock of golden hair back from her face.

"It's about ... Michelle."

Giulia sighs and her shoulders drop.

"You have had so much on your plate, so much that you were drowning. You couldn't handle Michelle at the same time ... but with this ... do you think maybe you're up for it?" I ask.

Giulia blinks hard but doesn't speak.

"I saw her today."

Giulia's eyes cut to me. "How is she?"

"Bad," I answer honestly. Giulia flinches at the news, throat bobbing.

"She asked me to give you a letter," I continue. I reach into my pocket, pulling out the sheets of paper and placing them in front of Giulia. "She just wants to talk."

"I... After so long, I don't know what to say," Giulia admits.

"She feels the same. But that doesn't mean you couldn't try," I nudge softly. Because Michelle and Giulia belong together. They make each other so happy, so strong... They both deserve the true, unselfish love they share.

"Fiora says I should let her go. Because I love her, I need to walk away. Fate has given her something ... special. I shouldn't deny her that. And she's right, what about the consequences of ignoring Fate? It's not like you. I'm not making the decision not to commit a murder. No one here is losing their life, and if Fate punishes Michelle for something I do—"

"Stop, stop." I quickly cut her off and take Giulia's hands. "These are Fiora's words, not yours. Fiora is a devotee of Fate to escape her own pain. To understand where her words come from." I quickly explain the story of how Fiora found her Soulmate. Giulia's jaw drops to the floor.

"No wonder she believes so strongly in Fate's decisions. I'd cling to them, too." Giulia shudders.

"But we don't have to." I grin, squeezing my fingers over hers. "You can love Michelle. If you want it, fight for it. She loves you so so much."

Giulia pulls her hands from mine and tentatively picks up the letter on her desk.

"What does it say?"

"I haven't looked. It's for you." Giulia sucks in two deep breaths before tugging the paper open. Her eyes flit back and forth, diamond tears clustering along her lash lines. I rub her shoulder, turning my head away patiently while she reads.

My heart is pounding in my chest as Giulia presses a hand to her mouth.

"Okay?" I ask quietly. She nods, reaching the last page. A sigh slips free as a single tear escapes and trails the length of her cheek. She turns the page over to me.

Zinnia flowers. The entire page is covered in them.

On their first date, Michelle asked Giulia for her favourite flower. Michelle didn't have any money, so rather than buying her flowers, she drew one and sent it to our house requesting another date.

"Can we go see her?" Giulia ventures quietly, taking a deep breath and cracking the first real smile I've seen from her in ages.

"Absolutely!" I grin, hopping up before she can change her mind.

We hurry out of the bank and walk arm in arm through the streets of Halice. A new bounce enters my sister's step – I can almost forget the horrors of the last few months. Giggling and gossiping, we wind through the darkened streets. A soothing violet sky stretches overhead adorned with diamond stars. The world feels so much better.

We reach the Garden quickly, travelling down the cobbled pathway. The wind tosses gold and burgundy leaves around our feet as the cool breeze pries roses from our cheeks.

When we get to Michelle's house, Giulia hesitates. The shutters are drawn, but the amber firelight of candles seeps through. She's still awake.

"Okay, here goes," Giulia breathes as she walks towards the door. She opens it widely, stepping inside but stops dead like she's been turned to ice. I hurry after her, fear clogging my throat, and find Royah sitting at the dining room table.

Crap.

"Oh ... I see." Giulia's voice is thick with tears as she stumbles back a pace.

"No. No, Giu, it's not like that." Michelle's face ripples with horror as she leaps to her feet. She was sitting on the other side of the table from Royah and nothing untoward was happening. Michelle runs towards Giulia with desperate stumbles.

"Don't," Giulia hiccups, recoiling as Michelle tries to reach her.

"It's not what you think," Michelle pleads.

"You're spending time with your Soulmate. As is your right." Giulia's voices shakes, and I can tell she's verging on numb. "But I won't torture myself. I can't—"

"No, sweetheart, please! I'm not in love with her!" Michelle begs. "It's not love!"

"Of course not. You only met a week ago." Giulia tries in vain to swallow her fresh sobs. "You're Soulmates. Clearly you want to be together."

"No, no, I don't! Giulia, please," Michelle sobs. "It's not like that! I don't look at her and feel how I feel with you. No one could make me feel that."

"She's your Soulmate!" shouts Giulia.

"I don't care!" Michelle shouts back, both of them shredded by tears and anguish. "It isn't love. It isn't romantic. It's nothing like the Church says it should be! Meeting Royah wasn't like falling in love, not like when I first saw you. Nothing could compare to the moment I met you. I knew I was in love. I fell so fast and so hard, I can't ever recover. I don't *want* to recover."

"Then what is it, Michelle? Why is she here?" Giulia sobs.

"I'm so sorry for the pain I've caused you both. More than you will know," Royah says soberly. "I came for closure, nothing more. I'll leave now." Royah eases to her feet and starts gathering her things. Giulia refuses to even acknowledge her as Michelle clings to Giulia like she might evaporate forever.

"Please, let's talk properly," Michelle begs. "Just hear me out. If you want to leave me afterwards, I understand. But, please, for everything we've ever had ... please listen to me. Please stay and hear me."

Fresh tears swell like opals in Giulia's eyes, her ragged breathing making her tremble. I don't know which way my sister will fall on this.

"Okay." Giulia swallows tightly. Michelle takes my sister's hand and pulls her upstairs so they can talk privately. Royah and I are left alone in Michelle's open-plan kitchen, dining room and workshop.

Royah rubs her eyes. I say nothing and wait. Eventually Royah sighs and heads towards one of Michelle's paintings. It's half-finished, and the way she's captured raw agony is a marvel. It is a depiction of reaching for the goddess in golden light and the desperation of falling short in the chase.

"She loves her," Royah finally says, breaking my study of the work. I nod.

"They are devoted," Royah says. "They are happy and enamoured. I want that for her, for them both. They seem ... perfect. I don't want to ruin that."

Royah pushes her braids over her shoulder, sniffing sharply and setting her hands on her hips.

"I'm going to go."

"Me, too," I decide. "They deserve privacy."

The two of us walk to the door, pulling it shut behind us as we head back down the winding path towards the city. The night is quiet and cold, not holding any of the bubbling energy it had only minutes ago when travelling with Giulia. The tension between Royah and me is stilted, until a sharp sigh from the warrior breaks the nervous silence.

"Why don't you banish me from the city?" Royah asks, sounding almost frustrated.

"Huh?"

"For your sister. You could, right?" Royah asks pointedly.

"I could," I muse, not pretending the thought hasn't crossed my mind. "But I won't. It would only make things worse. This question going unanswered would eat them both alive. Giulia with her insecurities, Michelle for missing that piece of her. They need you here to work it out, for better or for worse. To whatever end."

Royah shakes her head and her face wrinkles.

"I never wanted a Soulmate," Royah admits quietly. "I was sure I'd disappoint them. Sure I couldn't be what they need or give them what they want. But Michelle ... she doesn't want the things I can't give. She just wants to be my friend."

"What do you mean?" I ask curiously. Royah hesitates, running a few braids through her fingers as she talks.

"I ... I don't ... I don't like romance," Royah answers as she works out how to phrase it. "Or sex. Sometimes I think I'm broken, having never had those desires. Those things just don't sway me like they seem to capture others. I mean, I understand, as much as I can. But they've just never been things I've wanted, if that makes any kind of weird sense..." Royah trails off as though frustrated.

"More than you think," I answer softly.

"I was afraid of meeting my Soulmate, that she would need things I can't provide." Royah smiles softly. "But Michelle doesn't."

"What's it like then? Help me understand, so I can get Giulia to understand, too," I say quietly.

"It's like ... like I just met my sister. A part of myself, a piece I didn't realise I was missing. I love her like I love Tahira," Royah answers with a silly, raptured smile. "Like she's my best friend in the whole of creation. Conversation is so easy that it's like we've been together our whole lives."

I smile, linking my arm through hers.

"If you feel comfortable, you should tell Giulia that," I suggest quietly. "No pressure, but she'd understand."

"We don't have time," Royah says ruefully. "We're leaving the day after tomorrow."

"Maybe. Or maybe you'll be returning quicker than you think."

"What does that mean?"

I wink at her.

"Come to the dinner tomorrow night at my house. Bring Tahira and Karrius. And Idris, if you can stomach him."

As we step outside the gates of the Garden, a black cart passes, a large cloth draped over a body. An elderly woman weeps in its wake, but supporting her is a familiar face.

The lone priestess.

An idea springs to mind. A new one. Something to pursue after we secure Tahira's agreement to this new trade deal.

Everything is falling into place.

"See you tomorrow." I bid goodnight to Royah and hurry over to the priestess, hoping to extend a quick invitation.

CHAPTER 17

"This is unbelievable!" Rialta babbles. "You're gambling the entire bank on these people!"

"I quite agree. You can't trust these Coari barbarians," Agosta adds, folding her arms as I pick up my earrings.

My aunts barged into my room as I was getting ready for the trade dinner, hurling complaints and objections without pausing to draw breath. I've been preparing all day, organising displays of the wealth Halice has to offer a trading partner. All the Electi have been invited, so have Tahira and her key advisors. Hopefully the less formal environment of my back garden will keep everyone relaxed, as will the copious amounts of wine. I've brought in some of the best vintages, including some from our own Di Maineri vineyards.

"Renza, are you even listening to us?" demands Rialta.

"No," I answer curtly, threading the jewelled earrings into place. The long, dangling jewels twist and curl with every colour, reminding me of moonlight dancing over a lazy river.

I stand up and brush off my dress. The Halician style has a beaded halter neckline and long skirts made of intricately painted silks. Vibrant flowers of every creed bloom across the floaty material, layered with a fine, glistening piece of gossamer that flutters like fairy wings. Around my waist is an intricate gold metal belt, adorned with jewels of yellow, pink and blue, and finished with long decorative chains. Made of a thousand individually formed charms and perfectly set gems, some loop back and some dangle at various heights all the way down to my knees.

I lean towards the mirror, checking the light touch of make-up I've applied to my cheeks. My dark hair is piled up onto my head again, a few locks left loose to frame my face.

Perfect.

"Renza, don't you care we're here?" Agosta whines. "Last time these people went anywhere—"

"I would've thought you'd both be pleased," I say sharply, a warning lurking behind my words. "Isn't saving the bank what you want? Isn't a strong Halice what you want?"

"The bank is our family legacy," Agosta says, uncharacteristically serious. "Not just yours and Giulia's but all of ours. Anyone wearing the Di Maineri name for the last one hundred years has a strong history and connection to this bank. You're gambling all of us on these people."

"You don't even operate a bank, Aggie," comes Fiora's voice from behind them. They step aside to allow her into the room.

"So she can't care about her family because she doesn't involve herself in the family business?" Rialta demands, hands flying to her hips. "By all means look for fixes, Renza, but this isn't the way."

"This is happening. Get on board, or get out," I answer brightly. "Preferably both."

I push past them all, summoning a deep breath as I walk swiftly down the corridor. I pause at the top of our stairs, looking into the courtyard. The sun is setting, washing the sky with amber and butter, a smattering of fluffy clouds with red underbellies drifting by. Tables are set, the musicians are playing, and lanterns hang in the trees around the manicured lawn with the various product displays ready to go. Fabrics, dyes, lumber, art, metalwork – you name it, we have a display for it. Anything we might be able to trade is laid out to be admired and appraised. A sample of wealth in the Independent States.

Giulia is already here, mingling with Maggia and Ulrico. Leone is clearly in deep discussion with Savino, and it doesn't look like they're agreeing. I walk down the steps and enter the courtyard. All the wine is served in stained-glass chalices, another mark of the beautiful things we have here. I pick one up, sipping on the red as I go to Giulia's side.

"Maggia, you look stunning," I greet. "As do you, Ulrico."

Ulrico belly-laughs.

"You are too kind, signora. But what's this all about? Your sister won't spill the beans," he says, before taking a hefty swig of his drink. His cheeks are already beginning to pinken.

"All will become clear, Ulrico, I promise," I say warmly. "It'll be worth the wait. Please, go survey the tables. I've brought some of our best vendors together so they might inspire us."

"But inspiration has clearly already struck," Maggia says warmly, raising her eyebrow as a small smile flickers around her mouth. I'm about to answer when all eyes cut to the group walking in.

The Red Sands Bannerhood. Tahira is at the helm, a small group of her captains and generals escorting her, including Royah and Bashran.

Idris is with them. My breath stops in my throat and my mouth runs dry. No matter how my eyes itch, my fingers sting, my blood burns ... I can't take my eyes away. The rich violet of his jacket set against the blond of his hair is fixating. Burning torches lighting my courtyard throw rippling veils of gold and amber over his features, picking out the intricate silver embroidery decorating his clothes.

"What are they doing here? I thought they were leaving?"

Ulrico asks quietly, no malice in his voice. I can't say the same of Maggia's expression. Leone looks positively livid and Savino seems to be playing his cards close to his chest.

"Hopefully not empty-handed," I say quietly. "Trust me."

I walk towards them, putting on a welcoming smile.

"You made it," I say warmly, keeping my stance open as I reach Tahira's side.

"Thank you for the invitation. Your home is extraordinary," Tahira says, her demeanour friendly, but there is an amused suspicion in her eyes as she scans the scene.

"Thank you. It's been in my family for generations."

"Who did the piece in the hallway? The flowers and birds mosaic?" asks Royah, gesturing over her shoulder. "It's phenomenal."

"That would be my mother," I answer. "Before her passing."

"Oh, I'm sorry." Royah groans, mad she's put her foot in it already.

"Don't be," I answer warmly. "My mother would've loved knowing her work still makes people smile. Speaking of phenomenal work in Halice, please enjoy the food and wine this evening. You might not have had much chance to explore Halice in your short visit, so I have brought Halice to you. We have some of our best artisans and workmen here to talk over their trades. Spread out. Explore. Enjoy!"

Tahira gives her men a short nod of dismissal and they start wandering around my courtyard. Idris flashes me a wink, before steering a few of Tahira's generals towards a table filled with lumber.

Tahira doesn't step towards a table, instead standing at my side as she appraises the setting and studies her people.

"I'm surprised you wanted to risk this again," she whispers conspiratorially.

"This isn't formal, and I think you sent a clear message the last time something went wrong," I answer, before taking a sip from my wine.

"Are you going to tell me what all this is about? Idris has been evasive all day. I couldn't even beat it out of him when schooling his footwork."

The image of Idris and Tahira sweating with weapons in hand slams into my brain like a red-hot poker. Nothing dislodges it, save actively shaking my head and blinking hard for a few long moments.

"It'll become clear," I answer, chuckling at Tahira's wry snort.

"You're as bad as each other. I know when I'm being led to water, Di Maineri." She folds her arms, eyes jumping around the tables.

"You're also smart enough to decide whether you'll drink it," I answer diplomatically. "Come, let me show you some of the silks we have. I think you'll love them."

I take my time, showing Tahira around the stalls, displaying the dyes and skill in fabric-painting, the lumber, the wines, the glasswork. I pointedly ignore Leone Strossi's furious sideways glances all evening, and Idris's blistering gaze burrowing into the back of my skull at predictably regular intervals.

The only real point of contention is Giulia, who avoids Royah like the plague. I don't know where she and Michelle left things – but given she's not here I can't assume the best.

"Pretty," says Tahira, holding up a piece of glasswork and examining the intricacies of the colour.

"Hold it against the light," Maggia encourages, gesturing to one of the torches. "See how firelight bleeds through?" She's worked out what I'm up to – or at least part of it.

"If I may?" the trader says. We turn our attention to them and they pick up a regular-looking glass goblet. "Is this not the kind of glass you have in Coari, signora?"

"Yes," Tahira answers, amused. The trader tosses it and the

crystalised goblet flies over the table to land on the hard mosaic floor of my courtyard, shattering into a million pieces.

"Such a shame," the trader chuckles, a mockery of disappointment as they pick up a secondary glass. "Wouldn't it be nice if glass were somehow a little sturdier? Think how much more useful it could be."

The trader holds up a second goblet, almost identical to the first. He tosses it. I wait for the shatter, but instead it bounces and rolls across the stone floor.

A delighted gasp comes from the group as we clap for the trader who does a slight bow.

"We call it tempering, a new treatment that requires extreme heats but strengthens the glass beyond its usual means without impacting the quality of the end result," the trader explains.

"Wonderful!" Tahira answers. "This has been wonderful."

"Good, I am glad you like it. It seems as though the rest of your soldiers like it, too," I say, looking around the group.

"Indeed. So, are you finally going to tell me why you're showing off?" Tahira asks pointedly. I smile and tap a finger to the rim of my wine glass for a moment.

"Do you think these things would be enjoyed in Coari?" I ask lightly. Tahira pauses, her brain racing to catch up what that sentence means. She lets out a low chortle.

"I see..." she says quietly. "You mean, do we want to trade these back in Coari for you?"

"Your men want gold, do they not? This would be easier and safer than a fight," I say lightly. "Right here, you have a wealth of resources, skills and new materials you could be responsible for bringing to your people, with all the rewards that would entail."

"So we buy this from you and sell it for higher prices in Coari – is that the plan?" Tahira asks expectantly.

"I mean, it's easy money, isn't it?" I say seriously, turning to face her. I look into her dark brown eyes, waiting for the shift that lets me know I've hooked her. "You know these items would sell, particularly the lumber and the dyes, and we can work up to everything else in time."

Tahira's mouth twists like she's trying to stamp down a smirk. But the shine in her eyes tells me she's listening. Intently.

I lean closer, speaking softly.

"Your men are here mostly because they want gold, but also because the scars between your people and the Holy States run deep. Why not fill your pockets, becoming wealthy for relatively little effort, while giving the Holy States the middle finger at the same time?" I say quietly. "Safer work, richer work, easier work. And it settles some centuries-long scores. Doesn't it tick all the boxes to get your people on board? Couldn't you spend more time at home or in safer places, rather than seeking out conflicts? Wouldn't that make everyone in your party safer?"

Tahira sharply snaps her head around to me, eyes narrowing dangerously at that last statement.

"I know you're talking about Karrius. He is my priority in everything," says Tahira, a fight bristling in her words. I don't back down.

"I'd never doubt that. Giulia is the same for me," I answer instantly. "Which is why I know, while they are safe, they can always be safer. Money helps with that. This makes you richer, makes work easier, allows you to help out a friend, allows you to piss off the Holy States and protects your family – a five-way win. What isn't to like about that?"

Tahira takes a long, deep breath, her dark eyes narrowing. The wind rustles her curls as she thinks. Then slowly, inch by inch, a wicked smile blooms across her face. She laughs, throwing an arm around my shoulders.

"Alright, Di Maineri, let's talk details, shall we?" Her eyes dance as an infectious grin spreads onto my face, too.

"Excellent," Giulia says, holding up the papers. "Because we've already drawn them up."

"Why am I not surprised?" Tahira belly-laughs. I crack a smile. Excellent. And I'm not done yet. I have one more thing up my sleeve to help make things here better.

Perhaps I'll have a far better birthday tomorrow than I previously thought.

CHAPTER 18

"HAPPY BIRTHDAY!" Giulia's voice hits me the minute I step foot into the living room. Giulia, Michelle and Emilia are sitting across my sofas grinning at me.

Michelle! Michelle is here!

Perhaps I have more reasons than ever to be cheerful.

A smile wraps around my face as Giulia bounces over and engulfs me in a big hug.

"Thank you!" I laugh, hugging her back. It's so good to see her happy.

I turn my ear to her lips.

"Michelle's here?" I ask softly.

"We're going slowly," Giulia whispers back before releasing me. I nod at her, unable to contain the thrilled smile spilling over my face.

"We got you gifts," Michelle calls, patting the coffee table to gesture me over. I walk over to the sofa and sink down in front of the small pile of presents.

"You didn't have to do that," I protest. Giulia pours a mug of coffee and presses it into my hands.

"We wanted to," Giulia says warmly. "Come on, you're going to love what I got you!"

Giulia sits down next to Michelle, and my heart jumps for joy when Michelle takes her girlfriend's hand and squeezes it tightly. I look down, trying to hide the ridiculous joy at them both being happy and together again. Seeing Giulia back to her usual bright self ... it's better than any gift they could buy.

"Come on, open it!" Giulia says, waving her present in my face.

"Thank you," I say taking it. I open the small paper packet and pull out two tickets to a new play at the theatre.

"It's supposed to be a musical comedy," Giulia explains. "The early reviews have been really promising."

"Oh, thank you!" I beam. Reaching forwards for the next one, I pick it up and read the tag. From Emilia.

I smile at her. She nods, her smile tight as she folds her arms. Is she worried about something? Is there too much work on her shoulders at the moment? Have things with Serra got worse? She's not here so maybe. I should pay closer attention.

I open the muslin bag and pull out some gorgeous fabric. The purple, blue and green tones gently fold into one another with ease – it'll make an absolutely stunning dress.

"Oh, wow, thank you, Em," I say brightly. She nods again and sips her coffee. Yes, I will need to ask her about that. I reach for the next gift – this one from Michelle by the looks of it. She's got me a book, one of my favourites from childhood.

"Open it," Michelle says ardently. I do and my mouth falls open. She's painted on the pages. You can still read the words; they show through her beautiful depictions of the scenes taking place.

"Oh, Michelle, this is stunning!" I gasp, turning to show Giulia.

"Oh, wow," Giulia breathes.

"I hoped you'd like it. Something unique just for you."

Michelle beams, wiping a springy brown curl back from her eyes.

Fiora also got me a gift — a lovely new set of quills with vibrantly dyed feathers, some of which are even jewelled. There is one box left on the table. It's made of dark wood, etched and inlaid with silver to mimic a night's sky.

"This was on the doorstep this morning," Giulia says quietly. "No idea who sent it."

I pick it up, looking for the tag. No name. I frown, but then swallow a laugh. Of course! This is how he sent his last gift. The books on mind-stilling. Idris must think he's being funny. I open the latch and lift the smooth lid.

Nestled amongst midnight velvet is a gorgeous necklace. The silver chain is short and decorative with metallic stars leading to a large crescent moon. The moon is made from glass in dreamy blues and sleepy violets, cut to shine like a thousand glistening constellations.

"Oooh, that's pretty," breathes Giulia.

"Yeah, not one of Ruggie's, though. It's not his box," Michelle says, picking up the box to inspect it.

I smile; Idris has lovely taste.

"Help me?" I ask Giulia, who nods. I shift my hair out of the way, letting her slip the necklace into place. It sits perfectly, proudly, below my collarbone. It's a little heavy, but I like the weight. I gently run my fingers over it, a warmth spreading through my lungs. Idris is so thoughtful.

I walk to the mirror to inspect it, unable to help the smile stretching over my face. It sets off the pale lilac of my dress and the silver adornments I chose this morning. How could he have known?

"Listen, I have a lot of work, but we'll have a great birthday dinner tonight," Giulia promises. "We might have to dodge the aunties but it's going to be fabulous."

"Dodge the aunties?" Fiora glides into the room, eyes glistening. "Is that so?"

"Aunt Fiora, I didn't mean—" Giulia starts but Fiora chuckles, waving her down.

"It's alright, dear. You young girls want to spend time with your friends, of course you do," she says, although her gaze sticks on Michelle for a few beats longer than strictly necessary. She gives me a big hug.

"Oh, darling, happy birthday," she says warmly. "I hate to interrupt but your guest is already here. I set the tea up on the terrace for you both."

I crack a smile.

"Excellent!" I say. "Sorry, ladies, work waits for no one."

"Go, save Halice," Giulia only half mocks. "We'll see you later."

"Love you," I call back at them as I hurry out of the room. I stride confidently past the mosaic columns. The golden light of autumn spills across my home, giving everything a gorgeous warm glow as I head to the terrace. Sitting in a chair, looking slightly awkward as she gazes at the serenity of my garden, is the lone priestess.

Her eyes run over the trees sporting plumage of canary and cinnamon, the flowers offering their last blooms of the year with their tall purple stems or burgundy petals. The priestess is wearing her simple black dress again, the same white veil pinned to her warm hair that hangs loose down her back. Her head snaps around as I walk closer, the silks of my skirts billowing against my legs.

"Welcome," I say warmly. "Thank you so much for coming."

"Thank you for the invitation, signora," the priestess answers, a note of confusion in her tone.

"I'm Renza Di Maineri," I say warmly, sitting down.

"I know who you are, signora." The priestess nods, still clearly a little nervous. "Have I done something wrong?" The words explode from her mouth like she couldn't bear to hold them back.

"No. Not at all," I say, surprised. Her shoulders drop in relief. "How should I address you, signora?" I ask warmly.

"Ottavia, but my friends call me Otta," she answers. I reach over and pour some tea for the both of us.

"Then may I call you Otta?" I ask. Otta nods, taking a deep breath as she reaches for her tea. I set the pot back down.

"Thank you, signora."

"It's no trouble at all, and please, call me Renza. I've been wanting to talk to you for a little while actually. I hope I didn't interrupt anything important."

"The work of the gods is always important," Otta answers. I nod, sitting forwards.

"Of course, forgive me. I meant something more important. Being the only priestess left in this city, you must be in high demand. I'd hate to occupy you if you're needed elsewhere."

Otta sighs, her pink lips twisting as she looks at her tea, clearly seeing something else in her mind. "I wish the people had more."

"Soon there will be more," I say, confident in the knowledge of the deals signed last night. "Soon food and jobs and trade will be back."

"You sound ... certain..." Otta says, a sharp hope in her eyes as she studies my face.

"Do I?"

Otta smiles, sitting back in her seat and nodding slowly.

"If there is a plan in place, people will be very grateful, I'm sure. But why did you want to speak to me?" Otta asks, her face pulling slightly.

"Might I ask a personal question, Otta?" I say, setting down my teacup. Otta nods, her shoulders pinching as she waits for me to continue. I keep my body open and relaxed and give her a small smile.

"Why did you stay?" I ask gently. "The Holy Mother ordered the Holy Faith to leave."

Otta rolls her eyes at the mention of the Holy Mother.

"She ordered those who serve the Church to leave. I, however, serve a Faith," Otta says, surprising me with the strength running through her words, which are sharp and shining as iron. I wait patiently for a moment, but realise she won't reveal more unless I push gently.

"Forgive me, I didn't mean to offend. Perhaps my ignorance is showing," I say quietly, as though embarrassed. "But what do you mean?"

Otta presses her lips together, turning her eyes to the garden again before speaking.

"The Church is an institution made by man. There is power there and as such there's also struggle and the potential for injustice and corruption. It's controlled by a small, select few who are flawed humans, prone to pride and various hungers, fears and other selfish inclinations. As we all are. Through those few, the entire institution can be removed, reshaped, remade," Otta says setting her cup down. She moves her hands slowly as she speaks, and feeling pours into her next words. "I didn't take my Holy Vows to serve a Church. I took them to serve my Faith, my gods. The Church and Faith are not the same thing. Faith has a beautiful duality. It's both made and owned by one person and all people simultaneously. It's both a collective and an individual power. Ultimately you decide your own faith, but as a community we get to channel, challenge and change it for ourselves and others to make it what is needed. That is a fundamental power in the people. The institution of the Church tries to control that power. But it won't control me."

Otta smiles, then her eyes snap up to mine as though remembering where she is and who she's talking to. Her tone suddenly holds a nervous edge. "My faith tells me the people of Halice are suffering, and that my service can make a difference."

I sit back in my chair, a real smile slowly spreading across my face as I look at the small but passionate priestess in front of me. There is a fire and strength of will inside her that feels all too familiar. And that speech ... the power of the people ... could anything sound more Halician? For a woman not from our city originally – her mild Holy States accent makes that most clear – it's admirable.

"You *are* making a difference," I tell her. "I've listened to a few of your sermons. I've always come away feeling at peace."

She blinks, surprise fleeting across her face.

"You've heard me preach? When?"

"I try not to stand out. My presence tends to draw attention." I wrinkle my nose, but truthfully I don't mind it too much. In fact, more often than not it's useful. But at a religious gathering it feels distasteful.

"And you like what I have to say?" Otta says slowly, as though in disbelief.

"Tell me, what do you make of *my* situation?" I say, hand drifting to the necklace Idris gave me.

"You mean ... your Fated? You and Electi Patricelli?" Otta clarifies.

"Yes, and please, be truly honest. Everyone else gives their opinion freely – without invitation!" I chuckle. "But I really want to know what you think." Otta pauses, choosing her next words carefully.

"It's *my* belief that Father Fate doesn't give us our Fated as commands for actions to prove our loyalty," Otta says. She takes a deep breath before continuing. "Otherwise, Fate is nothing more than love or death. I think the Great Plan is a lot more complicated than that. I believe that Fate put you and Electi Patricelli together as Soulhates to teach you both something. Maybe to teach us all something."

"Teach us what?"

"That is for you to decipher. It's your bond. It's your

lesson," Otta says. "Perhaps about the power of doing what's right over self-gratification, perhaps about rethinking our enemies, perhaps it's supposed to get us questioning the things we know or think we understand. Or perhaps it's shaped your lives to give you the skills you need to live the life Fate intends."

I pause to mull that over. Now, that answer I like. I like it a lot, and am rather ashamed I haven't considered it before. Perhaps it isn't punishment for my blasphemy. Perhaps it isn't a sign of loathing or a test of faith. Fate is a father after all. Good fathers don't command, they teach.

"Priestess," I begin, "that is the most helpful and restorative thing I've ever been told about my faith. Thank you."

"I'm glad it could help." Otta smiles. "But that isn't why you brought me here, is it?"

"No," I say, picking up my teacup again. "No, I would like you to take over the Office of the Church. You can start by giving your sermons in the Watchtower in Market Square. I think the acoustics of that building will allow your message to reach even more people than your street sermons."

Otta's face is a picture of shock. She scrambles for words, setting down her teacup with a gentle clatter.

"I'm not a cardinal," Otta says hurriedly, brows pulling.

"Why not?" I ask. "You are the one serving the people. You are the one who stayed. You have a vision for a Holy Faith that serves the people of Halice. Why shouldn't you have the resources and authority to do some good?"

"But the Holy Faith—"

"You don't serve a Church," I repeat her words back to her. "You serve a Faith. Make your own Church, an independent Church. Preach for the people that need it."

Otta blinks hard, frozen in her seat as she tries to take in the position I've just offered her.

"Particularly with Agoi in just a couple of days," I say.

"Having a priestess lead the celebrations ... I think it would be a real balm to the people."

"Agoi is a festival of love and community," Otta says. "The people don't need me in order to know that. They'll feel their bonds of love to be at their strongest. The bonds of hate to be at their weakest."

"On the contrary, I think they could really, really use you," I say. "I know I have missed feeling at peace with my faith. I am certain others feel similarly."

Otta looks for something to say, blinking rapidly as she tries to find the words.

"There is no pressure. It's a lot to throw at you. But, please, consider it," I say patting her hand comfortingly. "At the very least, feel free to hold your sermons in the Watchtower. Particularly on Agoi."

Otta nods then bursts to her feet.

"Thank you, signora. I will consider it."

"Please, call me Renza," I answer warmly.

"Excuse me, I need to go. I have a funeral ... but thank you," Otta says again, as though dazed. I take a deep breath, watching her go for a moment. It will be interesting to see how that lands.

"Clever," chuckles Agosta, seeming to materialise out of nowhere before sitting in the seat the priestess recently vacated. I don't look at her, and instead sip on the last dregs of my tea.

"Funerals, weddings and naming ceremonies can take place again, with no Holy States oversight," Agosta continues. "A new Holy Faith."

"We should reward those who bravely serve even when others run in cowardice." I allow myself a small smile as I meet her sharp brown eyes. Agosta nods, a wicked smile blooming across her features.

"The Holy Faith will not be happy about that," Agosta councils, grinning. "They'll see this as an act of aggression, of undermining their power. People might see it as blasphemous."

"Not performing funerals because you want to conquer a land that isn't yours. Banning weddings and naming ceremonies for your own greed. That sounds blasphemous to me."

Agosta shrugs.

"I'm certainly no expert. More power to you. But if you want peace with the Holy States, this isn't the path," Agosta says seriously.

I nod slowly.

"You're probably correct. But I will not be blackmailed or bullied into submission." I set down my cup and stand up. "After all, I'm a Di Maineri. We never back down from a fight."

Agosta chuckles, although there is a dark cloud in her eyes as she rests her chin elegantly against her hand.

"Sometimes it's better to live and fight another day, dear. Survival sometimes requires compromises," she says quietly. I nod, turning around and heading back inside.

Again, she's right. But not today. Today we can win.

I plan to do just that.

CHAPTER 19

Today is going to be a good day. I've decided it.

I head up the familiar path to the Patricelli family home. The sun is shining, the birds are chirping, and we have a new trade partner to make the city stronger.

A fucking good day.

I knock on the front door, but as my last rap sounds, a loud cheer surges from the garden. Bemused, I walk around the side of the house and let myself in through the latched gate. Idris's guards don't stop me, my face all too regular a visitor here.

I stroll down the patterned stone path, winding amongst the flourishing lemon trees, their citrus perfume sweet and seductive. A large patio made of creamy stone slabs looks over the garden, and the large lawn slopes downhill with views of the city. A set of wide, shallow steps leads down from the patio to the lush green lawn, and standing in a circle on the grass at the base of those steps is a small group. Royah, Tahira, Karrius and Tiao are all in fighting clothes and they're standing watching two shirtless men wielding curved swords.

A noose of purring fire wraps around my throat when I realise one of those men is my Fated. My mouth goes dry and my pulse throbs hard under my collarbone. No matter how it burns, I can't tear my eyes away from sweaty, shirtless, chiselled Idris as he evades Bashran's vicious attack. Each sweep of Bashran's blade makes the bond purr and flex its claws in satisfaction, each near miss jolts through me as I simultaneously savour it and crave the sight of Idris's blood.

Both men are laughing, but their attacks are vicious as the swords swing through the air, their strikes skating past each other by mere inches. Idris moves with such speed – confidence and skill ooze off his every motion. His muscles flex and gleam in the sunshine, blond hair like spun firelight, his eyes blazing with purpose and determination.

Warmth spreads across my belly, my breath hitching as I fight to keep my breathing even. The whispers circle around my brain, pleading for violence, quivering with the anticipation of brutality. Idris all of a sudden snaps up straight. His head whips around to look at me, standing at the top of his patio stairs. He smirks, those golden eyes blazing with the fury of High Summer sun before he dodges Bashran's assault of opportunity and knocks him to the floor.

"Hey!" calls Tahira, waving up at me. "Come for the show?"

"I didn't realise I'd be getting one," I say, thankful my voice holds as I descend the steps towards the party.

"The boys are showing off," chuckles Royah. "I could kick their arses."

"Sounds like fighting talk," says Bashran as Idris helps him to his feet.

"I'm game." Royah grins viciously, flexing. Idris walks over, picking up a towel from the side and slinging it around his shoulders.

"Like what you see?" he teases. I roll my eyes, refusing to gape at his alarmingly close, sweaty, sculpted physique. If I do, all my purpose for today will be lost.

"Of course. Bashran is in excellent shape," I answer

brightly, causing the mountainous soldier to burst out laughing. "I'm sorry to interrupt the two of you getting hot and sweaty."

Idris's eyes gleam as Tahira snorts then quickly covers her mouth.

"Then don't interrupt, get involved. You're welcome to try your hand." Idris gestures to the space where the two men were just brawling. Fate's Fury, he's in a good mood today. Normally the idea of me in a fight would give the both of us hives and set him glowering into dark corners. I laugh, giving him a piercing look.

"Oh no, when I get Bash hot and sweaty, it'll be in private."

Bash chokes inelegantly on his drink, spraying it everywhere. Tahira and Royah descend into laughter. Idris's eyes gleam, not leaving my face for a moment. I raise a hand to the necklace around my throat, wondering if Idris will comment on the gift currently sitting there. His mouth twitches with amusement.

"Well then, I'd best whisk you away before you corrupt his training," Idris jokes, a bounce in his step as he leads me away from the group. I walk with him, desperately trying to ignore the tantalising, torturous heat radiating off him. Itchy goosebumps run across my arm, barely an inch from his as we walk inside the orangery.

The ceiling is made of a small glass dome, the thick walls a soft peach colour with pretty white flowers climbing around the corners. Large arched windows look outside, allowing so much light in we could still be outside enjoying the day. The floor is tiled with blue and white patterns, and several comfortable-looking chairs and tables fill the room.

Idris closes the glass door behind him then pulls the towel off his shoulders and drops it on one of the wooden tables.

"Did you want a drink?" he asks, moving towards one of the cabinets to pull out a tall vial of fruit juice.

"I'm alright, thanks," I say. "I arranged a new deal this morning I want to discuss."

"This morning? Already?" he asks, turning around. He leans against the cabinet, blue-stained glass in hand as he takes his drink. "You've been busy. After the success of last night you could've given yourself the morning off to enjoy it."

"Only thing better than one victory is a second, Idris," I tease, crossing to him. "Besides, there's never a day off when you work in politics. Haven't I taught you that by now?"

"Hmm." Idris narrows his eyes at me playfully, and my throat tightens. "I can think of another lesson you could teach me first."

"Did Tahira and Royah tell you about a priestess still preaching in the city?" I force the words out before his distractingly naked chest drains all sense from my body. An infernal pounding takes up residence behind my eyes. Idris shakes his head, brow puckering.

"No."

"I've been listening to her."

Idris stands up properly, all wicked intention washed away. He sets down his glass.

"I didn't know you were still attending services."

"I'm not really, but I stop to listen when I can, which isn't often." I sigh, folding my arms, suddenly feeling exposed to him. "She's not like any other preacher I've heard. She makes sense, Idris, and it made me realise how everything left this hole inside me where my faith should be. It's not just me, it's this city. I know you said we should promote a message of patriotism and Halician strength instead, but I already truly believe in that with all my heart and ... the gap of faith is still there."

Idris studies me with concern.

"I didn't know you were struggling," Idris says softly. I shrug, wishing his eyes didn't strip me naked with each passing second. I clear my throat awkwardly.

"Faith is a private matter," I answer gratingly. "I'm not a devoted believer, but I do believe."

"I know," Idris says as he takes my hand in his. He squeezes tightly, fireworks exploding along my palm. "I'm sorry, I should've realised."

"You're not religious. You have nothing to apologise for."

"Faith is important to you. And you can't deny that I am a very complicated piece of that," Idris says quietly. "I should've been checking in." Strings pluck painfully in my chest as I clear my throat.

"Your piece of my faith is decided," I say quietly. "The rest ... never quite seems to settle."

I look down at our locked fingers and try to crush my stampeding breaths into a regular pattern.

"The priestess is called Ottavia, and I've offered her the Offices of the Church, to create an independent Halician faith."

Idris freezes for a long moment, eyes locked on our joined hands before a sharp, amused breath leaks from his lips.

"So if the Church won't do what you want, you'll create your own? My-my, that won't go down well with the Holy Mother."

"She's playing games, and I don't lose games," I answer. Idris barks with laughter, stepping forwards. He raises his other hand to my cheek, his fingers planting hot, sizzling sparks that ripple all the way across my face and neck.

"What about peace with the Holy States?" Idris asks, mirth in his voice. His thumb slowly brushes along my jaw, branding me with each deliriously slow second that passes.

"If we don't stand up to them now, they'll try to bully us forever. We might be small, but we are mighty. Once they understand they can't manipulate us, that their cause is a doomed fantasy from another era, then we can create a lasting peace."

"Hmmm." Idris's deep voice sends dark, devious ripples

down my spine. "What happened to not acting alone? You just offered her the job without talking to anyone?"

"You were the one saying if we're going to save this city we should act," I remind him.

"Using my own words against me?" Idris smirks. "Okay, Di Maineri, if it's already happening, what do you want from me?"

"So many things," I answer softly, leaning closer to him. My breath is like fire as it leaves my lips tingling. "But namely, listen to her speak. Come with me on Agoi, to show support."

"I don't do religion," Idris says on a groan, face wrinkling with distaste. "I've listened to different preachers across the world – here, in Chalgos, Malaya, Coari, Kavas... It doesn't sit with me."

"I know. But, please, it could make all the difference if we're both there on Agoi to give her some powerful backers," I answer. Idris sighs, mulling it over. The silence between us swells to the point of painful. I don't back down, don't blink, just wait for his answer.

"Alright. One service. I might not have much faith in Fate," Idris murmurs softly, dropping his head down to inches above mine, "but I do in you."

"Thank you."

"But you owe me," Idris says, running a finger across my jaw towards my chin. His blistering breath crashes over my nose, his agonising, addictive touch hooking like thorns into my skin.

"Owe you?" I repeat softly, eyes fluttering. "Is that how we do things now?"

"Don't worry, all I'm asking for in return is the truth," Idris whispers, his lips so close I can feel them ghost across mine.

"Admit it," he practically purrs. Pins and needles dance across my skin, shuddering up my spine. Meeting his eyes is an addictive kind of torture. That wicked heat claws deeper and deeper into my chest.

"Admit what?" I gulp.

"Admit what you've refused to for weeks. What you felt last night seeing me all dressed up. What you felt this morning, sneaking into my garden to spy on me." Idris steps forwards, pushing me until my back is against the cool plaster of the wall. I swallow, my blood turned to racing lava under my skin. His hand catches my wrist and circles the dainty flesh in callous, sweltering fire against the harsh stone. The other slowly sweeps down my side, stealing a feel of my curves.

"Admit it. I was never just a distraction, was I?" His wretched lips brush tantalisingly against my ear, flooding my mind with fire. The air between us is thick and fizzing with dark energy. Tight and humid sparks spit in warning of the storm about to break.

"No." I almost whimper the word as his fingers dig into my hip.

"You've already had my confession. Now it's your turn. Tell me," Idris breathes. I'm awash with his scent of lavender and mint, the dark, dangerous heat of his body that makes me feel drunk.

"You ... you..." I gasp, wrestling the urge inside me that wants to dig my nails into his shoulders, to kiss him or throw him away still undecided, but both will be an inevitability soon. His hands press into my waist, trapping me against the immovable wall of his chest.

"Admit it," Idris whispers.

"You're my Fated," I manage to snap out, grabbing hold of the bite of these sparks and letting it run free on my tongue.

"You can do better than that."

Indignation flares inside me. My one free hand is buried in his hair and I tug to exert a modicum of control. Of power.

"Make me," I challenge, breathy and feverish.

Idris's mouth descends onto mine. Every nerve, every fibre, every tiny scrap of being explodes with fire and fury. The delicious, exacting movement of his lips melts my senses.

His strong hands move with confidence over the curves of my body, blissfully, blindingly igniting everything in their path. I'm drowning and devouring him, the divine poison of his lips, the punishing, paradoxical work of his tongue.

The war of our bodies is fought amidst burning breaths and fevered moans. My hands trail the landscape of his muscles, memorising every excruciating chiselled ab. He's a masterpiece.

He obliterates any space between us, the full length of his manhood pressing through his trousers and the silk of my dress to imprint against my thigh. Every long, hard, impressive inch sends my mind spinning to dark, dirty, devastating places. A hot, needy urge coils between my legs as the battle of our lips wages on. It is a war of clashing teeth and swiping tongues.

The noises escaping me are lustful and brazen as I thread my fingers through his hair, arching my back as his hands work their way around to my ass. He squeezes tightly, his fingers burning into the flesh like a brand.

"Ahem," Tahira's voice interrupts.

The pain hurtles to the forefront again, the bond roaring like lightning to blind me, battering like a sledgehammer to my skull. I recoil in pain, shoving Idris away. I press my hands to my face, blocking Idris from my sight as I desperately wrestle to steady my breathing. The voice of Fate screams rampantly around my mind, dominating its every corner. Every nerve is on a razor's edge, every bone in my body slicing and blistering.

"What?" growls Idris behind me, his voice an aching, roaring acid fraying at the threads of my control.

"This can't wait. It's Alfieri," says Tahira, her voice sober. A pang of worry stabs through me.

"What happened?" I suck in a short, bitter breath.

"He's hurt. Badly," Tahira says, looking between us both. Horror swells in my belly, churning like a violent storm.

No. No. He was working for me, for the bank. This is all my fault.

Idris springs into action. "We'll leave immediately. Have you got this?"

"I do now," I answer hotly. "Move!"

Idris nods and races out of the room, leaving me and Tahira alone together.

"Come on," Tahira says, gesturing with her head. "We can arrange the carriage while he finds his clothes." I muster a nod, my mind struggling to recover from the whiplash I just put it through. I hurry with her through the house, towards the front door. Everyone is readying to leave, except of course Karrius and Taio, who will remain where it's safest.

I stand by the front door, nervously chewing on my lip as my thoughts jump to Alfieri. My cheerful, steadfast friend.

How bad is it when Tahira says "badly"?
Will he be okay?
How on earth is Emilia doing? Does she even know?

A million questions fly around my head as image upon image of possible injuries stalk my imagination. I don't know what to do. Tahira squeezes my shoulder, trying to keep me calm as Idris reappears, a fresh burgundy tunic pulled over his workout trousers as we rush out the door.

To find our friend.

CHAPTER 20

The carriage ride is frantic. Idris sacrifices comfort for speed, and I'm grateful. The rattling wheels fly over the uneven cobbles and the silence inside is fraught.

I grip onto the plush velvet seat of Idris's carriage, knuckles turning white as my pulse races and I fight to stay in my seat. My earrings jangle and slap around my neck, tangling with my hair, and my jaw is locked to prevent me biting my tongue. Idris glowers out the window. It's impressive that half the buildings on our route aren't rendered to ash and cinders under that glare.

We pull up outside Alfieri's home, which is built of creamy Halician brick with gothic windows. Idris doesn't wait for the carriage to properly stop before throwing open the door. He hops down then turns back to offer me a hand. I take it, inelegantly dropping onto the path as we race for the door.

Idris's hand doesn't leave mine; our palms are welded as he pulls me up the wooden stairs until he comes to a room whose pretty panelled door is already open.

In a large four-poster bed, surrounded by silk sheets of navy and cream, lies a pale-looking Alfieri. The bay window allows soft sunlight to flutter into the room, highlighting the bloody bandages wrapped around his chest. My stomach falls. My eyes sting. Emilia sits next to Alfieri, holding his hand tightly as the doctor finishes his inspections.

"Alfie." Idris leaps forwards, his hand finally leaving mine as he hurries to his friend's bedside. My feet refuse to move. It's like I've melted into the dark wood floor. I gape at my friend, my heart thumping in my throat.

"What's all this? Causing a fuss over nothing, huh?" Idris's teasing doesn't mask the worry in his voice.

"Hardly nothing," the doctor counters reproachfully as he continues his work. Emilia starts crying, both hands clamped over her face as she folds over into Alfieri's shoulder.

"Hey, I'll be fine. It's okay," Alfieri murmurs softly, stroking her hair. But the drained colour of his face and the way the doctor refuses to meet anyone's eye takes all comfort from his words.

"Absolutely no moving from this bed. Lots of liquids, lots of rest. I'll be back in two hours to check on things but send for me if you start feeling even slightly worse. I'll leave you to your loved ones," the doctor says. "But I mean it, take things slowly. Don't rip those stitches, no matter what you do!"

The doctor gathers his things to leave. As he passes, I take his arm and step outside to speak with him.

"Doctor, how bad is it?" I ask quietly, where no one can hear us.

"He's not out of the woods. Fate's Fury, he can't even see the tree line." The doctor breathes deeply. "It's a coin flip right now. If he makes it through the next two days ... we'll know more."

My stomach drains through my feet as I swallow, but nothing moves the cold, frozen lump swelling in my throat.

"I'm paying this bill," I manage to croak. "Please send it to me."

The doctor nods before leaving.

"What happened, Alfie?" asks Idris darkly.

"We were ambushed by the Holy States, outnumbered four to one," Alfieri answers thickly. "They knew where we'd be and what we were carrying."

He looks straight at me. My cargo; the bank's cargo. I let out a shuddering breath, my hand going to my mouth. Idris looks between us, suspicion crawling onto his face.

"What were you carrying?"

"Bank tithes!" spits Emilia, fury contorting her features. Her face is red and carved with a rage I've never seen in her before. All aimed at me. Her dark eyes are bursting with tears as she throws herself to her feet.

"How could you do this?" Emilia yells at me. "How could you put him in danger like that?"

"Em, stop it," Alfie says, though the sharpness of his words doesn't hit true. "It's not her fault."

"You almost died! You were sliced open from chest to navel, Alfie!" Emilia is shaking with grief, her words swollen and raw. "I almost lost you, and for what? For her money!"

Tears sting in my eyes. My breath hitches and my throat swells. Idris closes his eyes and rubs his brow. He turns to look at me, his expression expectant but lacking the judgement I thoroughly deserve.

"It was for the bank. To keep it afloat," I manage, words trembling and watery with shame.

"I didn't know things were that dire," Idris says quietly. A fat tear falls to streak down my cheek. Shame at my tears, shame at my actions, they both clog my throat and shudder in my hands.

"If the bank goes under, Halice will crumble." I don't know how audible my breathy, half-hiccupping words are. "I never ... I didn't know it would ... I would never have done this—"

"Renza," Alfieri says seriously. "We made the deal. There are always risks in my work. I agreed. You did nothing wrong."

"She should've never asked you in the first place!" shouts Emilia, throwing out her hands in frustration as she turns her ire on me. "I've barely seen him because he's been running your money. I've been sick to my stomach every day, knowing he was putting himself at so much risk for you, for your bank!"

"This isn't about shallow profits. It's to keep it running. A collapsed bank would be a disaster." I hiccup, blinking hard as fresh tears spring to my lash line. I wish I could destroy them, press them back into my eyes like they weren't there. I deserve this. I deserve Emilia's wrath.

"She's right. That would be … an unmitigated disaster," Idris says quietly. Emilia's face creases, fury on her tongue.

"*This* is a disaster! Alfie could have died!" she spits. "That deal is done! No more!"

"Of course," I whisper. The hatred in Emilia's eyes could bury me alive.

"I hope the funds I've delivered have helped," groans Alfieri. I freeze, trying to process that before taking in a sharp breath.

"What funds?" I ask seriously. Alfieri blinks hard as all heads in the room turn to look at me.

"The tithes from the other banks," Alfieri says slowly, his brow furrowed.

"But you haven't delivered any yet..." I trail off as Alfieri starts shaking his head.

"This was my fourth run," Alfieri says quietly. "I've already dropped off three shipments. Emilia, could you grab my books?"

"Seriously? Right now?" hisses Emilia in outrage.

"Yes," Idris says insistently, looking at Emilia. "Because if Renza doesn't know about these shipments, it's because Giulia doesn't know about them. Which begs the question, what's happened to all that money?"

I scramble to catch up. "Someone is hiding the money or stealing it."

"Alfieri is lying here covered in blood and you're worried about money?" shrieks Emilia.

"Em!" snaps Alfieri, wincing as he does so. "This is important."

"So are you!" Emilia scowls. "More important than any of this!"

Alfieri's expression softens as Emilia holds her face in her hands and cries quietly. Alfieri reaches for her, holding onto her leg to comfort her.

"You're right, Emilia," says Idris quietly. "Alfieri is important, which is why we need to know what happened. Why did the Holy States find Alfieri this time? Why suddenly were they ready in overwhelming numbers to ambush him in just the right spot? Alfie went from making three runs completely undisturbed to this? That isn't an accident or bad luck."

"Someone told them," I say on a breath, horror swelling in my stomach like a flood. My pulse rushes in my ears as blood drains from my fingers.

"Someone sold Alfieri out?" Emilia asks in a brittle voice. Alfieri takes her hand gently.

"I'm okay. Sweetheart, look at me, I'm right here," Alfieri soothes, rubbing her hand with his fingers before turning his attention to me. "Who would do that?"

"I don't know. The same person hiding the money? Where did you deliver it?" I frown.

"Right to the bank doors," Alfieri says. "I have dates in my book, amounts, fees taken—"

"We need to go to the bank." I find a firmness returning to my words. "Find this traitor."

"Traitor?" Tahira and Royah have finally made it up the stairs to join us. I nod slowly.

"Bank stuff," I explain quickly.

"How can we help?" Tahira offers immediately.

"Are you sure?" I ask, surprised. "This isn't your problem..."

"That's what friends do, isn't it?" Tahira asks, a wicked

smile on her face. "Besides, if your bank goes under, so does the deal that'll make us all filthy rich."

"We can't let anyone know why we're there or what we're looking for," I say. "Idris, you stay here—"

"Not a chance. Someone did this to Alfieri. I want them found and justice delivered," Idris snarls.

"This information can't leave this room – except for Giulia of course. We'll need her. She'll find that money," I answer. "Anyone could be involved."

"There's no time to waste and a lot of papers to go through," Idris says. "Let's go."

"Emilia, want me to send for someone?" I ask. "I could ask Michelle or Serra—"

"You've done enough!" Emilia scowls. "Get out!"

I nod and swallow as I leave with my head down. Alfieri's injuries will not be in vain. I will find this monster and I will bring them to justice. Fate as my witness.

CHAPTER 21

"So this is the Di Maineri Bank." I pretend to be giving Tahira and Royah a tour. No one bats an eye, though a few people give the mercenaries guarded looks. I gesture around the light space, pointing out the accountants sitting at their polished wooden tables, the pale stone columns decorated in blue paint, the large blue glass dome that makes up the ceiling depicting little snippets of my family history.

No one can know the real reason we're here, and this seems like the most reasonable cover story. It's not nearly as funny as the last time I needed a cover story for being here, but I don't have it in me to yell at Idris today. Not with Alfieri as injured as he is.

"Oh, nice," Tahira says, real appreciation in her voice. "Who built this?"

"This building was commissioned by my grandfather, but my great-grandfather started the bank," I answer as we walk.

"The same grandfather that built the High Chamber?" asks Royah. I nod as we ascend the steps to my sister's office.

"Yes. Some say he built the bank to test his theories for the High Chamber. You can certainly see the influence of his favourite architect who ended up shaping some of the most signature elements of our city."

"More lemons," notes Tahira. I pause, a question in my eyes.

"The depictions," Tahira explains and gestures to a few old carvings gracing the walls.

"The lemon tree is on the Di Maineri family seal," explains Idris. "So it's fitting it covers their bank."

"So that's why they're all over your house, too!" says Royah. I nod, smiling. Before being bankers, my ancestors were citrus farmers, and my great-grandfather claimed the tree as our crest to remind us of our humble roots.

It doesn't take long to reach Giulia's office. I knock and push my way in carefully.

Sitting behind her desk, quill in hand, is my sister. Her golden hair falls over the table like a waterfall of sunshine and her head rests in her hand. On the sofa, a sketchpad on her knees and charcoal in her fingers, is Michelle. Both look up at my entrance.

"Are you two alone?" I ask.

Giulia nods, frowning. "Yes, what's going on?"

I open the door wider, allowing everyone into the room. Idris first, followed by Tahira and finally Royah. Michelle and Giulia tense as Royah enters the room. She hangs close to the door, a small, stilted smile on her face.

I close the door firmly, twisting the lock before going to my sister.

"We have a problem," I say seriously, taking her hands. "Alfieri has been smuggling money from the other bank branches here for a few weeks now."

"He what?" Giulia gapes.

"He's delivered three different shipments," Idris says, putting the leather ledger on the desk for her to read. "On the fourth he was ambushed by the Holy States."

"Oh my gosh, is he okay?" Michelle gasps.

"It's ... touch and go," I say, my voice thick. "He's hurt badly."

"Poor Alfie... But wait, wait, three shipments?" Giulia queries, poring over the information in her books. "Three absurdly large shipments – this is months and months of tithes! Fate's Fury, we haven't received this money! I've never seen a penny!"

"I know," I say seriously. "You've never seen it, but Alfieri swears he delivered it right to our door. Right to this building."

Giulia straightens, taking a deep breath as anger pools behind her features. Her face is a picture as her blue eyes narrow into slits.

"Seriously? Another traitor?" she hisses. "First Dorado and now this?"

"We need to find the money," I say darkly. Giulia nods, rubbing the back of her neck.

"Not to be a pain, but wouldn't it just be in the vault or something? Unless someone walked off with it?" asks Tahira with a frown. "Alfieri said he delivered it to the door."

"Yes, it's probably in there," I agree.

"Okay, so can't you just walk down there and find it?" Tahira asks, eyes darting around as though trying to understand.

"We have a lot of money in a lot of vaults with systems that move it about for accountancy reasons. The vault totals are counted every two weeks and verified by three different teams," Giulia says, shaking her head. "There's a whole counterbalance process to ensure accuracy. If the money is there, it's being reported but not correctly."

"What does that mean?" asks Tahira, folding her arms as she tries to keep up. "How do you hide that kind of money if it's being reported?"

"There are lots of ways but boiled down I would say it's been allocated somewhere we can't touch, making it practically invisible to our profit and loss books," Giulia says. "Money that should be ours – the bank's – outright, is being hidden in our system somewhere that we can't use it."

Giulia runs a finger down the totals again.

"Seven per cent handling fee?" Giulia murmurs, giving me a sharp sideways glance.

"I was trying to keep us afloat," I breathe. "I was desperate. I didn't know Alfieri would get hurt—"

"It's illegal. You don't stand for that!" Giulia hisses at me. "You're an Electi!"

"Exactly. The collapse of the bank would cause devastation across the city. Riots, starvation – not to mention priming us for invasion! It's not just about us!" I answer, but the shame takes the feeling from my words.

"What's done is done," Idris says, trying to stem the argument before it kicks off. "Let's find the people who hurt Alfieri and handle it."

"Would the money being reported correctly have made a difference?" asks Michelle, walking around the table to her side. She places a hand on Giulia's back in support.

"Yes!" Giulia laughs wryly, rubbing the scar on her jaw as she thinks. "While it wouldn't make our problems evaporate, if we sacrifice taking any profit like we have been, this could keep everything going for so much longer. I've been worrying about getting through the next three weeks, but this buys us months."

"Would the Holy States know that?" asks Royah quietly from the back of the room. "I mean, if the bank goes under then the chaos in the streets would make you ripe for a hostile invasion. It speaks to motive."

"Thanks to Dorado, they probably had a very detailed understanding of our bank before he died," I grumble. "It wouldn't be hard to work out."

"Dorado might've had collaborators here," adds Idris. "Maybe it's his collaborators doing this now?"

"I had everyone questioned. Everyone suspicious was let go," Giulia says. "I wasn't playing games."

"Maybe we missed someone." I groan, pinching the bridge of my nose.

"Well, first things first. Let's find the money. We have work to do," Michelle says. "I'll find Philo. Ask him to bring ledgers for accounts that received any income on these days."

"Who's Philo?" asks Idris instantly.

"My assistant," Giulia says. "Dorado's replacement. We can trust him. He's reliable."

"I'll go with you," Idris says to Michelle as the two head for the door. "We don't need him getting suspicious or alerting anyone."

As they reach the door, Michelle exchanges a long, awkward look with Royah as they pass.

The awkwardness lingers. I don't know what to say, wondering if I should do anything. But we need to work together, and there is no mind sharper for numbers than Giulia.

"Giu, if you were hiding the money, how would you do it?" I ask. Giulia sits down in her seat again, the chair creaking slightly as she considers my question.

"I would start by staggering the deposits, placing them in various accounts so a large influx wouldn't catch attention. I'd make sure all deposits were recorded and in place before the next vault count so nothing would seem amiss. I'd hide it in accounts under fake names or belonging to people I trust and I would keep the money moving. If the money is constantly moving around accounts, then the bank can't touch it even temporarily."

"Because it's not in one place long enough to assess how much can sit in the stationary funds," I finish quietly. Giulia nods.

"What are you talking about?" asks Tahira, confused.

"Banks don't make money by holding onto people's money

and doing nothing with it," Giulia explains, tapping the table. "We put the money to work. We invest it into trade, businesses, loans, you name it. That's how we can have accounts offering interest rates and make a profit."

"But if you're investing the money, what happens when people want to withdraw it?" asks Tahira with a frown.

"They can get hold of it," Giulia explains. "Because everyone comes together and puts all their money in the same place, everyone's money can be accessed as required."

"So it's a community-benefits situation?" Royah says, catching on quickly. "Because everyone comes together to keep their cash in the same place, provided everyone doesn't withdraw everything all at the same time, you'll have a certain steady pot of cash sitting there that you, as the bank, can use to make more money with various investments and loans. And that in turn benefits the community by giving them access to loans, making additional money from interest rates on savings, keeping their money safer and other things."

"We call the money the bank uses the stationary fund," Giulia answers, not really looking at Royah. "It pays bills, wages, is given as loans, everything. And it's been running on fumes, barely scraping by. We're mere weeks away from not being able to cover the fluid funds – the money people need day to day."

"And if that happens, people lose confidence in the bank, they race to withdraw their money and, poof! Everything implodes," I finish, running both my hands through my hair. I take a deep breath and bite my lip.

"Okay, so the culprit knows how the bank operates in order to hide the money," says Royah, approaching the desk. "So who has that kind of insight?"

"Several people," Giulia and I answer together.

"I didn't know banks worked that way," Tahira admits quietly.

"There are many ways banks make money. Facilitating

trade, like with yourselves, is another way," I say, shaking my head. Giulia starts riffling through the papers on her desk, gathering details on count dates and totals against the times in Alfieri's books.

I walk towards Giulia's window. Guilt swells in my throat, clogging my airways slightly as I look down over the city. I don't see the wide streets of Halice. I see Alfieri on that bed, bloody bandages stretched across his middle. I see Emilia's justifiable rage, the tears spilling down her cheeks.

Tahira stands next to me.

"You alright?" Tahira asks quietly. She doesn't have to be here but stands ready to help. She owes us nothing; she doesn't know much about banking, she doesn't really care about Halice or my family, but she's still here. To offer support. The princess in all but blood who came when Idris called for help and stayed when she didn't need to. Someone Idris trusts implicitly with a secret like this, not even questioning if she can keep it to herself.

The Princess of War leans against the wall, sunlight striking across her large, looping curls and angular features. Her dark eyes are intense as she studies me.

"I put Alfieri up to this," I say quietly.

"And if you hadn't, we wouldn't have realised you have a traitor in your bank," Tahira reasons.

"It was illegal. I knew it was wrong, and I did it anyway," I whisper, shaking my head. Tahira sighs, chewing on the words. She looks out of the window with me and hesitates before speaking.

"I've seen a lot of war," Tahira says quietly. "Seen a lot of leaders navigating crises. In times of hardship, all leaders have one thing in common: they make sacrifices and take risks. Sometimes it's morals, sometimes materials, sometimes lives. The good ones sacrifice for the greater good, the bad ones do it for themselves. You and I are leaders. We are the ones who have to decide what to sacrifice." Tahira turns her gaze back to me.

"You weighed up the options and you made the call. Someone had to."

"This isn't who I am or what I stand for." I swallow, shaking my head. "The law is the law for a reason. It stands to protect and defend. *I* should be better. I should've found another way—"

"Laws and rules and morals are all well and dandy when things are going well," Tahira cuts me off, her tone gentle but firm, "but we're talking about the literal survival of your entire city. That changes everything. What we consider justifiable risks and acceptable consequences shift into an entirely different world. Nothing is off the table. You had to act, and you did. You heard your sister; this money makes all the difference. Had we not agreed to trade, your actions with Alfieri could've made or broken *everything*."

"But now we have our trade with you—"

"Which you didn't have then, nor any inkling of its possibility," Tahira counters, dark eyes going sharp and serious. "Look at Idris. You know he's fierce over his friends. Does he blame you?"

I pause. Idris hasn't said a bad word to me at all.

"He'd be a hypocrite if he did." Tahira chuckles. "Idris has made rough calls on behalf of this city several times. He doesn't beat himself up over it. There was a need, and he acted."

"His actions almost started a three-way mercenary war in our city ... no offence," I answer. Tahira cracks a wicked grin and nods.

"None taken. There was risk, but he weighed it and made a judgement call. Survival was at stake, and he acted, just like you did. Now look where you stand, allied with the best military force in the world and the promise of money in your pocket." Tahira grins as she compliments her own soldiers. "The sacrifice of a few strangers' lives and a couple of stressful days was worth it, no?"

"I can't think like that. I don't trade in lives," I argue. Tahira presses her lips together into a line and takes a deep breath.

"You do now, Renza. Your city is at war."

My mouth goes dry, the weight of her words settling uncomfortably in my chest. Any week now I might be sending soldiers to their deaths on a battlefield to defend Halice. If the Holy States decide to invade, that order would come down.

"That's why we have a High Chamber." My voice is coarse. "We make decisions together, as a united people."

"Perhaps," Tahira says with a shrug, "but you exert serious power over the chamber. I saw it. Where you lead, they follow. Soon you'll have to make the choice."

Tahira reaches out to take my arm and looks me in the eye. She speaks gently.

"For what it's worth, I'm certain you'll do better than most. You're a warrior. You won't give up," Tahira says, dropping her hand and leaning back against the wall. I frown.

"I can barely hold a dagger—"

"You wield words better than many hold a blade. I've seen your words save lives, dismantle precarious situations, raise spirits and change hearts. A warrior of words is sometimes overlooked, but such a person is vital. Without them we'd never be able to stop violence before it starts."

I open my mouth to respond when the door is pushed open. Idris walks in, followed by Michelle and a very worried-looking Philo. He's tall and lanky, with dusty brown hair, a narrow nose and wide mouth.

"Philo?" Giulia asks sharply. Philo doesn't flinch.

"I'm bringing up the books. I've also asked for Roberta to come up when she gets in. She's been working the night shifts recently and she's supposed to report any night deposits," Philo says instantly. He walks over to Giulia's desk and stands next to her as he pulls out a fresh piece of paper. "How much are we looking for combined?"

"You know?" I ask sharply, narrowing my eyes at Idris.

"He worked it out." Idris scowls unhappily at the young man. "When we made the request to see the accounts."

"To see that many accounts at once means someone is doing something serious that they shouldn't," Philo murmurs, looking at Giulia's numbers. "And this is supposed to be tithes from the other banks? How did it get here?"

"Doesn't matter." Philo's eyebrows shoot up and he nods.

"Alright then. Let's get to work."

"What do we do?" asks Royah, stretching out her fingers.

"Get ready to do a lot of maths." Idris chuckles and Royah's face drops unhappily.

"We are looking to find the money that equals this amount," Giulia says. "Over a few days but always before the next full vault count."

The books start piling in. Books upon books upon books. Everyone pitches in, though it must be said that Giulia and Philo are the best at putting the pieces together, probably doing a solid seventy per cent of the work. Michelle, Idris and I contribute as much as we can, Tahira and Royah chipping in on occasion, too, very pleased when they add something of value.

Hours pass as we isolate the accounts. Seven of them, four of them new, three of them very, very old that have been dormant for twenty-five years before becoming active again all of a sudden with their deposits. The money is circulating between them all, constantly on the move, almost daily.

Who is doing that?

"Okay, well ... we've found it," Philo says, throwing down his quill and stretching out his neck. "Every penny. Once we close the accounts we can reallocate the funds appropriately."

"But who made up these accounts? Who is trying to hide it? Do these people even exist?" asks Giulia. Philo shrugs.

"Whoever did this can bypass the system and create accounts without any supervision," I say quietly.

"Someone high-up then," Philo says, tapping the table.

That's when a knock comes at the door.

"Enter," calls Giulia. In walks a young woman with thick brown hair scraped back into a neat bun. Her blue eyes are wide as she surveys the scene, all of us spread out with books and pages and pages of scribbled sums.

"I was told you wanted to see me?" Roberta asks, clearing her throat.

"Shut the door," Giulia instructs. Royah gets up from the floor as Roberta enters the room. She quietly slips over to the door, casually leaning against it to block the exit.

"Why didn't you report the large nighttime deposits?" asks Philo, the edge in his voice feeling uncharacteristic.

"I did." Roberta frowns.

"I didn't know about them," says Philo.

"I was told to report them directly to Signora Di Maineri."

"I didn't get them," Giulia snaps.

"No, not you, signora," Roberta clarifies. "Signora Rialta Di Maineri. Your aunt."

I could laugh. I raise both hands to my face, rubbing at my eyes ruefully as I lean back on the sofa. I take a deep breath.

Of course.

I exchange a look with Giulia, and oh, my sister. The rage in her eyes ... she could burn this place to cinders and commit atrocities far worse than murder.

"I didn't tell you to do that," Philo says, his voice dangerously quiet. Roberta goes pale.

"But ... but your letter was waiting for me. Signed by you. On my desk," Roberta insists.

"Do you still have the letter?" I ask dryly.

"No, I threw it away," Roberta says, her face dropping. "But it's your signature. I know your signature."

"Not well enough to spot a forgery," Philo says quietly.

"I can give you my records of deposit," Roberta says. "I always keep duplicates. They're in the office."

"Please, that would be useful," Idris says. "Royah will go with you."

Roberta turns, jumping when she sees the mercenary leaning against the door and smiling intimidatingly. The two women leave.

"Your aunt would really do this?" asks Michelle.

"Yes," Giulia and I say at the same time.

"Di Maineri infighting strikes again." I scowl, tossing my pages of calculations onto the table.

"I can't believe I didn't see it sooner." Giulia half groans, half laughs with exasperation. "All that pushing to sever this branch of the bank. To give her control of what's left so we don't sink the entire family."

"She was ready to sink the ship." I scowl. "Just to be captain of the crash."

"But she's your family..." Tahira asks, confused.

"Which is why we should've suspected her sooner," I grumble, standing up. "Never trust a Di Maineri, isn't that what they say?"

"There are a few exceptions – present company being a good example," Idris says, gesturing to Giulia and me. "Okay, so we have proof. We can convict her."

I press my lips together.

"We have proof ... but we could have more."

"What are you planning?" asks Giulia suspiciously. I give her a wicked grin before turning to Idris again.

"Ask Savino to meet us. It's time for my aunt to find out exactly who she's messing with."

CHAPTER 22

We're going to catch Rialta in the act. We've arranged to have Roberta report another delivery straight to her the very next morning. Hopefully Rialta won't have heard about Alfieri's injuries – it shouldn't be common knowledge.

When she gets the report from Roberta, she'll start covering it up and we'll have the City Guard ready to arrest her.

Giulia spent the night at Michelle's, opting not to tempt herself by looking our aunt in the face. I only just managed to hold my nerve at dinner as she babbled about options for the bank again.

Whenever things looked dicey, I turned my thoughts to Giulia. She and Michelle are back together. Together and happy! If the situation were any different, I'd throw a party. But the current mood makes that feel insensitive.

Fiora could tell something was up, but she didn't say anything with her sisters around. Her face when she learned where Giulia was made me bite my tongue. She looked half-ready to march to the Garden and retrieve her by force.

But now it's time. Rialta has been working in her office for almost thirty minutes. She'll be in the thick of it.

Idris, Savino and four City Guards are with me as we walk through the halls of the Di Maineri Bank. The guards' boots stamp on the polished floors, the swords at their sides glinting in the morning sunshine as we approach Rialta's office.

I don't knock. I just push through the door into the room.

Rialta is sitting at a desk, a ledger open and a quill in her hand.

"What is the meaning of—?" she starts to shout indignantly as the guards swarm the room.

"By order of the Electi, Rialta Di Maineri is under arrest for fraud and embezzlement," says Savino, producing the arrest warrant.

Rialta's face falls as the guards pull her from the desk, her dress sleeves trailing as the quill drops from her hands. I pick up the ledger, shaking my head ruefully.

"Yep, one of the seven accounts," I announce darkly, handing it to Idris.

"What are you talking about? I'm just recording deposits," Rialta argues, her face contorted with rage as her arms are forced behind her back and the chains are slapped into place.

"Don't bother lying. We have witnesses and evidence," I say. "You deliberately tried to sink the bank. You wanted your bank in the Wheel City to be the biggest, and you wanted to take over as Head of the Bank from Giulia."

Rialta throws me a withering look.

"You don't deserve it. Neither did Tomas. Neither of you was ever devoted to our family legacy! It was always Halice this and Halice that!" she spits as she's dragged towards us. The City Guards don't care about being gentle. "You'll ruin us all!"

"And you'll spend the rest of your life in a prison cell," I promise her. Rialta laughs once, the noise broken and bitter.

"You think the rest of the family will let me rot here?" Rialta sneers.

"Yes. They will. Because they only care about what they can get from you, and now that's nothing," I answer. A light of worry sparks in Rialta's eyes as they narrow.

"Get her out of here," commands Savino.

"Gather everything for examination," Idris commands the remaining City Guards.

I take a deep breath and turn away, pressing a hand to my throat. The person who put Alfieri in danger has been found. The villain – the traitor – came from inside my own house. Not on behalf of the Holy States, but on behalf of her own greed. Her own sense of entitlement.

I could punch a hole in the wall. Or in her face.

My fist trembles. My grip shakes. The bond purrs, grating against my mind as I battle the onslaught of violent urges screaming in my skull. Idris starts talking to the City Guards, his voice like a thousand nails scraping down my spine.

I squeeze my eyes shut, trying to focus on anything else. But all I can think of is my rage, the betrayal, my anger. The bond snarls and gnashes its teeth, gleefully ramming hot pokers down my throat and clawing at my eyes. Idris's voice throbs like a viper clamping its jaw on my brain.

I bend over my knees and pant as the violence chews on my limbs and sears down my throat.

"Renza?" Idris says my name.

"NO!" I scream at Idris, clamping my hands over my ears, digging my fingers into my scalp as I war with the loathing coursing through my limbs.

"Breathe, Renza, breathe." Idris's words fuel indignation and disgust as they bubble to life in my belly. His hand on the small of my back snaps my fraying control.

"DON'T TOUCH ME!" I shriek, wheeling around to shove him. I use all my strength, throwing him to the floor. He crashes against the desk on the way down, the wood screaming against the polished tile.

Blood drains from my face as Idris holds up his hands in surrender from his awkward position on the floor. I shake my head, breathing frantically as I stare at my hands. The compulsion to feel his blood slick on my palms, to curl my fingers tight around his neck—

"Renza, leave," Savino says quietly, his voice an anchor to reality. He steps in front of me, blocking Idris from view. "Come on, walk with me."

Savino walks me backwards as I close my eyes and wrestle the bond into fraught submission. Savino accompanies me all the way down the corridor, backing off only as I stagger to grip the wall two hundred paces from the office.

Groaning, I cover my face with my hands.

"I'm so sorry. I'm so sorry," I manage to choke out.

"I know. We all know, including him." Savino doesn't use Idris's name, uncertain what it might aggravate. I blink back hot tears, feeling entirely untethered.

"Why don't you get some fresh air?" Savino suggests.

I stand up, forcing myself to breathe slowly and control the rhythm.

"I'm sorry," I say again.

"We've got this. Clear your head," Savino suggests.

I nod sharply, not hesitating before running away.

I attacked Idris. I shoved him! I lost control. The guilt, the shame – it crawls and swells in my throat. The bond pleads to go back, to give in to the satisfaction of loathing.

As I get outside, Rialta is being loaded into the prison carriage, chains dangling from her bound wrists. Spectators are gasping and pointing at her as she sits down. This news will be all over the city before lunch.

There's only one person I want to inform before rumours

can twist the narrative, and he's lying in a bed with stitches holding him together. I can do that much good today at least.

The ride to Alfieri's house passes in the blink of an eye, my mind clouded with the last twenty-four hours.

I'm shown in by a staff member and I follow the path Idris had pulled me along before. Voices come from the bedroom. Nervously, I pause by the large wooden door.

Inside, Alfieri is propped up in the bed, his fingers linked with Emilia's, who is curled up by his side, along with another face I haven't seen in a long while. Serra looks rough but thankfully sober.

All three have suffered because of me, because of my failures. My family, my friends ... they are in pain.

All three turn as I linger at the door.

"Renza." Alfieri smiles. "Another visit? I'm beginning to feel important."

"You are important, Alfieri," I answer, clearing my throat. "I just wanted you to know, we worked out who betrayed us."

"Who?" Emilia asks coldly.

"My Aunt Rialta. She wanted to sink this bank branch so she could take control of the wider bank network." I sigh, not daring to step further into the room.

"Now, that I wouldn't have guessed." Alfieri chuckles, wincing as pain shoots through his chest.

"Is she in prison?" Emilia asks darkly.

"She's on her way. Charged with embezzling and fraud," I answer, struggling to force the words out around the lump in my throat. "I didn't want you to hear through the rumour mill, so I came to tell you myself."

"Is that all?" Emilia's words crack like ice. I swallow the bitter sensation. I shake my head and turn to leave but I pause, my hand on the doorframe, as Tahira's words yesterday echo back to me.

"You know what, Emilia? You need to get over yourself!" I snap.

"Excuse you?" Emilia narrows her eyes.

"You think I wanted any of this? You think this was my intention?" I demand, letting my frustration leak into my words.

"You know how I feel about Alfie's work!" Emilia all but growls at me. "You knew it was dangerous, yet you went behind my back and paid him to do it!"

"I didn't go behind your back, it simply had *nothing* to do with you," I retort angrily.

"Nothing? He could have died! I love him and he could've died!" Emilia yells, her cheeks turning red. "You lied to my face and hired him to do this!"

"I didn't lie. I just didn't tell you."

"Because you knew how hurt I'd be!"

"So where's your anger at Idris?" I bark back. "Idris sent Alfieri out time and time again. I didn't see you weeping and wailing when he brought you back pretty jewellery instead of cuts and bruises."

"This is far more than cuts and bruises!" Emilia snaps.

"Yes, but only now are you acting the self-righteous wounded animal!"

"Because I never thought you'd do this to me!" Emilia's eyes are shining with tears. "You, of all people, who espouse morals and duties and your dedication to the law like a lovesick musician. You tossed all that away, and my trust alongside it."

"I didn't do this to *you*!" I scream at her. "This was never about you. None of this is about you!"

"Of course not, because everything is always about *you*!" Serra jabs a finger at me. "You are the one who makes all the decisions for everyone. You get to decide when to break the rules, because you're *Renza Di Maineri*. You didn't want to rescue me from the prison because it went against your principles, but you'll send Alfieri to smuggle gold when it suits? You are a hypocrite!"

That hits me like a slap in the face. I look at stone-faced Serra. I laugh, shaking my head in disbelief.

"You're acting like children who've just learned the world isn't fair," I say incredulously. "The reason I make those decisions is because I was *elected* to do so. And before you forget, Serra, I *did* rescue you."

"Do you even hear yourself? It's all you. *Your* risks, *your* actions, *your* decisions," Emilia retorts. "You're not the one cut open. You haven't even said you're sorry!"

"Because I'm not!" I shout at her, fury rolling off me like a tide. "I regret that Alfieri's been hurt, of course I do. But I didn't pick up a sword and swipe at him. I didn't ask Alfieri to go out there lightly. I'm in a fight so great and so suffocating that I'm drowning every single day! So many lives are in the balance and it's my duty to save as many as I can. The situation was dire. If the bank goes under, the devastation will haunt the history books for centuries to come. So much agony and death for so, so many. The decision I made strangled me like a noose and sometimes I couldn't breathe for the guilt. But I am a leader, and I need to put my people first. Not just you, not just Alfieri. I am responsible for an entire city, and we are at war. A war for our very survival, and that changes the rules!"

Emilia shakes her head, her mouth wrinkling as tears roll down her cheeks.

"You play Fate, convincing and manipulating people to do what you want. You can always justify it, can't you, getting other people to risk their lives for your agenda? Well, Fate will fight back. Fate always has a price for those playing games."

"My agenda is the safety of the entire city," I remind her, seething with anger. "If you have a problem with that, that's fine. But don't act like you're somehow superior simply because you don't *have* to make those decisions. Hindsight is a bitch, and it's so easy to judge once the dice have been cast and we know the price we paid."

I step forwards, not backing down from the fight. Tears wet my words, but they still erupt angry and pained. "If it's so easy, look me in the eye and tell me what the other solution was. If you have one, perhaps you should be Electi, not me. I would gladly lay this burden down and cast it to some other unfortunate soul but I can't. I won't turn my back on the lives that are depending on me, just because I'm afraid of the cost. Even if it costs me everything. Even if it costs me you."

I turn around, shaking with anger as I march away. I race down the steps, rage and tears bundling in my eyes. I don't really know where I'm going, all I know is I need to move. I walk and walk, the Halician sunshine battering the top of my head as I weave through the blur of people on the streets. The cobblestones undulate under my feet as I follow a path.

Are they right? Am I really that selfish? Do I really make everything about myself? Did I betray Emilia by asking Alfieri to help? It felt that way in the moment, I can't deny that. I didn't tell her because I knew she'd be upset. But what other choice did I have? If there are always more options, where and what were mine?

My breathing is fast, my pulse throbbing in my ears when I find myself standing before Idris's door. I push it open and walk inside. I don't know why I'm here. My instincts pull me towards the man Fate decreed to be my enemy, the key to my destruction, the bane of my existence, the unravelling of all my joy.

But I need him. I need him like breath in my lungs and blood in my veins.

"Renza?" I look up the stairs as Tahira makes her way down. She pauses halfway, seeming to see the anguish on my face. She nods slowly and offers a pleasant smile.

"He's not here. How about we find a drink?"

CHAPTER 23

Normally if I were to order alcohol before noon, I'd get strange looks. If I'm with Tahira, however, there is no hesitation whatsoever. So now I'm at a random bar, sitting at a table by the window with a view over the narrow street below, sharing a bottle of brown liquor with one of the deadliest women in the city.

Tahira finishes her drink, setting the shallow glass back on the table.

Tahira winces after I finish regaling her with my encounter with my friends. "Oof, that sounds rough."

"Is she right, though? Did I betray her?" I ask. Tahira shrugs.

"I am not the girl to ask," Tahira says honestly. "You Halicians see things very differently. In Coari, if you choose to get into a fight, you can't complain about getting wounded. That's pathetic and weak. Choices have consequences."

"How do you do it?" I ask, tapping my glass with my fingers. "I mean, you send Royah into combat and she's your best friend. You knowingly thrust her into danger. And Bash and Taio and, heck, even Idris in the past. How do you do that and not drown in the stress and guilt of it all?"

"They're adults who make their own decisions," Tahira answers honestly. "They all signed up to follow me when they joined the Bannerhood. They can also walk away whenever they want to, Idris being a great example. Alfieri could've refused when you asked him. Would there have been retribution towards him if he'd said no?"

"Of course not," I scoff.

"There you go. He made his own decisions. The costs sit on his shoulders."

"But I knew it would hurt Emilia," I groan, resting my head on my hand.

"Maybe she'll come around and maybe she won't," Tahira says, leaning forwards. "But to me it sounds like she's angry at the situation. She feels powerless and scared and is seeing the consequences of violence up close and personal for the first time. She's probably terrified and misplacing it on you."

I sigh, running my fingers around the rim of the glass.

"Or she's hurt that her best friend sent her beloved into danger."

"He sent himself – you only asked," Tahira reminds me, refilling both our glasses. "If she's pissed at you then she doesn't get it. Being responsible for other people sucks."

"Urgh, tell me about it. And for the culprit to be my own family…" I rub my eyes. "I always knew that my bloodline was a worthless nest of selfish, greedy snakes, but to leverage a city in crisis just to steal more power for yourself is another level."

"No love lost amongst your kin then?" chuckles Tahira.

"I have a litany of stories about my kin, and I barely interact with them. Ask anyone on this continent and they will have tale after tale," I grumble, sipping on my drink. "If you ever meet someone else wearing the Di Maineri name, instantly be suspicious. That's my insider tip."

Tahira nods and then goes still, her head tilting sharply to one side, her mind's eyes somewhere else.

"Do you think she was responsible for bribing my men for that disastrous party?" Tahira asks quietly. "If she was in contact with the Holy States, it would make sense."

I sit up straighter.

"I mean ... she could've," I answer, my brow puckering.

What else does Rialta have up her sleeve? What other dominos have started falling?

I exchange a look with Tahira.

"I need to question her," I say quietly.

"After we look through her things," Tahira agrees. I reach for my purse to pay the tab. Tahira pushes my money back towards me, reaching for her boots and pulling out a small leather roll of coins.

"No, I've got this one." Tahira throws down a few Hali-Pounds and takes the bottle. I'm not used to others paying for me, and the change is certainly a nice one. Bottle in hand, we hurry out of the door. We hail a carriage and climb inside. I sit silently, biting my lip.

What will we find at my house?

"Hey, drink," Tahira encourages, pushing the bottle into my hands. "For that nervous energy."

I bark a laugh, taking a swig from the bottle before passing it back. Tahira grins wickedly, like I amuse her.

"What?" I frown.

"Nothing, I just ... you aren't the person I thought you'd be," Tahira admits.

"Oh, what did you expect?" I grin, leaning my arm against the side of the carriage. "What picture did Idris paint of me over the years? He kept tabs on me."

"I'm *very* aware." Tahira sniggers, before taking a swig of the bottle herself. She muses on my question before answering. "I was expecting a rich, smart, privileged woman. And you are, but not in the way I was expecting."

"Is the Princess of War, whose stepfather is a literal king and who grew up in a palace, calling me rich and privileged?" I retort.

"Yes, but I'm also saying you're not the haughty, entitled bitch I was expecting," Tahira argues and we both descend into snickering. I lean back in my seat and decide to take it as a compliment, because she's right. I am all those things.

"You aren't the woman I thought you'd be either," I admit.

"Now I'm worried. What did Idris tell you about me?"

"Idris painted you as some unmoveable, stone-faced master warrior, unrivalled with a blade and strengthened by a will of iron."

"And I'm not?" Tahira gasps in mock horror.

"Not in the way I was expecting," I answer back, taking the bottle from her.

Tahira chuckles. "Well, it seems Idris is utterly unreliable then."

"Not only does he name-drop, he does it badly," I muse. Tahira barks with laugher as the carriage pulls up at my house. I hurry inside, Tahira pouring in behind me. I barely take five steps towards the stairs before a shout stops me in my tracks.

"RENZA!" Fiora emerges at the top of the stairs like a fury.

Oh, right, I haven't seen my aunts since Rialta's arrest.

"Rialta betrayed the family. She was caught red-handed," I answer shortly as I ascend the stairs.

"Oh, I know," Fiora scowls, her eyes narrowing, "I heard all about it."

That's impressive, given it's barely been two hours since it all went down. Fiora and her informants.

"What do you want, Fiora?" I ask sharply. Fiora puts one hand on her hip, pointing a finger in my direction.

"Watch that tone with me, girl. I'm on your side."

"Are you? Then you won't mind putting your little spies all over the city to work finding the traitors who keep revealing our moves to the enemy. Have them do something useful for once rather than stalking me so you can scold me about Idris Patricelli."

Fiora takes a deep breath and folds her arms.

"I am worried about you and that boy," she says sharply. "Fate has a wrath like no other and constantly being together tempts it! You will pay a price if you continue to ignore him, to refuse him—"

"I do not have time for this." I scowl, and march past her towards Rialta's room.

I push open my aunt's door and see Agosta standing by the desk.

She turns her head to look at me, horror in her expression.

"Look at this," Agosta says urgently, holding up a letter and walking straight to me. I frown at her, taking the paper from her hands.

"What are you doing here?" I demand.

"Rialta betrayed us. She risked this entire family for her own greed. I wondered what else she was capable of," Agosta says, uncommonly serious. "Look at the letter. It was hidden in that drawer. She gave it a false bottom."

I look to the drawer she's pointing at, now open to view. Agosta points at the letter again. "It's only addressed to her 'friend', and there's no stamp or seal."

I look down at the letter, which seems innocent enough.

"Think it might be a cypher?" asks Tahira, looking over the letter from behind me.

"Keep looking." As Tahira starts moving through the room, I turn to Agosta.

"Why do you care? Your money doesn't come from the bank," I say quietly. Agosta lets out a sharp, offended breath and her hands go to her hips.

"I may not be a banker, but I am a Di Maineri," Agosta answers hotly. "I thought of all people you wouldn't throw that in my face, *Electi*."

I sigh, and nod once.

"It's been a rough morning," I grumble.

"Yeah, arresting your own flesh and blood can do that," Agosta mutters. "So what's the punishment? Are you taking the bank from her?"

"Life imprisonment," I answer. Agosta gasps and her eyebrows shoot up.

"Seriously?" Agosta asks incredulously. "But she's family."

"That makes it worse! You want me to go easy on her?" I demand. "She betrayed me, she broke the law, and now she must face the consequences."

"Says you?" Agosta asks, folding her arms. "If you can really claim you've never done something against the rules with a straight face, I'll eat my earrings."

"The difference is, I wasn't caught," I snap back. "And I didn't do it specifically to screw over my own flesh and blood. Now get out!"

Agosta shakes her head at me and rolls her eyes.

"Look at you, judge, jury and executioner. You really think you're the law-maker don't you?"

"My city, my house, my bank," I remind her. "I *am* the law."

I show her the door and slam it behind her, letting out an exasperated breath.

"I'm glad I don't have aunts," Tahira mutters as she starts throwing sheets off the bed and flipping the mattress. I get to work at the bookshelf, leafing through books and emptying drawers. I knock on the back of furniture and test every tile of her floor. We find stacks of letters asking for instructions from her banking branch in the Wheel City, but no personal letters and no correspondence from friends or anyone else. All business and all from the Wheel City.

"Here we go," Tahira says, upturning a small purse. Coins bounce and roll all over the bed. I cross to it, picking up the familiar currency. Not Hali-Pound or the Aureus of the Holy

States. These are stamped with a wheel and patterned around the edge to prevent shaving; they are Kerma, the currency of the Wheel City.

"Hmm, funny little coins," mutters Tahira, picking them up. "Why do you have so many currencies over here?"

"Banking histories," I answer quietly. "This is a lot of money."

"Perhaps that's why she was hiding it," Tahira muses. "Though there's nothing inherently strange about hiding your money."

"Agreed," I grumble, throwing them back on the bed as I think about my own personal stash hidden behind one of my mother's murals downstairs. Tahira and I stand there for a long moment together, looking around the overturned room.

I sigh and sink onto the ruined bed. "We're no closer to knowing if she bribed your men."

"No," agrees Tahira, sitting next to me.

"We could ask her anyway," Tahira proposes. "Pretend we found something."

"No, Rialta's too sharp." I rub my neck. "She'd see through that in an instant."

"Then we keep looking." Tahira nods firmly. "There has to be proof she's communicating with the Holy States."

"Unless she isn't working alone," I answer quietly. Tahira throws herself back on the bed, deep curls splayed over the immaculate silk sheets and rubs her dark eyes.

"She's not stupid enough to keep evidence like that in your house, but her counterpart might be," Tahira says.

"Exactly."

"Well then, who?"

"No idea. Someone she must've met up with."

"Sounds like a job for your aunt with all the spies," Tahira jokes, propping herself up on her elbow. The bed jiggles with the movement.

"If we can trust her," I argue.

"You can test that, too," Tahira muses.

That's not a bad plan.

"It's a shame you're not in politics. You have the brain for it." Tahira snorts and shakes her head.

"Nah, not for me. I like to solve my problems the old-fashioned way." Tahira pats the blade on her thigh. "I'll leave that to Kaz when he grows up. Perhaps he can learn a thing or two from you and Idris while he's here."

"Are you asking me to corrupt the naïve youth?" I chuckle. "I'll see what I can do."

That evening, my study crackles with a warm hearth. Gentle heat strokes the sides of my face as I review the first trade proposal for Tahira. It's good, starting with items she knows she can sell. We can focus on maximising profit later, so long as she brings food on her return.

A knock comes at my study door.

"Renza, is now a good time?" asks Giulia.

"Absolutely," I call back. Giulia slips inside. The gentle teal of her dress glides like water as she chews her lip. Her golden hair is hanging loose, gleaming like a sunset as she walks.

"What's up?" I ask. Giulia looks at Father's chair, her mouth twisting for a moment before she grabs it and pulls it over to the other side of the desk.

"Michelle," she says. I nod, waiting for her to elaborate. Giulia raises a hand to her jaw, rubbing the scar absentmindedly as her lips thin.

"Are you happy?" I ask quietly. Giulia nods and furrows her brow.

"We've talked. A lot," Giulia explains. "I need advice from someone who's denied a Fated bond before."

"Oh?"

"Michelle says she doesn't feel love for Royah. That it's not romantic or sexual. That it's more like finding her best friend or even a sister."

"What do you think to that?"

"I ... I believe it," says Giulia. "I mean, you and Idris don't work like we were always told Soulmates should work. Why can't society's understanding of Soulmates be flawed, too? What if Soulmates don't have to be romantic? What if some are truly platonic. It doesn't have to make them any less crucial or important. Every single relationship between people is different – none is exactly like any other. Why can't Fated bonds also be unique?"

"Have you spoken to Royah?" I ask curiously.

"I have. She came by Michelle's yesterday. Michelle refused to speak with her – refused to let her in. But she asked to talk to me," Giulia explains. "She was very kind, trusting me with that part of herself. And I understand – or as far as I can anyway. She's ... a good person."

"How does that make you feel?" I ask quietly. Giulia sighs.

"Unsettled?" Giulia offers, but it's clear the words don't express her feelings properly. "Unhappy? Not about Royah, obviously. But the situation ... I can't stop thinking about it. I mean, what's it like to defy a Fate bond?"

"Soulhates and Soulmates are different." I lean back in my chair and it creaks softly.

"But you're what I've got," Giulia insists. "Does it ... hurt?"

"Yes," I answer honestly, but not unkindly. "But it might be different for Michelle. Soulmates are different."

"But they're just as integral," Giulia counters quietly. "Would she be happier with Royah in her life?"

"Would you?" I ask without inflection. Giulia hesitates and shrugs, turning her eyes to the fireplace.

"I ... I feel so lost. When Michelle and I agreed to try, the terms were that she'd never see or speak with Royah again," Giulia admits. "But that was before. Now I know it's not like *that* ... I feel so guilty."

"Have you said this to Michelle?" I ask. Giulia shakes her head and looks at her lap.

"She's terrified she'll upset me, which doesn't feel healthy for anyone," Giulia answers clearing her throat. "I don't want that for her – or me. Or Royah."

"Giu..." I trail off meeting her eyes. She groans and leans back in her chair.

"I have to speak to Michelle again, don't I?"

"Sounds like the healthiest option," I agree, resting my head on my hands.

"We've had so many difficult conversations recently," sighs Giulia.

"Well, before you go in there, really ask yourself, could you be happy with Royah in your life? Would you ever feel safe and secure with Michelle if Royah is around? Before you broach the topic, know what you're suggesting and where you stand," I advise.

"Maybe we could come up with rules and boundaries?" Giulia muses. "At least for the start? I don't want Michelle to miss out on such an integral part of herself, not now I understand."

"Maybe try in a group setting – invite Emilia and Serra and Tahira as buffers."

"You'll come?"

I hesitate before answering.

"Probably best if I avoid Emilia and Serra for a while," I answer quietly. Giulia sighs.

"That won't fix things."

"I'm letting them cool off. We'll fix things in a few days. Let's not put too much pressure on one gathering." I try to dismiss her worries, but the rage in Emilia's face ... will I ever be forgiven? An ache forms between my shoulders. I sit back, stretching to try and relieve it as the flames trickle down my spine. I recognise the symptoms.

"I have half a mind to yell at them myself," grumbles Giulia. "I might not like what you did but to say such awful things—"

"Don't go starting fights on my behalf," I chortle.

"You're my sister. I'll happily start fights on your behalf – end them, too." Giulia grins. A knock comes against the polished wood as Agosta pushes the door open.

"Your Soulhate is here!" she announces in a sing-song voice, grinning at Idris who smiles back in his most charming manner.

"I'll leave you to it." Giulia smirks, getting to her feet. "Evening, Idris."

"Evening, Giulia," Idris says warmly as the two pass. Each of Idris's footsteps pounds like a war drum as Giulia closes the door behind her, leaving us alone. The fireplace crackles and the air between us thickens.

I can't find any words. Fate's Fury, I can't even look at Idris. Shame forces blood to my cheeks as I glue my eyes to the desk.

"So, I got your apology letter," Idris says, tossing the pages on the table. The remaining blue wax of the Di Maineri seal still clings to the page, the lemon tree cracked in half. I nod.

"Good," I manage to utter.

"You could've come to talk to me." Idris's deep voice grows tender and quiet, the warmth burrowing into my brain.

"I didn't know if you wanted to see me..." I trail off. Idris sighs.

"Renza—"

"I'm so sorry," I breathe, the words torn as they leave my lips.

"You have nothing to apologise for. That's why I came. I'm sorry. I should have checked how you were coping when I saw you struggling," Idris says quietly.

"My actions are my fault, Idris." I clear my throat, blinking hard. "I should have had control. I hurt you."

"No, you didn't. There isn't even a bruise," Idris teases gently. "Are you handling it now?"

I nod as Idris rounds the desk towards me. He leans against the wood and his hot fingers slip under my jaw, gently forcing my head up to meet his golden eyes.

"For the record, I always want to see you," he murmurs quietly. "No matter what."

A tear slips free of my lash line. I try pulling my head back, desperate to wipe it away but Idris's calloused thumb races over my cheek, skittering sparks across my face and up my spine. I swallow before summoning the dregs of my courage for the most painful, crucial question burning a hole in my mind.

"Forgive me?"

"Always," promises Idris. He lowers his forehead, pressing his blistering brow to mine. His searing fingers slip back to tangle with my dark hair as we sit there, basking in and battling with the bond for a long moment.

My heart races and my veins tingle in revolt as I push my jaw forwards. I capture his lips with mine, my hands sweeping up to grip his neck. Idris groans, the noise eliciting feral satisfaction as he matches my tender, devouring pace. My fingers twist into his blond hair as our breathing clashes and our tongues dance. My stomach warms and clenches, my head pounding and fierce.

"Renza," Idris breathes against my lips, the tethers of my sanity entirely undone in his presence. The fury with which I claim his mouth is second to none, the need and wanton desire building in me reaching deeper and deeper.

I slip out of my chair, pressing myself against him. He sits on my desk, me between his legs as one hand trails down my back, exploring the dip of my waist and the curve of my thigh.

My hands drop to the bulge forming in his trousers and I wrap my hands tightly around his thick, tantalising girth.

Idris half gasps, half growls as he pushes off the desk. A pace later I'm crammed against the bookshelves as my hand disappears down his trousers. He hisses as I begin to stroke, claiming this power, this punishment, this ecstasy for myself. Idris shudders under my grip, panting hard as I bite down on his bottom lip. I stroke, long and languid, enjoying every thick inch of him as Idris fights for control over the warring sensation I evoke.

Idris's hands leap to my wrists, yanking my hands away and slamming them back against the shelves. I gasp in shock as his mouth moves to my neck.

"What are we doing?" My words are a mangled groan. "We're Soulhates. We should stay far away from each other."

"I really don't care about what we *should* do," Idris growls, his hands gripping me tightly. "That's other people and their expectations. I don't give a fuck about them."

"Why is it like this? Why can't we help it?" I moan. Idris breathes against my neck, his movements stilling as he speaks.

"This bond is *ours*. Ours to define and ours to navigate. Our Fate to determine. I don't want to 'help it'. I embrace it, every excruciating moment. No matter how rough."

Idris lifts his head, breathing slowly as he hovers over my lips.

"We are inevitable," Idris whispers, his words like a vow. "I've known it for years. I'll wait until you see it, too. Because you will."

Idris kisses me before I can answer, long, languid and promising.

Then he backs away, offering me a rogue smile before heading to the door.

"See you tomorrow, Di Maineri. Remember what I said."

And like that, he's gone.

CHAPTER 24

The last week has been chaos – adjusting bank accounts, bringing new numbers to the High Chamber, officially signing the life-imprisonment order for Rialta. Exhaustion wraps its tiny hands around my eyes and squeezes.

Which is why I'm not impressed when I receive an emergency summons to the High Chamber. We only closed the session two hours ago, and now I have to go back? I just want an early night.

A yawn brews in the back of my throat as I stride up the painted steps. It's a closed session, thank goodness, so I don't have Agosta and Fiora trailing my every move and offering their unsolicited opinions. Their bickering has triggered more than one headache, and they're one sparring match away from being thrown out for a few nights, just so I can reclaim a semblance of peace.

I cross the polished marble floors, my steps clipping quietly. The skirts of my dress ripple in shades of burgundy and paprika, my low ponytail dancing along the back of my neck and the gentle dangle of my earrings brushing rhythmically against my neck.

"Ah, Electi Di Maineri," says Leone warmly as I reach the gate. "Thank you for coming on short notice."

"Of course," I answer, stepping inside. My gaze travels around the occupied chairs, again falling on the empty seat that once belonged to Cardinal Bellandi. My eyes jump to Idris's face which is drawn in shades of buttery yellow. Heat licks down my spine and my throat closes. He clearly didn't call this session.

I take my seat.

"We have received a response from the Holy States," says Leone, not bothering with the formalities of calling a session to order. He walks towards the central stage. He looks tired, his usually neat brown hair decidedly rumpled. Black smudges adorn his fingers as he holds up the letter, dark curtains lurking under his eyes.

"They have agreed to meet with one member of the High Chamber," explains Leone. "They have suggested a spot on their side of the border near the town of Barive. They said their party will contain no more than twenty guards and their speaker, and request we match in number. We need to elect a speaker and send them to negotiate on our behalf."

That seems perfectly reasonable.

"Did they say who they're sending?" I ask. Leone shakes his head, his lips pursing as he turns his eyes back to the letter.

"I suppose it'll be a cardinal. I doubt the Holy Mother would go anywhere with only twenty guards," he answers. "So the question is, who should go?"

"I'll go," volunteers Idris immediately, sitting forwards in his seat. My heart sputters at the thought. I curl my fingers into a fist and dig my nails into my palm. I snap my attention to him, the roaring itching of his presence screaming at me. Of course he'd volunteer, always the first to put himself in the line of fire.

"I think you're the worst person to go," Ulrico says curiously. "You have a clear dislike of the Holy States, and you objected to pursuing peace."

Wow, a startlingly valid response. Nice job Ulrico.

"Perhaps, but should events go sideways, I am the best equipped. This meeting is objectively dangerous. We would be crossing into enemy territory, walking deliberately into the arms of our foes. Any number of things could happen. Should violence break out, I have the experience to handle it."

"While you have extensive experience on a battlefield, Idris, many people here also know how to handle a blade," Leone counters levelly. "Besides, the retinue of twenty guards is there for exactly this reason. I'd also argue that going expecting violence will lead to its inevitability."

Leone coming in strong with another valid point.

"Then who should go?" asks Savino. "I'd volunteer but I'm needed to continue preparations with the guard should this not work."

"I think it should be Electi Di Maineri," says Ulrico suddenly. I lift my head to look at him, surprised.

"She's one of our best speakers and she's good with people from all walks of life. She's persuasive and calm in a crisis. We've seen her de-escalate violent tensions right here in this chamber," Ulrico explains.

"Thank you for your confidence. Should the Chamber agree, I will do my best to represent us," I say honestly, a little surprised by the sharp assessment of my colleague. Ulrico smiles at me.

"No," Idris says immediately. "No, it's too dangerous."

"It'll be dangerous for whoever goes," Maggia says. "Renza is a wise choice. She's got international recognition beyond this chamber and that commands respect."

"The only question, signora, and I don't mean to be insensitive, is whether you can put aside your personal grievances with the Holy States for this task?" Ulrico continues. "I lost my sibling to their schemes and admit I would find it hard to keep my senses should I meet face to face with their murderer. Do you believe you're able to do this?"

"Whoever they send won't have been directly responsible for the death of my father or colleagues before you," I answer, mulling it over. "For the sake of Halice, I can work past it."

"They'll likely send someone the Holy Mother trusts implicitly," Maggia says quietly. "They'll have known."

"Agreed," says Leone. "I was going to recommend I be considered, but Electi Di Maineri is an excellent choice."

"Not to mention sending Renza might signal that we are serious about peace," Maggia offers. "Given she has reason to hold grudges, if she can put them down, perhaps they can, too."

"No," Idris says, shaking his head emphatically. "It's too dangerous."

"I'll do it," I answer. "If you vote for me, I will go. But I need absolute authority to make whatever deal I think is best. Whatever I negotiate is the deal we will all accept and live with."

"Of course," Leone answers. "We should talk about what we are and aren't willing to compromise on before you leave, so we are all agreed on the hard boundaries."

I nod, picking up a sharp piece of charcoal to start scribbling notes. Idris closes his eyes and pinches the bridge of his nose in frustration.

"Firstly, we should confirm with a vote. Forget the stones, all in favour of our speaker being Renza Di Maineri, raise your hand," Maggia says.

I raise my hand, and so does everyone else in the room.
Except Idris.

He leans forwards, his hands cupping his mouth and nose as he glares at the wall opposite his chair. He looks like he's about to tear this place down brick by brick.

"It's agreed. Electi Di Maineri will go," says Maggia, eyeing Idris warily. "Why don't we take a few minutes to gather our thoughts before we continue."

Idris lurches from his chair and marches away. I sigh, watching him stalk towards a familiar door, a door that leads to the stairs spiralling up to the roof. The wood shudders as he slams it shut behind him.

I look around the group, all of whom refuse to meet my eye as they shift in their seats and make small talk. They're waiting for me to go after Idris and calm him down.

Fate's Fury, why am I his minder?

I walk towards the door behind which Idris disappeared, taking hold of the handle and pulling it quietly shut behind me.

Idris is breathing deeply but quickly, hands pressed to his face.

"No, Renza," he bites out. "Not now!"

"Oh, I see, so we're throwing tantrums when we don't get our way?" I tease softly. Idris rips his hands from his face, glaring at me.

"Don't mock me," he snaps, marching forwards. He's trembling; the tether of his self-control frays before my eyes. I swallow tightly, ripping my own gaze away, knowing it'll only provoke him further. I fix my eyes to a wall, and breathe slowly, hoping he'll copy the mind-stilling pattern.

"I'm not," I say softly.

"I don't have this!" he snarls. "I don't... Walk away!"

"Okay, but first help me understand." Although I know it, focusing on words rather than the bond might help pry him back from the edge.

"You can't go," Idris insists, his words sharp and solid as stone.

"I'm going," I respond firmly, keeping my eyes trained on the brickwork. "The vote has been passed."

"It's too dangerous." Idris's words shudder as the half-roar leaves his throat. His eyes aren't on me anymore, that familiar suffocating heat leaving my face. We stand so close I can smell him. His lavender and mint scent are simultaneously enraging and calming. The infuriating, oxymoronic nature of Idris Patricelli.

"I'm not going alone," I answer, hoping my gentle words land somewhere amongst the stresses raging in his mind. "I have twenty guards I can take with me. I have a few names in mind."

Idris sucks in a sharp breath.

"I could—"

"No," I say before he can start. "You can't come with me. They specifically said one member of the High Chamber. They will know you. You can't come."

"Then who—"

"Tahira," I answer. "Maybe Royah, too. I'll pay them, of course, but I hope they'll agree. You know how good they are."

"I do," Idris grinds out begrudgingly.

"You trust them, don't you? Besides, having Tahira there will also be valuable from a diplomatic standpoint," I muse, various strategies already coming together in my mind.

"Tahira's people won't like sending her." Idris scowls. "She's their leader and they protect her as much as she does them."

"Half Halician City Guard, and half Red Sands Bannermen, for her protection and for mine, and to prove the political point that we have allies and are not undefended," I say. "Not to mention we can have a larger retinue waiting for us just the other side of the border in case of trouble."

Idris groans, taking my hand in his. Boiling pins and needles stab across my palm as thorns bristle along my tongue.

"Renza, please, please think about this. Say no."

"It's decided, Idris. I'm going," I say seriously. His hand jumps up and his fingers gently brush across my right arm, over the wounded flesh. The bruises are faded now and the scar is forming nicely. The tips of his fingers spark infernal waves rolling through my bones. I shudder under his touch, knowing where his mind has gone.

"There has to be another way," Idris whispers.

"Maybe, but this is the path forwards. A possible peace."

"It's too risky. It's not worth it."

"Idris—"

"Risking you isn't worth it." Idris lifts his hands to my face. His grip it red-hot as he takes my head in his hands, lowering his forehead to mine. I force my breathing to slow as his skin burns into mine, incinerating my flesh and charring my bones. I take a moment to feel his presence, the simultaneous parts of me at war, my need for him and my revulsion rolling like battling storms.

"I need you to be safe," Idris almost pleads with me. "I need it. I need it."

I press my hands to his chest.

"I have to do this." I swallow and find his eyes. That maddening, seductive gold. Their attention could make me combust where I stand, but I'm unable to look away. "Will you help me? I need you to help me."

Idris's shoulders collapse.

"You have it," he whispers, his words deep and swollen. "You have me."

I smile, leaning up on my toes.

"Then let's make sure I'm prepared. That way I'll be home all the sooner."

CHAPTER 25

The sun slides from the sky as the session breaks, draining the dancing saffron and turmeric hues. Shadows encroach with the moon acting the eager general, advancing the night with a silvery grin protruding from a gauzy cloud.

I walk the streets of Halice quickly, having trodden this path a thousand times before. A nervous breeze sends fleeting kisses over my skin, tickling my nose and nipping at the ends of my hair. My bracelets jingle quietly with each footstep on the cobbles.

My skirts flutter behind me, the sound muted as I'm finally left alone to realise what I'm about to do.

I'm going to walk into the heart of the enemy and negotiate a peace for our people.

This might be the most important thing I do in my life.

My pulse itches under my skin, but Idris isn't close. I all but ran away after the session. My throat is tight and my breathing shallow.

I pass through the Garden gates, heading down the winding path that's peppered with fallen leaves that crunch underfoot.

The trees whisper as I pass, heading for a familiar front door. I reach the buttery house nestled in the corner and knock on the door.

There are footsteps inside, and Michelle opens the door. Her face lights up as she pulls it wider to allow me in. I look for my sister. To my surprise and absolute delight, she's sitting next to Royah at the dining room table.

"Hey, Renza, come and look at these." Giulia grins and waves me over. "She actually did some of these herself. Imagine tattooing your own skin!"

"I think Giulia might be angling to get one," Michelle says in mock-whisper.

"If you want, I totally could!" Royah grins. "I always love a new canvas."

"Royah's talented," I answer, clearing my throat. "Giu, do you have a minute?"

"What's wrong?" Giulia asks immediately, the smile falling from her face. I shake my head.

"Not wrong, but..." I take a deep breath and continue. "The Holy States have requested a meeting to negotiate terms of peace. They're sending a speaker, and so are we. I was voted to go on behalf of the city."

Giulia blinks hard, sucking in a breath.

"Where?" she asks faintly.

"The other side of the border, near Barive."

"When?" Giulia asks, her eyebrows somehow rising even higher on her face.

"I leave tomorrow. First light."

Giulia swallows, but it doesn't wipe the blank expression from her face. Royah pats her back comfortingly.

"Wow, Renza, that's..." Michelle clears her throat. "Who's going with you?"

"I'm allowed to take twenty guards with me. I was actually going to ask Tahira if she'd come, for moral support as well as for her skill. Do you think that'd be possible, Royah? I'd pay, obviously."

"I don't speak for Tahira," Royah answers, tossing her long dark braids over her shoulder, "but I'll go, and don't worry about money with me."

"Seriously?" Relief adds colour to Giulia's glassy words. "You'll go?"

"Sure. I get paid to get into trouble." Royah chuckles. "I can keep her out of it."

"And I will pay you," I reiterate.

"What about me? I could go," Giulia says, but I shake my head.

"No, you need to stay. Stabilise the bank."

"But—"

"Idris is putting together the rest of the team. It's the only way he'd even consider letting me out of his sight," I soothe, but my sister isn't mollified.

"Doesn't surprise me," snorts Royah. "He's rather possessive of you."

"Tell me about it," grumbles Giulia. I smile, warmth taking root in my belly as my hand drifts up to the necklace he bought me. I've worn it nearly every day since my birthday. There's something about it that helps fill the void his absence creates. It's like ... a piece of him.

"Wow, Renza, that's really something," Michelle says.

"I'll be fine," I reassure them. "It's a negotiation. The aim is peace. There are rules to these things."

I walk over to Giulia, who nods along with my words. Worry eats at her eyes as she gnaws her bottom lip.

"People can't know I'm gone from the city," I say quietly. "I need you to keep up a ruse in my absence."

"How long will you be gone?" asks Michelle.

"It's a two-day journey there, one day for the meeting, two

days back. Conservative estimate is maybe six days, to account for any delays?" I offer. Giulia nods.

"So you'll be back in time for Agoi," says Michelle, her eyes lighting up.

"Exactly, when we can all hopefully celebrate the end of this awful war." I try to be upbeat, giving Giulia a friendly nudge. She gives me an unamused smile before patting my hand.

"Aunt Fiora and I can keep up a ruse that you've been struck down with the flu or something. That'll be easy enough."

"You trust your aunt with this? After what happened with your other aunt?" asks Michelle seriously. Giulia and I exchange a look.

"Fiora ... is devoted to family. It's a little sharp and mean sometimes, and almost always bossy, but the love is real," I answer begrudgingly. Giulia rolls her eyes.

"You should've heard her talking about finding me a new girlfriend." Giulia smirks. "Lord, she was practically making a list."

"Well, throw the list away. You're taken," Michelle says firmly. "If this is your last night in Halice for a little while, what do you say to a drink, hmm?" she asks me.

"I should get back. I just ... needed to tell you in person."

I smile at Giulia encouragingly. She smiles back at me.

"Promise me you'll be safe."

"I promise to try."

Giulia sighs as Michelle opens up her cupboards and rattles around for wine and some glasses.

"I suppose that's all I can ask."

CHAPTER 26

Why in all of Fate's Mysteries are we setting off at the first crack of dawn?

The world is still cool and slow, and the rattling of the carriage is dull as I rock back and forth. We're almost at the meeting spot outside the High Chamber. Once everyone has gathered, we'll leave for these peace talks. Fate have mercy, let them go well.

The carriage comes to a gentle stop and I open the door. A crisp morning embrace sprints up my arm and pools in the wells of my collarbone. Stepping into the throng of people, I smile at those who bid me good morning. Soldiers from both Halice and Coari wear polished armour; they look over the horses, which are prepped and ready to go. Amongst them all is a sizeable, expensive carriage. I look around, counting people, a question pulling at my brow. This is far more than twenty.

"Hey there, sleepy!" A familiar, friendly voice interrupts my inspection. My head snaps around and my eyes bulge from my head.

What is he doing here?

"Alfieri?" I ask incredulously.

"Hey, Di Maineri." He beams, slipping his hands into the pockets of his high-quality travelling attire. Suspicion lodges unhappily beneath my ribs. I think I know why he's here and I don't like it one bit.

"How are you feeling? Shouldn't you be resting? What are you doing here?" I demand, immediately looking around for a seat for him. Alfieri laughs.

"I'm coming with you of course."

This has to be some kind of joke. He's still recovering! He is held together with stitches and willpower.

"No, you're not! You were almost dead a few days ago!" I lower my voice, not sure who might be listening.

"That was a whole fortnight ago," corrects Alfieri. "Besides, I'm one of your approved guards."

"No!"

"Yes." The word hits me like a wall of brimstone. Idris appears behind me and I jab a finger at him accusingly before turning back to Alfieri.

"You are still recovering."

"It looked a lot worse than it was," Alfieri answers brightly. "I'm fine."

"What part of 'rest and don't stress yourself' didn't you hear because I am happy to go get the doctor and have him repeat it!"

"The doctor gave me the all-clear," Alfieri answers innocently. I scowl.

"How much did you pay him to say that? Not to mention Emilia will have my head on a platter if I let you come!"

"That's for me to worry about," Alfieri says seriously, his face falling for a second. "Besides, you didn't ask me to come. Idris did."

"Alfieri—"

"We need him," Idris cuts me off. He slips an arm around my shoulder, the movement driving hot lacerations across my chest. He steers me away from Alfieri and towards the carriage. His fingers press into my shoulder, the material of my jacket offering no protection from the searing brand of his touch.

"Alfie is going as more than one of your guards," Idris whispers so fast and quick it feels like an assault. "I don't trust this meeting, or their intentions. So he's going to do some digging while you provide the distraction."

"Idris! He's injured! He's still recovering – he can't waltz into danger!" I hiss, pushing off his arm. Fate's Fury, the bond first thing in the morning will wake you up like nothing else! Meeting Idris's hazel eyes sends a flood of molten steel into every sleepy crevice of my body. "If he gets caught—"

"He won't. Trust me, and trust Alfieri—"

"He's injured."

"Do you think I'd let him go if I weren't certain he's okay?" demands Idris. "I'm not careless with my friends."

"Alfieri aside, if we undermine these negotiations before they start then they won't work."

"Hope for the best, prepare for the worst," Idris retorts.

"Idris—" I start.

"No arguing. It's all arranged," Idris says firmly. The urge to stamp my foot, fold my arms and scream at him almost wins out. Almost. "Right, you'd best get into the carriage. We can set off now you're here."

"We?" I repeat seething, irritation shuddering in my clenched arms. "You're not coming, remember?"

"I'll travel with you to the border," Idris responds as though it was all agreed yesterday and I've foolishly forgotten. "Then the chosen twenty will go with you from there."

"Idris—"

"That way I'm on hand quickly if I'm needed."

"Idris!" I shout at him, exasperation flooding my lips. He pretends I haven't spoken and opens the door to the carriage.

"Your carriage awaits," he finishes with a smug smile that

shows no remorse whatsoever. I blink hard, desperately waiting for my mind to catch up.

"What about you?" I sputter.

"I'll be riding," Idris says. "No need for us to be locked together in a box for hours. I think that would exhaust both our restraint. I prefer the freedom of riding anyway."

"I just ... I don't ... I..."

Fate's Fury, I need coffee. I can't even think straight. It's too early to form any semblance of a sane argument. I give up and climb into the carriage. It's going to be a long, long day. I should save my strength. This is a fight I'm not going to win; I can tell by his tone and the look in his eyes.

I sit down and Idris closes the carriage door for me. He presses himself against the door, head and shoulders leaning in the window.

"I'm just out here if you need me," Idris says softly. "All you have to do is ask."

"So what, I'm travelling in here alone?" I ask gesturing around the luxury carriage with its comfortable seats. That doesn't sit right with my friends riding out there.

"People will circle in and out, keep you company and rest the horses." Idris shrugs playfully. "I'll be here to convince you to trade places in the peace talks every hour or so, but we both know you aren't a morning person. I figured you'd prefer to start this journey alone, lest anyone be at the mercy of the morning Di Maineri wrath."

I roll my eyes at him.

"I'm not that bad," I scowl.

"You kind of are, though," Idris teases, straightening from his position at the door. "I'll be sure to get you some coffee at our first rest stop."

"I can get my own coffee. I'm perfectly capable. I am not some delicate, precious jewel that needs to be taken care of," I sigh.

"You are to me," Idris says quietly, no question of mockery or humour in his voice. He clears his throat and steps back. "Right, let's not wait around."

He disappears, barking orders, and I look around the carriage. To my left is a blanket. It's the blanket from the bed in his house – the soft blue fleece would be familiar anywhere.

Unable to tame my smile, I wrap its warmth around my shoulders and lean back in the carriage as we leave Halice behind.

∽

The sky is streaky with grey-bellied clouds and the wind is bracing and fresh. It carries the scent of autumn leaves and the rustling of gossiping trees. We stop by a lake for the night, and the water glistens as it swirls playfully with the sloping, muddy shore.

I stretch out my neck as I stand under a large oak. I press my hand against the coarse bark. All my limbs ache from the day spent being thrown about in a carriage on the unruly country roads.

The carriage is so slow – perhaps we can leave it behind and continue on horseback.

True to Idris's word, people took breaks to join me in the carriage. Alfieri was good company, and with me quite regularly. Though he tried to act like his wound didn't hurt, I could tell all this activity wasn't good for him.

I refuse to let him get hurt again, not because of me.

Rolling green hills stand proudly behind the lake. In the distance, foggy grey teeth jut from the ground, protruding against a blooming sunset – the first vicious peaks of the Steel Curtain, the mountain range that divides the Independent States from the Holy States. The natural protection of the Steel

Curtain has kept us safe for years, and also prosperous by forcing all trade through the Argenti Strait and Halice.

My fingers tingle. My throat itches. A dark, blistering star hovers out of my vision, growing larger step by step.

I smile at the grassy floor before lifting my head again, keeping my eyes on the glittering lake.

"Pretty spot," I say before he can speak.

"Glad you like it." Idris's voice is a deep rumble that jars down my spine like boiling tar. I gesture to the view.

"Makes you proud to be Halician, doesn't it?" I say quietly. "The beauty of our home."

"Says the woman who rarely leaves the city," teases Idris.

"I have duties. I want to, I just … can't." I frown. "But the Di Maineri family owns vineyards out this way."

"I didn't know that," Idris mumbles.

"They're a day-or-so's ride southwest of here. I go see them in the summer, when there's a break in the Chamber," I say quietly. "Although recently I've visited our coastal properties on my breaks."

I steady my breathing as I look at him. His expression is tight. He won't stop worrying until he sees me safe and sound on Halician soil after tomorrow's meeting.

"You can still change your mind," Idris says quietly, starting up this old conversation yet again, though his tone sounds hopeless. "I can go in your place."

"You have such little faith in me," I half tease.

"You know it has nothing to do with ability," Idris answers, as if I've offended him. "I agree with every reason why you were chosen. I even have a dozen more. I just wish it could be someone else."

"Don't bring this up now," I sigh, leaning into the rough bark of the tree and letting my shoulders sag. The day has sucked the energy from my bones.

"Then when? You cross that border tomorrow and ... I have a bad feeling about all of this. Nothing is ever this easy."

"Perhaps you're right," I muse with dry humour. "But my life is worth the risk if it saves Halice."

"You can do far more for this city alive than you can dead." Idris almost snarls the words.

"Maybe, but if I do die, use it. Renza Di Maineri, martyr of peace," I joke. "Not a terrible ring to it."

Without warning, Idris invades my personal space. I gasp at the fire washing over me with renewed, visceral intensity. It cuts off my words as his abrasive hands cup my head, his fingers intertwining with the strands of my hair. His eyes are twin suns bearing down on me with relentless fury.

"Don't talk about your death, Renza. It won't happen. I refuse to let it," Idris says darkly.

"How presumptuous. I shall do with my life what I please," I retort as he closes the space between us even further. My throat squeezes to the point of choking and my skin teems with sizzling, stinging sparks.

"Fate gave your death to me, Renza Di Maineri. He entrusted it to my care. It's mine," Idris vows, a feral growl behind the words.

"I thought you weren't religious."

"I don't care for Churches or preachers, but I will never deny the sacred nature of our bond. Its weight, its purity, its sanctity," Idris murmurs as though hypnotised or entranced, running a scalding thumb over my bottom lip. "I would be bereft without it, without you. So much of my life has been shaped by this gift and I am thankful for it."

The air is thick and spitting with hot, rabid energy that digs into my skin and tugs at my blood.

"So don't joke about your death with me, Renza, because it's not funny." Idris's words are deep and rumbling as they fuse with my bones. "Because it's also my life at stake, and I protect what's mine."

Ringing takes up residence in my ears. My hands shake and my vision swirls red. I dare not move, dare not speak. I'm teetering on a knife's edge, and I'm terrified of falling.

Idris backs away like it takes all of his self-control to put the inches between us. I scramble for my senses, latching onto the fading of our bond like a lifeline as Idris steps back. His eyes don't leave mine, and I'm trapped. But I don't want relief. Not from him.

Then he turns and walks back towards the camp being set up. I gasp for air like I've been underwater for far too long. I press my hands into fists as I yell after him.

"Your death is mine, too, Patricelli. It's a two-way bond."

Idris freezes, then turns, smirking.

"Good. I'd have it no other way."

CHAPTER 27

We reach the border the next day. We're far closer to the mountains now, their staggering peaks towering over us like giant, barbed blades. The pitches and valleys of this terrain made the last part of this journey impossible to navigate in a carriage so I convinced Idris to let me ride, for the sake of time, and I was continually corralled to the centre of the group.

The border here is a large, deep ravine with a rushing white river at the bottom that'll eventually meet a larger river called the Semita a few miles downhill. It froths across its grey stone bed, its giggling chatter echoing up the sharp walls of its rocky prison. A long, weathered rope bridge, anchored on both sides, is the crossing point.

On the other side of the bridge, on Holy States soil, a small retinue of guards waits before a large wall of grey rock.

My stomach convulses. My breathing is tight.

I can do this. I'll be okay.

I took the time to properly freshen up before the crossing. Appearances matter. I check myself in the small looking-glass. My hair is fashioned into its usual low ponytail, adorned with beaded hair jewellery and a few decorative twists and braids. I wear a luxurious crimson tunic, the loose, wide sleeves made with white silk and embroidered with every swirling colour under the sun. Paired with smart black boots and trousers, an artisanal metalwork belt finishes the look. It is practical, yet empowering – at least that's what I'm going for.

I reach my fingers up to Idris's necklace. Brushing the jewellery piece sends a surge of surety down my spine. Even if he's not here with me, a piece of him rests on my skin.

Okay, time to move.

I step out of the small tent and the material flops back into place with a little slap. Idris hasn't left the door for a moment. He glares across the gaping ravine like he could make it combust or shatter or simply evaporate. Perhaps with that intensity he can.

His head snaps around to look at me as I emerge, his expression falling slightly.

"What?" I ask, touching my face with worry. "Have I messed it up?"

"No. No, you look great," Idris says, clearing his throat.

"Good." I smile. "Pack everything up. Hopefully we won't need more than a few hours to agree things. If talks go into tomorrow, I'll come back this side to sleep, but let's aim to get moving and put distance between us and them sooner rather than later."

Idris nods sharply.

I reach for him and give his forearm a squeeze as I take a step away. Idris's hand leaps out to catch my wrist. He tugs me back, drawing me against his chest. His arms wrap tightly around my body and I'm swallowed by fire. I arch my back, gasping against the sudden sensation. Idris leans towards me, closing the distance between our heads.

"Stay safe." I can't decide if his words are a plea or a command.

"If you insist," I tease softly.

Idris doesn't laugh. I reach up, taking his head in my hands. I nod slowly, waiting for him to release me. Idris's face is a warzone as he slowly withdraws his arms. I wink at him before stepping away.

"Don't worry, I'll be back to tempt Fate with you in no time," I promise as I retreat. I turn around and head towards the bridge. The men are ready, as are Tahira, Alfieri and Royah.

Fate's Mercy, this is the first time I've seen Tahira and Royah in their armour. They look formidable, deadly ... and incredibly attractive! Wow, the Coari know how to dress for every occasion!

Tahira in particular has transformed. Her hair is pulled back into a thick, neat braid. The leather she wears is stained a deep, rusty maroon. Pads of leather-covered steel scale down her shoulders and arms, with separate pads for her forearms with a lip that stretches to protect her wrists. Two blades are secured across her back, with more blades strapped to both her arms and legs like a second skin. Dressed like this, she has become her namesake: the Princess of War.

"Ready for this?" I ask her. She flashes a wicked grin at me.

"Let's make peace so we can all make some money!" she cackles. I nod and face the bridge.

This rope bridge is just wide enough to cross in single file. Some of the guards start moving first, going ahead to make sure there is somewhere safe on the other side. The order of things is deliberate. Alfieri will be one of the last to cross and will hopefully go unnoticed. It's strange seeing him dressed in the uniform of a City Guard, and his usual easy charm does nothing to settle the guilt crawling around my stomach at the idea of him with us.

Focus. I have a job to do.

This is my duty, my honour as an Electi. I am here to make peace for us all.

I start across the bridge, Tahira in front of me and Royah behind.

The bridge sways softly from side to side, but not unnervingly so. The footsteps sound heavy against the wood and the order not to march in time with each other is called a few times up and down the crossing.

When my feet touch the grass on the other side, I steal a deep breath.

Please, Fate, let me only have to cross that again once.

A retinue of five guards in black and white stand ready to receive us. If they're surprised or unhappy with the Red Sand Bannerhood in our party, not one of their entirely blank expressions shows it. One guard marches forwards, every motion neat and sharp.

"Electi, we are to escort you and your companions to the meeting."

"Please, lead the way," I say. They turn as a unit and march forwards.

"Not very chatty," mutters Tahira, and I smirk. We follow them around the rocky outcrop and to the open space of their camp. In the centre, surrounding a tent larger than all the others, waits a fierce ring of Church Militia. Standing to attention, their positions are perfectly still but their eyes are cutting. They're an intimidating force. Our guides stop their march outside the tent entrance.

"Please enter the tent, signora," says the speaker.

I nod, looking at Tahira as we start walking towards the tent together. But the Church Militia move to stop us going further.

"Please enter alone, signora. Your protection may wait outside, as will we," the speaker informs us. I swallow tightly, unnerved by this change to our plan. But I suppose I can't blame the cardinal inside, if they also don't have soldiers. Perhaps it sets the wrong tone to talk of peace with so many fighters in the room.

I turn to Tahira, my pulse wild under my ribs. She hesitates, her hand falling to a small dagger at her waist.

"Your call," she says softly, her eyes assessing the men in front of her with distaste – no doubt remembering the vicious events in Malaya. I assess the Church Militia, their black and white robes pristine, their weapons gleaming viciously. We need to give this a real chance; not to mention we need to allow time for Alfieri to do his work. A show of trust.

"It's okay," I say, clearing my throat. "I'll shout if there's a problem. Just ... stay close."

Tahira doesn't look happy but lets me continue alone.

I pass the Church Militia but hesitate outside the tent entrance. I look back to the group. Royah and Tahira watch carefully and I nod at them. I push the fabric door to one side and enter.

The tent is quiet as the fabric door drops close behind me. The floor is layered with dark rugs, and the cream-coloured tent stretches high overhead, allowing me to stand tall. To one side is a patterned fabric screen that sections off a private recess from view. I walk towards a large wooden table set in the centre of the room that has two plush chairs placed before it. The wooden table is heavily laden with food of all kinds, and two large pitchers of wine. Do they really think I am fool enough to eat any food they provide?

I drop my hand to the polished wooden surface and look around the tent. Towards the back is a dark velvet curtain that has a small gap between its edges, revealing a large, low bed piled high with pillows and blankets.

Something moves behind me and I turn as someone walks out from behind the screen to stand between me and the door.

My blood turns cold, frost swells in my stomach, and a tight noose forms around my throat as I stare disbelievingly at the figure before me. He steps forwards slowly, like a hunter stalking cornered prey. A knowing smirk stains his face. Green eyes glint with savage victory.

"Hello, Renza," Nouis says deeply.

"No," I breathe, staggering backwards but the table blocks my retreat. My breath is hurried as I shake my head, throwing out my hands as he steps closer. "You can't ... how ... but..."

"How am I alive?" Nouis asks, sounding amused as he closes the distance between us, hands sliding into the pockets of his trousers. "After you stabbed me in the back?"

Horror fills my every breath and blood drains from my face as my stomach churns. My feet refuse to work, refuse to move as I stare in dread. The man I murdered – the betrayer, the traitor, the killer – is back from the dead.

"Oh, Renza." Nouis chuckles darkly, the sound sending a swarm of nauseating tremors through my body. "Look at you. Did you really think you'd killed me?"

"Next time I'll try harder." The words are brittle as they leave my lips. Nouis barks with laughter, stepping closer and pressing his chest against my outstretched hand I raised to warn him away. As his body connects with my fingers, I want to cry. This is no awful spectre, no ghost or nightmare. He's real, he's here. A monster back from the grave.

I shake my head as I recoil, but he grips my wrist. His fingers dig into the flesh to keep me from moving.

"Don't be like that," Nouis purrs. Bile pools at the back of my throat. "It's okay. You're here now. Once you've had a chance to calm down, it'll all be okay. We can fix things."

Fix things? Fix things? *What on earth is he talking about?*

Nouis pulls my hand away from his chest but keeps hold of my wrist as he presses me further back against the table. I hate how I'm shaking; I hate how I'm fighting for each shallow, racing breath not to be accompanied by vomit and screams.

"First we'll eat and drink. Catch up on everything we've missed," Nouis continues, a sickening look creeping into his eyes. "Then we'll seek some privacy in the next room – we could even start there. Hmm, now there's an idea."

He means... He wants...

Fate save me! Save me or kill me or anything else. Get me out of this! Please, Father Fate, do something – anything!

"There is one thing I can't figure out, though, so if you'd be so kind as to explain before we start? How did you know?" Nouis continues like this conversation is entirely normal, like he's asking after the weather or how my weekend was rather than how I discovered his betrayals.

"What?" I gasp, frantically fighting to think my way out of this.

"How did you work it out?"

"Let go of me and I'll tell you," I snap, finding strength in the memory of defeating him once before. Nouis brushes off my comment and lifts his other hand to draw a possessive finger along my jaw.

"Oh, Renza, there's no need for hostility. Or fear," he croons softly. "I forgive you. For everything. For what you did to us, for what you did to me. Everything that followed. It's forgiven."

"Forgive me?" I cry, unable to understand what in Fate's Fury he's talking about. "*You* forgive *me*?"

"Of course." Nouis sighs. "That's what relationships are about. Forgiveness."

He's delusional. He's insane.

"You murdered my father, and you expect forgiveness?" I shout at him, throwing my hands against his chest. I try to push him back, push him away from me, but I'm battling stone. In a flash, Nouis traps my arms against his chest, pulling my face close to his.

"The fire did that. I saved you. I even saved Giulia." Nouis frowns like I'm being ridiculous. This close to him, he surrounds me. I can't escape and fear clogs my throat like poison.

"You kept her in that coma!"

"She would've woken up, once things were settled," Nouis argues. "After things at the bank were fixed. We couldn't have suspicions after all. And Dorado was making such a mess of the books. From one banker to another, it was an abomination. He had to go. I hear you saw to that."

I shake my head, fury and disgust tinging the cold, hard terror that's lodged in my throat.

"You didn't see what I was trying to build for us. Somehow you still don't," Nouis says, disappointment clear in his words. "I thought you'd see it for yourself, but that's okay. I can show you. I can take the lead for a while longer. Your grief clouds your vision, my love."

His last two words make me want to retch.

"What vision?" I hiss. "What possible reason can you have for the horrors you've brought, for your betrayals against me?"

"I have *given you* what you always wanted." Nouis's anger flares in his tone. "Think about our future. Together, you and I can rule this continent. We can bend it to our design. With our banks combined, we'd be the real wealth and the real power across the entire land. A few years under the yoke of my aunt, combining our banks and building our power discreetly, then we can exert our influence. Build a High Chamber exactly to our wills and push our power over every State, fiefdom and city. You and I would rule over everything, free from command or consequence. As it should be."

He's sick. He's twisted. He's depraved.

Nouis searches my face.

"You see it, don't you? The world and the power that we could build together."

He leans his head closer to mine and I arch backwards as far as I can, but it isn't much.

"It's okay. Don't panic. We can still have it all," Nouis breathes softly. "All Halice has to do is fall. Briefly. You and I are together again now. We can get everything back on track."

"You're mad."

Nouis sighs, rage appearing in his eyes.

"Don't be stupid, Renza. I'm giving you what you want."

"No, I never wanted this." I hate how watery my words are, how close I am to pleading with this monster. "I don't want this."

"I'm doing this for you!" he growls.

"You're delusional! I almost died when mercenaries attacked the High Chamber. Bellandi tried to kill me! My people are starving and you almost sank my bank!" I shout at him.

"That's your fault!" Nouis snaps at me, giving me a sharp shake. Pain cracks up my spine and pushes tears to my eyes. "Wake up, Renza! If you'd let the army take the city, if you had stayed by my side and trusted me, you never would've been harmed. By now we'd already be rebuilding, and all the pain and loss would be a thing of the past."

I can't fight the sob so I turn my head away and close my eyes tightly.

Idris was right. I should've listened to him. I should never have come here. This was all too easy.

"Shh, don't cry," Nouis croons, lifting one of his hands to my face and wiping away a tear that escapes my lashes. Then his fingers grab my jaw, planting the seeds for bruises as he forces my head back around to look at him. "I can fix your mistakes. We're together now."

A commotion starts outside and Nouis's head snaps towards the noise. I thrash my body backwards, finally able to pry an arm away from his grip. I scrabble around on the table behind me, fingers wrapping around a plate and I channel all my strength into my arm as I swing around. I slam it into his head, the metal clanging with a thwack. I throw my weight at him, shoving him back. I break free and sprint for the door.

I burst outside to find myself faced with a brawl. Tahira and Royah are fighting for their lives, the Church Militia closing ranks around them. The dead lie strewn across the ground, glassy eyes staring endlessly at the sky.

"RENZA!" roars Nouis, barely paces behind. I run, charging into the violence as I aim for Tahira. I stoop, fingers closing around a dropped sword as I run. I try to dart around the individual brawls, but a hand grabs the back of my tunic. I scream as I'm hauled backwards, the hand ripping at my hair and pulling the necklace so tight it cuts off my airway.

"I thought you were smarter than this. I thought you were braver," Nouis snarls in my ear, a sword now in his hand as he brings it up. I try swiping at him, but he shoves me forwards so hard I hit the ground on all fours. My arms ache with the force of catching myself, the prickly ground scraping against my palms.

I spin around, gasping for breath as Nouis looms over me. I scramble backwards frantically. Nouis raises his blade, pointing at me.

"Come with me, Renza. You know this is what you want."

"No."

"You've already forgiven me! You know you have. Why else would you be wearing my gift?" Nouis sneers.

Fresh tears spring to my eyes as the necklace suddenly becomes a noose around my throat.

A hero in maroon leather leaps forwards, knocking Nouis's blade to the side. Tahira stands between me and Nouis, ready to fight, already breathing hard.

"You?" Tahira laughs shortly, loathing in her tone. "I heard you were dead. Pity. Though now I suppose I get the pleasure of killing you myself."

"Your kind should've stayed across the ocean," Nouis hisses, launching himself at Tahira. Tahira is an artist with a blade, vicious and smart. But so is Nouis. Their styles are so different: Tahira favours sharp, fluid movements versus Nouis's raw power and pristine form.

I scramble to my feet, remembering what happened the last time I distracted the person fighting Nouis. I flee, desperately looking around and spying Alfieri sprinting towards us as fast as his athletic form can carry him.

Oh, thank Fate's Mercy.

I race towards him, away from the bridge that would lead us to Halice and the remainder of our forces.

"We've got to go!" I shout at him.

"Agreed. Watch it!" Alfieri shoves me aside as one of the Church Militia swings for him. He pulls out his blade, but the man gets too close and the blade sweeps down the side of Alfieri's head.

No!

I roar, lunging forwards with my sword to drive it through the soldier's side. Alfieri takes advantage of the wound I deliver and finishes the job.

We need to get out of here – now!
I can't let Alfieri get hurt again. I can't!

"Retreat! Retreat!" shouts Tahira. *Don't need to tell me twice.*

Alfieri and I sprint for the bridge.

"Come on! Get to the bridge!" shouts Tahira. She and Royah are so fast they're already gaining on us. We sprint as fast as we can for the small rope structure. I gasp for breath; my legs scream with the effort.

Alfieri pulls ahead and tears across it first, the structure strong but swaying under the violent movements. Royah and Tahira are perhaps a few paces in front of me when Royah throws herself forwards, crossing the bridge maybe three steps ahead. Tahira finds her footing on the rope crossing when—

Thump! Thud!

The world spins as I trip and fall. I hit the grassy floor and it knocks the wind out of me. I gasp and pick myself up from the dirt. Royah and Tahira are already a decent way across the bridge, both skidding to a stop.

"Renza! Renza!" shouts Tahira, turning back to get me.

I look at Alfieri on the other side, gripping his stomach wound as the Halician forces charge towards the crossing. Royah is already making her way back from safety, blood streaming down her face.

I'm a distraction. A liability. I'm too slow, I'm unskilled. I'll get them killed. The Church Militia are so close behind us. My gut turns to steel. I get up, sword in hand.

"HOLD ON!" I shout at them and swing the blade down on the rope securing the bridge in place.

"NO!" shrieks Tahira as the bridge drops beneath her feet. I watch her fingers grab hold of the rope as she falls from view. She'll make it, she'll be okay. They can hold on and climb up the other side to safety.

Now I need to get moving if I'm going to stand any chance at all.

"GET HER!" roars a sickeningly familiar voice that is far too close for comfort. I break into a panicked run, gasping for breath as I sprint along the side of the ravine. The remains of the Church Militia chase me down. I dart around trees, pushing hard as I follow the edge of the steep hill. Their heavy armour makes them loud and slow. I know exactly where they are, but I'm not built for this kind of thing. The thick, springing bushes seem to be trying to stop me, thrashing and clapping as I force my way past each leafy limb.

My lungs ache and my blood pumps cold and desperate. I can't let them get me. I can't. I don't know what Nouis will do to me after this, but with his level of delusion it won't be pretty.

Gasping for air, scrambling for space between me and the monsters on my tail, the rocks beneath my feet start to skitter and slip. The fear strangles my voice as suddenly I'm sliding inelegantly down the steep grey ravine, rocks turning to blades as they carve up my arms, legs and face as I try and steady my graceless tumble.

I roll off a small ledge and land in the river. At this point, it's not quite deep enough and I hit the pitiless riverbed of unyielding stone. Thankfully, it isn't full force, but it's still sharp and jarring. The water smothers my pain with cold, mocking giggles.

I flail in the water as I lurch inelegantly for the Halician side of the river. I claw my way up the rocky land, heaving water from my lungs and then up the other side of the ravine. I look behind me. The Church Militia are still coming after me, though their descent is far more careful and slower – I have some distance now.

The world is woozy and wet. I've lost my scavenged sword somewhere but I don't have time to waste.

I run. Following the path of the river and hugging the treeline, I move as fast as I can. Every step is punishing, every breath is fraught as I battle the fear threatening to strangle me. My clothes are torn and soaked, and mud is caked to my battered and bleeding limbs. There's just one thought in my mind, the word racing over and over and over again.

Run.

Run.

Run.

CHAPTER 28

I follow the river. While it might be winding, it does move in a specific direction – towards the coast. If I follow it, I know where I'll end up eventually. Which is also helpfully away from Nouis and his militia.

They are relentless. Every time I think I've put some distance between us, every time I dare to stop and try to catch my breath they show up, they appear like spectres amongst the trees, their black and white outfits signalling their approach like smoke, their blades brandished like poisoned teeth.

The sun sank from the sky many hours ago. Wild, hostile shadows now pool in all directions. Eyes lurk in every crevasse. Strange, haunted moans fill the cold night air, my breath shuddering as it leaves my lips.

The moon hides behind patchy grey clouds, deigning on occasion to toss a handful of moonlight over the world and taunt me with sight for a few paces. I keep moving, as fast as my aching limbs will allow. My feet are numb, my lips are cracked, and my is mouth dry. For hours and hours I stagger on, trying to find a path between the unknown danger lurking in the trees and the threat of visibility by the riverside. Even though my tunic is ruined – slashed open and covered in mud, thanks to my fall down the ravine – it's still brightly coloured. It's a beacon in the dark, so I must stay in the shadows.

I groan, pausing to lean against a tree as I try to catch my breath. I want to throw up but refuse to allow my body the concession. My stomach aches, howling almost as loudly as whatever animal is lurking in these woods. I press a hand to my mouth, desperately searching for some kind of strength to keep going. Exhaustion runs heavy in my bones, like a lead anchor trying to drown me.

Eyes. Eyes are stalking me.

My blood runs cold as I spin around, but I spy nothing in the unyielding darkness. I swallow, my dry mouth offering no comfort. But I know this beast is there. Something awful is drawing closer.

I'm being hunted.

I study the darkness again, my gaze flitting across the threatening navy trees swallowed by shadows. My bones shiver and thrust my heart into my mouth. No torches, no men. No sign of anyone.

But the gap is closing. I have to move; I have to run.

My life depends on it.

I break into a run, my lungs weeping for the effort as I throw myself faster and faster through these woods. Cold feet trudge carelessly over the roots, dirt and stones. My ankles twist and undulate, my arms pump through the cold air. My limbs protest every movement and tears of frustration build along my lash line.

I can't keep doing this. I'm not going to make it.

Exhausted and brutalised, I'm scraping the barrel for any semblance of energy. Fresh tears brew in my eyes as my limbs refuse to obey. Gasping and weeping, I stagger to a stop, leaning over my stomach as the stitch that has haunted my steps decides to rear its head again, biting vicious teeth through my stomach.

I can't keep going. I have nothing left.

It's getting closer. So much closer.

I turn to the yawning black jaw of the forest, scanning the near total darkness. I have no choice. I need cover. I can't keep moving. I don't have the strength. All that's left is hiding. Hiding and praying.

I stumble into the treeline, salty tears streaking down my cheeks as I push through the gloomy, veiled trees. Their tall, murky bodies loom overhead, leaves rattling like gnashing teeth, their spindly arms and bony black fingers reaching out to swallow me whole.

A dead tree lies on its side, a mass of roots and dirt ripped from the ground like splintered bones, left bare to decay. That'll work. I hurry for its cover, my pulse throbbing in my ears. My feet crunch over fallen leaves as I round its base and fold myself low into the darkness, a frozen lump of dead roots and dirt.

I attempt to fight the noise of my frantic breathing. I'm shaking so much my vision is blurry as I desperately clamp my fingers over my mouth. Hot tears burn along my lashes as they weave down my face. My aching body is entirely broken.

I stare deeper into the forest, not daring to blink. Deeper into the sneering sea of ebony and navy hues.

It's getting closer; the predator is coming.

Every muscle trembles, every sense screams. I think my heart might erupt in my throat. Every corner of my mind is begging and pleading with me to run. Run, run, run.

A shriek splits across the darkness and echoes through the forest. I crumple myself down as small as possible, pushing myself deeper into the mud and roots that jab cruelly into my beaten back. I close my eyes, silently crying, curled in a cold, muddy, bloody ball on the ground as the danger stalks closer.

The entire world is silent, that bold emptiness a

punishment from Fate trying to give me away. Ghostly hands wrap around my bare neck, as I silently pray for salvation. For mercy. For a swift ending.

"Renza!"

My eyes fly open and relief surges through me, so euphoric I could drown in it.

IDRIS!

Kneeling before me like a golden knight, examining me from head to toe, is the miracle I prayed for. The miracle Fate sent me.

I throw my arms around him, the sobs wrenching free of my throat as I bury my face in his chest. Idris's arms snap tightly around me, his blistering warmth and strength holding me together as I fall apart. I can't hold back the bubbling, ugly sobs I release, holding on as tightly as I can. Relief ripples on the babbling gratitude falling from my tongue. I can't stop shaking. Why can't I stop shaking?

"I've got you, I've got you now, I've got you," Idris repeats softly into my filthy hair, holding me close, like he'll never let me go. I breathe him in and – even now, even out here – the faint perfume of mint and lavender burns my nostrils. My nerves are entirely shot, but if anything will calm them it's him.

"Are you okay? Are you hurt?" Idris demands, his hands performing a methodical search along my body, carving a path of blistering destruction down tired, frozen limbs.

"Battered and bruised. A few shallow cuts," I hiccup, fighting to regain some fragment of control over the trembling teary mess I've become.

"Thank Fate for his mercies." Idris's words escape like a prayer, his hand returning to my head as he holds me closer.

"How—?" My question is interrupted with hiccups, making it next to inaudible. Idris somehow deciphers my meaning.

"Tahira saw you running as she climbed the bridge, so I knew the direction you'd gone. I prayed you'd think to follow the river. Why the hell would you do that? Why would you leave yourself behind?" Idris scolds, his voice laced with fear and panic.

"We couldn't get away if I didn't," I babble, desperately trying to wipe my eyes. "I would have got us caught. I couldn't do that, I couldn't—"

"But why didn't you get on the bridge before cutting it? You could've held on, too," Idris interrupts sharply. I gape, the bottom falling out of my stomach as a wave of self-loathing hits me square in the chest.

"Because I didn't think of it," I whisper, shame coiling in my throat.

Fate's Fury, I'm stupid! I'm so, so stupid.

He's right. I could've done that. Idris sighs, pressing his forehead against mine.

"It's okay. You're okay, that's all that matters. You're all that matters. Come on, let's get you out of here."

Idris encourages me to stand, his arms never leaving my back. I lean on him, perhaps more than I should, as we head back towards the river. His horse is waiting impatiently and the mottled black and brown mare tosses her mane as she sees us approaching.

We leave the dark embrace of the trees. The sky begins to warm, a faint yellow glow kissing the ghostly treetops. Dawn is coming.

I've been out here alone all night. *How far have I walked? Where are we?*

"Okay, first drink this." Idris pulls his waterskin from the saddle and hands it to me. I do as I'm told, taking a mouthful of the water. Pure nectar gushes down my throat, soothing the raw, rough flesh. I indulge in another mouthful before handing it back.

Idris helps me up into the saddle, then mounts behind me. He presses himself against my back, his arms coming around me to gather the reins. I lean back into the warmth of his embrace. Vicious needles nip at my fingers and my pulse thrums a hot, impatient rhythm in my ears. But it's him. Every itch, every whisper, every flicker of the flames. It's Idris.

It's safety.

"Eat this," Idris says softly, pulling out something that looks like a dried biscuit from his pocket. I take it gratefully, my withered stomach desperate for any offering.

"Where are we?" I croak around a mouthful of food.

"Back in Halician territory now, thankfully," Idris answers as he leads the horse on. "I think there's a road not too much further away. Once we find it, we can follow it to a town and get your wounds properly seen to – and get some real food."

"What happened to the men chasing me?" I ask, shuddering. "Are they still behind us?"

"No. Tahira and Royah decided to hang back and tidy them up for us," Idris says. "So I could focus on finding you."

"Should we go find them?"

"No, that was hours ago," Idris admits. "They agreed to go back to Halice when they were done. If I don't get a message back to Halice in a day's time, they'll raise a search party."

I nod, relaxing back into the warmth of his body. I raise a hand to my eyes, the exhaustion and fear of the night catching up quickly. If I'm not careful, I'll fall asleep in this saddle and tumble right off the horse.

"It's okay. You can use me," Idris whispers softly. "I'll keep you safe. Rest your eyes, just for a bit."

I shake my head. Idris has been awake all night, too. He is every inch as tired as I am, so if he can stay awake, so can I. At least until we get somewhere more populated.

"Still stubborn, I see." He chuckles in my ear.

The sun climbs steadily higher in the sky as the river swaps its sinister whispers for gleeful giggles. Then, after an hour or two following its direction, we come to the road Idris promised.

Made of mud and stones, it carves a bumbling path through

large, open plains and tall, wavy grasses. Soon we spy livestock in fields, and even other travellers pass us on the road. The sun is bursting and brilliant, chasing the chill from the air when we crest a hill, and discover a large town nestled at the base of a valley.

I could sing for joy.

We ride down the worn cobbled roads into the settlement. It's bursting with activity and noise as people flit about their work. The buildings are made of local grey stone, their roofs thatched with thick beige straw. Bright decorations hang across windows, bunting leaps across the open streets, and wreaths of autumnal flowers explode over doors and walls. We arrive in the centre of town, where preparations are fully underway for a huge celebration. The stage is almost constructed and large tables are being laid out for the feast. The most divine smells leak from every window.

Idris pushes the horse onwards until we find an inn. Idris slips off first, then helps me down from our faithful steed. I stagger as my feet hit the ground, gripping onto him tightly as I steady myself.

We enter the pub, which is brimming with people. We wind through the patrons towards the bar. A plump, cheerful barkeep flashes us both a wide smile and lays his hands on the surface.

"Welcome, welcome. What'll you 'ave?" he asks, though he eyes me warily – assessing the state of me.

"Two plates of whatever is hot and ready, with two pints to wash it down," Idris answers warmly. "Any rooms available? We've unfortunately had a rough time while travelling."

"Oh, you and your wife are lucky, signore. We just had someone leave their room – which, let me tell you, doesn't happen this close to Agoi. Most of the town is booked up weeks in advance." The barkeep chatters happily as he sets about getting what we've asked for.

"Excellent. We'll take it. We'll be needing baths, too, if you can arrange it? Sooner rather than later is preferable." Idris handles everything as we ease onto the available barstools. My elbow props up my head as I fight the exhaustion long enough to have the hot meal Idris has bought me. The barkeep nods, eyebrows lifting.

"Yeah, you look like you need it. What happened?" he asks, setting the cheap ale down in front of us.

"Got lost," Idris sighs, "and my wife had a really nasty tumble down the hill. Don't suppose you know a good doctor to check the wounds?"

I almost choke hearing Idris call me his wife. I force myself not to look up lest our lie be caught out.

"No! That's dreadful. Are you alright?" the barkeep says, looking mildly horrified. "I do know a good doctor, and I'm happy to send word?"

"I'm fine," I reassure him. "Nothing a bit of rest and a good meal can't cure."

"If you're sure. Well, here you go," he says as a young woman brings over two hot bowls with a side of bread. I dive into the bread, dunking it into the delicious soup. This might just be the greatest meal I've ever had.

"We need to send a message to Halice. It's urgent," Idris says.

"This close to Agoi? No one will want to go all the way there. They won't make it back in time for tomorrow." The barkeep frowns. "Can't it wait?"

"I'll make it worth their while. Anyone willing to go can name their price – within reason of course." Idris chuckles. "Not to mention, Agoi in Halice is beautiful. Could be a once-in-a-lifetime experience."

"Ah, you're from the city." The barkeep chortles to himself as though he should've figured. "Well, I can ask around."

"I'd appreciate it," Idris answers.

Idris keeps conversing with the barkeep as I devour my

meal. It's all I can do to fight the heaviness of my eyelids, now weighted with invisible lead. I finish my meal, washing it down with the bitter ale.

"Is it alright if I have that bath now?" I ask weakly, once every drop is gone from my flagon.

"And the room key," says Idris, paying generously. The barkeep nods and yells at a woman who I think is his daughter about showing me where I can bathe. I follow along a narrow corridor to a room, and she hands me a clean towel.

"Water and fire to warm it is in there. Heat up as much as you want," she says before leaving me alone. I lock the door and set a large pot of water over the roaring fireplace, being sure to stoke the flames to keep it hot. Then I set about the work of peeling off my clothes.

There is a skinny, cracked mirror at one end of the small room. I look at myself in the reflection, my mouth falling at what I see. My hair is wild and wound with leaves and sticks. Mud coats the right side of my face, merging with the bruises that float along my jaw. More bruises streak across my ribs like painful violet clouds. My stomach has several shallow cuts, and there's another one on my arm. It's a miracle I haven't contracted an infection. Around my neck is a vicious, ragged red line where Nouis's necklace cut into my throat. The culprit still sits there, hanging like a brand on my chest.

I rip it off me and hurl it across the room. I pant furiously as fresh tears come to my eyes. The memory of his hands on me... The look in his eyes... The necklace hits the wall with a dull thud, then clatters to the floor. It's gone. He can't touch me. He won't touch me again.

I finish setting up my bath with shaking hands and climb into the narrow metal tub. The warmth against my frigid toes is painful and I let out a muffled groan as I sink into the heated embrace. I don't want to waste time. The promise of a warm bed is calling to me. I need it now.

I work methodically, starting with my face and hair, and moving down my body. I find myself emptying and starting new buckets twice. No point scrubbing myself with dirty water. When I'm done I put on my undershirt again, the hem just long enough to keep me decent. Everything else is logged with too much mud and dirt to go back on my body.

Finally, with hair wet around my shoulders, I open the bathroom door. Idris is waiting outside, half asleep where he stands.

Is he standing guard for me?

He opens his eyes, a shadow of exhaustion lurking around the fierce hazel. He smiles at me softly but it's short-lived as he takes in the obvious bruising that mud and poor light can no longer hide. He furrows his brow, lifting his hands towards my chin but stopping just short of touching me. His eyes drop to the vicious red mark wrapping around my neck, certain no fall could make those marks. Fury flares behind that maddening hazel.

"Which way is our room?" I ask, clearing my throat. Idris gestures down the hall.

"Number fifteen. I won't be long. I could use a quick wash myself," Idris answers. I take the key from his hands gratefully as I slip my body past his.

The room is small but warm. A fireplace is laid ready; the bed is made with clean linen sheets and a thick, colourful woollen blanket. There is a deep-set window framed by heavy curtains, and an old wooden table with two chairs pushed up against the other wall.

I drop my ruined clothes and boots in the corner and hurry towards the bed. I peel back the cover and crawl underneath, wet hair splaying over the pillow behind me as I lay my head down. I swear I only close my eyes for a minute, only a minute, and yet the sound of the door opening again has me bolting upright.

Idris walks in, his blond hair dripping water as he closes the door and locks it tight. His loose shirt hangs half tucked from his black trousers as he puts his belongings on the side. He smiles at me, his exhaustion unmasked. He walks towards the bed, stopping short of getting in.

"Is this alright?" asks Idris cautiously, like he's worried his very words will strike me with more wounds. I nod.

"Of course. You're as tired as I am," I say, patting the empty side of the bed. Idris sits, holding up his hand. My stomach drops when I see the necklace.

"I found this and thought you might want it back—"

"I never want to see that again!" I spit, my fingers launching to my throat. Idris flinches, his fingers closing over the jewellery to hide it from view.

"You've been wearing it every day lately." Idris frowns. Fresh tears spring to my eyes, and my mouth trembles as I speak.

"It's *his*," I manage. I press my hands to my face, trying to physically hold back the tears as they well behind my eyes. Idris sucks in a sharp breath.

"What?" he demands.

"I thought it was from you." I hate how frail and stupid the words sound as I wipe the hair from my face. "It arrived on my birthday, outside my front door. No name, no note, just like when you gave me those Malayan books on mind-stilling. I thought you were being ... you. But it was him."

"Bastard," hisses Idris, glaring at the necklace between his fingers.

"I'm so sorry," I babble, eyes stinging as the water wells. This is my fault. I thought I'd killed him. I thought he was gone for good.

"Hey, it's not your fault," Idris says seriously. I wrap my arms around myself, leaning back against the headboard.

"He said he did it for me," I whisper, the memory of his words haunting me. The ghost of his fingers makes me want to vomit. I close my eyes, but a tear breaks free to slip down my cheek. Idris reaches for my shoulder, giving a reassuring squeeze.

"What else did he say?"

I sigh, swallowing as I force myself to relive the details.

"He said that this is what I wanted, that it wasn't too late. He wants to join our banks and be the de facto power in the continent." I force the words out, suddenly feeling cold all over. "He said he did it all for me, to give me what I wanted. He said this is all my fault."

Idris mutters unintelligibly under his breath, but it sounds rude.

"What's worse ... is he still ... *wants me*." I hate how saying the words makes them real. "He kept saying he forgives me. That he could fix things. He expected us to... He set up a bed..." I can't finish as my entire body shudders. I have no breath left; it's walled by the storm thrashing to escape my lungs. Idris's entire body turns to stone at the words. I wipe the stray tears away with trembling fingers, wondering how on earth I'm supposed to sleep knowing that lunatic is out there.

"Forget him. We can talk once we're rested. You're safe now, and he won't get you," Idris promises. I nod, but can't seem to throw those disgusting words from my mind. They cling like slime to the inside of my brain.

Idris shifts closer, slowly wrapping his arm around my shoulders.

"Is touching okay?" he asks quietly. I nod, even though his touch brings sharp flames rolling over my skin. I suck in a shuddering breath as he pulls me closer against his chest, lying us both down in the bed. Between the boiling heat of his chest and my bare cheek is his shirt, the thin material somehow withstanding the inferno.

"Focus on your breathing," Idris suggests softly, his voice deep and steady. "Focus on the bond. Something familiar, something controllable. I'm right here, feel that. Feel me."

I nod, blinking hard as I focus on mind-stilling. It takes all the control of my exhausted mind to keep my breathing slow, to let the writhing heat and flying sparks of pain wash over my body and not find a place to root. I focus until I drift off into uneasy slumber.

CHAPTER 29

Slowly, sunlight slips between the curtains of this room. It falls over my face, which is pressed into a warm chest that breathes slow and even. I blink a little, then remember the chest in question.

I freeze, not daring to move a single inch as my pulse throbs in my ears. But not like normal – not in the way Idris normally elicits, the way that thrashes and punishes and stabs through my veins.

His chest is warm ... but it's ... just that. Warm. Comfortable. There's no fire that threatens to burn me alive. No searing pain, not even the stinging of pins and needles. His warmth is pleasant, like soaking up the first beautiful day of spring after a long, cold winter.

I dare to turn my head to look up at Idris has he sleeps.

No vile whispers. No revulsion so sharp I want to claw my skin off. Nothing.

It's him.

A grin stretches wide across my face as I push up further to look at him properly. Idris shifts in his sleep, consciousness floating to the surface as his full pink lips part slightly, those long lashes fluttering softly.

The rumours are true. I thought they were just silly stories made up to tease children. But they were right: for one glorious day, we're free.

Joy fills up my belly, as I gently shake his shoulder.

"Happy Agoi," I whisper with bated breath. Idris's brow buckles for a moment, but then his eyes fly open and that sleepy, beautiful hazel gaze finds my face. His mouth falls open for a long moment, his mind racing to make sense of the unusual silence of our bond.

"Happy Agoi," Idris answers, a wild grin splitting across his face as we both start laughing. I don't know why, but it seems to be the only thing we can do. Bounding, unrestrained laughter pours from our lips. I collapse back down into the bed, soaking in the divine feeling of freedom.

"Wow," Idris says, rolling to his side to face me. A small giggle leaves my lips.

"I know, right?"

"It's ... it takes a moment to get used to," Idris barks, incredulous.

"I didn't move a muscle for like a minute, afraid it was a trick," I admit before biting my lip.

"It feels kind of weird," Idris breathes. "To hear your voice and not feel..."

"So weird!" I agree, meeting his eyes. "To see your face without..."

Idris and I smile, our eyes ensnaring each other for a long moment. No battle, no abrasion. Just shared warmth, shared relief ... shared jubilation.

"Well, we should probably make the most of it," I say, sitting up in bed, throwing off the covers to get up. "Get some food and get on the road."

"Or..." Idris draws out the word as he sits up. That sounds like trouble. I smile at him, raising an eyebrow expectantly.

"Or?"

"If you want to make the most of it, we could stay another day," Idris suggests. "Explore the local festival and head back tomorrow instead."

"We can't do that." I frown. "We have to tell the others—"

"I sent a rider with a message yesterday, although the price was extortionate," Idris snorts. "They know we're safe and heading home."

"But what about Nouis—?"

"No! No. Let's not think about that stain on humanity for a day at least." Idris walks around the bed to my side. He sits next to me, holding out a hand and waiting for me to take it. I do, settling my fingers into the cosy warmth of his grip with a small smile.

"Come on, just ... one day." Idris rubs his thumb over the back of my hand, tracing wonderful patterns. "One day away from wars and politics and problems we have to solve. We have today with no bond. We should celebrate. Let's take just one small day for ourselves. Don't we deserve that much?"

I groan. This isn't fair. Without the bond in the way, his voice really is deep and charming, his smile so seductively persuasive. I nod, relenting.

"Alright. One day," I agree as Idris grins in victory.

"Yes! Right, you stay here," Idris says, grabbing his jacket and shoes. "I'll scrounge up some clothes for you and find some breakfast."

"Alright," I say as he heads for the door. He flashes a disarming wink in my direction before whisking from the room. I laugh, falling back against the covers and grinning to myself like an idiot. I feel almost euphoric.

About twenty minutes later the barkeeper's daughter

knocks on my door with a bundle of clothes. Idris is nowhere in sight.

I thank her, unfold the items, and set about getting ready.

The dress is a cheerful cherry red, with a fitted lace-up bodice and sweetheart neckline. The skirt is made of tumbling layers of red and white with a lace trim that falls to just below my knees. The sleeves are fitted to the elbow, where they trumpet outwards with a few ruffled layers of white lace.

I tighten the bodice using the strings at the front, finishing them off with a little bow and pulling the simple patterned leather belt over the top, and fasting it in place to hide the knot. Idris has also sent new boots, though perhaps new isn't the right word. The worn brown leather is comfortable as it reaches up my shins. My dark hair tumbles free and wild around my face as sleeping on it wet did nothing to help tame the frizzy waves. At least it's clean.

I leave the room, locking it behind me and slipping the key into a pocket on my bodice. I head towards the main restaurant area and find the room stuffed to the brim. Already the drinking is underway, with raucous noise and laughter in every corner.

It takes me a long moment to find Idris amongst the crowd, unable to use the bond like I usually would. He's standing amongst a group of men, laughing and drinking like they've been the best of friends their entire lives. I take a moment and smile at him. Now I can see him as everyone else does: a warm friend, a charismatic and inviting person; someone always welcome, always inviting.

Idris looks up eventually, spying me standing by the door. The fact he couldn't use the bond to feel my attention really is something. I grin, folding my arms as I wait. He doesn't hesitate to weave his way over to me, leaving his drink behind.

"Ready?" he asks excitedly, that golden gaze sparkling with anticipation.

"Ready for what?" I ask.

"For an adventure. I got all the gossip about the best places to go," Idris says, taking hold of my hand. "Come on."

We hurry out of the pub together, stepping out into the warm autumn day.

The streets are packed and everyone wears strong, vivid colours, and it looks like a rainbow as they pass from stall to stall in the streets. A small crowd has gathered at one corner, and we stop to watch a man performing magic tricks. He pulls a rose out of a lady's sleeve, makes one gentleman's hat fly over the crowd, and then he starts making small balls appear in other people's closed hands and pockets.

I clap in delight as a woman opens her palm and a small colourful bird flies away. Further down the street, music starts.

"Come on." Idris grins, his warm fingers intertwined with mine as we hurry to watch. I lean closer to him, my other hand gripping his muscled arm as we continue our exploration. The sun bounces off the stone walls, washed with simple yet brilliant decorations of every design.

Idris stops off by one of the stalls. The table is overflowing with beautiful flowers combined with hair jewellery. He picks up a headband wound with white chrysanthemums and indigo aster flowers. He turns around, reaching up to put it in my hair for me. I laugh as it settles in place across my crown.

"There, perfect!" he announces with joy, reaching for his gold purse. I turn back to the table as I find the perfect one for him.

"This one, too!" I tell the seller as Idris starts to pay. I lift up the garland of salvia and crimson petunias. I set it amongst his blond hair, tugging gently to be sure it's fixed into place.

"There we go. Now we both have one," I tell him.

"Good, I wouldn't want to be the only one without." He grins. "Come on, I know you love dancing."

We follow our ears all the way back to the centre of town.

Up on the stage, which is strewn with streamers of green, yellow and red, is a brilliant local band. The drums are fast, the strings and accordions lively and full of gusto, and the wind instruments pick out fantastic harmonies. The small square is packed with bodies, either crammed at tables, chatting and downing food, or spinning across the dancefloor in their loved ones' arms.

I take Idris's hand and pull him to the dancefloor.

"I don't know this one!" he protests.

"No one does." I laugh, taking both his hands as I spin us around. "Just enjoy it!"

The smile on his face is infectious. The music builds and soars, seducing us with it in merry symphony. We dance and dance, spinning and sweating and smiling until our faces ache and our limbs are spent. I spin, and twirl, feeling my loose hair fly around me. I'm giddy, light and free.

Fate's Fury, when was the last time I went out dancing?

Not since my aunts arrived in town, that's for sure.

Idris and I drift on and off the dancefloor, grabbing drinks and quick, delicious snacks from the nearby vendors before getting back to the dance. My feet ache, but in the best way. The beat and tunes pull and push in wonderous harmony. Time races and stands still all at once. Today is detached from reality as we enjoy the performances and explore this beautiful town while the musicians take their breaks.

As the sun stains the sky with bronze and wine hues, Idris and I sit at the end of a wonky wooden table in the centre of town. Sweat coats the back of my neck and face, the trifling breeze occasionally sending delightfully cool kisses across my body. I tear into the hot, sweet roll Idris has bought, my large flagon of cheap ale half-empty.

"Oh, here we go." Idris nudges me, pointing behind me. I turn around, seeing that the game is about to start. Apparently, it's a local Agoi tradition.

"Alright, blindfolds on everyone!" the game master instructs as Soulmate couples line up on opposite sides of the square and everyone ties their blindfolds into place. "Okay, everyone set? On your marks ... get set ... go!"

The crowd erupts into laughter and cajoles the couples, as they stumble blindly towards each other. The goal becomes clear: find your Soulmate above the noise and the chaos of the games.

"Look, look!" Idris comes to my side of the table, and I scoot up to make room for him. He points to an elderly man in the corner with his hands out in front of him as he walks confidently towards an elderly lady. People have stumbled, people have got tangled. Apparently, walking straight with a blindfold on after lots of drinking is really difficult. Lots of people bump into each other, and there's fits of giggling as the crowd cheers them on.

"Come on! You've got this!" I call, stamping my tired feet on the ground as the elderly couple get closer and closer.

"Yes! That's it!" Idris encourages. They're paces from each other, moving slow and steady. Their hands connect and a bell sounds. Idris and I leap to our feet, cheering with everyone else. As the first couple to find each other, they're the winners.

The couple embrace, love shining in their eyes as they're reunited.

"Okay, we need that game in Halice!" says Idris, laughing as he sits back down next to me. His other arm rests behind me as he swigs his ale.

"We don't have a square big enough for every Soulmate couple in Halice." I laugh before finishing my sweet bread and reaching for my own drink.

"Then loads of smaller games," Idris counters, leaning closer so I can hear him over the din of the crowd.

"Well, I'll leave you to organise it." I grin. "You haven't seen the river parade in years."

"Oh, the parade!" Idris sighs wistfully. "That was my favourite as a kid."

"It's still one of my favourites." People in Halice create beautiful paper floats of the most vivid and creative scenes and send them bobbing down the river and into the ocean. People are so inventive.

"Have you ever made a float?" asks Idris.

"Of course. Giulia and I used to compete when we were kids, until one really nasty fight. Then my father forced us to collaborate for a few years." I smirk at the memory.

"Not anymore?" Idris asks. I shrug.

"We both got busy. Maybe next year." I laugh and reach up to push my hair back behind my ear. The curls tickle my bare neck, my fingers brushing against the dog-eared flowers. After a day of dancing, drinking and sweating, they can't be looking their freshest.

Idris finishes his drink and gets back to his feet.

"Come on then," he says, taking my hand. "One more dance?"

"Oh, go on then!"

Idris and I dance to three more songs before, tipsy and happy, we stumble back to the inn. We stagger through the crowded bar, giggling like naughty teenagers as we head back to our room. I fumble with my bodice, producing our room key before deftly turning it in the lock.

We hurry inside and I lean on the arm of an obliging chair before bending down to pluck at the clasps on my boots.

"Oh, my feet!" I groan in good humour, already feeling the blisters from the straps.

"Let me." Idris chuckles and kneels down. I slide into the seat, smiling as his warm fingers deftly pull the boot from my foot. He tosses it over his shoulder, reaching for the other one.

"Oh, that feels so much better." I sigh, resting my bare foot flat against the cool wooden floor, the muscles slowly uncoiling.

"Good. Begone foul footwear!" With that, he tosses the offending boot over his shoulder. I snort as I rest my other foot on the ground. I look to Idris and laugh as he stands up. He's somehow got powdered sugar all over his cheek.

"How did you even manage that!" I stand and reach up to wipe it away. My fingers tingle with a softly fuzzy warmth as I brush them against his face, my breath catching as I meet the trap of his eyes. We stand barely an inch apart. I swallow, blood racing to my cheeks. My heart pounds so loudly I'm sure he can hear it.

"Don't look away," Idris whispers as his hand skims up the outside of my arm. A delicious shiver ripples like falling stars along my spine. His hand gently falls to my neck, his touch so delicate and warm on the sensitive skin.

His thumb carefully presses into my jaw and he tilts my head upwards to properly face him. My breath quivers as it leaves my lips, trapped in the allure of his study.

"Your eyes are stunning." He barely moves his lips, the words coming out breathy, like a prayer. "Like a polished midwinter sky."

I reach up to touch his face. The fingers of one hand slowly dance across his brow and around his eyes, a smile pulling at my face as I take him in. His eyes remind me of High Summer sunsets and molten honey, so warm and soft and inviting.

I've never been able to hold his gaze this long. To study him so freely and without restraint or distraction. I knew he was handsome, tall and fair. But I didn't know that when he's lost in thought a dimple appears between his brows. I didn't know about a small, barely visible scar that skims the outside of his left eye. I didn't know about the way his lips quiver before he smiles.

Idris lets out a quiet, shaky breath. His fingers slip down my neck to brush the ugly bruise that decorates the ridge of my collarbones.

"I am never letting you out of my sight again." His deep voice takes on a sacred tone, like he's swearing an oath.

"This wasn't your fault. You don't have to protect me just to prove a political point," I whisper softly.

"Protecting you has nothing to do with politics." Idris sounds almost offended. I'm about to respond when he drops his head closer to mine.

"Don't you get it yet, Renza? How else can I tell you?" Idris breathes, a hand slipping behind my waist as he pulls me against his warm, solid chest. I gaze up at him as his fingers tangle with my hair. "Fate bound us together in life and in death."

His head slowly sinks down, those golden eyes never leaving my face. My heart hammers in my chest.

"Everything we are, belongs to each other," he murmurs. His breath runs over my lips, a ripple of tingles covering the sensitive skin.

"Two halves searching to become whole," I whisper back, my eyes half-closed. His mouth is an inch from mine, our breaths mindless with the scent of ales and sweet bread.

"Please, tell me." Idris's hands go to the back of my head, fingers intertwining with my hair. "I need to hear you say it."

"You're mine, and I am yours." I whisper the words that have plagued me for weeks. Words I didn't dare admit even to myself. Words I can no longer deny. "We're inevitable."

"You're mine," answers Idris. "My sweetest rival, my divine nemesis. My Fated undoing."

His mouth descends on mine and his lips move like a man starved. The ambrosia of his tongue drowns any sense and shrinks the whole world to him and only him. His hand moves down my back to pull me flush against his body, a trail of pleasure shuddering across my skin like melting stars.

I knot my fingers in his thick blond hair, matching his

tempo. This kiss is not tame or soft. I need more. I crave all of him.

My hands go to the buttons of his jacket and quickly pull them free, and Idris reaches down to yank his shirt over his head. He throws it to one side, his mouth off mine for barely a moment before it returns to its rightful place. His tongue plays rapturous tricks along mine, but I return his devotion in kind.

He reaches down, picking me up as though I weigh nothing at all before laying me down on the bed. Through his trousers I can feel every long, thick, delicious inch of him pressed against my hip. His warm, chiselled body leans over mine. The softness of his skin, the roughness of his five o'clock shadow, the fervour of his hands blocking all else from my mind…

His hand slowly slides down, reaching the hem of my skirt. His fingers seek out naked skin, before slowly drifting up my body. His lips move to my neck, attending to the sensitive flesh with faithful attention. My moan encourages the path of his fingers, higher and higher until they reach the pulsing, needy wetness between my thighs.

I buck, gasping as his fingers drift over my entrance. His groan of approval and hunger thrums with excitement. He starts his tease, making my knees weak and my heart pound. My bliss builds and builds, the artistry of his fingers an all-consuming work.

His other hand quickly does away with the belt at my waist, tugging on the strings of my bodice until he can pull the dress apart. His mouth and hands explore the fresh skin on offer, his dedicated exploration occurring with touch and tongue.

He relents on my core, using both hands to pull my dress over my head, leaving me completely naked underneath him. His eyes burn with hunger as he looks down at me.

"Fate's Mercies, your breasts are perfect. You are perfect," he moans, descending to devour them with kisses. I arch my back, mewling as his tongue dances across my nipple. A deep growl of need leaks from his throat and he presses his groin against mine. Only the maddeningly thin material of his trousers separates us.

I push off the bed, throwing him flat against the sheets as I lower myself to his waistband. I push his trousers out of the way and wrap my hand around his shaft. Idris emits a string of profanities as he watches my tongue travel from the base of his cock to the tip.

"Renza," he pants as I swallow him into my mouth. Damn, I'm not sure how he fits, but I feel him at the back of my throat. I suck hard, letting my tongue work around the skin as I slide up and down with deliberate, teasing slowness. His hands tangle in my hair. Fate, I love hearing him writhe against the sheets. He throws his head back, his golden hair a mess, his face twisted with ecstasy building higher and higher.

After several, long, delicious moment he pulls himself away. But there is a fevered light in his eyes as he climbs on top of me, his mouth returning to demand mine. I'm captivated by him.

"The first time I have you, I will have you properly," Idris almost growls in my ear as his hands grab my thighs. He presses his long manhood against my core, swallowing my moans with devouring kisses. He rubs, pressing every inch of him against my wetness, rubbing and teasing until his hand sweeps lower.

He positions himself, pausing to look into my eyes. I reach up, knotting my fingers through his blond hair. He thrusts, pushing all the way to the hilt, and I'm sent spinning. Delirious, divine ecstasy thrums through my entire body as he fills up every single inch of me.

He starts moving, in and out. He drives me hard, desperately and deliciously. I feel something akin to madness. I grip him tightly, holding on for the ride. His perfect arse is clenched as he pounds into me, his sweaty, muscled body working against mine. Again and again, he slams home with building waves of starlight forming inside me. Our moans answer one another, our panting mingles.

"Idris!" I cry as the mountain shatters, sending blissful stars exploding across my body.

"Renza!" Idris answers, following me with his own release. The two of us ride the waves of climax until we collapse, sweaty and reeling on the mattress, limbs entwined.

Together.

CHAPTER 30

Searing talons slash relentlessly across my body. My skin blisters and boils as I lie on top of a roaring bonfire. Agony spasms up my spine, sharp and vicious as barbed wire.

I gasp and bolt upright.

Naked, I scramble away with raw, unadulterated revulsion curdling my blood like a malevolent toxin. Sitting on the edge of the bed, I glare at the wall and fight to control my breathing. I grasp the sheets to cover myself with one hand, the other flying to my throat like I could force the air back into my lungs.

Idris stirs at my mad scramble. He flinches sharply and lurches himself to the other side of the bed, fighting for his own breath. The two of us sit silently back-to-back on the bed, glaring at the floor, fighting to control our freshly reignited bond.

The wave of pain surges through me, mingling with the stinging in my eyes as reality settles back in.

Water wells along my lash line like shattered glass.

"I'm sorry. I didn't mean to—" I whisper, but I'm interrupted.

"It's not you," Idris answers. His voice has regained its virulent itch.

I grip the sheets so hard it feels like my knuckles might break. Misery swells, rushing up towards my face. I press a hand to my mouth, desperate to swallow my sorrow.

It's back. This awful, terrible Soulhate bond. The desire to claw out his eyes, the urge to feel his warm blood coating my fingers, it's all returned. This is our brutal reality. Yesterday was a cruel, fleeting reprieve. Dancing and laughing and kissing ... a merciless delusion. This is our life; this is our truth.

Fated enemies. Each other's promised ruin. This is what we are.

"Idris..." I start my whisper coarsely.

"No. Just a bit longer." Idris's voice is thick. "I don't want ... I don't want to feel this. I want to pretend ... for a bit longer."

I close my eyes, my breath trembling as tears freely spill down my face. My heart pounds in my ears, each throb breaking harder and sharper than before.

"I don't want to feel this either." I let out the half-sob.

Our confessions hover on the air between us. I wrestle with the urge to look around at the black sun roaring behind me. The biting at my fingertips, the whispers of violence hovering at the edges of my ears, it's all back.

"Fate plays a cruel game. Those that deny him always pay a terrible price." My breathy words can't conceal their woeful pitch. "Yesterday was a wicked, spiteful lie."

"No," Idris growls. "This is the lie."

Idris's hand moves amongst the bedsheets, the rustling growing closer. I suck in a breath as his sizzling fingers wrap around mine, a jolt of fire racing up my bones to assault my chest.

"Yesterday was us." Idris's voice is dark and deep and filled with quiet rage. "Yesterday is who we really are. Without the interference of Fate. We were exactly who we chose to be. We were us."

"It was an illusion."

"It was freedom, a revelation. For a single, beautiful day we had freedom and chose each other. And it was *everything*." Idris's voice is rough, but his fingers lock tighter with mine. "Don't lie. Don't retreat and put up a wall pretending it was anything different. Don't take that from us, too."

"I won't." I hate the swollen, watery words but they're true as they leave my quivering tongue. "Yesterday was … it was amazing."

"You meant what you said to me," Idris declares. "I know you did. Don't regret it, don't hide from it. Not from me."

"We're Soulhates, Idris," I cry, hating how my voice breaks. "There's no escape."

"I don't want to escape you. Fate bound us together and I am glad for it, for you are mine in a way no one else is. And I am yours."

I look up to the ceiling, cursing whichever of the gods will hear me. My shoulders buckle as I curl myself inwards, knees drawing to my chest.

"You might be my Fated, Renza Di Maineri. But I choose you. Now and always, I choose you," whispers Idris.

I let out a bubbling sob. His words fill me with simultaneous joy and despair.

"I choose you, Idris Patricelli. You're my choice, my Fate, my future. Whether it's to victory or ruin, joy or misery." I grip his fingers with all my strength, but it still feels brittle. "We will do it together. My Fated, my chosen."

Our hands shake in the sheets. I press my other hand to my face as tears stream from my eyes, falling silently to my lap as I cry.

Because we're stuck. Without him I'm drowning and alone, unmoored in a storm. With him I'm battling an inferno that threatens to consume me. There is no break, no peace. This is forever. This is us.

Idris turns in the bed towards me. I bite back my cries. He pulls on my arm, waiting patiently as I gather myself enough to face him.

Looking at him is like looking at the raw, punishing majesty of the sun. He leans closer, his brow furrowed as his hand skims up to cup my face. My lashes flutter against the flames that twirl across my cheek as his thumb slowly wipes away my tears. His head lowers closer and closer to mine, each torturous inch closing with a throbbing pulse and screaming whispers echoing through my mind.

"Renza Di Maineri, my dearest destruction, my beguiling foe," Idris whispers softly. "My Fated choice."

His mouth is fire and burns into mine with a fierce, defiant fury that dominates me. I grip onto him tightly, terrified to let go. Because he's mine. I choose him, now and always. My Fated. My choice.

My Idris.

CHAPTER 31

The journey back to Halice is a long one. Thankfully, after the first three hours, the roads begin to flatten and widen, their condition improving significantly as we get closer to the city. We stop for lunch and to give the horse a rest by a large lake.

Idris and I lounge by the water, soaking up the autumnal sunshine that will soon bow to the cool winds winter will bring.

Though it didn't come with the ease that Agoi gave us, spending this time with him away from Halice is beautiful. While we both have to be careful of our self-control, our looks, our touches, at least we're still together. The stresses of the city can justifiably be ignored; we can simply be ourselves. Idris tells me about some of his adventures abroad and I tell him about my favourite adventures at home. We offer small pieces of ourselves for the other to see a little better.

The sky glows with the glorious gold and amber as we come to the top of a hill and see the enchanting beauty of Halice. From our vantage point, looking down, we can see every vibrant colour, every gleaming, domed roof, every twinkling candle prepared for the night that's slowly settling in.

"Welcome home," Idris says, his warm voice rippling down my neck. A small prick of disappointment hums in my chest, but guilt and shame make me shove it way, way down. This is our home; these are our lives.

Idris and I ride through the city, the horse hooves loud on the cobbles as we finish the final part of our journey. People look as we pass, calling out in greeting. But the look in their eyes isn't joy. Instead, there is alarm and concern.

What happened while we were away?

Idris turns up the road to my home and stops the mare outside the front door. He slips off first, reaching up to help me down. I hit the ground, my arse hurting from the long day of riding, my legs and feet sore from celebrating Agoi and from my arduous midnight trek.

I steal a glance up at Idris, to find him looking at me. The wall of dark, sticky heat hits me, and I control my breathing, forcing it to wash over me like nothing. But it's not nothing. It's him.

"RENZA!" I turn just in time as two arms wrap tightly around me, and golden blond hair smothers my face.

I wrap my arms around my sister, hugging her back.

"I was so worried," Giulia gasps as she holds me tight. "I thought I'd lost you. I thought you were gone."

"I'm okay. A bit worse for wear, but I'm okay," I reassure her, patting her shoulders. She lets me go, making a study of my condition for herself before nodding. A large group of people waits by the door to my house: Michelle, Emilia, Serra, Fiora and Agosta.

Emilia runs towards me, her eyes welling with tears as she throws her arms around me.

"I'm sorry. I'm so sorry," Emilia cries. "I thought I'd never see you again."

"Alfieri, is he home? I didn't have time—"

"Yes," Emilia says, pulling back and wiping her face. "Yes, you got him home. Thank you."

"The way he tells it, you saved their lives," Serra says, walking towards me. She has dark bruises under her eyes. She hugs me, too, and I realise just how much weight she's lost.

"Only the Fates know that for sure," I answer quietly.

"Modesty doesn't suit you." Serra chuckles. "And seriously, you need to stop with the self-sacrifice plans."

"Maybe when they stop working," I answer jokingly as she releases me.

"Fate help us," Idris mutters. I ignore him and instead smile at Serra. Every apology we needed to share passes between us in an instant.

"Come inside, dear," Fiora says hurriedly. "We'll call a doctor to look at you."

"Idris, thank you for getting her home. You should come inside," Giulia says warmly.

"No," Fiora interrupts sharply. "He should go home. You've both tempted Fate far, far too much. There will be a wicked penance if you flaunt your blasphemy much longer."

"I should let Tahira and Royah know they can stop worrying," Idris agrees, a tone of unease in his voice. "I'll see you tomorrow, Renza?"

"High Chamber, bright and early," I answer, turning to see him leap into the saddle. He gathers the reins and he winks at me.

"Looking forward to it," he teases as he encourages the horse to turn around and walk away.

"Inside, come on." Fiora grabs hold of my arms and steers me into the house. I am ferried into the sitting room and pushed towards one of the sofas with Fiora and Giulia fussing over my various bruises and scrapes.

"Tahira told us everything," Giulia says, impersonating a limpet as she clutches my hand. "About Nouis..."

The room grows thick and heavy.

"What happened?" Agosta asks quietly. She's uncharacteristically serious.

"I'd rather not relive it," I answer honestly, as Fiora hands me a glass of wine. "What about you? How was your Agoi?"

"Eventful," Serra says ruefully. "The river ran black in the middle of the Float Parade."

"What?" I gape. "How black?"

"Pitch-black, like liquid coal," answers Michelle with a shudder.

"People lost their minds," Serra says, running a hand over her black curls. "They started saying it was a sign from Fate, a bad omen. Fate had abandoned us once and for all. That priestess, Otta, was trying to calm everyone down."

"Did she succeed?"

"To a degree, yes," says Michelle, surprised. "Otta is quite a powerful speaker."

"How did the river run black?" I ask, narrowing my eyes.

"Turns out someone dumped loads of Cavidum powder upstream, perfectly timed for the Float Parade," Emilia answers scathingly. "We went to investigate because *something* had to have caused it, and I doubted Fate himself was the culprit. We found the site not too far out of town."

"I use Cavidum powder in some of my paints," Michelle says. "It's a persistent stain – a tiny little bit gets smeared over your hands and it's fixed there for weeks. I'd know it anywhere, and it was all over the banks. It covered the mud, the rocks, the grass. Everything."

"And there were also signs of a contraption like a water gate, similar to one I designed a while back," Serra says quietly. "It was used so they could dump everything all at once. We found the remains of a bonfire still smouldering not too far away – I reckon that's what they were burning."

"That's not all," Fiora says, just when I think my eyes could not get wider if I tried. "While the girls were investigating the river, we had an issue in the High Chamber."

"Oh?" I ask worried.

"Leone Strossi tried to put forward a bill to throw the Red Sands Bannerhood out of the city now that peace with the Holy States was 'likely'," says Giulia and my eyebrows jump up my face in outrage. "He argued that we don't want foreign armies in this city now we are on a path of peace and should cancel the trade contracts and bar them from the city."

"But that makes no sense." I frown.

"Well, he wanted to call a vote," Fiora explains. "He was very persuasive and taking advantage of the panic in our streets over the river incident, which many blamed on the Coari fighters."

"Thank goodness Fiora was there to, ah, ruffle some feathers." Giulia grins and the girls in the room giggle. I turn to my aunt who shrugs.

"I had to stop the vote; I couldn't let it happen without you," Fiora justified, entirely not sorry.

"How did you do that?" I ask suspiciously.

"She released a flock of pigeons into the High Chamber before the vote started," Serra cackles.

A delighted laugh erupts from my lips as I grin at Fiora.

"Seriously?"

"It was pandemonium!" Giulia giggles.

"Well, I had to do something!" Fiora says. "It was all I could think of on short notice."

"How did you have a flock of pigeons on short notice?" I press.

"That's what I do. I know things and I find things," Fiora responds evasively. "It's one of the ways I serve this family."

"If that's true, I have a shopping list you could take a crack at," teases Agosta who walks over with a fresh bottle of wine. "So, Renza, how was Agoi with your Soulhate?"

"Stop it," snaps Fiora. "It's best if we all pretend that never happened."

"Yes, but are the rumours true?" Agosta asks, sitting forwards on the sofa. "Everyone knows that Soulmate bonds vanish on Misos. Do Soulhate bonds vanish on Agoi?"

"Yes," I answer honestly. Fiora takes in a sharp breath.

"What was that like?" Giulia grins.

"I could finally see Idris the way you must see him," I answer evasively. "Without that wall of loathing between us. I suppose he's that charming to all of you all the time."

"He has his moments," admits Emilia.

"Is that all?" Michelle teases. "Nothing more? He's just … *charming*?"

"Forget it," says Fiora sharply, giving Michelle the stink-eye. "That's not the point of Agoi."

"It's also not the important thing we need to focus on right now." I redirect the conversation before Fiora can begin preaching. "Who stained the river and spread the rumours about it being a bad omen from Fate?"

"That we're not sure about," Emilia answers.

"I mean, the Holy States is the obvious answer," states Serra.

"Yes but who specifically on their behalf?"

"I mean, we already know of one traitor for the Holy States operating inside this city," offers Emilia quietly. "Who's to say she wouldn't have more information?"

Fiora and Agosta go very still and exchange a look at the mention of their traitorous sister.

"It's worth a try," I muse, sitting back in my seat.

"Are you sure?" Agosta asks warily. "You can't trust her."

"No, we can't, but that doesn't mean she can't be a source of information," I agree.

"Why don't I go?" offers Fiora. "I'm sure I can get her to speak—"

"No, I'll go. But if you don't mind, I'm going to have a bath first. I've been on the road too long and this dress is starting to itch."

"Alright, dear. I'll call that doctor—" Fiora says getting up.

"Great – for after my bath," I say firmly.

Agosta and Fiora walk with me out of the sitting room towards the stairs. They wait until my foot is on the first step before speaking.

"We wanted to talk to you about Rialta," Agosta says quietly.

"Oh?" I ask, unimpressed.

"Does she have to remain imprisoned here?" asks Fiora tentatively.

"She's a criminal who brought this city to the brink of disaster. She's lucky it's life imprisonment and not worse."

"She's family. Di Maineri," Agosta says rapidly. "We test each other, weed out the weak—"

"Are you really trying to justify her actions?" I hiss in anger.

"No," Fiora answers, voice as forgiving as stone.

"But we are family," Agosta continues. "We bicker and fight and scheme amongst ourselves – it's what we do. But when it comes down to the wire, when someone moves against our family, we have each other's backs. That's something Rialta understands and right now people are moving against our family."

"Yes. *She* is," I snap back at both of them. "It wasn't just me or Giulia she attacked. If this branch of the bank had fallen, how long until all the others followed? It would've led to the decimation of the Di Maineri family. Our legacy would have been over because of her own insatiable greed. I am the head of this family. I am the Head of the Bank. She tried and failed to take what is rightfully mine and now she suffers the price."

"Rialta was simply the first. Had it not been her, it would've been someone else. Your father suffered similar insults when he first inherited his position from our father," Fiora says, her hand reaching out to stop me as I walk towards my bedroom. Her brown eyes burn with serious intent as she speaks. "It's practically customary – a tradition of sorts. Why do you think I came? You're so busy looking at the storm coming for this city that you forgot to mind the wolves we call family looking to test their new leader."

"Do you have a point you're getting to?" I scowl.

"Rialta has been chastised, beaten, exposed on the world stage," Fiora says calmly. "But she's a Di Maineri. We can't let her rot."

"So what? Let her go?" I scowl. "She broke Halician law so she faces Halician justice. That's got nothing to do with me."

"Says the Electi who had her arrested," Agosta counters quietly. I narrow my eyes at my aunts and grit my teeth.

"Rialta will spend the rest of her miserably pointless life – however long or short that is – in a prison cell," I say, letting the venom of my threat crack loud and clear. "I don't care what names the wolves or vipers wear, if you attack me you don't get back up. Ever. If this doesn't send a clear message, then I'll have to make a clearer one. I suggest you don't volunteer."

And with that I turn my back on my aunts and walk away, seeking the comfort of a warm bath, a good meal and my own sweet bed.

CHAPTER 32

A blood-red sun hovers at the horizon line, striking upwards with a firm amber fist. The stars flee back to their sky dwellings, the watery smirk of the moon retreating in cowed defeat.

The prison is a hive of activity, with boats carrying workmen and materials descending on the small island. The prison has been undergoing significant renovations, not just to make it more secure for the prisoners and jailers, but also to act as a sea watch and naval defence position.

The crooked old brick structure is being reinforced by all kinds of new columns and structural components; I'm impressed with Emilia's designs. I didn't much mind about its outward appearance, only its functionality, but when it's done, it'll certainly present an imposing face.

The boat sways as a member of the City Guard rows me towards the small island. We don't say a word as we listen to the gurgling ocean and the cries of swooping seabirds starting their morning scavenge.

I spent the night tossing and turning. How is Rialta doing this? How and why? She's been caught, so what is the point of the continued sabotage? Is she hoping for rescue? Is she planning an escape?

The boat docks in the rocky port and I'm escorted past the line of workers having their information checked. I'm greeted at the door by the Night Captain.

"I'm here to see Rialta Di Maineri," I declare.

"Yes, signora. May I do a quick search?"

It's perfunctory as I've brought nothing with me, and I'm soon being escorted inside to Rialta's cell. The Night Captain slams her fist against the bars.

"Visitor."

Rialta scowls, her eyes narrowing as she spies me. She stands up and stretches her back out. Her hair is an absolute mess and she's still wearing the dress she wore on her arrest.

"I must be special to warrant such an early visit," Rialta snipes as she makes her way to a simple desk. She sits in the chair, boldly meeting my gaze. The Night Captain and City Guardsmen retreat but stay nearby for my protection.

"You're not important enough to take worthwhile time from my day," I answer coolly. Rialta rolls her eyes at me then picks up her quill and pulls a fresh piece of paper towards her. She begins to write.

"But still important enough to come and see me in my disgrace. Honestly, dear, look at it." Rialta gestures around the dark, dank little room they've got her in. "It's not befitting a Di Maineri."

"You got a window." I point to the tiny carved crack in her bedroom wall overlooking the ocean. "That's more than you deserve."

"Oh, don't be such a sore winner," Rialta scorns. "We're Di Maineri – what did you expect?"

"I don't care how the Di Maineris act throughout the rest of the continent. Squabble and fight, betray each other and debase our bloodline all you like, but not here. Not with me. I would rather burn our family legacy to the ground," I answer with venom.

Rialta's chair creaks as she sets down her quill and folds the paper in half. She seals it with wax before starting another.

"You make it sound so terrible. So I played a little game of hide-the-money." Rialta shrugs. "You worked it out and now you'll be all the wiser next time. Honestly, you're overreacting. Think of it as a life lesson."

"There won't be a next time. This cell is for life." I knock on the metal bars to ram the point home. "You're guilty in the eyes of Halice for fraud and embezzlement. You're lucky the cell isn't in the basement."

"We'll see," Rialta answers quietly.

"But there are things we can do, to improve your conditions," I say, gesturing around her narrow little cell. "Tell me how you're still communicating with the outside and why. Perhaps we can get you a proper bed, maybe some fresh clothes."

"You think you can bribe me?" Rialta smirks, finishing her second letter and sealing it. She throws her quill onto the desk with a clatter, sitting back to survey me.

"I think things can also get a lot worse for you. That basement cell is still an option," I remind her, tone cold as ice. "That is, if you're not executed for treason."

"I've not committed treason," Rialta answers sharply.

"Prove it."

Rialta pauses for a moment, mulling on that.

"Fine, ask your questions." Rialta sighs, looking expectant as she crosses one leg over the other.

"You have been collaborating with the Holy States for quite some time, haven't you?" I accuse. "Sending them after the smugglers so they'd kill my friend, acting on their behalf to hire the mercenaries that almost killed me? And the river ran black on Agoi, spreading vile rumours."

"The little Coari traitors were paid with *which* currency again?" Rialta sounds like she's lecturing an errant child. I clench my hands into fists.

"Gold Aureus."

"Why would I pay with Gold Aureus?" Rialta asks, a smirk on her face. "I'm from the Wheel City. The cash I brought with me is Kerma or Hali-Pound – which you no doubt already found amongst my belongings – and I'm not stupid enough to pay men to commit crimes in incriminating currencies. I had access to the bank, practically unrestricted access. Why wouldn't I just use Hali-Pounds? Way more difficult to trace and practically invisible in this city."

She's telling the truth. The mercenaries weren't under her command. Which means there's another traitor in this city.

"You're not working with the Holy States," I state, watching her face carefully for a response. Her stance is relaxed. There's no surprise, no caution in her gaze. She really doesn't have anything to hide.

"No," Rialta answers seemingly honestly, eyes almost glittering with mirth. "They have nothing to offer me. Your little friend getting hurt wasn't on my orders. Hiding the money was going so well – why would I jeopardise it? You're vicious protecting those you deem worthy of it, and you only cottoned on to my scheme because he got hurt. Besides, Giulia was on the precipice of giving me rightful control of the bank. Just a few more days and it would've been mine."

"We would've worked out you were hiding the money eventually." I narrow my eyes at her. "When Alfieri and I spoke or when the other banks confirmed they'd sent the money."

"By then it'd be too late. I'd be home again, out of your reach and legally, rightfully, the Head of Bank. As I should be." Rialta scowls at me.

"My sister is a brilliant woman and an excellent banker."

"Giulia inherited her role; it was handed to her as one of

your castoffs. I started with nothing and built the most profitable bank branch across the entire continent in the Wheel City — and yet *you* get to control us? The woman who can't be bothered to manage something so important herself? We have to send you tithes. We have to listen to your rules? I have proven that I am better suited for the role so why shouldn't I be the leader?"

Silence fills the space between us and I nod slowly.

"You're a good banker," I agree quietly. "But terrible at most everything else. You don't understand people at all."

"Says you? You entrusted our tithes to a criminal!" snarls Rialta, getting to her feet.

"It worked. I compromised the rules of this city, the compass of my morals, all to keep my bank afloat. So tell me who really doesn't deserve it? The snake that would steal it or the woman that would sacrifice everything to save it?" I muse. Rialta doesn't answer. She throws me a cold look.

"Everything was going well for you, until you told someone about the deposits Alfieri was making," I say. Rialta stills slightly, her mind drifting over my statement. I see the moment when the pieces fit together in her head. Slowly she approaches the bars, her shoes clipping quietly over the unforgiving floor.

"How much is it worth?" Rialta asks with a sly smile. "How much does that name buy me?"

"You're still trying to bargain?"

"Honestly, darling, sometimes I wonder if you're really a Di Maineri." Rialta chuckles, wrapping her fingers around the bars. "Di Maineris know that everything has a price."

I nod slowly, a dark smile taking hold.

"Guard, remove all furniture from my aunt's room," I say, stepping back from the bars. "Oh, and take the shoes from her feet. Then take her to a basement cell. Maybe a week in the dark, alone with nothing but her thoughts, will make her more amenable."

"Wait, wait, alright!" Rialta scowls as I hold up a hand to stop the guards carrying out my order. "All I want is for you to deliver my letters."

She crosses to her rickety desk, plucking her two letters off the surface and handing them to me. I take them, looking down at the names. One is to someone at her bank, and the other is to Fiora.

I raise an eyebrow.

"Just a little thing." Rialta smiles. "Do we have a deal?"

"That depends on how good the name you give me is."

Rialta leans against the bars.

"I was talking with my sisters one evening a couple of weeks ago. Fiora mentioned she'd come back from the soup kitchen and things were improving. Agosta was surprised and asked where they were getting their food, given that city supplies were thought to be running low. Fiora answered evasively, saying the city must have extensive reserves." Rialta cracks a wicked grin. "Which might've been when I mentioned that perhaps the city might have employed a smuggler to move things through the blockade. Though I never mentioned the bank of course."

My heart skips several long beats as the pieces start slipping together.

"Of course, one conversation is far from proof," Rialta continues. "And you do so love your proof, don't you? Your Halician processes. But that would be where I'd start my search."

I nod slowly. A good starting place indeed.

I look down at the letters in my hands. I step back out of her reach and towards the light of the torch. I crack the seal.

"Hey!" snaps Rialta throwing her hand through the cell towards me when she realises what I'm doing. But she can't snatch the letters back. I quickly review the words on the page.

This one is to her second-in-command in the Wheel City, instructing him of his next course of action: to call in debts with people who might be able to leverage the bank here to insist upon her release for diplomatic reasons.

I crack open the seal for the next letter and open it. It's to her sister, insisting she convince me to let her go for the good of the family by leveraging some shared memory from their childhood to create sympathy.

"You're a good banker, Rialta, but terrible with people," I say lifting the letters up to the torch and setting them on fire before dropping the burning embers to the cold stone floor.

"We had a deal!" snaps Rialta, her face torn apart with anger.

"It's your own fault that you were stupid enough to believe me," I answer coldly. Rialta's face is a picture as she steps away from the bars, glaring at me with fury.

"This is why I'm head of this family," I explain. "It's not about the bank, or the money. It's about the people. Controlling them, motivating them, removing them. People are power. When it comes to your people, well ... they're mine now. Your second in the Wheel City? He's been given authority over his own banking branch in Rhone. He jumped at the opportunity. As for Fiora, well, she's already writing to your friends and associates to tell them of the disgraceful and deceitful things you've done to your own family. Not to mention how Giulia is now digging through all your bank records to discover if your illegal activities began at home. We'll find something, no doubt, and let the relevant authorities in your home city know. Though, it must be said, exile from the Wheel City seems a moot point when you'll be spending the rest of your life in here."

The rage is wiped from Rialta's face, the cold frozen reality of her future settling into her mind as she swallows.

"Y-you c-can't do that," she stammers quietly. "It's not who you are. You believe in family. You believe in change."

"I am Renza Di Maineri," I answer, the words biting and

frozen, lacking even a drop of remorse. "I am devoted to my family, and I am ruthless to my enemies. But what you failed to realise is that family isn't a bloodline. Family is a promise between loved ones to protect and cherish. You could've been my family, but you chose to be my enemy. Terrible mistake. You should've learned from the Great Rebellion what I do to those who harm my family."

"You can't keep me here!" shouts Rialta as I turn around. "Renza! RENZA!"

I smirk, not bothering to turn and face her.

I meet up with the captain. The two of us start walking back towards my boat.

"Keep me informed when she tries something," I say, the gravel crunching beneath my boots as I head back towards the boat.

"*When* she tries something?" the captain asks, looking for confirmation. I meet her grey eyes with a short nod.

"When," I confirm.

After that, I climb back in the boat and return to the city, our boat one of the few moving against the tide of builders coming to improve our prison.

As we grow closer to shore, my pulse hikes and my skin crawls like I'm being eaten by a thousand midges. Bile swells and starts the suffocating climb up my throat.

The skies are now a blushing pomegranate, the horizon crowned with a ring of gold. That gilded light bounces off the familiar head of Idris Patricelli, who stands, arms folded, at the dockside. Silently, he offers me a hand out of the boat. I take it, not meeting his eyes. His palm is blindingly hot, but our grip lingers. I clear my throat and pry our melted fingers away from each other.

"You're here early," I say.

"I run several businesses. Daylight hours are working

hours," Idris answers quietly, irritation lurking in his voice. "You stole my boat."

"No. I found your boat and have returned it safe and sound," I tease. Idris doesn't go for the bait.

"You saw Rialta?" he asks.

"Yes."

"Anything interesting to say about the antics that took place in our absence?" Idris has clearly been filled in. I hesitate, noticing the various ears hovering around our exchange.

"Can we meet at yours later to talk about it?" I ask. Idris nods curtly without saying anything further. An awkward beat of silence passes between us. I scratch my wrist, trying to work out what I've done to anger him.

"Are you cross about the boat?" I ask quietly. "I'm sorry. I didn't think it'd be a problem. I should've asked—"

Idris groans and lets out a low, mirthless laugh.

"It has nothing to do with the boat," Idris says softly. He steps closer and slowly runs his knuckles down the side of my cheek. I catch a breath, shuddering under the searing ache of his touch.

"After everything in the last few days ... I don't like you not being in the city."

I frown. "The prison is in the city."

"Only just." He closes his eyes, his forehead hovering above mine like a dark, torrid magnet.

"The bond puts all these awful images in my head," he admits. "Images of you in trouble, of you in pain or dying. It's torture."

I know because I get it. The voices that whisper foul concoctions whenever he's present fill me with simultaneous dread and obsession. I take a deep breath, controlling myself before speaking.

"I'm right here," I reassure him, pressing my hands against his chest. "I'm safe, here with you." My fingertips are ablaze the minute they connect with his rock-hard body. His lavender and mint sent mingles with the salt of the sea on my tongue, tantalising and tormenting in a violent clash that leaves me reeling.

"RENZA!"

With a snap I jump back to see Fiora marching towards us, face bright red and absolutely furious. Drawn cheeks, thinned lips and dark eyes burn as they target Idris Patricelli.

"Aunt Fiora? What are you doing—?"

"When you weren't in your room this morning, I figured you had gone to see your aunt without me!" Fiora scowls, folding her arms and giving Idris such a stink-eye it's unmissable. "What are *you* doing here?"

"I'm working," Idris explains calmly. "I have business—"

"I'm aware of your businesses, Signore Patricelli," Fiora throws at him. "None of which should involve you being anywhere close to my niece! Particularly not unsupervised!"

"Fiora," I warn. She turns to jab a finger at me.

"No. No. Laughing at Fate will lead to ruin! This is not a game. We're going home. Now."

"Watch your tone when you're talking to me!" I scowl, narrowing my eyes at her. She huffs and squares up like she isn't afraid.

"I can't believe I have to explain this to you. This man is your Soulhate. Why on earth can't you stay away from him?" Fiora demands. "You refuse Fate, mocking him with your defiance. His ire will come for you in ways that will devastate all of us!"

"Enough!" I snap, letting anger fill my voice as I stare her down. "I respect your beliefs, Fiora, but no one asked you. Keep your unsolicited opinion to yourself."

Fiora balks at my sharp words, but her mouth presses into a firm line.

"Home. Now." She all but glares. I raise an eyebrow. I am done taking orders. I am done being pushed around and yelled at and being called a fool from all angles for doing my damn best. I'm sick of it.

"You are a guest," I remind Fiora, through gritted teeth, "in this city and in my home. Speak one more word and you'll outstay your welcome."

Fiora lets out a sharp breath and shakes her head. She folds her arms, glaring at Idris who hasn't said a word. Clearly she's not leaving until either he does or I do.

"I have errands. I'll see you in High Chamber," I mutter to Idris as I head back towards the city. As I leave, I know he's watching. His attention is like all the focused pressure of a black sun, roaring and gnawing at the back of my neck.

I have a traitor in my city. Maybe more than one.

I don't have time to waste bickering with an aunt who might just be the very person trying to bring it all down.

Time to get to work.

CHAPTER 33

"Ready to go?" I ask quietly. Giulia nods as she comes out of the living room. The two of us are trying to leave without sparking attention from either of our aunts. We received a note from Michelle to meet at the Amica tonight. It sounds like we're getting the old group back together, to face the traitors in our city. Again.

I wonder if Paula will give us a discount for the next coup we avert?

Giulia checks her hair, and I see a large trail of mud up one side of her skirt.

"Giu," I tease softly, taking hold of her skirts and pulling it out to show her. Irritation flurries across her face.

"Give me two minutes," she huffs and hurries as quietly as she can upstairs. Knowing my sister will likely take more than two minutes, I head back to my study. Fiora has been distant ever since our altercation at the dock. *Good.* I am done tiptoeing around my own home.

I push the door of my study open and pause two paces before my desk.

Sitting square and centre is a box, the same as before. Dark wood, engraved with tiny stars. On top rests a letter.

The whole world shrinks to the horrifying sight. *How did it get here? How is it on my desk?* I swallow tightly as my hands shake.

I force myself to step closer, fighting to keep myself from running out of the room. I put one foot in front of the other until I'm before my desk.

I reach down, the paper dry between my fingers as I touch the black wax seal. With a crack I snap open the letter. That odiously familiar, elegant black handwriting sprawls across the page.

My Renza,

> *Do not fret. I have already forgiven our misunderstanding. I understand that the love of your life coming back from the dead is a greatly confusing time. I thought that you were sturdier, but now see that the exhilaration of finally being together again clouded your senses. You struggled to adjust to the staggering reality of your secret fantasies being before you. So do not languish in your devastation, we will still have all we desire.*
>
> *My men attempted to rescue you from the forest after you fell, but were thwarted from your aid by those ghastly foreign barbarians. I take it they stole you back to Halice, away from me. But do not dwell in your pining for me, my Renza, or linger in the pit of regret you will be cursing yourself with now. While your heedless outburst has forced our parting for longer, it will not be forever. I have everything in hand.*
>
> *I swear my blood oath to you that we will be as one soon, my Renza.*

Patiently waiting,
Nouis.

"Renza?" Giulia asks, her voice thick.

I look up at her and see her new lilac dress is gentle and sweet, and brings out the yellow hues in her golden blond hair. Hot tears brim in my eyes as the letter shakes.

Oh, wait, I'm the one shaking.

I gasp as a single tear springs free of my lash line. Giulia hurries to my side, an arm around my waist as she takes the letter from my hands. Her blue eyes cut across the words, determination falling hard on her face.

"We're going to the others," she says, folding up the letter and picking up the box. "Now."

"But—"

"Come on." Giulia's tone takes no prisoners.

I follow her, trying to shake off the dark, sticky cloud of Nouis. I feel watched from every angle. The air is thin as my breathing turns shallow, invisible walls closing in around me. I study every corner, certain I can see eyes amongst the shadows. No surface, no place, no action feels safe.

Giulia's anchoring hand in mine is all that keeps me from screaming as she pulls me briskly along. The hoods of our cloaks are high over our faces as we head down the street. We can't have anyone knowing where we're going. Not with the topic of the evening's discussion.

Giulia whisks me to a familiar building.

The Amica.

Giulia knocks, dropping her hood as the door is pushed wide.

"Is everyone here yet?" she demands, marching into the restaurant and stopping dead. I follow, my mouth falling open as the inside is bursting with scented candles and vivid flowers.

Michelle stands with our friends, all of whom are dressed to the nines and grinning like idiots. Serra walks over and presses a finger to her mouth, letting me know I should be quiet. Beaming like she can hardly contain it, she takes my hand and pulls me over to stand with Emilia, who's already got tears in her eyes.

"What is this?" Giulia asks, confused, as Michelle walks closer. She pulls the box and the letter from Giulia's hands and puts them on a nearby table.

"This is all for you," Michelle says softly. She coaxes her further into the room. "Giulia Di Maineri, I love you. I love you more than anything in this world. You are the light of my life, the meaning of my days, and I never want to lose you ever."

I gasp and clamp my hand over my mouth as I realise what's happening right now. I think I might cry. Giulia gapes as Michelle drops onto one knee, realisation cracking like dawn across her face.

Michelle holds up a small box – one of Uncle Ruggie's. She pulls open the little wooden top to show off the most gorgeous ring. The artfully placed swirling design is adorned with glittering diamonds, rubies and emeralds.

"Giulia Di Maineri, will you marry me?" Michelle asks.

"Yes!" Giulia all but screams the word, dropping to her knees with Michelle and throwing her arms around her. The two hold each other tightly, both crying and laughing as they hold on to each other.

The three of us spectators break into applause, cheering for them as they laugh and hug. Giulia frantically wipes her eyes as Michelle prises the beautiful jewelled ring from the box and slides it onto my sister's finger. It's a perfect fit.

"You're engaged!" Emilia squeals with delight.

"We're engaged!" Michelle agrees, planting a loving kiss on my sister's lips. Giulia can't stop giggling, switching her gaze between her adoring fiancée and the gorgeous ring on her finger. They get to their feet and we race over to congratulate them. I wrap my sister in the biggest hug ever, the two of us laughing like lunatics.

"You're getting married!" I squeal.

"I'm getting married!" Giulia giggles in my ear, finally letting me go. "Did you know about this?"

"No," I answer. "But I am so, so happy for you. There is no one better."

I turn to Michelle, hugging her tight.

"You sly dog, how long have you been planning this?"

"Since before everything..." Michelle admits. "But everything is as it should be. Giulia and Royah are friends, and I just know nothing else will ever test us like that."

"Oh my gosh, we have to talk weddings," Emilia gushes. "Wait, what do we do about brides' parties? I want to be in both your wedding parties!"

"We'll work out a switching system," Serra suggests. "This is so exciting."

I beam at Giulia, but it isn't long until my gaze falls back on the discarded contents of Nouis's box and his letter. An invisible noose tightens around my neck, a cold bubble of ice forcing its way up my throat.

"Ladies, this is the best. I wish I could stay and celebrate but I need to find Idris. I thought he'd be here," I admit.

"He will be." Emilia beams. "Alfieri is bringing him and the others in a bit, but Michelle wanted it to be just us girls first. So we can celebrate the five of us."

"Not to be a party pooper, but does Royah know about this?" asks Serra quietly. Michelle nods, winding her arm around Giulia's waist.

"She actually found the ring by accident a few days ago." Michelle snorts. Giulia laughs suddenly.

"Wait, when she opened that drawer in the kitchen and gasped like someone dropped a brick on her foot?" Giulia demands. Michelle nods, hand going to her face.

"I thought it was going to ruin the whole thing!" Michelle groans. "After you left, she demanded that I plan my proposal to you immediately, or she'd do it for me."

"She was asking me about my favourite flowers," Giulia recalls, looking around at the intricate decorations of zinnia in every overflowing bouquet. Paula walks out with her congratulations and a tray of drinks for everyone. Serra looks a little sheepish as she accepts the drink.

I smile to myself, looking at my own glass as the conversations and celebrations continue. They debate the merits of dress styles and colours, decorations and flowers, big versus small, indoors versus outside. I follow along with the discussion, not wanting to take one shred of Giulia's joy in her big moment away from her.

But I can't help it. Nouis's gift taunts me like acid, eating away at my brain. The unopened box sits in the corner, a foul witness to something so pure and wonderful.

It isn't long before Alfieri arrives with Tahira, Royah and Idris in tow. Everyone welcomes them in and congratulations fly all around. Idris's presence starts a war of dark suns between the two taunting, infuriating presences, splitting my sanity in two.

Eventually I set down my wine and take the box and letter from the table. I go into the back room – I don't need to ruin the celebrations. This is Giulia's night, but I have to know. Whatever ghastly monstrosity lurks inside, I will handle it. I won't let Nouis's vile insanity plague me any longer.

I close the door behind me and throw the box onto the table. Breathing sharply, I reach with a trembling hand and unlatch the lid, quickly flipping it open.

I peer into the box, and my stomach turns over.

Nestled amongst cushions of black velvet and coated in his dried blood is a rusted knife with a familiar wooden handle. The ghostly memory of my fingers is still smeared in crimson over hilt. The blade glints in the low light like a rotten orange tooth.

I bend over, scrambling for a nearby bin as my stomach empties. I hurl again, my stomach contracting as bile burns through my throat and nose. The memory of that wicked blade is stuck in my mind's eye and I can't get rid of it.

"Renza!"

Sweltering fingers are in my hair, holding it back from my face as I fight for breath between my convulsing stomach and the raging inferno Idris's presence elicits. Footsteps hurry to the door and I groan between torrid breaths.

"Fate's Fury!" cries Serra. "That sick freak. That's the knife I gave her."

"The knife she killed him with? Or tried to?" asks Michelle in horror. Giulia swears violently. She comes to my side and presses a glass of water into my hands.

"I'm sorry," I moan, pressing my hands to my lips.

"It's okay. He can't touch you here. He can't," Giulia soothes, taking over from Idris as she sits me down. I grip the glass nervously, swirling the cool liquid around my mouth in a vain attempt to soothe the burning.

"Go back to your party, Giulia, go back to your night. Celebrate," I try to tell her, but she gives me a look and I drop it, knowing this is a battle I won't win. I turn my head, the cruel, smouldering ache of Idris filling my vision as he picks up the letter next to the knife. His face is a mask of fury as he reads, his fingers clenching the letter till it wrinkles.

Emilia marches over to the box and slams the lid firmly shut.

"Who delivered it?" she asks, turning to look at me. I shake my head and shrug.

"It was waiting on my desk," I say.

"In your house?" Idris's voice holds more danger than I've heard before.

"I've had people watching the house," Tahira says. "No one unusual has come or gone."

"Ask them about this box. Maybe they saw it being carried inside," Royah says.

"Don't bother," I breathe, rubbing my brow. "Rialta isn't the one who passed messages to the Holy States. She didn't set people on Alfieri. But she suggested to Fiora and Agosta that maybe I was using smugglers." I turn my eyes back to the water between my fingers. The top jiggles as I struggle to stop the tremor in my limbs.

"You weren't kidding when you said your family was a bunch of snakes," mutters Tahira.

"I found letters," Alfieri says. "At the camp. Letters to Nouis, reporting on Renza and her movements in one handwriting, and then the outcomes of things going on in the city like the High Chamber votes and bills in another."

"Two traitors," scowled Serra, folding her arms.

"Would you recognise the handwriting if you saw it again?" asks Idris.

"Yes." Alfieri nods as Emilia moves closer to stand with him. I pause, an idea coming to mind.

"Alfieri, would you be able to talk to Michelle about the handwriting and the language of those letters?" I ask. Alfieri nods.

"Want me to forge something?" asks Michelle, a smirk already on her lips.

"Two letters. From one spy to another, asking to meet. 'Come see me, it's urgent' – or something along those lines," I muse, getting to my feet and setting my water aside. "And then we leave the letters for Fiora and Agosta to find."

"The real spy will do what the letter says. The other will be confused and we can rule them out." Serra says, catching on quickly.

"Then we can follow your aunt as she complies with the letter and she'll lead us to the other traitor," Idris realises. I nod, folding my arms.

"Oh, very cloak and dagger," chuckles Tahira. "I'm in. I'll

double the watch on your house, make sure nothing slips our notice again."

"Yeah, about you watching the house..." Giulia begins uncomfortably.

"With all the traitors in the city, I'm glad of it," I murmur, pinching the bridge of my nose. Her people are motivated by gold, and our trade deal keeps their pockets thickly lined for relatively stable, steady work.

"We'll get to work straight away." Michelle smiles. "When do you want the letters?"

"As soon as possible," I say. "But start tomorrow. Celebrate tonight. Enjoy the evening. You're engaged. We can't stop celebrating things, especially not things this important."

"Sounds like a plan. Now, who wants to try some Coari spirits?" Royah beams as people filter back into the other room. I turn to Giulia before she leaves.

"Hey, I don't want to spoil the evening any further. I think I'll just head home," I say softly, feeling a familiar shadowy inferno stepping closer to my back.

"I'll go with you," Idris says immediately. "Make sure you get there safely."

"Are you sure?" Giulia asks. I take her hands and squeeze them tightly.

"Yes, absolutely. And tomorrow morning you'd better be filled with wedding ideas because we have so much to plan. Your wedding is going to be the event of your dreams, everything you can imagine – so dream big."

Giulia pulls me close, holding me tight for a moment.

"Love you, Renza," Giulia says gently before letting me go. I smile and step back towards the door. I force my fingers around the vile wooden box, picking it up and folding the letter exactly as it had been before.

"Love you, too, Giulia. I'm so excited for you." I beam before making my exit into the night. I fill my lungs with cold air, unable to shake the ghostly, icy fingers of Nouis stroking at the back of my mind.

That is until the ferocious, blinding heat steps into the alley beside me. It chases away all dark thoughts, sending the vile haunting slithering back into the darkness.

I push down the bile pooling again in my throat, fight to ignore the sensation of acid eating through the soft flesh of my throat.

"Are you sure you want to go home?" asks Idris quietly. "You could come back to mine. Your bed is still there—"

"No. I can't act like anything is different. I can't have my aunts on edge or speculating that I'm even suspicious of them."

"If they ask about it?" Idris asks, taking that infernal box from my white-knuckle grip. I'm grateful.

"I'll make something up. I'm good at coming up with things on the spot," I answer, clearing my throat as we walk through the darkened streets of Halice. He's like a blinding torch in the darkness, a focus point that sends the hidden eyes and vicious schemes running away.

My pulse pounds in my head, my skin crawls, and my breath is hot. He is fire incarnate. But fire cleanses. In the most brutal way.

"Thank you," I breathe, my hand going to his forearm. The connection of our skin together erupts in a dancing firework, burrowing sparks deep into my bones.

"For walking you home? I'm a gentleman, you know. Besides, I didn't really feel like celebrating much this evening either. Not with traitors lurking in your own home."

"We'll get it sorted."

"How many more times will this happen? Bellandi, Nouis, Rialta..." Idris growls in frustration. "Some of the things Alfieri reported on – they're things only we know: numbers of troops, positions, the upgraded defences we've installed across the city, the lie of the land between here and the border if they march troops in."

My stomach churns in answer. Two of the names on his list have lurked under my very own roof. And now a third is likely betraying us. What does that say about me? Have I really been so ignorant of what's going on around me? I tried to give my aunts the benefit of the doubt. I should've been more suspicious from the beginning. We're at war; we're in crisis. Some of our principles have got to change. For the sake of our survival.

"Either they're spying on closed sessions or have found a way to spy on an Electi or their documents," Idris finishes his thought.

"Who do you think it is?" I ask. Idris lets out a small sigh and shrugs angrily.

"The Electi probably doesn't even know they're doing it," Idris answers.

I rub my brow and groan.

"I don't think it's likely to be Savino. So we should have him with us when this all goes down. And City Guards to seize and search rooms and belongings," I answer quietly. "Having three Electi to witness this plan and see it through should make for a relatively short trial if we need one."

"I'll speak to him tomorrow about everything. He's already up to date on the important facts, about there being information passed back to the Holy States."

"Good," I murmur, eyes swinging to a dark corner as we pass it. What monsters lurk in the shadows? Which of Nouis's cronies are reporting my every move to him?

Idris reaches out. The backs of his fingers skim softly from my elbow down to my wrist, trailing a blaze of molten iron that causes me to suck in a breath. I bite my lip as his boiling fingers slowly lace with mine. Our footsteps on the dark cobbles are the only sound, the dancing torch light peppering the navy streets to spotlight our walk home.

The world is quiet. It's just me and him.

"Calm your breathing," Idris murmurs quietly. "All of this can wait until tomorrow. We will have answers soon."

"You're right," I answer, my voice catching in my throat as I look down at our entwined fingers. I soak into that fire, focusing on the pure, searing sensation to chase all else away. Idris is here. We're together and we have a plan. Stressing and worrying does nothing to help.

Idris lifts our joined hands up to his face. I follow their path, hounding red stars throbbing at the corners of my vision as he brushes a sweet, incendiary kiss across my knuckles. My bones start to melt as my heart picks up a new disjointed beat.

"Do you need a distraction?" Idris asks, a twinkle in his eyes.

"I thought we agreed." I step closer, words leaving my lips like dragon fire. "We are more than a distraction."

Idris groans, dropping his head to hover above mine.

"I crave hearing you say that." Idris's words brush across my lips. "Say it again. For me."

I lean up on my toes, so my lips barely brush against his as I whisper, the words turning into a teasing, fiery tempest between us.

"You are mine," I breathe. "And I am yours."

His lips consume mine, the inferno of his mouth obliterating all thought or reason. His tender kiss leaves me breathless, our linked hands now melded into one.

"My Fated. My choice," Idris whispers before stepping back. We walk home hand in hand in the dark night.

CHAPTER 34

"Ready?" Tahira asks me. I nod.

Fiora sits outside. From our seats inside, positioned behind a curtain to keep us from view, we can see her but she has no idea we're here. She has a pot of herbal tea on one side and a book balanced across her knee to which she's paying no attention. She's clearly lost in thought, the cup in her hands quickly losing its warmth.

I nod to our staff member, Leo, who knows his role well. He holds up the letter and schools his features before walking outside. I know we can trust Leo; besides, we just told him about his job. There's no way he can prewarn my aunts.

I watch Leo cross the patio, the sun bouncing off his clean cream uniform until he gets to my aunt. I can read his lips as he bows and hands her the letter before walking away.

Good, nothing but what we rehearsed.

Frowning, Fiora deftly opens the letter and scans it, that brow furrowing further into confusion. The blank bewilderment on her face tells me everything I need to know as she stands up and looks back to where Leo disappeared in search of answers. She starts to go after him, letter still in her hand, a myriad of questions painted across her lips.

As she steps inside, she spots Tahira and me sitting by the window, a staged game of tiles spread between us.

"Renza, dear, did you see which way that attendant went?" Fiora asks, walking towards me. I move a tile, suddenly aware I never bothered to explain the rules to Tahira.

"Why?" I ask. She walks over and hands me the letter.

"He just gave me the strangest letter..." She trails off and narrows her eyes as Tahira and I exchange a look. She looks to the window and clearly spies our excellent view of her previous position.

"What kind of game are you playing?" she asks quietly, holding back the wobbling accusations from her words.

"Sorry, Aunt Fiora, but now we have our answer," I say, folding up the letter and throwing it on top of the tiles.

"What do you mean? What answer?" Fiora demands, crossing her arms and raising an expectant eyebrow.

"Rialta hasn't been working with the Holy States," is all I say in response as I stand up. Tahira joins me. Time for part two of the test.

"So you thought I was?" Fiora demands. She moves to step in front of me, to prevent me from leaving as she studies my expression, but it softens a touch. "No. But someone in this household is..."

"Fiora, on this occasion, if you truly are innocent, I recommend you stay out of it." My words hold a quiet, lethal kind of authority. Fiora takes a beat before nodding and letting me pass.

Tahira and I walk away. As we pass a burning hearth, I throw the first letter into the flames. One down, one to go. Let's see how this shakes out.

That evening, Agosta returns carrying a veritable fortune of a shopping spree. Fabrics, jewels and decadence pour from her fingers. She babbles her tales of the market in town before sweeping upstairs to her bedroom.

We're sitting in the living room, Fiora on her own by the back windows with a notebook on the table and inked quill between her fingers. Giulia and I are playing a game of tiles on the coffee table as Tahira being here at this hour would be suspicious.

"Look at this!" Agosta beams, her turquoise beaded earrings swinging against her neck as she sweeps a beautiful bolt of painted silk over the table next to me.

"Oh, very pretty. This'll make a stunning dress," I muse, spying Leo awaiting my sign. I give him a subtle nod.

"Oh, won't it just." Agosta chuckles to herself. "I've been meaning to get a few in the new Halician style. Much more flowing—"

"Sorry to interrupt, signora," says Leo quietly, bowing properly at Agosta's side. "Urgent note, just arrived for you."

Fiora freezes for a second, her eyes still on the page of her journal as Agosta takes the letter. Agosta opens it, casts her eyes over it, and her expression falls.

"Everything alright?" asks Giulia.

"Oh, yes," Agosta answers brightly. "Seems I made a miscount with a payment. How dreadfully embarrassing. I really should go and fix it. I'll be back in time for dinner."

Traitor.

I quash the surging roar of outrage swelling inside me and nod calmly, offering her a nonchalant smile.

"See you later," Giulia calls as Agosta turns on her heels and hurries out the door. I turn my gaze over to Fiora. I wait, forcing her to meet my gaze. She lifts her eyes to mine and defeat radiates from them.

"Now you know," she says softly.

"Now I know," I answer firmly, without room for hesitation or mercy. She nods as though accepting what has to come next. I head for the door.

"Don't wait up," I tell Giulia and she nods.

Agosta's carriage pulls away, and a second later I step outside. Idris and Savino round the corner on horses, along with six members of the City Guard. Idris dismounts and my heart races as his sweltering hand sweeps gently down my back before he gives me a boost up. Now settled in the saddle, he climbs up behind me and presses my back against his scorching, chiselled chest. I focus on my breathing as Alfieri's black horse whips past us, hooves somehow whisper-quiet against the cobbled road. He'll be the one to follow Agosta more closely – our larger retinue is too easily spotted.

Idris's strong, smouldering arms hold me close. My spine quivers and my stomach goes molten. His fevered breath falls on the back of my head, erupting into a river of fire that pours down my neck. I resist the urge to turn around and gaze at the torrid, dangerous bonfire holding me safe in his arms, fighting tooth and nail with the part of me that longs to melt into the expert crafting of his chest. I have to focus. This is important.

The horses move quickly. Alfieri whips back and forth like a dark beacon to show the way. We wind down the dark streets, my pulse thready and throbbing under my tongue.

Alfieri comes to a stop at the corner of a road and my stomach sinks as he points to a building. Idris swings down, his searing hands coming to my waist as he makes sure I land steadily on my feet. Savino joins us, his face grave as he looks at the building.

"Whose place is this?" I ask. It's clear that both men recognise it.

"You're about to find out," Idris mutters. Idris pushes the door open and Alfieri grabs the attending servant, silencing them with a serrated blade pressed against their soft, fleshy throat.

"Where?" demands Alfieri, the threat in his voice so different to the fun, easy-going man I know and love. The servant points towards a room and we creep forwards. Our steps are silent as we come to a door that's open ajar.

"—what you're talking about!" comes a familiar voice and my stomach drops.

"This note!" Agosta shouts. "It's from you."

"No. It's not. You idiot—!"

Agosta's conspirator races to the door, throwing it open. He stops short when he sees us waiting. Agosta's face is a mask of shame and horror, that of her partner in crime a mixture of outrage, irritation and disgust.

Ulrico.

"You bastard," I hiss. Ulrico? The bumbling fool? He was conspiring with the Holy States all this time?

"You're under arrest for treason," Savino announces as the City Guards sweep into the study.

"No, no!" shouts Agosta as two guards force her arms behind her back. "No, Renza, you can't, you can't—!"

I ignore her, glaring at my colleague as my aunt is dragged out of the room. Ulrico looks down his nose at Idris and me.

"Why?" Idris asks. Ulrico doesn't bother to fight the City Guards as they clamp his hands in chains behind his back.

"No one ever believed I would be capable of this job. No one ever believed I was as smart as Yelena, as good a politician. But *they* did, *he* did." He smirks.

The way he says those last two words are meant as a jab at me. I want to vomit, seeing the true architect of this betrayal.

"I did a brilliant job, even if I do say so myself. Were your aunt not so stupid, you wouldn't have worked it out until it was far too late. I suppose good sense doesn't run in your family."

"Nor loyalty in yours," I answer.

"You knew she'd meet Nouis at the peace talks. You knew it was a trap." Idris makes the statement quietly, with so much violence lurking in the words, but Ulrico doesn't seem to register the threat as he laughs in his face.

"Why do you think I suggested she go?" Ulrico laughs. "My job gets easier when she's off the board, and Nouis was never going to let whichever delegate that went return. At least he wants her alive."

The closed fist flies like a cobra as Idris swings his body around with the force of an avalanche. The slamming sound has me gasping and jumping back as Ulrico sags forwards, blood dripping from his mouth and broken nose.

"Get that stain to a cell. Now!" shouts Savino as Idris heaves, anger emanating from him like vicious steam.

"Idris—" I take a step towards him.

"No!" Idris barks, his entire body trembling as he throws up his hands to stop me. He turns around, gripping hold of the wall, knuckles white as he fights the roaring breaths in his throat. His pupils are pinpricks as his face contorts with a violence that sends a surge of blood to my head.

"Idris—"

"OUT!" roars Idris, slamming his balled fist into the wall. My vision goes red as I force myself to take a step backwards.

"Perhaps you should..." Savino begins and I nod, ripping my eyes away from Idris. I don't say a word as I trail outside. I hurry, sucking in a breath from the cool night air as I break free from the traitor's home. Agosta is outside of course, and she starts yelling at me again – begging, really, to talk to me. I can't bring myself to look at her.

"You alright?" Alfieri asks, surprise evident in his voice as he seems to materialise in the dark. I offer him a tight smile as I take another shallow breath, letting the cool night air soak into my lungs.

"Yeah, things with Idris ... the bond got strained," I manage, clearing my throat. Alfieri nods slowly as a moment of silence passes. My eyes turn to Ulrico who's sneering at everything and everyone in his path. His mouth is folded in disgust as he's pulled away by the City Guard.

"How about I take you home. It's been a long day."

I nod as Alfieri guides me to his horse. He pats the mare's neck before offering me a hand up. I turn over Agosta's betrayal again and again in my head. Why did she do this? What did I do to offend her? What was she promised out of this?

She'll die for this. It was my plan that got her caught, my plan that proved without a doubt that she's been working against us all this time. Whatever her reason, whatever her bribe, her actions are her own. And she will pay the price. She has to.

The horse's hooves are soft on the cobbled street as Alfieri walks us home. He's back to his normal, easy-going, thoughtful self.

"Your business is a family business, isn't it?" I ask quietly.

"Yes..." he answers warily.

"How do you ... have you ever had to...?" I trail off, not sure how to form the question. Alfieri sighs. I can't imagine an international smuggling operation comes without its brutal requirements. And when the organisation is all family based...

"Those that betray family are not family," Alfieri says quietly, the words spoken with an air of familiarity, like the phrase has been told to him a hundred times before. "Family isn't blood, it's a bond. It's a silent promise. Those who choose to take advantage of that promise or cast it aside, they are not worthy of the title. Blood ties mean nothing until our actions make them worth something."

I've always been proud to wear the name Di Maineri. We are successful, rich, smart, driven. Di Maineris have influence and intelligence in every country across the continent; the name is known in almost every home.

But today, I am so ashamed of my blood. One aunt is imprisoned, the other is to die. Betraying their own and not feeling bad about it. Like I should expect this kind of behaviour. Is that all the Di Maineri name really means? Schemes and plots. Do our family ties really run so thin?

Giulia and I must be the exception to the rule.

Alfieri stops outside my house and I go inside to see City Guards marching up and down the corridors, searching for any further evidence. Tahira leans against the wall with folded arms. Fiora is nowhere to be seen, but I imagine Giulia is keeping an eye on her.

"So?"

"Not who I expected. But perhaps I should've," I answer. "Anything here?"

"These," Tahira says holding up some letters. "And a significant amount of Gold Aureus. I think you should read them. Some of the details might be ... interesting for you."

I nod and take the letters out of her hands.

"I'm ... I'm done for today," I say quietly. Tahira nods, a sympathetic look in her eyes.

"We've got this," she says, jutting her jaw towards the City Guards. "Get your head somewhere better."

I head up the stairs for my room. I close the door behind me, throwing the letters on the side as I crawl over the blankets of my familiar bed and collapse. I wrap my arms around a pillow and close my eyes, hoping the memory of Agosta's face will stop haunting me.

CHAPTER 35

I come down late for breakfast the following morning. I walk into the dining room and pour a large coffee. Giulia is halfway through a bowl of fruit as Fiora sips on her herbal tea. The silence is swollen and bruised, neither party wanting to needle the wound with careless words.

No, I won't be uncomfortable in my own damn home.

I deliberately sit across from Giulia and fix her with a bright smile. I reach over, catching her left hand and holding it up to the light. Her engagement ring sparkles like a captured rainbow on her hand.

"I love it more and more every time I look at it," I say. Giulia grins, admiring it again as though it were the first time.

"She knows me so well." Giulia sighs in blissful contentment. "Although I was worried about the cost – it can't have been cheap."

"No," I agree as I serve myself some food. "But Michelle is responsible. She'll have saved to get you exactly what she wanted. I wouldn't worry about it. All you need to worry about is making your wedding exactly the way you want it. Any plans yet?"

"We're thinking we'd like to hold it as soon as we can, after all the tension resolves itself – so we can all actually relax and celebrate," Giulia says, her eyes going a touch glassy as a wistful, joyous smile fills her lips.

"I take it then that Michelle's Soulmate is leaving the city?" Fiora says, clearing her throat. "Going back to Coari before the wedding?"

"She might make a visit, with the new trade deals. After all, she has to work, but she'll be at the wedding," Giulia answers without looking at Fiora. "She's very happy for us both."

"I see," Fiora answers, her tone forcefully inflection free. "That's been … decided?"

"It's what we all want. Royah is a *friend* to us both. I've explained this before," Giulia answers shortly. Fiora nods and clears her throat then gets to her feet.

"Of course, my mistake. Well, I am excited for the big day. Perhaps you'll be gracious enough to invite your cousins for the party at least? My boys have never been to Halice, and I'd love to show them where I grew up."

"Family is always welcome home, Fiora," I say, giving her a levelling look. "As long as your boys know how to behave." She meets my eyes and a steady, genuine smile slowly grows.

"My boys remind me of the two of you sometimes," she says quietly, turning her eyes to Giulia. "Being here has made me miss them."

"Does that mean you'll be leaving us soon?" Giulia asks. Fiora hesitates.

"Would you like me to leave?" The quietness of her tone holds so many questions and inflections I can't unpick them all. Understanding masking hurt, willingness to agree but wanting to stay. All wrapped up in six little words. Perhaps Fiora should've considered a career in politics rather than managing our bloodline, given she's able to convey so many messages so simply.

"That depends," I answer, linking my fingers together and focusing on her. "Answer me honestly. With all the whispers you collect in this city and outside it, did you really know nothing about Rialta and Agosta's motives?"

Fiora sighs, but she's expected this. Her gaze holds steady.

"I knew nothing of Rialta, though I had an inkling. She's been irritated with the bank set-up for a while, but she's always been so devoted to it. I didn't suspect she would deliberately try to sink it for her own greed," Fiora explains, her brow furrowing as she talks. "I was also aware Agosta was often out in places she didn't tell us about, but there is nothing inherently wrong in that. She shops and wanders – she's always been a free spirit. But now I revisit a story or two, there are new questions around them. At the time it all seemed innocent enough..."

"Stories?"

"Questions around her most recent husband's accident in Kavas have been circling. Agosta was seen speaking with Red Sands mercenaries when they first came to the city. But then again, there is nothing inherently wrong in that, and no one could say if they were the attackers or not. Agosta has always been so nosy and curious, and they were something brand new..." Fiora trails off. She shuffles her shoulders and meets my eye again. "That's everything I have. But if you need me to look into more—"

"Well, we all suspected the accidents," Giulia mutters quietly. "Three dead husbands?"

"Do you think she did it?" I ask Fiora point-blank. She takes a measured breath before answering.

"It's distinctly possible."

Giulia and I exchange a look, and I raise an eyebrow.

"One aunt came to take the bank, one aunt came to destroy my city. Why are you here, Fiora? Why did you really come?"

"I've told you. For you. For our family," Fiora answers, her eyes blazing. "After Tomas's death, with everything happening to this city ... you girls need someone who's not looking at the bank, who's not looking out for the city. Someone who's just focused on you. You don't have parents or family outside each other here anymore. Did either of you have a chance to grieve your father when he passed? Giulia wasn't even awake for his funeral."

"We've grieved. We still grieve," Giulia answers hotly. "But we have each other."

Giulia links her fingers around mine and we smile at each other.

"Good," Fiora answers with genuine warmth. "You have me, too."

I'm about to speak when a hot, tingling sensation spreads across my tongue. I cough as prickles rise up my throat and goosebumps crest across my arms. Needles tear into my fingertips.

Giulia smirks.

"Let me guess, Idris is here?" Giulia says softly. I nod as Leo enters the breakfast hall.

"Signora Renza, Signore Patricelli is here to see you. He's in the foyer."

"Thank you, Leo," I answer and get to my feet.

"What is he doing here?" Fiora asks irately.

"I don't know. Hence me going to ask," I answer, brushing off the crimson silk of my dress to make sure it's straight. The beads on my dangling belt chatter softly as I walk past the familiar mosaics and paintings that grace the creamy stone walls. The burning in my extremities picks up, a familiar searing taking a root behind my eyes. My teeth feel like boiling stones in my gums.

I come to the large front foyer to see Idris who stands admiring my mother's mosaic on the floor. Golden sunshine gushes through the patterned windows to bounce off his white tunic which is trimmed with pretty silver and blue adornments.

The pins on his sleeves twinkle like stars, his golden hair transformed into spun sunshine itself.

I clamp my teeth shut as his gaze sweeps around, a cheeky, teasing smile half filling his lips. Those hazel eyes study me for a long minute as we both just breathe.

"I'm sorry," Idris begins softly. "For yesterday."

"Tensions were high," I answer. "It's fine."

"Did it...? Are you hurt?" The roughness of his words shows the depth of his guilt.

"No," I answer immediately. His shoulders drop with relief.

"Good. Well then, I suppose you should get your shoes."

"My shoes? Where are we going?" I ask suspiciously. Idris cracks a wild grin.

"To see your birthday present of course. You don't really think I didn't get you anything?"

I blink, my mouth falling open.

"My birthday was a while ago."

"Things ran late." Idris shrugs. "Blame the state of affairs in this city, if you like. Or me being picky. But do you want to come see it or not?"

"See it? Now I'm worried." I chuckle and fold my arms. Idris walks closer, linking his hands behind his back as he stops before me, a playful expression on his face.

"Trust me, Di Maineri?" Idris asks lightly, the challenge clear in his tone.

"Do you want an honest answer?" I tease right back.

"Hmmm." Idris leans down, his blistering lips hovering just above my ear. "Well, your present is there either way, so the question is will you let me show you first or leave it undiscovered?"

"I've had enough of secrets. Lead the way."

The carriage jostles over the cobbles. The dark wood interior is adorned with plush green velvet cushions and beautifully embroidered white and gold curtains. Idris sits by my side as we travel, his knees occasionally brushing against mine, sending a bolt of hot lightning up my entire body.

I keep my hands folded over my lap, wondering what kind of gift Idris could possibly have got me that requires travelling to retrieve it. Idris seems relaxed as we both measure our breathing – vexingly so.

"How are you doing ... after yesterday?" Idris asks quietly. "With your aunt and Ulrico?"

I press my lips together.

"I'm sad," I answer. "Agosta ... I don't understand why."

"She lived in Kavas for years with her husband. Perhaps she was swayed," Idris says quietly. "Will you speak to her before...?"

Before she dies tomorrow.

It had been a quick conviction, with three Electi and members of the City Guard all providing evidence and acting as witnesses.

Leone had been utterly rattled, his face paler than the stone of our city for the entire event.

"It's the responsible thing to do," I answer quietly. "To see if she knows anything else."

"I could do it for you," offers Idris. I look at my fingers and shake my head.

"No. That's a discussion I need to have. Di Maineri to Di Maineri. I owe her at least that much."

"You owe her nothing; she betrayed you," Idris answers hotly. I keep my eyes fixed on my linked fingers, guilt bubbling up my throat to the point where my tongue struggles to reach for its words. I just shake my head.

"I have to," I manage. Idris sighs and nods.

"Well, put it from your mind for today at least," Idris says softly, leaning closer. I shudder as his hot breath rolls down my neck. He chuckles, spotting my reaction. His fingers slowly trail across my thigh, sending a tide of sparks rushing through my blood before his hand closes over mine.

"Any guesses so far?"

"I honestly have no idea." I frown at him. He grins at me, unabashed and a little smug. I look out the window, recognising where we are.

"Are we heading to the bank?" I ask, astounded. Whatever he's got me, is it so pricey that it needs to be kept in our vaults or safe boxes? Already my stomach churns at the thought of it. The Patricelli coffers are vast to be sure, with investments, dividends and profits pouring in from a variety of businesses and transactions surrounding their docks and trade across the continent. So whatever it is, I'm sure he could afford it. But still, extravagance isn't necessary. Not when all businesses have question marks at the moment.

"Maybe." Idris chuckles in amusement, his free hand reaching to play with one of my stray curls, running it slowly between his fingers before tucking it back in place. I turn to look at him.

"Maybe isn't an answer," I tell him softly.

"You really don't like not being in control, do you?" Idris teases. I sigh, puckering the corner of my mouth.

"Less and less as the days pass," I admit. It feels like everything I'm not taking charge of goes wrong.

"Here we are," Idris says as the carriage comes to a stop. I reach for the door but his hand whips across to cover mine. I pause, my heart jumping to thud in my ears. I breathe slowly as Idris moves to block my exit.

"Close your eyes," he instructs.

"You're kidding." I scowl at him. He doesn't move his hand but his fingers close tighter around mine.

"Close your eyes, Di Maineri," Idris says again, leaning closer to me. "For me."

I narrow my eyes at him and bite my lip.

"What, don't you trust me?" Idris snorts.

"That awkward little question again," I tease but Idris doesn't take the bait.

"Go on. Let me take the lead for a bit. I promise you'll like it." Idris is almost purring. I huff and close my eyes.

"How many fingers am I holding up?"

"One," I answer shortly, though I have no idea with my eyes firmly shut. "Right in the middle – oh no, wait. That's me."

"Oh, testy this morning. I thought you wanted your gift," Idris says and opens the carriage door.

"As stated earlier, I'm not a fan of secrets."

Idris gets out first and takes both my hands in his. His skin against mine is like clutching burning cinders. His words drip like smouldering acid in my ears as I follow his instructions. One of his arms comes around my waist as I slide out of the carriage and I can feel the length of his tall, muscled body against mine. I swallow, that infuriating wall of fire commanding me to melt closer and recoil all at the same time.

"Okay, just a few steps," Idris says as I let him lead me forwards, following his blazing path with careful steps until he comes to a stop. He moves around me, his hands searing as they come to my shoulders. Shudders ripple up and down my spine as he turns me slightly. Fiery fingers appear on my chin and lift my head upwards.

"Okay," he whispers softly in my ear. "Open up."

I open my eyes.

Oh. Fate's. Fury.

This is beautiful.

Standing in the square, at the base of the steps in front of the Di Maineri Bank, is a new art installation. I knew they were building something the last time I was here, but this is astonishing.

Huge panels of stained glass stretch tall in gilded stone frames; it's all intricate, vivid glass pouring with colour and light.

Gasping, I step backwards, straight into Idris's chiselled, caustic chest. His strong arms come around me, their fiery grip barely distracting me from the beauty. Each panel is so intricate, so expertly put together, I can barely believe it's real.

One is undulating blues and tall ships down at the docks as they bathe in sunlight. Another explodes with all the vibrant wonders of the Garden. Another captures the ethereal majesty and splendour of the High Chamber, crowning it in a ring of brilliant gold. There's the Old Church Building, the river filled with vibrant floats for Agoi, bursting vineyards and rolling hills, the sun setting over the city as viewed from outside the front gates. It's all astonishing.

But most of all, in the centre, is perhaps my favourite piece. Giulia and me, together. Hands linked, her gold hair cascading one way, my dark hair cascading the other. Surrounded by an explosion of blues, pinks and yellows, we're both given an almost spiritual look. The detail in our faces … the intricacy is astonishing. The way the artist has captured our likenesses, displaying us together as the equals and team that we are, is breathtaking.

"Happy Birthday," Idris whispers, his words sending a flood of fire down my neck. I laugh, my hand coming to my mouth.

"Idris this is … this is beautiful." I gasp, not sure where to put my eyes. Each piece of work is phenomenal.

"I know you love the stained glass in the High Chamber, so I got some. Just for you," Idris murmurs quietly, pressing his lips to the side of my head. His sweltering warmth soaks through my hair and into my head.

"It's … it's…" I'm so speechless there are almost tears in my eyes. My heart thumps at a million miles an hour. I want to scream and giggle and rush over to examine each piece all at the same time.

"It's perfect," I manage. Idris kisses the top of my head, arms tightening around me for a moment before answering.

"Good. Come on, let's get a closer look."

Idris takes me around each panel, showing me how the light cascades through each piece. We're not the only ones admiring the new installations – loads of people walking by stop to admire the new art gracing the forecourt of the Di Maineri Bank. At the side of each piece's thick framing is a little bronze plaque explaining the scene and listing every single person who contributed to the design and construction – such a brilliant touch.

We stop in front of the one of Giulia and me. It's so elegant and perfect. I stand there, soaking in the rich, exquisite explosion of colour, admiring every artisanal twist and curve. There are tears in my eyes when I turn back to face Idris.

"Don't cry," he says softly. He runs a hot finger under my eyes to catch a fleeting escapee.

"Thank you. Thank you so much," I breathe. Idris wraps his arms around me and leans closer.

"Of course, anything for you," he says softly. He drops his head down to mine, his forehead resting on mine, his presence burning through every dark corner of my brain, consuming me with his lavender and mint smell, searing through any other possible distraction. There is nothing else, only him.

His lips fall against mine, soft and tender. Their heat licks along my tongue, provoking and yearning, destruction and desire boiled together.

I wrap my arms around his neck and press my mouth harder against his, letting my tongue sweep across his own. Idris stops, a deep, rumbling groan leaking from his lips.

"I'm glad you like it," he whispers. I take a slow deep breath, forcing my heart to slow, demanding the bile in my throat retreat, that the whispers fall silent in my head.

He takes my hand and pulls me back to the carriage. I look over my shoulder at the beautiful art as we walk away. I'll be back, and soon. I could sit and study these pieces for hours.

Idris pulls me into the carriage next to him and closes the door. He gives some quiet instructions to the driver while I look out the window, admiring my last few glimpses of this art, which stands basking in the glory of Halician sunlight.

When it's finally out of view I lean back in my seat. I don't fight the smile on my lips or the giddy jolting of my heart.

Idris is behind those wonderful pieces. Idris did it.

For me.

The air in this carriage is practically fizzing. My heart pounds in my throat, my pulse sprints like its life is on the line. Idris leans closer, his arm slipping around my shoulders.

"I like you in this colour," he whispers, the words a sultry growl. I look down at my red dress.

"Oh?" I ask, trying to clear my throat. "You think it suits me?"

"You look good in everything. And without anything at all," Idris answers, planting hot, fiery kisses along the side of my jaw. I laugh at the blind audacity of this man to whisper such naughty things.

"Should I prove it?" Idris challenges. His hand comes up, turning my face towards his. My hands leap to his golden hair, knotting myself in the fire. Breathless, his sizzling kisses mould with my mouth. His tongue battles with mine, our dance addictive and torturous. His hands move over my body, blazing a fierce, aching tail across the dips of my waist and over the curve of my ass.

He pulls me onto his lap, my legs spread wide to pull me flush with his chest. My trembling, wet centre is just a few layers of fabric away from the straining length of his manhood that stands at full attention in his trousers.

He pulls his lips from mine and I moan as he begins his assault on the soft flesh of my neck. My breathing is haggard and rapid as one hand squeezes my arse harder, the other slipping up like a river of fire to my breast. His fingers slip inside my dress, the tender, gentle flesh left to the savage mercy of his whims.

I gasp, arching my back as his fingers find my nipples. The straps of my dress fall from my shoulders, exposing both breasts to his attentions. He kneads one breast as his mouth descends upon the other, gently playing and biting down. My mewling response is so brazen, so breathy, I'm barely aware of the sounds leaving my throat.

I pull his mouth against mine again, desperate for more of him. Somehow I find room between us, my hands working their way down to his straining cock, every thick, solid inch of it. I grab it, and he bucks, swearing as my fingers search their way over his trousers towards his waistline.

Then he's moving. I gasp as I'm suddenly back on the bench. He's kneeling on the floor between my legs, his hands pushing up the silky layers of my dress. His fingers trail up the insides of my thighs with excruciating slowness, the agonising path sending my head spinning as his lips follow.

He grips my thighs with two hands and tugs, pulling my legs over his shoulders. With no mercy or warning he descends on my wet, trembling centre. I cry out as the blistering euphoria of his mouth licks and nips and dances along the sensitive flesh. My moans are breathy and high, savouring the incendiary bliss of his touch. His lips and tongue work together in a master plan, teasing and stroking and building higher and higher and higher.

One hand reaches up to my exposed breasts while the other grips my arse, holding me firmly against his face. I'm utterly at his whim, his games with my body unsparing and fierce. My hands knot with his hair, pulling and clamping down with disregard, my ecstasy intensifying with each brazen sweep of his tongue against my clit, with each ruthless dance of his lips.

"Idris!" I all but screech his name as I drown in the violent shuddering waves of pleasure. I climax against his mouth but he devours it down, savouring every savage convulsion. Every spark and wave is so vicious I see stars ... I forget to breathe ... there is nothing else in the world.

Gasping, I collapse back against the bench as Idris looks up, grinning with wicked delight. He comes to sit next to me on the bench, a smug expression on his face as I straighten myself up and desperately try to catch my breath.

I look towards Idris as he rearranges his clothing, that smirk both irritating and making me grin all at the same time. I lean forwards, my hand going to his thigh.

"Your turn," I whisper, but he scoops my hand off.

"Later," he murmurs as he plants a sweet kiss on my lips. "Believe me, I'm not letting you go any time soon."

I snort, leaning back against the seat as he intertwines his fingers with mine.

I slow my heart, control my breathing, ignore the whispers and focus on him.

My Idris.

CHAPTER 36

Noon comes swiftly the next day, and soon the High Chamber stands just outside my carriage door. Grey clouds mar a fleeting sun from looking down at the sorrowful scene. A crowd has gathered, the noise deafening and utterly inconsequential all at the same time. They're shouting and talking, many gesturing to the gallows constructed on one side of our great building. Far on the other side stand the other members of the Electi. Leone, Maggia and Savino are already there. I can't see Idris yet.

My fingers tighten on the door handle, blood draining from my face and pooling cold and slick around my ribs. I breathe slowly and force myself to twist the handle. The City Guard are waiting for me, ready to protect me from the crowd as I exit.

Some of the crowd look my way, some yell, some defend me to their counterparts. I blink rapidly, my gaze turning to the hastily erected and heavily defended grey tent set off to one side. Agosta will be inside there, as will Ulrico. Their last few moments of privacy before...

I swallow tightly, but the icy stone lodged in my throat

doesn't shift. I force myself to take a step forwards, flanked by Halician City Guards. I move towards the tent. Proceedings can't begin without Idris anyway. I have time. I don't owe her anything, but I'll give her the courtesy of a chance to explain. Purely for the city.

The jostling crowd eventually parts as I head for the grey tent. I'm relieved when we get to the clear space around it. The Night Captain from the prison is there. She gives me a respectful nod.

"A moment with the prisoner, please."

"They're both in there," she lets me know. I nod. It won't matter what Ulrico overhears now. He'll soon be too dead to tell anyone anything.

I step towards the flap and push it open.

Two large, caged structures are parted by a slim walkway. One person stands in each. They've each been given a chair and a desk with paper in case they have any last words they wish to convey.

Ulrico sits at his desk, glaring at the paper on it with a grim expression, a vicious bruise marring half his face. Idris's work. I don't care about him.

Agosta paces back and forth in her cell, her arms hugged tight to her chest. Her dark hair is wild and unkempt. Both flinch the moment I enter, their eyes locked on me.

"Well, well, the executioner is here," Ulrico snarls.

I ignore him and walk towards Agosta. She's statue still. Her eyes are wide and tired, her lashes damp like she's only recently stopped crying. My stomach turns over; my lungs shrink as I stand a pace from her bars.

We look at each other for a long moment. She swallows tightly; fear fighting for complete control over her face. I break the expectant silence.

"I can't pardon you," I say honestly. I won't lie to her. Not now. A whimper escapes her lips as she looks at her hands, blinking rapidly.

"You betrayed me. I'm your family and you betrayed me," I continue. "This is the city where you grew up, your first home. And you betrayed her. We have the proof, Agosta. I can't save you now."

Agosta nods, but she's trembling. The curls on her head quiver.

"I understand," she says with a wet whisper.

"Why?" I ask, letting the pain ring in the word. She laughs, fear strumming fast and fierce.

"I had to," Agosta breathes, walking away and refusing to meet my eye. "They had proof of my late husband's death. They took *everything*. I was penniless."

"They were blackmailing you?" I whisper, letting the words hover. Agosta rakes a hand through her hair and clenches her fingers.

"If I gave him information on you, on this city..." Agosta sighs as I realise exactly who she's talking about. I swallow, a fresh wave of betrayal quivering on my tongue as I speak.

"You knew Nouis was alive."

"He's the one with the proof," Agosta admits with a helpless shrug. "He said he'd give my money back if I did as he said. I tried to give him things I thought were irrelevant. I hired Red Sands Bannerhood mercenaries as instructed but conveniently forgot to tell them Idris was the target. I passed on a vague whisper about smugglers when I thought nothing of it. I told them about your new priestess Otta for Agoi. I didn't realise the damage he would do with it."

"You knew. You may not want to admit it to yourself, but you knew the damage he'd do," I counter. Now is the time for hard truths. She shouldn't go to her grave lying to herself.

Agosta takes a sharp breath and folds her arms, turning to face me as she holds herself tightly.

"I suppose," she answers morosely.

"All of this ... was about money?" I sigh, pinching my brow. "We're the richest family across the continent. You could've gone *anywhere*."

"I couldn't turn to family, not without admitting it was true. What I did is illegal everywhere. Everyone would've used the proof Nouis sent them to control me, manipulate me... If I was going to be under someone's thumb it wasn't going to be a Di Maineri. I know that monster too well." Agosta shakes her head violently and her face crumples. "I couldn't marry again, not with the evidence looming over my head. If I tried anything but what Nouis asked, that evidence would be sent..."

"We've suspected for years your husbands' deaths weren't accidents," I say quietly. "You know that."

Agosta laughs, the noise brittle like cracking glass. She closes her eyes, as though to pretend I'm not there and she can remove reality of what's about to happen.

"My first husband's was," Agosta whispers. "Not that people believed me. It was a marriage all about money. I thought I'd be free of the family with him. But the idiot's lifestyle was well beyond his means. His extortionate debts became mine when he died. The second marriage was to save me from ruin, but he owned me. All he needed was my Di Maineri name for his business prospects, and as his wife he decided I belonged to him. I was to be controlled by whatever means necessary. A toy for his brutish whims. I had to get away from his hands..."

Agosta trails off for a moment, her face folding as she winces at a memory too vivid to describe. I don't speak, waiting for her. She takes a steadying breath before continuing.

"Alphonsus, my third husband ... people mocked our marriage from the start. Almost thirty years between us... There were whispers and sniggers everywhere we went but it was a marriage of real companionship. Not love, but friendship. We were friends for years beforehand. We both knew what the marriage was when we entered it. Alf didn't want someone to marry him for his money, no matter how well they treated him in his golden years. He wanted a friendship of equals, and for a few years that's exactly what we had. Alf had the best stories, and we'd talk and laugh all the time. He was happy to share his home with me and I with him. But he was old, and so unwell, and the illness progressed so cruelly. His pain grew blinding. He asked me to end it for him because he was unable to get out of bed and do it himself. I refused at first, perhaps selfishly. I knew what people would say when he died, I knew exactly how it would look. But his life was torture, every breath excruciating. His screams still haunt me. They used to echo down the corridor and at night I'd just listen. If you had seen his agony, his pleading with me... The end was a blessing for him."

Agosta opens her eyes and turns back to me.

"Perhaps he used me, too. He had to have known how it would've looked, what I would face afterwards."

"Only you can know if that's true," I answer honestly, quietly. Agosta takes a shaky breath and nods slowly.

"I am sorry, for what little it's worth," she breathes. I bite down on my tongue, expecting my gut to twist or my heart to twinge. But there's nothing. Just an empty black hole swallowing the place where my empathy or compassion is supposed to sit.

I pull out the small pill from my sleeve and hold it through the bars for her. Chains rattle as she takes it between trembling fingers.

"Not until the count starts," I instruct her. "You owe me that much."

She looks down at the small white capsule then lifts it to her nose, taking in the dark, floral scent. A strangled relief flitters across her face at the hopeless mercy I've handed her. At least she has the surety there will be no long, drawn-out death, no scrabbling at her throat as she asphyxiates. Instead she faces a sudden, gentle death akin to falling to sleep.

I don't expect a thank-you. I don't want one. I'm doing this as much for me as I am for her.

I take a step back but hesitate before turning to leave.

"For what it's worth, I wouldn't have used it against you," I tell her. She looks at the pill and laughs dryly, before levelling me with a gaze that strips me bare.

"Yes, you would," Agosta answers, so confidently that I'm unnerved. "You're so blind to your true self, thinking you're better than our blood. But you're a Di Maineri. You're no different from the rest of us."

I don't say another word before turning around and leaving the tent. The square is lined with armed City Guards as I walk through the crowd. There are a few of the Red Sands Bannerhood around, but not many. Just as I asked. This needs to be a Halician affair, for the Halician people.

People notice me as I walk, the two City Guard soldiers who flank me making people move out of my way as I march towards the High Chamber. Some are yelling up at the wooden platform that has been erected for the traitors while others levy curses on the Electi, all of whom have gathered to pass the sentence of treason.

I reach the base of the steps. A dark, familiar revulsion curdles at the base of my throat and I stare at the steps for a moment, not moving upwards. It's time.

The crowd is roaring. Blood rushes around my ears. My breath echoes in my skull. I want to clamp my hands desperately over my ears, to shut out the vile, sharp ringing that threatens to drown me. I fight with my pulse, battling to force air into my lungs.

I can't look up. I can't. It's too—

"Hey." Idris's hand appears in my vision, his pale fingers wiping any other sensation from my head like a lightning strike.

He's so close that my skin crawls, my throat burns, and my blood runs molten. But it's familiar. It's him.

I look up at him as he surveys the crowd. Seeing him hits me with that devouring, dominating fury. It roars through me like a poisonous tide, searing away any other sensation but him. I rip my eyes away, forcing my deep breaths and battling with my warring pulse as I put my hand in his.

He walks me back up to the other Electi, placing himself between me and the crowd.

"Let Savino take the lead," Idris says quietly. "All you have to do is walk to your mark and pull on the count."

"I know," I answer, bristling, even though he's trying to be helpful. *Blasted Soulhate bond.*

I join the group. Maggia raises an eyebrow and gestures behind me. I turn sharply and watch a familiar dark head fleeing the grey tent.

Fiora.

I turn back and shake my head. We don't need to do anything. I won't begrudge her saying goodbye to her sister.

"Okay," Savino says quietly. "It's time."

I turn back to the tent and the City Guards bring out Ulrico and Agosta. Both wear terrible expressions. Agosta's is almost blank, like a fearful acceptance. Ulrico's is rage and denial. They are marched through the crowd and towards the gallows. Savino steps forwards, indicating he's ready. The traitors are brought to the front of the stage, so people can see them for what comes next.

Savino starts to speak and the abrupt silence of the crowd is a gut punch. Idris stands next to me, his hand in mine feeling like a blistering anchor holding me in place. I lean into the bonfire of his presence; I tackle the fight I know how to handle.

Savino is succinct and to the point as he announces the crimes, the proof we have, the terrible consequences. Then the verdict. His words crack through everything, the rage, the revulsion, the burning.

"I, Member Savino Collier, today's speaker for the Electi, pronounce the accused guilty of treason and sentence them to death. May Fate grant them mercy."

Idris's hand tugs on mine, leading me the short walk to the gallows. I keep my head up as the crowd springs back into life. Ulrico and Agosta are walked to their marks, the ropes fitted around their necks.

Each member of the Electi takes position behind a waist-high wooden lever sticking up from the ground. It's our job, as Electi. If we pronounce someone guilty of treason, we must be the ones carrying out the sentence. For accountability. To show the severity of the actions taken. It can't be done out of sight; it can't be hidden away. It's for all to see, to ensure the system cannot be abused.

Only one of these five levers actually opens the trap door beneath their feet. But each will be weighted the same, so we'll never know who exactly it was. It spreads the consequences of the actions, be they personal guilt or anything more extreme, across the group. No one person alone holds responsibility for the fallout.

Idris's hand falls from mine as he takes his position.

My hands go to the lever. The wood is dry and itchy under my fingers. My palms tingle, my mouth is thick.

Why does it feel like this? I've done this before. I killed Nouis – or thought I did. But that was in self-defence. I killed Bellandi – I hanged him off the Church building with Idris. I didn't flinch and I didn't waver. But then, I was consumed with anger and adrenalin and determination to save my city.

I look up. Agosta's eyes are focused high above the crowd, on the grey Halician sky. She could've cost us everything. Alfieri almost died because of her. She knew Nouis was alive. She knew what he was trying to do and who the traitors were. She came here to betray me. To destroy the safety of this city. She could've killed everyone. She knew that and she didn't care. She did it anyway.

I let out a deep breath as the count starts. I grit my teeth.

"Three. Two. One."

I pull, my eyes wide open as the doors disappear beneath both their feet.

It's done.

I let go of the lever and stand back a pace, my shoulders heaving.

Idris hisses sharply. I snap around to see him reaching up, pulling something from the back of his head.

"What is it?" I ask, crossing to him. Idris frowns as he shows me a small metal projectile. It's sharp and spiked.

"Someone threw this at me." Idris rubs the back of his neck. His fingers come away tinted crimson.

"They must've done it with a slingshot or something, because that hit quite deep," Savino says as he inspects Idris's wound.

"I think ... it's wet..." Idris starts to slur his words and drops the object.

My stomach empties, blood screaming in my ears as Idris buckles sideways.

"IDRIS!" I scream, collapsing to his side. His eyes start fluttering as he fights to stay awake and his breath becomes laboured.

"No, Idris, fight it. Fight it!" I plead with him, tears gathering in my eyes. He raises a hand, clumsily cupping the side of my face. His touch blisters but horror pounds an icy contrast. He tries to say something, but the words get smothered. His eyes slide closed and his head tilts to the side. His hand flops against his chest.

Something dark, cold and desperate snaps beneath my ribs.

"Find them! Find them!" I scream at the City Guard, tears

streaming freely down my face as I cradle Idris's head to my chest. Chaos swarms the square as people scream and run and the City Guards charge into action.

I look down at Idris's blank face, watching in horror as his lips turn a scary shade of blue.

"Hold on," I plead, clinging to the fire in my fingers like a lifeline. "Please. Hold on."

CHAPTER 37

I *can't breathe. I can't think.*
My heart throbs and my pulse screams in my ears. Every fibre of my body fizzes and roars with a vicious, agonising energy, looking for something – anything – to dig my nails into and claw and claw and claw.

I tug my hair, the pressure a relief to the ringing whispers and the cold, twisted shards of fear coiling around my sternum.

The doctors are gathered around Idris in his room. I've never been in his room before, but it's just like him. The top half of the walls are made of creamy stone, the lower half adorned with expensive wood panelling. A huge, antique four-poster bed is made up with cream and navy silk sheets, facing a large stained-glass door leading to a narrow balcony.

Idris lies on top of the sheets. I took off his shoes myself, fingers trembling over the laces as the doctors pored over their work. It was all I could think to do to help, useless as it was. He'll at least be more comfortable, surely, so maybe it will help a little.

Taio and three other Halician doctors gather around. They

are constantly checking his pulse, his temperature, testing one substance and then the next; examining the projectile and swabbing for remnants.

He's so pale. Looking at him sets off a blinding war across my head, splinters of white-hot iron stabbing through my eyes to bury in my brain, but I can't look away. I can't bear it. Not when every fragile, battled breath could be his last. Not with the violet tinge taking hold of his mouth. Not with the black, bloodless look around his closed eyes...

It's been hours. He hasn't woken. He hasn't spoken. He's ... fighting, but he's doing it on his own. *Fate's Fury, I wish I could help.* I would do anything to take this fight for him. But I can't. I'm entirely helpless and I hate every second of it.

I stand at the end of the bed. My eyes feel so dry I feel like they might grind to dust with each blink. I have no tears left. I can't stop staring; if I stop looking and he stops breathing...

The minute we arrived, Tahira and her team were off. The fury combing through the city right now must be extraordinary. The rage in Tahira's expression, the raw, violent determination to find who did this, was unmistakeable. She doesn't care what she has to do, she will find this foul assassin that got into our city; that hurt her friend and my...

I grip the corner of the bed, forever grateful for its support as Taio sighs and looks in my direction. I meet his gaze and he gestures for me to follow him away from the bed. I barely realise I'm walking as I move to his side, the world slightly spinning as he speaks.

"We're not sure what it is," Taio admits quietly. "Your doctors think it's a plant from the north of your continent, perhaps a place called Rhone. But we can't know for certain."

"Will he be alright?" I ask. That's the only question I care about. I see the slump of his shoulders, the defeat in his dark eyes... I barely hear the words as ringing takes up residence in my ears, almost swamping what comes next.

"Even if it is what they think, they don't have the antidote. It's rare. It takes a long time to brew and some ingredients are difficult to get hold of. We're simply out of time. Now he just has to fight it ... and he's getting weaker. He's not doing well," Taio says, reaching out. Both hands gently squeeze my forearms, but whether he is holding me upright or keeping me from running away from the terrible words that follow next, I'm not sure. "You need to prepare yourself."

"No," I whisper, somehow finding what's left of my tears. I turn back to the bed, my breathing choked as my vision goes blurry. He's a glaring star, in perfect, blistering clarity.

"My prediction is that he won't survive the night," Taio continues.

I shake my head violently and my hand leaps to my mouth. My entire body is trembling. My world turns upside down, then tumbles and crashes to the ground. Every fibre of my blood screams and shrieks in my head, snarling at me to fight, begging me to take action. But what action? And where?

I stagger backwards, away from these doctors and their awful, awful words. My lungs can't get enough air and my stomach churns and forces its way up my cold, empty throat.

I push through the doors and into the corridor.

"Renza! Renza!" Alfieri shoots after me. He's been waiting outside, acting like a bodyguard. He sees my expression and his face crumbles.

I can't do it. I can't tell people. I can't do this. It makes it real. And it can't be.

IT CAN'T BE!

I fold myself onto the stairs, gripping hold of my throat like I can physically pry it open to let the air in. The ringing in my head gets louder and louder and louder. I want to scream. I want to smash things. I want to burn the world to the ground.

The front door opens and in marches Tahira. There's a dark

glint in her eyes as she looks around. She spies me on the stairs and her eyes narrow.

"Got the bastard," she announces, and she holds up a vial of something in her hands. "And he had this. I think it's the poison."

"Bedroom. Now!" I point as she races up the stairs. "Where's the culprit?"

"Basement cellar," Tahira shouts back as she marches into the bedroom with her prize.

The monster is in the cellar.

A cold rage, sharp and steely, settles in my bones. The tears stop and my pulse drops. My head empties. I get to my feet and march down the stairs, out the back of the property and towards the cellar entrance. A myriad of Red Sands mercenaries stand guard, including Royah.

"You sure you want to see him?" Royah asks as I reach for the door. I don't answer as I yank the door open, heading down the narrow stairs with her barely a pace behind. Orange-tongued torches line the dark stone structure. My steps echo as I walk, my shoes clipping against the cold, unforgiving ground.

I come to the door and Royah's hand leaps out to stop me.

"Renza." Royah's voice is thick and torn. I turn to look at her. Her dark braids are gilded with amber, those brown eyes brimming with pain but also worry. For me.

"He's a hitman for hire. He was paid to go after Idris four days ago. He wouldn't give up his buyer, no matter what Bashran tried – and he tried a lot," Royah says quietly. "You don't have to see him. You don't want to see the work Bash did—"

"You have the evidence?" I interrupt, my voice devoid of emotion.

She gestures to a large table at the back. I see weapons, more of those small, bead-like projectiles, and some kind of slingshot system. There are clothes, a few letters – if they were important Royah would've told me. Or Tahira. But they could be useful. Very useful indeed.

"We have the evidence to convict. You don't need to go in there," Royah says gently. "Please reconsider."

"No," I answer quietly but firmly. "But first get me some paper, and some charcoal."

Royah frowns before nodding towards one of her colleagues who goes off to comply.

"What do you have in mind?" she asks, folding her arms.

"If it yields anything, I'll let you know," I say. "How bad is he in there?"

"He could probably use a doctor if you insist on sending one."

"He'll live without?"

"Long enough to hang for attempting to kill an Electi," Royah answers begrudgingly, "but uncomfortably." I nod before taking a burning torch off the wall. The heavy, dry wood scrapes against the stone as I haul it free, extending the rapidly spinning flames out to the side as I close my fingers over the frigid iron handle. I twist, yanking the door open. The heavy door groans against the worn wood floor.

I look inside, waiting expectantly for the monster who's done this.

Sweaty, dirty, bloody. This skinny man is chained to the floor, buckled over himself in the dark. Firelight bounces off the clammy sheen to his head as he lifts his face up. It's smeared with red. It drips from his nose, his mouth, his ears, mingling with the dirt that clings to his face and is trapped in his short beard.

I toss the torch to the side, letting it hit the floor. It'll keep burning for a while at least, even lying on the floor. I don't need long.

"Alone, please," I say without turning to Royah. The door wails and slams closed behind me, locking me in this dark, dank room with this vile piece of filth.

The man doesn't speak. Neither do I for a long time. I just look at him, not sure what I was expecting. This rage is burning with a glacial, bitter chill. Cruel, cold loathing sits at the front of my mind like a storm.

"Who hired you?" I say, breaking the silence.

"You think you can make me talk?" The assassin's words are pained but there is strength behind them. It doesn't matter. "Better have tried."

"Different have tried," I counter, stepping towards him. My steps ring off the stone, as I stand over him. I crouch down, narrowing my eyes.

"You aren't afraid of pain, are you?" I say quietly, meeting his pale eye. "You think we'll keep you alive as long as we need something, and alive you have hope. Even if that life isn't worth living."

The man's face crumbles, blood brimming between his crooked teeth as he speaks.

"I won't tell you a damn thing."

"No need. Your work is distinctive. I'll find your job history quite quickly. Find where you come from, where you were born and raised. Anyone you might've left behind. Perhaps a parent, a sister, a brother—"

His brow wobbles ever so slightly at the last word. So there *is* someone out there then. I push on that weakness.

"I'll find your brother," I say, and the assassin's gaze turns wrathful. "I'm Renza Di Maineri. There's no corner of this earth I can't reach. My family are spread across every inch of this continent – our webs are everywhere. You know our brutality, our cruelty, the wicked games we play. I'll find your brother ... and that's where I'll make it hurt."

"You bitch!" he spits, spraying his blood over my face. I wipe a speck from my eye as though unbothered.

"You take those I care for; I'll return the favour. That little poison you used, it seems the doctors here don't know much about it. Perhaps your brother can be a case study for our medics to learn more. Perhaps we can open up his chest and watch his veins turn black. Perhaps we can crack open his ribs so we know the precise moment his heart stops—"

"You're a monster."

"Idris Patricelli is mine," I snarl, my hand leaping for his throat as I squeeze, letting my nails find root in his grimy flesh. "His life and his death belong to me – Fate decreed it so. You took what's mine from me. I cannot let that stand. So if I can't protect what's mine, I have no choice but to avenge it. People can't think they'll get away with this. Your little family can be my brutal, vengeful example on the world stage."

The man is breathing hard and rapidly, his mouth puckered with disgust.

"Unless you're just a tool, of course." I let my words soften as I search his face. I release my hand from around his neck and lean backwards. "If my anger ought to be directed elsewhere, then tell me. Present another target. Save your brother."

"I was hired by the Holy States. I don't have a name," he bites out instantly.

"No," I say coldly. "That's a lie."

The man lets out a short breath.

"Why protect them? You know I won't let you go. All you can do now is choose where I find my revenge," I say darkly. I stand up straight and step back, hands falling to my sides as I wait. Curled up on the floor, he breathes heavily before speaking.

"I don't have a name," he says quietly, but this has the ring of truth. Something in the way his eyes dart to the side as though he's summoning a memory ... the defeat in his shoulders, the slightly lower tone to his voice and slower pace to his words. "It was a woman. A small thing. Dark eyes. Dark hair. Warm complexion. Lots of curls."

My stomach drops as I realise who he's describing.

"Anything identifiable?" I ask quietly. He shakes his head as though trying to remember.

"She never let me get a good look at her face. I only saw it for a fraction of a moment, but when she handed me the money, I saw a wound on the back of her arm. An old burn by the looks of things."

Fiora.

My heart stops for a long moment. My blood goes quiet as the pieces move into place in my head. My jaw clamps down, and it's all I can do not to break my teeth.

"You know her," the man says, a smirk in his voice. "Oh, you've been betrayed..."

Again. I've been betrayed yet again.

Three solid thumps come at the old door. Right on time. I step back and rub my face. The torch sputters on the ground, rapid flames writhing back and forth as I open the door. I take the papers and charcoal and close the door without another word.

"You are going to write a statement in triplicate," I tell the assassin. "You'll confirm that it was Fiora Di Maineri who hired you. You will use her name. You will state details. You will write everything down."

"Why?"

"That's my business."

"What do I get for this? You already have your name," the assassin snarls. "You won't let me live."

"No ... but I can ensure that your brother gets a little ... financial boost. Perhaps a mortgage document gets mysteriously but permanently lost, or a surprise windfall finds its way to his pockets..."

"You Di Maineris, always using your money to get your way." The man scowls but takes the papers and the charcoal I offer him and starts to write. I step back in the dark and watch. Pulse itching, mind whirling, I wait and I plan.

That's it. No more betrayals.

This ends now.

CHAPTER 38

The moon is baring her teeth as I arrive home. Violet claws crawl over the golden torches of my home, battling the dark onset as I march on.

I slam the front door behind me, the heavy wood shuddering in its frame. The sound echoes through the house like thunder.

"Renza? By Fate's Fury, what happened?" Giulia comes running along the hall from the living room. Her blond hair ripples with the golden fingers of candlelight and her porcelain brow is carved into a deep frown. She is the only family in this world I can actually trust. The only one worth anything at all.

Over her shoulder, that traitor hovers in the living room doorway, a shallow crystal glass filled with wine in her hand. Her lips are a tight line as she studies me. Her back is poker straight, her knuckles turning white against the glass.

My stomach turns over. The need to scream builds in my lungs like an explosion. My fingers itch and my blood crashes like thunder in my ears.

I surge forwards.

"Renza, dear, you look—" Fiora starts, words daring to

strike a scolding tone. The roar rips free from my teeth as I grab her, ramming her against the wall with all the force I can muster. The glass drops to the floor, shattering with a scream at our feet. Her head thumps satisfyingly against the plaster, her dark hair flying around her face.

Pain slips through her lips, the whimper mostly shock. She stares at me with wide eyes, her arms trembling under my hands.

"Renza! Renza, what is this?" Giulia stands at my side. She tries to place a hand on my shoulder, to create some distance between me and the traitor under our roof. I don't move an inch.

"Three aunts descended on my home. All three were snakes lying in wait!" I spit, digging my nails into her bare shoulders and watching her wince. "You should've learned your lesson from your fallen sisters."

Fiora shakes her head, her lips wrinkling with sorry determination. There's no regret in her, only resignation.

"What did you do?" breathes Giulia. Pre-emptive anger bristles in the words.

"Idris..." His name is all I can choke out before the rage wraps a stranglehold around my throat again. Giulia stiffens behind me.

"I did it for you. To save you!" Fiora begins. My backhand cracks against her face so fast I barely see it. The force knocks my aunt to the floor, where she cowers amongst the glass fragments and spilled wine.

My hand races with stinging waves, but I crave the pain. The reddening of my palm is almost forgotten when I stare down this mockery of family. She scrabbles to pick herself up, the glass fragments scraping against the mosaic. She turns to look at me, her cheek turning vermillion as she looks up through her long dark tresses.

"He needs to die. It is Fate's decree! Fate will take the life he is owed, one way or another," Fiora insists. "It must be one of you, and I won't let it be you!"

"You had no right!" I snarl.

"There is only so long that you can keep taunting Fate until it takes revenge. Until it comes for our family." Fiora gets to her feet, her breath coming sharp and fast.

"You have to believe that," I snap back. "It's how you justify marrying your husband's murderer. It absolves you of the guilt that must eat you alive, claiming that Fate forced you. That you had no choice. It's Fate's fault. So it's okay to build a happy family in the puddle of your first husband's blood."

"Don't you dare—!"

"Does Marino even know who his true father is? Or do you pretend even for him that there was never another? Do you justify your lies by blaming Fate? Does he know what really happened?"

Fiora's face falls.

"You are not a cruel woman, Renza. This is heartless," Fiora says, her tone bruised. I laugh.

"Says the callous killer."

"I didn't do this out of malice," Fiora counters. "I bear Idris no ill will, but this family has to come first. You, my niece, are the one I care about. The one I must protect. You come first."

"So you saw fit to murder him."

"Is he dead?" Giulia gasps.

My fingers curl into fists as I stare at Fiora, wanting to do nothing more than punch her face in and keep going until her teeth join the glass fragments scattered over the floor.

Fiora sighs deeply, shaking her head in disappointment.

"He is my Fated." Tears brim in my eyes, the roar of my anguish barely contained in my breaking voice. "Idris is mine. He is mine by the decree of Fate, and he is mine by our free choice. *No one will ever take him from me!*"

Fiora's eyes go wide and glass cracks under her feet as she takes a horrified step back. Her head shakes as if she can deny my words.

"You cannot ... you cannot love him."

My heart cracks under my chest. *Love. Yes, that's it.* That's what this bleeding, screaming pain is that threatens to swallow me whole. Fiora is right.

I have to tell him. Fate's Fury, I have to find a way to tell him! He can't die not knowing. He can't.

I study my aunt and a tear springs free to roll down my cheek. I shake my head, a shallow laugh slipping off my tongue with my shuddering, uneven breaths.

"The gods chose hate, but I choose love. We. Choose. Love." I walk closer, each step punctuated by crunching glass shards over the mosaic, until my nose is inches from hers. I stare her down, threat bristling on my every word. "And no one, not all the powers of Fate nor the meddling schemes of pathetic mortals can ever change that."

"A brave effort, my dear." Fiora shakes her head. "One I'll endeavour to applaud. But it's doomed."

"Then I shall walk hand in hand with him into the jaws of doom," I promise, feeling that oath turn to steel in my chest. "And I will regret *nothing*."

I step back, my lip wrinkling as I stare her up and down.

"So what happens now?" Giulia steps forwards, her hand linking with mine. I squeeze tightly, soaking up her strength as we stand shoulder to shoulder. We both take the measure of our aunt, whom to her credit doesn't run or plead.

"She attempted to murder an Electi," I say, cold and detached. "We already know the price of that crime."

"Do you have proof?" Giulia asks, her voice just as cold. She isn't asking for herself, but for the court where we'll have to prove it in front of the other Electi.

"A confession signed by the assassin she hired, in triplicate, with letters found on his person that confirm both his hand and his name."

Giulia nods slowly, her chin jumping a little higher. "That'll do it."

Fiora barks a laugh and shakes her head ruefully.

"Three sisters, two dead and one rotting in a jail. It seems the Di Maineris don't do so well in Halice these days," Fiora says dryly, clamping her fingers together to keep from trembling. Her eyes cut to me, the dry sarcasm clear in her words. "I wonder why?"

"Because our family is a pack of treacherous wolves," Giulia retorts sharply. "Your actions are your own, and so are the consequences."

"Besides, you're wrong. There won't be two dead," I say quietly. "One imprisoned, one dead ... and you. Exiled."

"What?" Giulia flinches in shock. I stare down Fiora who narrows her eyes in suspicion.

"I hate you. I will always hate you. But I also believe you." I swallow the bitter taste building in my mouth. "You betrayed me to save me. In your own twisted way, you did it for the family. You work in the interest of the Di Maineris; you'll even go to extreme diabolical and evil measures to do it. I clearly can't trust you anywhere close to me. But perhaps from afar you can yet be of use."

"Of use?" Fiora asks, the word hovering nervously in the air.

"You have spies. Resources. Whispers. You'll use them all to get the deceitful relatives we call a family to fall in line. You will report their actions to me. You will remind them of the Fate that befalls those who cross me. One imprisoned, one dead, one exiled."

Fiora straightens, one eyebrow shooting up. "You want me to be a cautionary tale?"

"That's just an accidental benefit." I smirk. "I want you to do what you are so passionate about. You will serve the family interests abroad. I am the head of this family, meaning you will serve me. You will go where I send you and fix whatever issues we face. You will never return to Halice, on pain of death. If I find you have in any way tried anything like this again, you will die. You disobey an order? You die. You fail to comply? You die. Do I make myself clear? You have a sword hanging over your head because I hold evidence of a crime that will strip not just you but your husband and boys of everything they have. I will not hesitate to let it swing."

Fiora hesitates, then takes a long, slow breath before the corner of her lip twitches upwards.

"Perfectly clear."

"Get out. You have one hour before I hand my evidence over the City Guard, and they begin their hunt. Await my instructions for the next phase of the plan."

Fiora doesn't waste any time. She doesn't even go upstairs to pack her things. She walks along the corridor and turns at the front door, looking around her childhood home for the very last time.

She flicks her dark eyes back to us, to Giulia and me, standing side by side as we glare matching daggers of loathing her way.

"Before I go, allow me to give you one last piece of advice my dear," Fiora says quietly. "You are two steps behind in this war, reacting to assaults instead of taking charge and setting the course. The swords will be at your door before you know it. You're running out of time."

With that, Fiora closes the door behind her.

"What now?" asks Giulia. I swallow tightly and find that my eyes are watering. Her words echo in my head. Her words, Agosta's words, Rialta's words.

I'm running out of time.
Desperation changes the rules we think we know.

Survival is the only thing that's important.

"I know what I need to do," I say. "Send letters to the Electi to meet me in the High Chamber."

"In the morning?" Giulia asks sceptically. I shake my head as I march towards my study.

"They have an hour. I'm calling an emergency session."

CHAPTER 39

Layered grey clouds mottle the sky in shadowy charcoal and indigo. Their swollen bellies hang low and expectant, dragged north by the night air. A stray chill nips over my shoulder, tugging the end of my dark ponytail with it. Goosebumps swarm over my arms, the hairs standing on end against the assault as I march up the steps, my tunic swaying silently with the movement. I refuse to look sideways, at the spot where the gallows sat only hours ago. At the spot where Idris...

Idris.

I swallow tightly, my eyes set on the large arched doors as I stride forwards. I push them open, the ancient wood dry and rough against my fingers. I move inside, eyes locking on the far end of the hall.

Maggia, Leone and Savino stand by the white marble stage in the centre, each holding an orange candle, their own meagre shields against the encroaching night. The tiny orange flames fight valiantly, their traces jumping off the torn faces of my colleagues as they watch my approach.

"Is this about Idris?" asks Leone instantly.

"I've no more news ... but I have been told..." I take a deep, shuddering breath and clear my throat. Maggia reaches for me, rubbing my back gently.

"I'm so sorry, sweetheart. I know you two ... meant a great deal to each other." Maggia speaks gently.

"He's still fighting," Savino says brusquely, but even I can hear the sorrow in his words, the bleak denial of the most likely future.

"He is," I agree and gesture around the group. "Look around."

I step towards a chair that normally sits before a beautiful red window.

"Bellandi, traitor, dead," I say, pointing. I move around the circle gesturing at each chair in turn. "Morteselli, dead. Yaleni, dead. Ulrico, traitor, dead. Gattore, dead. My father, dead. Jacopo, dead."

I come to stand before Idris's chair. My eyes sting as the bottom of my vision blurs. I suck in a sharp breath, letting my hand fall to the arm of his chair. I turn to look at them.

"Idris..." I falter then move back towards the group.

"Twice now the Holy States fed their traitors into this very circle, into the apex of our leadership, and twice they succeeded. The results were cruel, violent deaths. We are all that is left. If one more of us falls, we will be running on a mere technicality, right when the survival of our entire city is on the line, and hundreds of thousands of lives are in our hands."

I pause and press my hands to my chest, looking each of them in the eye.

"I *love* our High Chamber. I think our democracy is one of the most beautiful things we have in this city. I will die defending everything this chamber represents. But we can no longer pretend that our enemies aren't abusing it. That our system isn't running too slowly to be truly effective and responsive. That we aren't vulnerable to attack. We are at war. This is a crisis. We need to act like it."

"You're talking about ... choosing a Maestrus," Savino says quietly. The air hangs heavy in the room as I nod.

"It's time," I say, the words burning in my throat as I meet their eyes.

"Halice is a democracy," Maggia says gruffly. "It's what makes Halice so special."

"It would only be temporary. Only until the fighting is done," I remind her. "This is a crisis, and we need a crisis leader."

"A crisis which could take months – maybe even years – to resolve. One of us would have absolute power over everything," Leone says quietly. "All decisions. All orders. Everything."

"Yes."

"We're still standing," Maggia says quietly. "We hold elections, fill the empty seats. We regain our strength and continue."

"How long did it take all of you to get up to speed? To be truly effective in this place?" I remind them. "We don't have time to hold the hand of a frightened new recruit. Not when the violence is already here and it's not going away anytime soon."

"And two of the traitors in our city have been Electi themselves," Savino answers thickly. "We have all proven ourselves to be trustworthy. But who says the newcomer wouldn't be another Holy States plant?"

"Besides, it just offers the Holy States more targets to take aim at," I reason quietly. "How many more Electi do we offer up to die?"

"Having many members is what makes us strong," argues Maggia. "There is no linchpin. No single point of failure."

"All they need to do is destabilise this chamber enough that we can't mobilise against their armies effectively," I counter. "Armies that are already gathering at our borders."

"What about the rest?" asks Leone. "When we choose someone, what happens to the rest of us?"

"You're still Electi. Your job is still to represent your people and protect this city," I argue. "That won't change."

"If we do this, we're potentially ending Halician democracy," Maggia says, her throat thick. "Leone is right, who knows how long this conflict will go on. Who knows what will happen once we make this call?"

"We won't win this war if we continue as we are," Savino says quietly. "We are too slow, wasting time bickering instead of building, preparing, planning. Our wheel of progress is moving too slowly to defend ourselves."

"And if we lose the war, our democracy will never return," I say. "And we will be responsible for the death of the free, independent Halice."

Silence hovers around the room as I take a deep breath.

"I nominate myself for Maestrus," I say quietly. Savino sighs.

"Of course you do," Maggia says softly.

"Savino would also make a good choice," I continue, "but we need him to have his eye firmly positioned on the army. His expertise in defending our city doesn't need to be split with other responsibilities right now."

"Your aunts betrayed you! One tried to bankrupt us, the other literally sold your secrets to the enemy. *While living in your house*," Maggia points out.

"And she caught them," Leone responds quietly. Surprised, we all turn to look at him. He's staring at the candle in his grip, speaking with quiet gravitas. His head eventually snaps up to meet my gaze.

"Di Maineri found the sources of betrayal and brought them to justice. She didn't shield her family; she rooted out the problem and handled it. No matter how she felt, no matter how it hurt. She did what had to be done for this city. If it weren't for her, Ulrico would still be handing out secrets to the Holy States and I would be set up to take the fall for his treason."

Leone takes a deep breath; the last few days have clearly shaken him to the core.

"I second your nomination, Di Maineri."

That wasn't what I expected at all. I nod my thanks his way and turn to Savino. He nods slowly.

"To be clear, you're giving me full command of the armed forces?" he asks quietly.

"You report to me, but yes. No more money management, no more debates in this chamber. All your time would be focused. And when the fighting comes, Savino, I am going to lean on you heavily. You need to make battle plans and draw our lines. Tell us how to win this when the armies start marching."

Savino nods.

"Alright. Agreed. But I can already tell you we're going to need more men. The Coari mercenaries agreed to protect our trade routes with this new deal, not fight an army for us."

"Let me work on that," I answer. "I already have a plan."

"Sounds like you've got it all figured out," Maggia grumbles.

"Were you to vote for this, I would want you in charge of civilian preparation," I tell her. Her eyebrows shoot up.

"What?"

"We need to start stockpiling food and medicines, and evacuating rural and remote villages in the enemy's path. Not everyone can fight, so what can we do about the young and the vulnerable? Please, take control of the civilian preparations."

Maggia shakes her head.

"You think you can bribe me with a title?"

"No. I think you're passionate, fair, and already experienced doing exactly what I need you to do, but on a much larger scale. If I am Maestrus, this is how it would work. You should know exactly what you're voting for and how things would operate."

Maggia's face crinkles, her lips puckering as she mulls that over. She meets the steady gaze of Savino, then Leone. Then she turns back to me and closes her eyes, sighing as her shoulders drops.

"Alright. We're doing this."

"Then, as speaker ... I'll make it official," I say with a thick voice. "For obvious reasons, I'll abstain from the vote. All those in favour of nominating me as Maestrus, say aye."

"Aye," says Leone quietly. There's a small pause.

"Aye," says Savino steadily, nodding with determination as all eyes turn back to Maggia. She doesn't open her eyes.

"Aye," she whispers, the orange flame in her hands jumping.

"The Di Maineri movement is called and ratified. I am now our Maestrus," I say quietly.

The silence that hovers between us is screaming.

"So, what's our first move, Di Maineri?" asks Leone. All their eyes turn to me expectantly. I nod.

"Maggia, Savino, review your areas and report. I want proposals yesterday. Leone, I need you to start evacuating rural communities immediately. I also want you to leverage your contacts to see what resources we can claim for the city. Coordinate with Maggia and Savino on this." I let out a shaky breath as my hands fall to my hips. "Let's start winning this war."

CHAPTER 40

They left me a candle.

A tiny yellow flicker frolics alone against the encroaching darkness, balanced on top of an ivory pillar as it slowly descends to a pool of wax in a shallow bronze dish. The little buttery flame will reach the end of its life in the next twenty minutes or so. I should leave. I should go home. But I can't stop watching it.

Savino, Maggia and Leone didn't hesitate to jump into action. They left the High Chamber hours ago and sprang into their new assignments with gusto. I'm alone, with only a single doomed light amongst the shadows.

I'm Maestrus.

I sit in my Electi chair, gripping the beautiful wooden arms. The chairs of my colleagues are still placed in their circle around the central stage. Cloaked in midnight ebony, only their outlines are plucked out by quivering threads of candlelight. The gilded columns loom in the dark. Feral winds battle against the dainty windows. Rain spatters aggressively against the glass panes. I let out a shuddering breath, the cold air curling like icy smoke as it leaves my lips.

I'm Maestrus.

I'm in charge. I have control.

No more debates. No more waiting around. No more betrayals.

It's time to start fighting back.

I should leave. I should walk home. Perhaps the rain will suck this cold, relentless energy from my veins, or slap some strength into me. Perhaps Fate in its cruelty might allow me the mercy of sleep. Yet my fingers are moulded to the wood armrests. My eyes are glued open, staring at the candle as it dances and frolics in the dark, naively oblivious to its impending doom.

Goosebumps prickle across my skin. I sigh, looking down as I run a hand over the rough skin in a vain fight against the cold. I still as bile collects at the back of my throat and my teeth begin to grind in an aching jaw.

My mouth goes dry.

Needles begin to stab my fingers as a thousand ghostly eyes stalk my every step.

Ancient metal hinges groan as the High Chamber doors push open into the dark, a rush of cold wind billowing in from the dark storm outside. My head whips around. My heart spikes. I leap to my feet as I gape at the sight before me.

"Idris!" His name pours from my lips on a sob.

Fate's Fury, he looks like death! His mouth is tinged blue. His golden hair is still bed-swept, his skin a violet hue. He breathes tightly, shoulders rising and falling at speed as his eyes lock on me. His walk across the polished black and white marbled floor is laboured.

Tears break free of my eyes. My chest swells and feels light, elation running warm and welcome through my veins like a drug. My feet move of their own accord and I hurl myself towards him, potent relief smothering my pounding heart and the racing, vile whispers. I throw my arms around him, clinging to him as I bury my head against his chest. Invisible flames explode across my body at his touch. His flames, his fire. I gasp for breath, basking in his inferno, my joy furiously drowning the agony of his presence.

Idris staggers back at my grip, sucking in gasp of pain.

I recoil sharply, mentally slapping myself as my mind catches up with my senses.

"I'm so sorry. I should've been more careful," I babble, reaching to steady him on his feet. "You're still recovering. Sit down—"

Idris prises my hands from his upper arms, his face a stony mask of absolute fury. His hands are tight as he squeezes my fingers together – so tight they could crack my bones. Those golden eyes are a fierce, fiery hurricane as he looks at me.

"Tell me it's not true," he growls, his voice dark and deep and on the precipice of a complete abyss. I frown but a white-hot slap of realisation hits a beat later. This is why he came here, in the middle of the storm, instead of recovering at home.

He knows.

I take a deep breath and lift my head.

"It's true," I say quietly. "I'm Maestrus."

Idris shakes his head, his face puckering with disgust. He drops my hands in revulsion, turning his back to me as though he can't stand the sight of me a second longer.

"No!" he growls, his voice somehow rising above the booming thunder crashing outside.

"It's done. The vote is cast, called and ratified. I am Maestrus."

"NO!" he roars, his voice bouncing off the dark, empty chamber. He stalks back towards me in the shadowy, frosty room.

"Give it back," he demands, jabbing a finger at me.

"Not yet," I answer.

"Give it back!" he shouts, stepping so close there is barely an inch between us. The air is thick with dark, dangerous lightning. I don't step back; I don't flinch at his rage. Instead, I glare up at him.

"No."

Idris looks like he wants to rip this building apart stone by stone. He's panting with his wrath as his face turns red. The veins of his neck strain as his shoulders shudder from the effort of holding himself back.

"How could you?" Idris snarls, his mouth contorted in a wretched mix of outrage and disgust.

"How?" I repeat, my words thin with disbelief. I fight to keep my voice level and reasonable with every breath. "What other option was there? We are at war. We are in crisis. We need a Maestrus."

"We've been in crisis for months! But you wait until I am unable to get in your way to seize power?" Idris hisses at me. I suck in a sharp breath, staggering back a pace at the heinous accusation.

"You really think me so corrupt?"

"What else should I think? You have robbed Halice of its democracy!" roars Idris. "You have stolen this city!"

"I'm trying to save this city!" I scream right back.

Why doesn't he understand? Why can't he see that I had no other recourse?

If we can't control things, it goes wrong. We need that control.

I back away from Idris, breathing hard as I pull my hair in frustration. The skies scream outside as wind and water assault the exterior of this hallowed hall. I turn back to face him, the space between us tense and taut.

"What is the point of saving this city if you've obliterated its soul?" Idris hisses. "Our democracy is sacred. I thought you of all people knew that. I thought you of all people respected its sanctity!"

"I do!" I growl back. "It is our treasure!"

"You threw it away!" Idris roars, throwing his arms wide with rage. "You have betrayed the people who elected you, you have betrayed yourself and everything you've ever stood for, and you betrayed me while I was dying alone."

"You weren't alone!" My words are torn and thick with fresh pain. "I was there. I watched as that vile poison stole your life away from me with each torturous second. It was an agony watching you die, an excruciating masochistic delirium I can't even begin to explain because no one but you could possibly understand."

"So you ran away. You turned your back on me, on your people and on your own principles to crown yourself a de facto queen."

"No!" I spit, flinching at the word queen. "I was fighting back. You couldn't anymore, so I did what I had to—"

"Don't you dare claim you did this for me," Idris spits. "Don't you bloody dare!"

"This was me taking the power to fight for all of us! If our positions were reversed, are you really telling me that you would've done differently?" I ask him, the words choked. "I watched you die today, Idris. As this chamber has bickered about this plan or that plan, traitors have infiltrated our city. They have struck again, and again, and again. My father, your father, Giulia, Alfieri – the list of the wounded and the dead goes on and on and on and is soaked through with Halician blood! The blood of our friends and family. Today I thought I was adding your name to that list. I had to do something! I had to stop the cycle. I had to fight."

I throw my hands wide, searching for something to say.

"So tell me, Idris," I almost plead with him, that single dying candle barely strong enough to highlight the ridges of his face against the overcast night. "What else should I have done? What other move is there?"

"You could've waited."

"For what? To be certain you were in your grave?" I ask faintly, fresh tears painting a path down my cheeks. "Taio said you would die. What sense was there in waiting?"

"Taio was wrong."

"I couldn't have known that." I want to scream at him. *Why can't he understand?* I did this in desperation. I'm not proud, I'm not happy. This was a wretched act of survival, but it will work. We can focus now; we can do what we have to. The good, the bad, the ugly. Whatever is needed.

Lightning flashes outside the window, slapping bright white light across the room before returning the marring darkness. Idris is glaring at me, panting hard as his limbs tremble with rage. His hands are clenched against his sides.

I fight to keep myself steady, my throbbing heart flooding my veins with fire.

"Had you been forced to watch as I slowly turned from blue to black, hearing each fleeting, agonising breath, desperately praying it wouldn't be the last but knowing, despite the anguished fight, regardless of each desperate, fitful second you clung to life, that you were going to lose, what would you have done, Idris? What other option was there?"

"I don't know!" Idris shouts.

"You would've done the same. Don't lie to me! Don't pretend! You said yourself that we need to move quicker, that we were wasting time in this Chamber. You would've done the same, you would've found a way to fight!" I say, hands trembling at my sides. Lightning flashes again, showing me the rampant torment on Idris's drained face.

"Maybe," Idris answers darkly, his voice cracking against the storm. "But you're supposed to be better than me."

A loud slam comes from behind me, the wind slamming a door shut perhaps? I spin around, shocked at the noise. I turn back and realise Idris is gone. The main door hangs open still, water splashing down from the heavens and seeping across the polished marble.

"Idris. Idris!" I shout, running after him, my heart throbbing in my throat.

He's so fast he's already at the base of the stairs as I tear into the rain, each frozen assault sending a spear of ice into my flesh.

"IDRIS!" I shout again. I race down the steps, but the water on the stone takes my foot from under me and I tumble down to the bottom, landing in a dirty, cold puddle in the square.

Groaning, I pick myself up, grimy water dripping from my hair and dirt smeared across my skin. The storm continues its hostile deluge, soaking through me in a second. On all fours, my own salty tears mingle with the storm as I watch Idris's retreating figure fade from view. Thunder crashes around me, echoing off the dark, empty streets and sleepy stone walls.

Sobbing breaths race from my trembling lips as I turn back, looking up at the High Chamber from my knees. Rain slices like iron daggers from the sky, striking hard against the stone sluiced in dark, ebony shadows. The gale howls a war cry that shakes the air in my lungs.

"I'll give it back," I promise with a sob.

I have to save Halice. Whatever it takes, I am prepared to pay that price. If my life is forfeit, I give it gladly. My comfort, my principles, my sanity – so be it. A greater evil is coming, something that will devour and destroy until nothing I love or value is left. I have to fight it. I have to protect it.

"I'll give it back," I scream into the gale, hot tears competing with rainwater for dominion of my face. Their paths immediately join as they drop like liquid silver from my chin. I gaze up at the drowning High Chamber.

This is my sacred duty. My solemn vow.

I'm Renza Di Maineri, and I will save Halice.

Or I'll die trying.

Acknowledgments

I can't believe that I have finished my second book in the Soul Hate series, and I can now say I have multiple books published! This is a serious dream come true, and as such, I have so many people to thank!

To my completely amazing husband, thank you for absolutely everything. From encouragement to chatting over plot holes to celebrating cover art – your support on this journey has made a world of difference and has meant the world to me. I love you so much.

To my mum, thank you for finding the time to celebrate and support my dreams along with finding success in your own. I love that we are achieving our dreams together, in tandem. I know it make us both ridiculously busy, but I love that we still find time to support each other.

To my dad, thank you for everything you have done for me, for supporting and encouraging me ever since I was small. I know fantasy romance books aren't your thing, but I know despite that you've read every word. (I'm going to pretend this book is completely PG appropriate.)

To the rest of my family, thank you for your unending support and encouragement. Both the readers and the non-readers have been real champions, celebrating the successes of this journey and encouraging me through the difficult parts, too.

To Georgia, one of my nearest and dearest friends in the whole world. Thank you for celebrating and supporting me in everything I do, even though books aren't your thing. From coming to book signings and events with me to celebrating the little wins together – you're the absolute best!

To my brilliant and endlessly patient agent Saskia, a huge thank you for absolutely everything you do. I know that I often have a lot of questions and queries, and spring random book ideas on you, but a huge, huge thank you for everything you do. Having your support in this has been amazing.

Thank you to my amazing editor Rosie and all the fabulous and wonderful people at One More Chapter. You guys are utterly brilliant and have been truly amazing throughout the entire publishing journey. I couldn't ask for more! Thank you for answering all my questions and helping make this book the absolute best it can be.

Also, thank you to everyone who has ever supported my small business. I love books in all their forms, particularly those with sprayed edges. To be able to sell luxury, limited edition sprayed edges is beyond amazing, and the support I've received for all bookish endeavours is amazing. Thank you to everyone for making that possible, too!

And finally, but certainly not least, to my cat Billy. Somehow, I completed this book despite your constant demand for attention and multiple attempts to occupy my keyboard. Thank you for every midnight cuddle, biscuit-making session and for listening to my every character dilemma with an utterly unamused expression.

Follow me on Instagram and TikTok for more bookish updates!

@KingdomBookDesigns
@HannahKingsleyAuthor

WHAT IF YOU FALL FOR THE ONE YOU ARE FATED TO DESTROY?

The Holy States teach that everyone is born with a Soulmate. But every coin has two sides...

Renza di Maineri is the youngest elected leader her city has ever seen. Devoted to the citizens of Halice, she is determined to finally step beyond her father's shadow. But her world falls apart when she meets her worst nightmare, Idris Patricelli.

It's bad enough that Idris is her main political rival, but fate is playing a cruel game. Idris is also her Soulhate, the person she is fated to destroy, and every moment in his presence she fights an urge to rip his throat out.

As gossip spreads and her ability to lead is challenged, Renza is desperate to salvage her reputation. But fate is not quite finished with her yet... can she uncover who can be trusted among those closest to her, when she cannot even trust herself?

AVAILABLE IN PAPERBACK, EBOOK AND AUDIO!

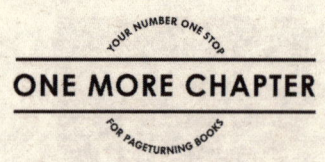

The author and One More Chapter would like to thank everyone who contributed to the publication of this story…

Analytics
Imogen Wolstencroft

Audio
Fionnuala Barrett
Ciara Briggs

Contracts
Laura Amos
Inigo Vyvyan

Design
Lucy Bennett
Fiona Greenway
Liane Payne
Dean Russell

Digital Sales
Laura Daley
Lydia Grainge
Hannah Lismore

eCommerce
Laura Carpenter
Madeline ODonovan
Charlotte Stevens
Christina Storey
Jo Surman
Rachel Ward

Editorial
Janet Marie Adkins
Rosie Best
Kara Daniel
Charlotte Ledger
Lydia Mason
Laura McCallen
Jennie Rothwell
Sofia Salazar Studer
Helen Williams

Harper360
Emily Gerbner
Ariana Juarez
Jean Marie Kelly
emma sullivan
Sophia Wilhelm

International Sales
Peter Borcsok
Ruth Burrow
Bethan Moore
Colleen Simpson

Inventory
Sarah Callaghan
Kirsty Norman

Marketing & Publicity
Chloe Cummings
Grace Edwards
Katie Sadler

Operations
Melissa Okusanya
Hannah Stamp

Production
Denis Manson
Simon Moore
Francesca Tuzzeo

Rights
Ashton Mucha
Alisah Saghir
Zoe Shine
Aisling Smyth
Lucy Vanderbilt

Trade Marketing
Ben Hurd
Eleanor Slater

The HarperCollins Distribution Team

The HarperCollins Finance & Royalties Team

The HarperCollins Legal Team

The HarperCollins Technology Team

UK Sales
Isabel Coburn
Jay Cochrane
Sabina Lewis
Holly Martin
Harriet Williams
Leah Woods

And every other essential link in the chain from delivery drivers to booksellers to librarians and beyond!

One More Chapter is an award-winning global division of HarperCollins.

Subscribe to our newsletter to get our latest eBook deals and stay up to date with all our new releases!

signup.harpercollins.co.uk/join/signup-omc

Meet the team at
www.onemorechapter.com

Follow us!

@onemorechapterhc

Do you write unputdownable fiction?
We love to hear from new voices.
Find out how to submit your novel at
www.onemorechapter.com/submissions